MW01048528

Angel of Death

(A Love Story)

By Anna Erishkigal

Copyright 2013 – Anna Erishkigal
All Rights Reserved

SERAPHIM PRESS

CAPE COD, MA

This is a work of fiction. All of the characters and events portrayed in this novel are products of the authors' imagination or used fictitiously.

Angel of Death (A Love Story). Copyright © 2013 by Anna Erishkigal. All rights reserved. Printed in the United States of America. No part of this book may be reproduced in any form or by any electronic or mechanical means, including information storage and retrieval systems, without permission in writing from the publisher, except by a reviewer, who may quote brief passages in a review.

Published by Seraphim Press, P.O. Box 440, East Sandwich, Cape Cod, Massachusetts 02537-0440.

v.3

SERAPHIM PRESS

CAPE COD, MA

www.seraphim-press.com

ISBN-13: 978-1489545992

ISBN-10: 1489545999

Cover photo: 'Angel of Death.' Copyright © 2012 by ~xartez. All rights reserved. No part of this cover art may be reproduced in any form or by any electronic or mechanical means, including information storage and retrieval systems, without permission in writing from the artist.

http://xartez.deviantart.com/art/Angel-of-Death-35266069

DEDICATION

I dedicate this book to the unsung heroes of war, the medics, trauma nurses and military doctors who forsake high-paying careers at home to keep the men and women of our armed forces alive … while under fire.

Thank you!

ACKNOWLEDGMENTS

I'd like to thank the people without whose support this novel would have died a plot bunny hopping around on a hard drive.

To my wonderful husband ... who tolerates my nocturnal writing bouts and strange musings about 'I can't talk now ... my bad guy is talking to me...'

To my lovely children ... who instead of asking 'mom ... why are you listening to the same song over and over again' on a car trip instead ask, 'mom ... tell us about the scene you're writing today?'

To Cindy Leppard Green, who helped beta read and provided invaluable grammatical support (not my strong point)! Thank you so much!

To my writing critique group, *Plot Bunnies and Edit Demons*, who provide that invaluable feedback and social support that you don't get anyplace else! And special thanks to the Barnes & Noble in Hyannis that hosts us every week ... and Jules for setting up our favorite table!

To ~xartez, who kindly let me use his photograph of the Wjortez Angel of Death as the basis of my cover. I hope readers will visit his deviant arts page and view his other works at http://xartez.deviantart.com/art/Angel-of-Death-35266069

To Sensei Donna and my fellow karate students at the *Feisty Lion USA Gojudo Karate* studio in Wareham who've tolerated my conscripting classes into live re-enactments of battle scenes so I can reality test the action.

To my patient friends, who tolerate my launching into conversations about fictional characters that do not really exist and do not call the police when I fade off mid-sentence and mumble 'excuse me ... I have to go home and kill somebody now...'

And to all my fellow authors at the WG2E who've given me education, encouragement, a sanity check, and support. Thank you!

Part I

Whoever he be ... that gives any of his seed unto Moloch;
He shall surely be put to Death:
The people of the land shall stone him with stones.

And I will set my face against that man,
And will cut him off from among his people;
Because he hath given of his seed unto Moloch,
To defile my sanctuary,
And to profane my holy name.

Leviticus 20:2-3

This book is a work of adult fiction. It contains subject matter some people may find upsetting, including death in all of its incarnations, tragic historical depictions of human sacrifice and torture (including child sacrifice and Jesus's crucifixion), rape, war and all the inherently unpleasant things which go with that topic, moderately graphic depictions of wartime surgery and injuries, sex, and creative reinterpretations of religious ideologies some people may find offensive or blasphemous.

Some people, especially devoutly religious ones or survivors of the wars in Afghanistan or Iraq, may find portions of this book to be upsetting.

If this book were a movie, it would be rated R.

This book is <u>NOT</u> religious fiction!

Prologue

And the Lord said unto Satan,
Hast thou considered my servant Job?
That there is none like him on Earth?
A perfect and upright man...
Then Satan answered the Lord, and said ...
Put forth thine hand now,
And touch all that he hath,
And he will curse thee to thy face.

Job 1:8-11

Galactic Standard Date: 155,525.07 AE
Ascended Realms

"Black pawn to E-8."

Shay'tan shifted a black pawn representing some hapless mortal into position to overtake one of the Eternal Emperor Hashem's seed worlds. The old dragon's tail twitched like a cat stalking a mouse as he waited to see what his ancient adversary would do. The white-robed, bearded figure that played opposite him stifled a yawn as he grabbed the nearest chess piece, a small, white pawn, and pondered his next move.

"Does something trouble you, old friend?" Shay'tan craned his serpentine neck across the chessboard. "You seem rather lethargic lately. Are you ill?"

"Oh, I don't know." Hashem twiddled his pawn. "Things have been going so well since we signed the Armistice."

The two old gods stared across the chessboard, united in their boredom. Technically the enormous spinning hologram of the galaxy was supposed to be a map delineating what territory belonged to which old god's empire, but the two had gotten into the habit of using it for a game they called Galactic Chess. Each solar system was a square, and within those squares, planets could be played for by moving their resources against one another. Despite millennia of playing, the two old gods were always in a perpetual stalemate.

"Things *have* been rather dull," Shay'tan commiserated. "Nobody ever warns you when you become a god how *tedious* eternity can be." The old dragon flared his leathery wings. "Perhaps we could start a border war?"

"Tempting, you old devil," Hashem yawned again. "But my subjects would never stand for it. You give them free will and what do they do? They vote you're nothing but a ceremonial god!"

"No respect!" Shay'tan belched a puff of fire. "It's almost enough to make you long for the good old days when they let us amuse ourselves by praying for us to go after one another all the time."

"A war of wits!" Hashem said.

"Pitting our armies against one another to prove which god's vision of the universe is right!" Shay'tan rumbled.

"Epic battles!" Hashem exclaimed. "With Moloch on the prowl!"

Shay'tan touched his forehead, snout, and heart in the same gesture he made his subjects use to worship *him.*

"Don't even -say- that name!!! It's all Lucifer can do to keep the bastard locked up in Gehenna!"

Hashem snorted.

"I told you to never mention that name to me again!"

"Who? Moloch?"

"No! That other … *name!*" Hashem crossed his arms in front his chest and glowered.

Shay'tan picked up a black bishop and examined it. A prince. *His* prince ever since Hashem had spurned the piece and cast it off. Much to Hashem's chagrin, Shay'tan shielded Lucifer from his wrath because he owed a debt, and everyone knew that dragons always paid their debts.

"Lucifer is your son," Shay'tan said softly. "Isn't it time you forgave him? It could have been one of *us* Moloch seized."

"Never!!!" Hashem waggled his finger at Shay'tan's snout. "This is the one and only time I will ever admit you were *right* about humanoid nature! No good deed goes unpunished!"

"True," Shay'tan toyed with the black bishop. "But there was nothing altruistic about your raising Lucifer to be your son. He was just another one of your experiments into the Seraphim gene pool."

"I raised that boy as though he were my own!" Hashem slammed his fist down upon the chess board. "And he thanked me by trying to steal my empire! He should be the one locked up in Gehenna!"

Shay'tan raised one eyebrow ridge with a bemused expression.

"For a god who preaches forgiveness," Shay'tan rumbled. "You sure know how to hold a grudge."

Hashem turned away, arms crossed. A rare scowl marred the face he took great pains to manifest as a kindly, fatherly one.

"I'll tell you what," Shay'tan put the black bishop back where it belonged ... banished where it could do no further harm. "Let's pick a random subject and bet on how we think they'll react to something. Whoever bets the closest reaction, wins."

Hashem absent-mindedly rolled the white pawn he'd been toying with between his thumb and forefinger.

"Wins what?"

"How about that resource planet we keep squabbling over?" Shay'tan's snout turned up in a toothy grin. "If *I* win, you'll let me pillage it. If *you* win, you can turn it into a protected seed world to see what evolves."

Hashem tossed the white pawn into the air and caught it again; his bushy eyebrows furrowed in thought as he examined the map of the galaxy.

"Who will we bet on and what will we get them to do?"

"Why not that pawn you're holding in your hand?" Shay'tan pointed to the piece Hashem toyed with. "Who does that represent, anyway?"

"Oh ... hah!" Hashem's bushy eyebrows rose with delight. "That's a young scientist I've been nurturing! His mother is a fierce proponent of hands-off natural evolution."

"What would happen if you sidetracked him from the science academy for a year and stuck him in the military?" A knowing grin lit up Shay'tan's snout. "Get him out of the ivory tower, so to speak. I'll bet you that planet you want that if you throw him into the real world, he won't be so hands-off."

"He's just a boy." Hashem studied the pawn. "Barely seventeen cycles. I'd need to send him to basic training so he doesn't get himself killed."

"You're his god," Shay'tan tempted. "Tell him you're sending him on a secret mission to Earth to watch them go at each other."

"Earth?" Hashem glanced at the accursed black bishop. "You know the terms of the Armistice. No one goes in, and no one comes out unless they ascend out of there on their own power. Even if *we* agree, Lucifer will never stand for it."

"You're entitled to one observer," Shay'tan said. "Pull out your regular guy, stick your pawn in, and then one year from now our wager will end. Lucifer will be none the wiser."

Hashem toyed with the little white pawn.

"I don't even know what's going on there right now," Hashem groused. "Human behavior baffles my observers and the General is too busy to babysit them."

"Why it's war, of course," Shay'tan smirked. "Warlike little buggers, those humans. The Phoenicians wage war against the Carthaginians; the Carthaginians battle the Sicilians; the Sicilians harass the Romans and the Romans are at war with the Phoenicians."

"So we'll, what? Pick a war?" Hashem said. "Drop our guy into the middle of it? And then what? Tell him he can't interfere?"

"Exactly," Shay'tan's gold reptilian eyes sparkled with excitement. "Only we'll … I don't know. Up the ante. How about this? The first thing that bothers him enough to report back to his commanding officer, you'll order him to observe and not interfere. No matter what! If he breaks protocol, I win. If he lets the subject go down in flames, you win."

Hashem looked down at the pawn in his hand. A budding scientist who would one day further the interests of his Alliance. A young man with a unique genetic profile he had gone through enormous lengths to procure. A subject who might be tainted by the knowledge Hashem had been forced to come out of his ivory tower and eat his hat when it came to humans and the malignant deity imprisoned within their home world; knowledge both emperors had gone out of their way to erase from the history books and deny.

On the other hand, Hashem was so bored he wanted to scream…

"It's a bet," Hashem said. "White pawn to Zulu-3."

He plunked the little white pawn down into the middle of the chess pieces guarding Earth.

Chapter 1

And the daughter of Tyre shall be there with a gift;
Even the rich among the people shall entreat thy favor.
The King's daughter is all glorious within;
Her clothing is of wrought gold.
Psalm 45:12-13

Earth: 311 BC – Carthage

Death from above. That's how the 101st Angelic Air Force 'screaming eagles' thought of themselves. Avenging angels sent in whenever the Emperor needed to hit the enemy hard and hold ground until the Alliance military could establish a base. Cannon fodder to flock from the sky and be ground up and spat out by the enemy. It was funny how staring death in the face made you appreciate the little things in life, such as Mom's terrible attempts at home-cooked meals instead of using the replicator, or the way his pesky little sister rifled through his things and followed him around like a shadow. *Especially* his little sister...

"Private Thanatos," the communications officer called into the comms unit pressed into Azrael's ear. "Have you found the source of the suspicious energy signature?"

"I've found no signs of unauthorized technology, Sir," Azrael said. "Are you sure these are the right coordinates?"

"Whatever we're reading has been broadcasting from somewhere inside General Hanno's house," the comms officer said. "You know the rules. No unauthorized technology is allowed on that planet. Keep looking until you find what's sending that signal."

"Yes, Sir," Azrael mumbled without enthusiasm. Some idiot must have dropped their communications device and now a human had picked it up and was playing with it.

The tall, slender Angelic crouched lower on the flat, woven reed rooftop and tucked his dark wings against his back to remain inconspicuous. Dawn had brightened into daylight, condemning him to spend the entire day here since the moment he took to the air people would spot his enormous 30-foot wingspan. The last thing they wanted was for humans to realize they were being watched by aliens from outer space, or, as was the more common mythology on this planet, watched over by angels.

The hot Mediterranean sun pounded down upon Azrael's ink-dark feathers like Shay'tan's breath. Why couldn't he have been born with white wings like *most* Angelics possessed which would have reflected the solar photons and helped him hide amongst the clouds? He had drunk the last of his water hours ago and his mouth had taken on that nasty, pasty flavor indicative of dehydration. In the courtyard below, a statue of a bull-man taunted him from the center of a fountain, its ruby-inset eyes glittering like some ancient demon. Why had *he* been sent to the unicorn planet, fresh out of the academy and still wet behind the ears instead of someone trained to do this kind of job?

Flies buzzed around the mud he'd smeared through his feathers to be less conspicuous; mud he hadn't realized until *after* he'd spread it all over his body smelled faintly of goat dung. Even, worse, his wings had developed a serious infestation of sand fleas!

"Bugger!"

Azrael twitched, trying to shake off the feeling of cooties crawling through his feathers. His skin crawled with the sensation of fleas burrowing into the soft flesh and feeding upon his blood. Oh! How he wished he had some sort of superpower!

'Die!'

He visualized the bugs vanishing into uncreation. It didn't help. No matter how much he pictured zapping the fleas, they kept right on biting.

Argh!!! He was conducting sneak-and-peek special operations recon on Carthage's de facto emperor. He was supposed to be still! He was supposed to remain unseen. He was…

Crawling with sand fleas!

He flapped his enormous black-brown wings, attempting to shake off the blood sucking parasites, but nothing helped. Desperate to be rid of the skin-crawling sensation, he moved to the edge of the roof and rubbed them against the coarse stone edge. Ahh…

"I see you," a little voice chimed, translated through his universal translator.

Azrael froze. He was under strict orders not to interfere in this planet's culture. The mere sight of an alien species could alter the course of human evolution. All because he, Azrael, a Private fresh out of the Angelic Air Force Academy, had allowed himself to be irked by a tiny insect!

"Are you really an angel?"

The little girl's voice was high and sweet. A face looked up at him from the courtyard below and smiled. She had curly blonde hair, pale skin, high cheekbones and a slender build; the face of a purebred Angelic, only without the wings. Here, in a city where the average inhabitant had dark hair and an olive complexion.

And the most compelling silver eyes he'd ever seen...

"No." Azrael tucked his wings against his back as though he was a person of importance. "I am a figment of your imagination."

Perhaps she'd think she only imagined him? Humans had legends of their species visiting their planet, but had come to view stories of half-human hybrids with the *same* skepticism his species viewed legends of a human home world. So long as he wasn't seen by an adult, the child's story would likely not be believed.

"Why are you up there on the roof?" the little girl asked. "Are you sick? Do you have a broken wing? I could go get a servant to help you."

"No!" Azrael shooed her with his hand, his mind racing to find a way out of this predicament. "I'm fine. Just ... go away."

The little girl hurried over to a ladder consisting of a log with wooden stakes drilled in at regular intervals and scurried up to the rooftop like a precocious little monkey.

"You really *are* an angel!" She wiggled like an excited puppy. "Can I touch your wings?"

"No." Azrael hoped she'd go away without raising the alarm. He could simply fly out of here, but the two emperors were diligent about enforcing the terms of an Armistice which he didn't have a high enough security clearance to know more than the fact it existed. He'd be in hot water if they found out he'd had his cover blown by an eight-year-old human child.

"Don't worry," the little girl held out her hand. "I won't hurt you. Would you like something to eat?"

The scent of cooking food wafted up from the kitchen, making Azrael's mouth water. His rations had run out hours ago and he'd been lamenting his parched throat only moments before. At this point his cover was already blown. Would it be so bad if he enlisted her help to make his stay here more comfortable?

"Please," Azrael croaked. "I'd love some water."

The little girl listened as he spoke in Galactic Standard, and then his translator rendered a translation in the local Punic language.

"*Uisce* ... water," the little girl said. "Hey ... I know that word!"

"You speak my language?"

"*Labrhaionn tu* ... you speak," the little girl beamed proudly. "Sorry ... that's all I understood. My tutor said it's important I learn to speak the language of heaven so someday I can become a priestess of the gods. Any god but Moloch!"

The child pointed down to the bull-man statue which lurked in every courtyard in this city. Azrael's skin began to crawl. Now he understood why the icon gave him the creeps. Moloch. Another legend.

"You're studying to be a priestess?" Azrael scrutinized her. "What's your name?"

"Elissar," her eyes sparkled with pride. "After my ancestor who founded this city. Papa insists I learn the same things a son would learn even though I am a girl."

"Why would it matter if you are female?"

"Why ..." Elissar scrunched up her nose as though pondering that question. "I don't know. Just ... because."

"Because why?"

"Because ... everyone says so."

"That's not how we do it on Haven."

"Then you'll have to tell me all about it." Elissar tugged at one of Azrael's long dark primary feathers. "Can you fly?"

"Stop that!" Azrael tucked his wing over the edge of the roof where she couldn't reach it. "You're not supposed to ... uh ... touch me. I might ... um ... bite you ... or something!"

"You look too kind to bite." Elissar gave him the same patronizing grin his little sister often gave when she was being a pest. "Besides ... you're an angel. You're supposed to be one of the good guys."

"How do you know so much about Angelics?"

"My ancestor was queen of Tyre until her brother killed her husband. Tyre was founded by an angel. Lucifer. He's my ancestor, too."

Azrael's mouth dropped as he sputtered, "The Eternal Emperor's adopted son was your ancestor?"

Thirty-two hundred years ago, the Emperor's son had gone missing amongst rumors of a hoax about rediscovery of the human source race. A hoax Azrael now knew was true after being reassigned *here*. Rumor claimed the son had staged a coup d'état, an allegation the Emperor adamantly denied. The diplomatic flagship which had gone missing had been named *'Prince of Tyre.'*

Elissar's angelic-like features curved up into a patronizing grin.

"The Eternal Emperor?" Elissar laughed. "You're silly! My *daddy* is the ruler of Carthage. He said if anything happens to Himilco, then I should rule. Like Queen Elissar did when she founded this city."

Azrael looked more closely at the child. Unless Lucifer had been genetically evolved enough to ascend to Archangel status, he would have died out 2,500 years ago along with the other Fallen, long before this city had been built. But her resemblance to a mortal Alliance Angelic was uncanny. In fact, her resemblance to the photographic history of Lucifer was uncanny! Right down to her eerie silver eyes.

Azrael's nostrils flared, an enhanced sense of smell gifted to *all* half-human hybrids by the Eternal Emperor. But not for the absence of wings, the little girl even *smelled* like an Angelic.

"Elissar!!!" A female called from the courtyard.

"I'm coming, Mama!!!" Elissar called. She bolted to the edge of the roof like an eager little dog. "Mama! Guess what I just found?"

"Shhh!!!" Azrael hissed in a panicked voice, wildly looking around him for a way to escape. "I'm not supposed to be seen! You'll get me in trouble with … god."

"What did you find, little one?" the mother asked. "How many times do I have to tell you not to climb up onto the roof?"

Azrael flattened himself against the rooftop, but one dark wing remained draped over the edge. He looked, pleadingly, into Elissar's silver eyes.

Elissar gave him a knowing wing.

"I saw a great big bird, Mama!" Elissar pointed in the opposite direction. "Over there. Look!"

Azrael yanked his wing up and pressed it against his back, thankful he'd camouflaged himself with the goat-dung infested mud just as they'd trained him to do at the military academy. Silently, he mouthed the words 'thank you'.

"I don't see any bird," the mother said. "Now please, Elissar. Come down. Papa will be joining us for supper tonight."

"Papa's coming?" Elissar rushed eagerly to the ladder, pausing only long enough to give Azrael a fetching smile before skittering down.

"You and your imaginary friends." The mother shepherded Elissar towards the house. "I didn't see any bird."

"Funny," Elissar glanced over her shoulder before she disappeared into the doorway and gave Azrael a conspiratorial wink. "I could have sworn I saw wings."

Chapter 2

Did we take them wrongly for a laughing stock?
Or have our eyes missed them?

Qur'an, Ch.38, v.3

Dwarf Planet Ceres - 311 BC
Dual-Empire Base

Ceres Station was a subterranean military base dug deep within a dwarf planet in the asteroid belt which orbited the Sol system one planet removed from Earth. In this base served not only Alliance military, but for reasons known to only a select few, it also served as a base for the competing Sata'anic Empire.

Azrael felt like a small, slender boy as he stood at attention and tried his best not to cower in front of the angry, enormous ten foot long Spiderid who was also his commanding officer.

"I can't go back there! My cover's been blown!" Azrael tucked his dark wings against his back in shame. "Now they know we're watching them."

"Did anyone come out to challenge you?" Major Skgrll asked. Spiderids were enormous, sentient arachnids. At the moment, all eight his eyes glowered at Azrael with disapproval.

"No, Sir." Azrael stiffened his spine. "I remained hidden until nightfall so I could fly away without being seen."

"Did you notice anyone peeking up to see if you were there?" Skgrll's palps twitched in annoyance.

"Just Elissar … um … I mean the child, Sir. She … um … brought me out some water before her father got home."

"She brought you water?"

"I … um … might have mentioned I was thirsty." Azrael tugged at the collar of his uniform which, despite being too large for his slender frame, had suddenly become unbearably tight. "In the … um … interest of distracting her from screaming."

Snickers erupted from the flight hangar. Under the terms of the Armistice, Ceres station was shared with the Royal Sata'anic Navy. Several lizard-soldiers clustered behind a shuttlecraft, eavesdropping while Skgrll reamed him out, their mottled green skin waxing pink with laughter. Ensign Zarif, a Sata'anic naval officer he'd grown friendly with, gave Azrael a knowing grin. He flicked his transparent inner eyelids, the equivalent of a lizard-person rolling his eyes.

"From what you describe," the C.O. growled, "the child was curious about you. Did she exhibit any further knowledge of Alliance vocabulary?"

"She … um … might have given me some bread," Azrael confessed. "She knew it was called 'aran,' as well as that fruit the Emperor likes so much. Olives."

"And did she feed you anything else while you were there?"

Azrael felt as though he'd just stuck his foot into a trap. A foot that practically swam in the too-large Angelic combat boots they'd given him to wear when he'd completed basic training.

"They … um … have this really flavorful meat called chicken," Azrael shot his commanding officer a sheepish grin. "It was very good."

"And how did you eat this meal? Did you eat it alone?"

"Not exactly." Color flushed his high, pale cheeks. "She … um … brought company."

"I thought you said she alerted nobody else to your presence!" the C.O. roared. "If you were seen by more than one person, I need to know!"

Out of the corner of his eye, Azrael noticed the others had stopped doing whatever they were doing and begun to throng closer to eavesdrop. Sata'an lizard soldiers. Spiderids. Mantoids. A Centauri officer. And worse! Three fierce Leonid multi-purpose fighters. Alpha-males. The toughest of the tough.

"Not so much anybody else," Azrael hemmed with mortification. "More … playmates."

"Other children?"

"Dolls," Azrael whispered, hoping the other crewmen didn't hear.

"You sat on the roof of this girl's house and played with dolls?!!"

'Dolls dolls dolls dolls' echoed through the cavernous launch bay loud enough for the entire galaxy to hear. Laughter erupted as every man on the base heard that he, Azrael, a lowly private sent on a reconnaissance mission to the fabled unicorn-planet, had just spent the afternoon having a picnic on the roof of his quarry's house playing dolls with an eight-year-old girl.

"Um … yes," Azrael whispered, gulping to fight the sensation of his heart pounding in his ears. "I was trying to humor her, Sir. So she wouldn't make me fly out of there in broad daylight. I figured with her, my cover was already blown. It was better than letting the entire city know I was there."

The three Leonid males elbowed each other in the ribs, giving him a toothy grin. One took the afterburner he was repairing and pantomimed cradling a baby-doll while the second one grabbed a small cylinder and, pinky-claw outstretched, pretended to take a sip out of a cup of tea. The third walked as though wearing high heels, giving his hips an exaggerated waggle, and flicked one paw in Azrael's direction in the universal symbol of a man who enjoys relations with other men.

"That's how I always ... uh ... distract my little sister," Azrael said softly. "It ... uh ... worked. Didn't it? She didn't tell her parents."

Ensign Zarif doubled over, slapping his haunches as he tried to catch his breath. Major Skgrll made a heroic effort to keep a straight face, but the twitch of his feathery chelicerae betrayed he found Azrael's explanation wanting. Throughout the launch bay, every crewman in two empires laughed at him.

Azrael wished he could evaporate into a black hole right this instant. Death. By mortification. Why in Hades had the Emperor personally requested that he, a nerd straight out of the bowels of the science academy with no prior military training whatsoever, go on this mission?

"Maybe you should ... um ... send someone more qualified?" Azrael mumbled, staring down at his feet. "I'm just a private. I'm not very good at this sort of thing."

Major Skgrll paused, two of his eight spiny legs wavering, and then resumed the stiff stance of a commanding officer.

"I already requested that," the C.O. glowered at him with all eight eyes. "Several times. Including earlier today when you first radioed up from the planet requesting to return to base. For some reason both emperors insist that you, and *only* you, are qualified to complete this mission! Do you have some secret qualifications hidden beneath the act of a bumbling idiot I should know about?"

"No, Sir." Azrael stared at his too-large combat boots. In a hybrid army where every super-soldier was larger-than-life, the slender, slow-to-mature Azrael appeared to be little more than a child himself. The C.O. had spat puppies upon learning he'd been ordered from the top of the food chain to send a Private to do reconnaissance on Earth.

"The Eternal Emperor *himself* just ordered that you are to be sent back to Earth as soon as you delouse the sand fleas out of your wings," the C.O. bellowed loudly enough for everyone to hear, "and continue your reconnaissance of General Hanno's household, looking for the source of the unknown energy signature. Do you understand that, Private Thanatos?"

"Yes, Sir." Azrael gave the C.O. a weak salute.

"And furthermore," the C.O. shouted. "You are hereby ordered to remain hidden and not to interfere!!!"

"What if … um," Azrael shifted his weight from one foot to the other, "what if the little girl sees me and she wants me to … um … play dolls again?"

"Then you will do whatever it takes to earn that child's trust and pump her for as much information as you can get about what in Hades is broadcasting that energy signature! Including, if it keeps her quiet, playing dolls!!!"

The crew burst into laughter. One Leonid soldier pretended to kiss his 'baby doll.' The other two sat on their haunches and pretended to scratch behind their ears as though they were dogs loaded with fleas.

"Yes, Sir," Azrael's face turned purple with mortification.

The C.O. rose on four rear legs, gave Azrael a salute of dismissal and marched away, the spiny bones of his legs clacking on the polished stone floor. Azrael edged towards the access hall.

"Hey, Az!" Ensign Zarif trotted to catch up, his green tail bobbing from side-to-side as he ran to counterbalance his weight. "Wait up!"

"What?" Azrael choked. He wiped his eyes as he hurried away so the others wouldn't see his tears.

"Don't pay them no mind," Zarif tasted the air with his long, forked tongue. "They're just a bunch of jarheads."

"Did he have to yell it for the whole base to hear?" Azrael's voice filled with anguish. "You have no idea what it's like, not fitting in!"

"You're right." Zarif grabbed Azrael by the shoulder and forced him to stop. "I don't know what it's like. I'm one of six hatchlings from a single clutch, from a mother who's laid dozens of similar clutches, from a father with three wives. But I *do* know what it's like to have one of your own brothers embarrass you in front of the others."

"Why did the Emperor even give me this assignment?" Azrael cried out. "I'm just a geek from the science academy. If he'd … if he'd asked me to study amoebae, I could understand. But just watch? And do nothing? Why?"

"The gods work in mysterious ways." Zarif touched his clawed hand to his forehead, his heart, and then his lips. "Shay'tan be praised. Perhaps it's some sort of test? Our emperor loves tests. Maybe yours does as well?"

"More like a big fat wager," Azrael scowled. "I've heard about Shay'tan's bets. But Hashem is too idealistic to be cruel!"

"Maybe he's thinking of advancing you to some other position and wants to see how you'll perform under fire?" Zarif suggested. "It's the only explanation that makes sense."

"Maybe. At least it would mean the Emperor isn't simply being sadistic. I don't think I could bear it if he went around toying with people."

The big, green lizard-man's dorsal ridge tucked down in a Sata'anic expression of thoughtfulness. His serpentine eyes turned serious.

"I don't think they mean to be cruel." Zarif said. "They're immortal. They don't think about how using mortals as pawns upsets our lives. To them it's all just a game."

"Well I hope there's a reason he wanted me here," Azrael said. "In the middle of east butt-crack, twiddling my thumbs. I don't even know what I'm supposed to be doing!"

"Sure you do," Zarif said. "The C.O. just told you. Remain a hidden observer. Watch how people act. Get to know the one you've befriended while maintaining your cover. And don't interfere. If that doesn't sound like an anthropological experiment in the making, I don't know what is."

"Oh?" Azrael's perspective suddenly changed. "You think I was sent here to observe? For scientific purposes?"

"You *are* from the science academy, nimrod!" Zarif slapped him on the shoulder. "Send a budding scientist whose mother is an expert in studying pre-sentient species to replace the jarheads to observe behavior? Sounds like a post-doctoral fellowship to me."

"Hey? How'd you know my mother is an expert in her field?"

"Um," Zarif hedged. The lizard man fiddled with the button-band of his uniform. "Word gets around."

"What word?

"They're … um … saying the only reason you got this assignment is because your mother bribed someone in the royal palace to put a bee in the Emperor's ear."

Anger boiled up in Azrael's veins and dissipated. Now *that* made sense. His mother had always kept him and his little sister firmly under the protective arc of her enormous white wings. She'd homeschooled him while out in the field collecting data so he'd get into the science academy years ahead of his peers. In the regular educational track, he wouldn't even be old enough to go to the science academy, much less graduate from it and also get through boot camp. It would explain how he, a mere cadet, had suddenly been sidetracked to where the action was. Hashem wanted him to follow in his mother's footsteps.

And so did he…

"Thanks, Zarif!" A smile lit up Azrael's face as he resumed his hurried pace, trying hard not to flap his wings lest he float through the halls. "I think I know what I'm supposed to do now!"

"Where are you going?" Zarif shouted as Azrael disappeared around the corner.

"To go get de-flead!" Azrael shouted. "I've got to get back down to the planet. The Emperor has entrusted me with figuring out what makes his pet project tick!"

'Notebooks to track data,' Azrael said to himself, his mind spinning joyfully as he thought through the list of supplies he would need to bring with him. 'Binoculars, to observe behavior at a distance. Recording device to record conversations that may prove significant later. And … some sort of treats to reward desired behavior…'

"Glad I could be of assistance." Zarif watched the young angelic bound down the hall, practically taking flight as he ran.

"Angelics!"

Chapter 3

And he said, take now thy son,
Thine only son Isaac, whom thou lovest …
And offer him there for a burnt offering…

Genesis 22:2

Carthage: 311 BC

"Daddy says Bormilcar isn't to be trusted." Elissar's curls surrounded her rosy cheeks like a golden penumbra as she handed Azrael a flatbread on the rooftop to feed his doll. "Mommy thinks I'm too young to understand, but she's really worried."

Azrael glanced down to ensure his recording device caught their conversation. Elissar was a wealth of information about the inner politics of Carthage, the various political factions, their family dynamics, as well as those of the surrounding empires. The child was like a sponge, drinking up whatever gossip the adults around her foolishly presumed she was too young to understand and making her dolls chatter about the political intrigues of generals and kings, economics, and the movements of armies.

"Why?" Azrael pretended to play nursemaid to his crude wheat-stalk doll, wrapping a bandage around its leg. Thank the goddess none of his barracks-mates were here to observe him playing dolls with a precocious eight-year-old. Especially because, truth be told, he enjoyed her company more than theirs.

"Agathocles … that's the Sicilian general." Elissar tied a tiny rag sling onto her own doll's arm. "Daddy says he's too wily to stay contained with a simple blockade. But Bormilcar insists we'll be safe if we just pray to the old gods for salvation."

"The old gods?" Azrael glanced down at the malignant statue of Moloch which dominated the family compound. "You mean *that* old god?"

"Nobody in their right mind *really* worships Moloch," Elissar said haughtily. "We keep a statue of him in our yard because it's expected. My tutor taught me the real history of our ancestors who came here from Tyre."

"And what was that?" Azrael hoped to get something on cassette since his C.O. kept denying his requests for enough security clearance to learn about the real reason for the armistice.

"My ancestor," Elissar said. "The one who was like you? He helped lock Moloch in hell. Hezekiah says we're supposed to protect our cities from Moloch! Not sacrifice the children of slaves to him."

"Wh-wh-what?" Azrael sputtered.

"Oh … everybody does it," Elissar nonchalantly splinted her dolly's leg. "The little boy you sometimes see? The one Mommy won't let me play with so I don't get attached to him? He's my Moloch-brother. Daddy bought him from a slave woman so he'd have a son to sacrifice the next time the citizens get nervous about some military campaign."

Azrael's eyes widened in horror. His mouth opened, but no sound came out. A shudder of revulsion rustled through his feathers, communicating to his observant young research subject that what she'd just said was *not* acceptable.

"All the noble families do it." Elissar's lips trembled as she realized she must have said something wrong. "Otherwise, the priests would expect them to sacrifice *me*."

"Elissar!" Azrael recovered his wits and flared his wings to their full 30-foot wingspan. "That's … just … wrong!!!"

"But all the gods demand sacrifice!" Elissar squeaked, trembling with fear.

"God doesn't want those kinds of sacrifices!!!" Azrael shook with anger. "Not even the child of a slave!!! Such ideas are an … an … an abomination!!!"

Elissar cringed as though she expected to be beaten, fearful of him for the first time since he'd known her. Tears sprang to her silver eyes, instinctively clutching her baby doll to her chest. Azrael realized he was acting like a bully.

"I'm sorry." Azrael tucked his wings against his back and suppressed his anger. "It's just that you humans have some really strange ideas."

"You sound like my tutor," Elissar said. "Hezekiah warned me to never tell anyone he thinks the same things that you do. Not even my father."

Why would a tutor risk shaping the ideas of such a young student when one slip of Elissar's tongue would get him killed. For that matter, why did *Azrael* trust Elissar to do the same thing? One word would have archers hidden in the courtyard before dawn. General Hanno was their nation-states highest ranking military leader and Azrael was essentially a spy. And yet the child remained silent, even though she understood what spying was and how it undermined empires. She understood he played with her because he was here to observe, and yet she knew the difference between *his* observations and the washerwoman she'd turned in for eavesdropping when her father discussed naval blockade strategies with his admirals.

"Your tutor is right." Azrael gave his most disapproving look.

"I'm sorry," Elissar wept. "Please don't go away! You're the only friend I have." Her tearful eyes were those of a child forced to become wise before her time. She was only eight years old!

"This Hezekiah sounds like a wise man," Azrael said. "But you must never repeat the things he teaches you to anyone but me, or the bad men who kill children will have him killed, as well."

"Hezekiah says one day I'll marry a powerful nobleman," Elissar said. "He hopes I'll influence him to get rid of Moloch as the patron god of Carthage. Then children won't need to be scared their parents will sacrifice them if they're disobedient anymore."

Azrael realized Hezekiah planted seeds of political change that would not flourish for decades, until Elissar matured enough to start wielding influence of her own. Who was this tutor?

"You're just a child," Azrael stared at his makeshift doll. "It's wrong to force you to grow up before you're ready."

Guilt sat like rotten meat in his gut. *He* also used her, pretending to be her friend so he could pump her for information.

"But that's what's expected of me," Elissar said. "None of the other nobles have daughters. They sacrificed them in return for favors from the gods. Mommy said it's so they don't have to pay the dowry to get rid of them. It's why ... it's why you're the only person who will play with me!"

Azrael realized he was no better than the humans! Exploiting a child for his own gain! She thought of him as her friend, while *he* deliberately tried to maintain his scientific impartiality by simply referring to her as 'the subject.' Well ... it was all a lie. Truth be told, Azrael looked forward to the time he spent with her and had begun to agonize about how much he would miss her once this assignment ended. He clicked off his recorder.

"Come here." Azrael held out his arms. Elissar crawled into his lap, bleating like a lost little sheep, every bit as heartbroken as his little sister had been whenever he'd been cruel to *her*.

"I'm sorry I frightened you." Azrael's heart filled with a feeling of protectiveness. "I would never hurt you. It's just ... your tutor is right. You shouldn't worship the bull-man. Ever. He's the most evil creature the universe has ever known."

"Do you have stories of him?"

Azrael wasn't supposed to divulge information that would interfere with human evolution. On the other hand, Elissar already had a source of information, the elderly tutor who came each morning to teach her reading, rhetoric, and reason. He would plant a listening device and shadow the man home. In the meantime, since his own knowledge was little more than legend, he'd tell her a story.

"Once upon a time, there were two gods. Ki ... a goddess of chaos. And Moloch ... a god of creation. They were married..."

"And lived happily ever after?" Elissar asked. Her face was eager with curiosity as she snuggled into his lap the same way his little sister used to sit with him to read a story.

"No," Azrael said. "Moloch was a bad husband. Ki gave birth to many children, but when Moloch saw they were made of light, he grew so hungry that he devoured them. Then one day Ki gave birth to She-who-is. Ki didn't want to lose any more children, so she sang the Song of Creation to entice the darkness to protect her. He-who's-not. Primordial chaos."

"My tutor has told me of She-who-is," Elissar said. "And her husband, the Dark Lord. But he's warned me to never speak of them. He said she's the real goddess who rules the universe."

"Your tutor is right," Azrael said. "But there are lots of other gods. People who were once like us, but were so good and pure they became gods, too. Like the Eternal Emperor. He's a god, but he'll be the first to tell you he's not perfect. He tries really hard to always do the right thing."

"I think I'd like your god," Elissar gave him a shy smile. "Maybe someday he'll come and rule our city?"

"In a way," Azrael said. "He already does. But so does another god. Shay'tan. They're always squabbling. They disagree on just about everything that can be disagreed about except for Moloch. The bull-god is bad. Your father shouldn't be raising a slave child to sacrifice to him."

"I'll tell him that when I see him again," Elissar said. "Though Mommy says we won't see him for a while."

"Why not?"

"The council appointed daddy and Bormilcar to go conquer the Sicilians together," Elissar said. "Mommy's really worried. She says Bormilcar will double-cross daddy the first chance he gets."

Elissar's silver eyes filled with worry. She adored both of her parents and her two elder brothers. She couldn't have chosen a better family in all of Earth to be born into, and yet with this privilege came acute loneliness. She slid out of Azrael's lap and resumed her play with her dolls.

"Don't you worry," Elissar told the doll, snapping a twig to make a makeshift crutch. "Azrael is our guardian angel. He's going to make sure everything is all right."

Azrael wished to reassure her, but he was forbidden to interfere. The only reason he spoke with this child at all was because the Emperor had ordered it. The fact this little girl reminded him of his little sister Gazardiel, the one he missed so terribly it made his heart ache, was irrelevant. He was here to do a job.

Azrael clicked on his recording device, resuming his friendly 'interrogation' under the guise of play. He did, however, decide he would contact his mother and request a certain item be included in the next mail shipment.

"Tell me more about your tutor…"

Chapter 4

And when the king of Moab saw that the battle was too sore for him …
He took his eldest son that should have reigned in his stead,
And offered him for a burnt offering…

2 Kings 3:26-27

Carthage: 310 BC

"Elissar will love you."

Azrael talked to his little sister's cast-off doll as he flew under the cover of pre-dawn murkiness. It was the simplest doll his mother had been able to scrounge up, one Gazardiel had long ago become bored with because it didn't walk, talk, eat, or wear fashion clothing. It was more elaborate than any human doll, but could be explained using current technology. If anyone pulled it apart, they might notice the delicate wire that shaped the doll's wings. Steel. Not yet in use in iron-age Earth, but giving it to Elissar would only *bend* the Emperor's prohibition against interference, not break it. It was, after all, only a toy.

"My thesis is complete." Azrael recited to the doll the goodbye speech he was about to give Elissar. "A whole year's worth of data! The Emperor has recalled me back to Haven to present my theory to the Council of Thrones where, if I'm lucky, I'll be inducted into the Eternal Science Academy as a novice member."

The doll, of course, did not answer. Its soft cloth wings fluttered in the breeze, as though it were flying, too. He felt … good. Like an adult, finally! He'd just completed extensive research about the wars humans perpetually waged against one another and compounded credible theories about how their warlike tendencies might be tamed, research which had been helped, in no small part, by a precocious nine-year-old with unusual silver eyes. He would miss Elissar terribly, but already he had begun to think of fascinating future studies to get the Eternal Emperor to grant him leave to conduct another tour of duty here.

As soon as he reached the outer ring of houses he noticed the strange, lingering smoke which overhung the city, offending his nostrils with a scent which sat on the back of his palate like burnt garbage mixed with overcooked meat. Off in the distance, a bonfire raged, along with the sound of drums, cheers, and singing. Azrael pushed the uneasiness which clenched at his gut out of his mind. It was most likely just a party which had lasted through the night. As soon as he circled Elissar's house to land, her tutor came running out and collapsed.

"Oh … please!" Hezekiah reached imploringly towards the roof where Azrael crouched out of sight. "Thank the gods you've come, Private Thanatos! She said you would come for her and you have!"

Azrael peeked over the rooftop. He smelled blood. The old tutor had been stabbed, but his blood smelled … odd.

"How do you know who I am?"

"She told me you were here," Hezekiah said. "Please! There's no time for questions! She's been taken!"

"Taken?" Azrael's heart leaped into his throat. "By whom?" He'd only been on Ceres station a few days!

"Agathocles circumvented the blockade and invaded Megalopolis," Hezekiah wailed. "His troops are on their way here!"

"Where's Elissar?" Panic gripped Azrael's heart. Elissar was the daughter of the de facto ruler of Carthage. "We can get her out of the city so the Sicilian king can't get her!"

"You don't understand," Hezekiah shrieked in anguish. "THEY took her! The priests! Of Moloch! Bormilcar murdered her father and claimed Moloch is displeased the nobles sacrifice slave children instead of their own. The mob has seized the youngest child of every noble in the city! Three hundred of them! They're sacrificing them to Moloch as we speak!"

"Sacrifice?" Bile rose in his throat. "Is she…?"

"Not yet! They began the sacrifices last night, but her mother hid her from them. They just found her! I called for backup, but they won't be here for hours! *You* might be able to save her!"

Hezekiah held out an ancient communications device, Alliance by design, but of a type Azrael had only ever seen in history books, thousands of years old. It was the source of the energy signature which had brought Azrael here in the first place.

The tutor reached for his eyes and pulled out contact lenses, revealing he possessed the gold-green eyes of a serpent, and unfurled his tail from beneath his robe. Hezekiah possessed Sata'anic eyes? Like his friend Ensign Zarif had back on Ceres Station? And a tail? Only Hezekiah was … human? Half-human? Nobody had told Azrael anything about human-Sata'anic hybrids numbering amongst the Fallen! What in Hades was going on here?

Screw non-interference! Azrael pulled out his comms unit and called back to base. "Papa Bear, Papa Bear, this is Baby Doll calling with a Code-1 emergency. Over."

"Baby Doll ... this is Papa Bear. What's your emergency?"

"These nutcases are sacrificing 300 children to Moloch!" Azrael called. "Request backup."

Azrael had learned one thing from being forced to commingle with the 'warrior class.' Even the Sata'anic lizards loved giving a good tail-kicking when it came to protecting hatchlings ... um ... kids.

"Baby Doll, this is the C.O.," a gruff voice came on. "You know the policy for that planet. No interference. Repeat. No interference. You are not to interfere."

"They're killing children!!!" Azrael screamed into the radio. "To Moloch!!! Three hundred of them. The Emperor will make an exception!"

"You are not to interfere. I don't like it, but you know the Emperor's policies. Non-interference is his highest law."

"The evil bastard is searching for a new host body so he can escape!" Azrael shouted. "This kid is a direct descendant of Lucifer! She just might be the one!"

There was silence at the other end of the radio. The C.O. pushed the push-to-talk button, pausing as he thought on his feet. In the background, Azrael could hear the other soldiers shouting they drew the line of noninterference at letting innocent children get murdered. The C.O. was about to have a riot on his hands.

"Baby Doll, Baby Doll, this is Papa Bear. Stand by and await further orders while I clear this with the Emperor. I repeat. You are to stand by. You got that?"

"She'll be dead by then!"

"Private Thanatos, you are to stand by until..."

Azrael never heard the rest. He dropped the microphone and took to the air, streaking towards the malevolent bonfire where humans murdered their own innocent children and cheered.

Thirty feet tall and clad in bronze, the statue of the city's patron god dominated the city with its body of a man and head of an enormous, sneering bull. Built on top of a platform, at its center was a brazier for lighting a bonfire. The statue possessed moveable arms suspended over the bonfire with chains so the priests could manipulate the gears to make it appear the sacrifice was bringing the statue to life.

Unlike most cultures which made burnt offerings by slaughtering an animal humanely and *then* cooking it, usually a 'sacrifice' which was merely ceremonial as the participants then feasted upon the meal the way they would any other cooked meat, the Priests of Moloch placed *live* animals upon the statue's hands and cooked the poor creatures alive. *Including human victims…* It was a gruesome way to die, one designed to cause the victim horrific pain.

Azrael spied Elissar being led up the steps along with other child-victims to stare up at the Evil One who was about to devour them. It was not to Hashem that he prayed, the immortal Emperor he knew could not hear him, but a much older goddess. One legend said had stripped Moloch of his ability to recreate his own physical body and rendered him a disembodied wraith. One who might sympathize with a lowly Angelic's prayer to save the life of his young friend.

"Ki … I know you're too high and mighty to listen to the likes of me. But please! She's just a child!"

The Priests of Moloch beat drums to rile up the citizens of Carthage into a religious fervor. The people were not fearful because they watched their own children being murdered, but because their god had sent an invasion and *this* is what the Priests had told them must be done to appease him. The crowd sang hymns to drown out the screams of a little boy who'd just been placed upon the Devourer of Children's outstretched hands.

The arms slid down, casting the hapless child into the flames below. The boy screamed. Tears sprang to Azrael's eyes. His wings pounded the air, his heart pumping so fast he feared it would burst, but he was too far away to save the boy just thrown into the pit to burn alive.

"Elissar!!!"

As he got closer he saw the priests no longer held onto the chains, but somehow the arms of the statue moved. How? This was a pre-technological planet. The statue's red eyes sprang to life as its mouth moved into a satisfied sneer. The head tilted downwards to look at Elissar who had been led by priests to stand before it. Azrael realized there was real intelligence in those eyes. Whatever the priests were doing somehow *fed* the ancient evil and acted as a power source, giving the Devourer of Children strength. Bits and fragments of legends he had researched sprang to mind. The last piece of the puzzle fell into place.

The tutor possessing unauthorized technology. Passing along secret knowledge to the direct descendent of Moloch's last unwitting host, Lucifer. Preparing her with knowledge she might need to one day lead her people as the new Morning Star should Moloch ever escape. Knowledge to resist Moloch.

"Let me go!" Elissar screamed. She stomped on the priest's foot and bit him as he placed her upon Moloch's outstretched hands.

The statue's eyes flared with malevolent glee as the mouth moved. Azrael realized it was more than a statue, but a golem, a robotic prosthesis of some sort which could be animated given the right sacrificial spirit to speak to Moloch's followers.

"*Quaerebamus inter nost est* [this is the one we've been looking for]." Moloch spoke in a horrible, deep voice that made the stones in the city shudder. "*Ego devorabit vitae industria et capere corpus meum* [I shall devour her life energy and seize her body for my host]."

A cheer went through the mob. Priests signaled the band which played instruments and beat drums to play louder to drown out Elissar's terrified screams. Azrael realized Elissar was about to be consumed, not by a fire lit beneath a statue of the ancient malignant god, but by Moloch *himself*. Whatever Elissar had, Moloch needed it to escape.

"Let me go!" Elissar fought against the metal fingers which clutched her small body, but she was too young to defend herself!

'*They –have- to be young,*' a voice spoke in Azrael's mind. '*Otherwise their spirit develops enough to resist possession. Moloch keeps himself alive by feeding upon the life energy of others. Lucifer was taken when he was fifteen years old. Elissar is only nine!*'

All of a sudden, Azrael understood that death was the least of Elissar's worries. There were worse fates than death…

And also that these thoughts were not his own.

"I understand," Azrael said, thankful the goddess had heard him. Ki asked something of him, offered him a choice.

The hands of the ancient god slid down to drop Elissar into the brazier, the trial-by-fire that would cause enough pain to separate her spirit from her mortal shell so Moloch could seize it for himself. A dark-winged blur streaked down from the sky, following her through the putrid green dimensional portal the brazier hid straight into the fires of Gehenna.

"Azrael!!!" Elissar screamed. Her small hand reached up towards his as her body slid into the flames. For so long as he existed, he would never forget the look of terror on Elissar's face as she disappeared beneath the sea of molten fire.

Azrael sped in behind her.

It hurt! It hurt! His feathers caught fire as he pressed his wings against his back and raced into the pit after her. He grabbed her hand, pulling her against his body and wrapping himself around her, his arms, his wings, trying to protect her. He understood they were no longer on Earth, but the trans-dimensional prison known as Gehenna, the reason for the Armistice.

"I've got you." Azrael wrapped his very soul around her, refusing to let her go as they sank into the magma to die together, every nerve fiber screaming with agonizing pain. Let Moloch deal with *his* stubborn soul! Not that of a nine-year-old child!

The most powerful energy source in the universe was not fission, or fusion, or even the clash of anti-matter or gravitons, but the energy cast off by the life-spark the gods called 'consciousness' and human legend called the soul. Ascended beings were merely soul-sparks which had grown powerful enough over the course of many lifetimes to use their *own* energy to manipulate matter. It was a source of power more potent than a hundred million suns, especially at the moment a lifespark transformed from one type of matter into another.

The flames parted and Azrael saw, not the effigy of a bull-man, but the Devourer of Children himself. Moloch towered above them, an enormous, muscular creature whose hand was so large he could fit the both of them into a single palm. His snout had a bovine flare and he had horns and ears like a bull, but no ruminant had ever had such sharp teeth or snorted fire the way that Moloch did.

"Heac mea est! [she is mine!]" Moloch clutched at Azrael's body with fiery claws. *"Da-te ei mihi!* [Give her to me!!!]" The hell dimension shook as Moloch tried to force Azrael to release her.

"Go to hell!" were the last words Azrael was able to form as flames incinerated his face. He felt Elissar shudder and die in his arms. She was dead. But her spirit still clung to his, intertwining with it so Moloch could not take her from him, his young friend who he loved more than his own existence. Together they were a larger morsel than Moloch could digest. The Evil One tried to tear them apart, but Azrael held on.

He heard a song. A beautiful song. Not Moloch, but the song which underlay the thoughts which had urged him to cast himself into the fire to save Elissar from a fate worse than death. It was the song which underlay All-That-Is, the Song of Creation.

'Give her to me,' Ki whispered into Azrael's mind. *'You will see her again. I promise.'*

Azrael used the energy released by his own death to punch a portal out of the hell-dimension and push his little friend into the welcoming arms which reached down from the highest realms. Safe. Although Elissar's mortal shell had expired, because he had protected her at the moment of expiration, the life-spark containing her spirit was safe. It was the only thing that mattered. That ... and making sure Moloch didn't have enough left of *him* to use *his* body as his next mortal vessel.

With his dying breath, Azrael flapped what was left of his wings to dodge Moloch's fiery claws and cast himself into the unearthly fires of uncreation where even Moloch couldn't follow him. His body turned to ash as pain stripped his spirit of the ability to recreate his own mortal shell.

The faint melody of the Song of Creation rang like a lone cello, filling his soul with joy even as it was being destroyed.

So beautiful.

Part II

And if the people of the land do any ways hide their eyes from the man,
When he giveth of his seed unto Moloch,
And kill him not:
Then I will set my face against that man,
And against his family,
And will cut him off,
And all that go a whoring after him,
To commit whoredom with Moloch,
From among their people

Leviticus 20:4-5

Chapter 5

In the beginning …
The Earth was without form, and void.

Genesis 1:1-2

Time: indeterminate
Highest Ascended Realms

The life spark drifted upon the Song of Creation like an infant rocked in a boat upon a gentle sea. Although he sensed his twin-spark was far away, her spirit remained tethered to his like a lengthy mooring. She was okay, and so long as he knew she was okay, he was content.

He fed upon the Song like a newborn suckling at the breast, gathering sub-atomic particles of primordial chaos to the consciousness which had survived the fires of Gehenna. He reconstituted his being until, at last, he regained awareness.

'Azrael,' Ki whispered. *'It's time to awaken. I need your help.'*

He nestled deeper into the Song like a small boy protesting his mother's command to get up for school, not wishing to remember. He didn't like it when he remembered. It hurt. He stretched his spirit across time and space, stroking his twin-spark's mind, reassuring himself she was still there. He couldn't understand why Ki wouldn't let him go to her.

'You will destroy her in your current form,' Ki said gently. *'If you wish to see her again, you must evolve enough to act as her protector.'*

The twin-spark urged him to do as Ki asked. As soon as he had the right building blocks in place, she would join him. He signaled his assent, stretching millions of tendrils of consciousness as he finally began to awaken from his long slumber. Images played upon his mind. *A mother. A sister. A best friend. Agape. Unselfish love.*

The memories changed. Fire. Gigantic arms reaching towards him. The scream of a helpless child as a bull-like maw chewed upon the souls of the innocent. Elissar! He'd sped down into the flames to prevent the evil god from consuming her.

He opened his mouth to scream and realized he had none. He reached towards Elissar's mind and found his arms no longer existed. He flapped his wings and discovered thousands of tendrils of spirit now took their place. Pain. So much pain. He directed the flow of primordial matter which drifted in the Song to give voice to the scream he no longer had a mouth to shout.

Azrael had his own song to sing now. The Song of Destruction. As he recognized his own existence, twenty-seven solar systems went supernova. Luckily, nothing more evolved than bacteria existed on those worlds. Ki had foreseen his panic and nurtured him back to sentience where he could do little harm.

'See, sweet boy,' Ki whispered. 'Your power is too raw and new. You must learn to control it.'

He sent a query to the mother-consciousness who sang to him, asking what she needed him to do. Images jumped into his mind of a small, nimble gnat biting a great bull until it became so exasperated it bucked and twisted like a rodeo bull. Hatred flared for what the bull had done to his twin spark. Azrael signaled his assent.

Ki began to teach him how to bait the bull…

Chapter 6

For we will destroy this place,
Because the cry of them is waxen great before the face of the Lord;
And the Lord hath sent us to destroy it.

Genesis 19:13

Earth: 146 BC **(165 years later)**
Carthage

Death from above. A creature of nightmare sent in whenever Ki needed someone to slip in, sever the consciousness of a Moloch-worshipping Agent from a host it had hijacked to remain corporeal in this realm, and drag it back into the fiery hell-dimension that was now as familiar to him as breathing had once been. Gehenna. The place where he had died.

It was funny how staring death in the face every day made you miss the little things you'd experienced when you'd still been alive. Like Mom's delicious home-cooked meals. Or the endearing way his little sister had rifled through his things and followed him around. Or Elissar, feeding him honey cakes and chattering about the intrigues of generals and kings as they'd played dolls upon the roof.

Elissar! Her name was a sob upon the lips he no longer possessed. He missed them. Mama. Gazardiel. But for some reason, he missed Elissar most of all! The best friend he'd ever had…

The Roman army had no idea he trailed behind them, watching them pull the city apart stone by stone; Carthage, whose Moloch-worship had grown so abominable her neighbors had finally set aside their differences and united to destroy her. Death. Death from above. Death to those who worshipped the Evil One who fed upon the souls of children. It was his job to make sure no Moloch-worshippers escaped as the Romans razed the city to the ground.

Ki's voice had grown faint once she'd sent him back to this realm, the lonely cello whose notes would grace his ears whenever she wished to send him on a mission. It was like experiencing the same beautiful memory over and over again. The Song Ki had sung to keep him alive. If he was alive…

Was he alive?

If feeling satisfaction at watching the Romans enslave the descendants of those who'd beaten drums and sung songs to drown out Elissar's screams meant he still existed, then perhaps he *was* still alive? No. Loneliness more accurately described his feelings than revenge. Or hunger. A great aching void which nothing could fill. He clutched the spot where his heart would be if he still had a heart to break. It sure *felt* like a broken heart, even though his spirit passed right through the nothingness that had once been his physical form.

Anti-form, he corrected himself. He was the opposite of a physical form. A creature of the void. Whatever he touched simply ceased to exist. Death incarnate. Only the life spark itself possessed immunity to his loathsome touch. Consciousness. What humans called the soul.

Soldiers herded women and children towards slave-galleys waiting to convey them into a life of involuntary servitude. Azrael wafted through the shadows, invisible, a darkness only those close to death could perceive as women wailed and babies screamed in terror … or the genetically evolved.

"Help us," a boy cried. His eyes filled with tears as he reached towards Azrael. "Ml'ch, set me free."

Azrael shuddered. Ml'ch. Moloch. The child reminded him of the boy who'd preceded Elissar into the flames, the one he hadn't been able to save. The one whose *spirits* he hadn't been able to save. Elissar was lost to him, but somewhere she still existed. He could feel her as though, any moment, she would pop out from behind a bush and chime 'I see you.' The others had been devoured, a fate worse than death.

Azrael faded back into the shadows. The Romans were brutal oppressors, but they were also an empire of laws. Even slaves had rights. They did not sacrifice their children as food for a malignant god. He pried himself away and floated above the city, letting fate take him where it may. So much had changed in the years since he had died.

Fate brought him to a house which was familiar. *Her* house. The dilapidated structure was no longer the house of a nobleman, but like him, it still existed. For now. The Romans had set fire to it. Azrael watched, his thoughts dark as flames licked through the tired roof, turning the structure into ash. Consumed by fire, just as *he* had been consumed by fire. Azrael floated without form; a billowing black storm cloud so dark none would ever mistake him for smoke.

No cloth dolls or honey-cakes adorned the roof where they used to play. No more colorful chatter about how one doll's empire could pit another doll's subjects against them and compel change. He missed her. Oh, how he missed her! She'd been a bright light shining in the pre-dawn sky. Her loss was not just Azrael's loss, but her entire world's.

"I'm sorry," Azrael whispered as the roof collapsed into the gutted building. Sparks flew up into his non-physical form and were absorbed. He had it within his power to simply touch the flame and extinguish it, to suck up the energy until it could no longer burn, but for some reason he did not. Ever since Ki had sent him back to protect this world, he had avoided this place. This accursed city where his anger at what they had done to the only real friend he'd ever had threatened to upset the delicate equilibrium which enabled him to exist in this realm without destroying it.

Destroy. The first thing the Romans had done was smash the statue where Elissar had met her death and dump it into the harbor. But the smaller statue in her courtyard was still here, shoved off its lofty pedestal, but otherwise unharmed, a reminder that Moloch still continued to exist. Its ruby eyes glittered against the flames, taunting Azrael's sorry state of existence like laughter. The air around him shuddered as he suppressed the perpetual dysphonic vibration which could uncreate worlds whenever he lost control of his emotions. It was better to act against the source of his anger than suppress it and lose control. He roiled towards the offending statue like pyroclastic flow and solidified into dozens of tentacles, wrapping one around the statue and relishing the feel of it dissolving into his ever-growing consciousness.

"Take that!"

The sound of stones crunching beneath a boot disturbed his ruminations from somewhere behind him. Azrael turned and froze at the first sight of one of *his* kind he'd seen since the day he'd been rendered a disembodied wraith.

"Get back!" the Angelic soldier ordered. His eyes glowed with an unearthly blue light as his sword poised ready to strike.

"I mean you no harm," Azrael said. "But please don't strike me. If you touch me you will die."

"I'm not afraid of you." The unknown Angelic's features were devoid of emotion, but he was big. The biggest Angelic that Azrael had ever seen.

"It's not a threat," Azrael spoke softly to convey he meant no harm. "I'm ... damaged. Everything I touch dissipates. Only the Song of Ki enables me to survive."

The Angelic cocked his head as though listening to someone speak even though Azrael could detect no listening device implanted in his ear. Although he wore the armor of a Roman legionnaire, he had the unusual black-brown wings of a Seraphim descendant. Wings like Azrael, himself, had once possessed, although the Emperor had never told his mother who his DNA-sire had been.

"Why hasn't your mate healed you?" the Angelic asked.

"I have no mate." Azrael tucked his tentacles in front of his form like an enormous resting cat to appear as non-threatening as possible. "I was rather young when I died."

A niggling sensation registered in Azrael's consciousness. Not only did he feel he should recognize the Angelic standing before him, but he felt the way he did whenever Ki was trying to tear his attention away from some fascinating butterfly he studied to alert him Moloch's Agents were on the prowl.

Only it wasn't Ki's energy he sensed…

"You lie." The Angelic flared his wings. "Only a mated pair can hear the Song of Ki." His fist gripped tighter around the hilt of his sword as feathers stretched into the wind, ready to catch it at a moment's notice and leap into the air.

Azrael had no idea who could or could not hear the song which perpetually vibrated like a radio playing softly in the background. All he knew was that whenever Ki wished to send him on a mission, the Song would grow louder.

"I have no mate," Azrael repeated. "But the Watchmen Ki asks me to save so they can bear witness against Moloch say they can hear it, too. At least for a little while."

The Angelic had no insignia of rank on his armor, but the gold breastplate indicated he must be a very high-ranking Angelic, indeed. Who was this guy, anyway? Perhaps he could find out what had been going on within the Alliance since his death and rebirth? Or was that death and … death? If nothing else, it would give him a chance to make small talk and reduce the likelihood the Angelic would rush at him and cause his own demise.

"Perhaps you have news of my mother?" Azrael asked. "She's a sociobiologist on the Eternal Emperor's staff. Janiel Thanatos?"

Mortal Angelics could live a thousand years … *if* stupid wars against Shay'tan didn't cut short their lives. His mother had still been young when he'd died. He'd teleported to every place they'd ever lived, but Mama and Gazardiel were long gone. With no way to convince terrified mortals to speak to him and no ability to touch electronic equipment without shorting it out, Azrael had finally given up searching. Ki needed him here.

"What's your name?" the Angelic asked, his demeanor changing.

"Azrael Thanatos. Or at least it was. Now … well … I guess my name is still the same. Not that anybody's called me anything but 'monster' since I came back. If they call me anything at all. Actually … usually they just scream and run away. You have no idea how good it is to actually speak to somebody for a change instead of ... well ... killing them. But they deserve it. If I do. Kill them. That is..."

Azrael realized he was doing that nervous run-on talking thing. He was normally rather shy, but it had been so long since he'd actually spoken to someone who wasn't dead, near-dead, or an Agent of Moloch that an enormous dam of talk sat all bottled up, ready to spill out at the first person unfortunate enough to ask, 'so ... how are you doing?'

Azrael decided maybe it would be better if he shut up....

The Angelic lowered his sword, the point resting against the ground, but he did not sheath it. His wings relaxed, slightly flared, ready to spring into action if Azrael so much as twitched. Azrael recognized the 'ready stance' they'd tried to teach him at Basic Training.

"Who's your sire?" the Angelic asked.

"I don't know," Azrael said. "Mama ... she had difficulty. The Emperor ... she'd been working for him for a long time. Mama liked to say instead of a commendation, he gave her me."

The sword still pointed into the ground between them, but by the subtle relaxation of the Angelic's wings, he realized he must have told him something he'd already known.

"Who are your siblings?" From his demeanor, it wasn't really a question. The Angelic already knew the answer and was testing to see whether Azrael knew.

"Gazardiel," Azrael said. "My baby sister. I suppose she's married by now. Unless she was like Mama. Nobody wants to marry a sterile hybrid."

Once more, Azrael felt that peculiar feeling when Ki wanted to reach him. Or if he was extracting a particularly nasty Agent that was squatting on a human host-body like a tick. Those were the worst. Of all the squatters Azrael had been forced to reap, the demigods were...

Oh ... shoot!

"General Mannuki'ili!" Azrael blurted, suddenly realizing why the Angelic looked familiar. "I'm ... I'm ... I'm ... S-s-sir!!!"

Azrael lurched up out of his catlike pose, fumbling his tentacles as he tried to figure out which one he could use to give the Eternal Emperor's highest-ranking general a proper Alliance salute. He had neither a hand, nor a forehead to salute against. Mikhail. The Angelic who had thrown Moloch into Gehenna.

The General burst out laughing, a most unexpected reaction given how serious the Angelic ... scratch that ... Archangel ... had been until this very moment. Unlike Angelics, who were mortal, albeit long-lived compared to humans, Archangels were ascended beings; like the Eternal Emperor, only younger. A lot younger. The General had been the first.

"You're supposed to be dead, Private Thanatos," the General said. "How long did Ki keep you in the upper realms before she let you go?"

Azrael lost form. Every tentacle except the one he'd chosen to give some semblance of a salute deteriorated into a roiling black thundercloud.

"I'm not sure," Azrael said. "Time moves differently there."

"It does," the General agreed. "Why didn't you report back to your commanding officer?"

"I ... um ... tried," Azrael stammered. "In case you haven't noticed, I'm kind of ... dead? Undead? Besides ... Ki asked me to stay ... and ... um ... I'm not even sure who I'd report to now. The day I died I'd just been transferred back to the Eternal Emperor's scientific division. When Ki released me, it was 160 years later. The only reason I was on Earth that day was because…"

Azrael trailed off. Ensign Zarif had cooked the books so he could make one last trip down to give Elissar the doll and say goodbye. Zarif. Another friend ... lost. His shorter-lived Sata'anic soldier friend was also dead and in the grave, as was his former Spiderid commanding officer. There had been no one at Ceres station to reason with when he'd teleported there in the hopes someone would remember him long enough to stop screaming in terror and shooting at him.

"We've been getting reports of an unknown entity punching holes directly into Gehenna to deposit Agents," the General said. "Witnesses described a young void-creature, but your behavior didn't match that of a void creature."

Azrael had no idea what void-creatures did or did not do. In fact, he hadn't even been aware there were others of his kind. But he realized the General had never answered his initial question.

"You do realize there's a front gate you're supposed to be using?" the General asked, his eyebrows raised in bemusement.

"N-n-no s-s-sir," Azrael stammered. "I didn't ... um ... Ki didn't tell me much when she sent me back. I just ... um ... that's how I got out ... I think ... I'm not really sure how I got out the first time because I don't remember ... but I think ... um ... you mean to tell me there's really a front gate?"

The General stared at Azrael as though he were a puzzle he wished to decipher. Azrael could practically hear the wheels turning in his mind as his expression turned from bemusement to curiosity. Yes. Why had a mere cadet been sent to do a man's job?

"Sir?" Azrael interrupted. "About my mother?"

The Archangel's expression changed from curiosity to sympathy.

"I'm sorry," the General said as gently as he could. "She passed away when word reached her you had died. The Emperor himself performed the ... uh ... he said she died of a broken heart."

A strangled cry of grief escaped into the air, causing the matter around Azrael to vibrate like a discordant note. Whenever his emotions became aroused, he destroyed. Even if he didn't mean to. He backed away lest he inadvertently destroy the General.

"I've got to go," Azrael choked, trying to stave off sobbing until after he'd gotten out of earshot of his commanding officer. Actually ... Ki was his commanding officer now. But Azrael didn't wish to blubber in front of the personal guardian of the Eternal Emperor.

"Private Thanatos," the General called as Azrael rose into the air, preparing to leap between the dimensions before he destroyed half the Mediterranean. "Wait!"

Azrael paused, his tentacles trembling with emotion. He could feel the molecules around him pick up harmonic sub-frequencies of the discordant vibration his emotions were broadcasting and multiply them like rings circling out like a stone dropped into water. The Song of Destruction. Sparks flew off his non-physical form as electrons collided with the antimatter he was comprised of and simply blinked out of existence.

The General appeared to understand what Azrael had become, and he was not afraid.

"I'll find you," the General gave him a salute. "As soon as you've had time to grieve. The Regent will want to meet you."

The air around Azrael reached the breaking point. He darted between the dimensions to the farthest end of the universe, where suns had long since transformed into white dwarfs and the planets which surrounded them were devoid of life.

Wailing like a little boy who had just lost his mother, Azrael destroyed a dozen stars.

Chapter 7

And the temptor came ... and saith unto him,
If thou be the Son of God, cast thyself down:
For it is written, he shall give his angels charge concerning thee:
And in their hands they shall bear thee up,
Lest at any time thou dash thy foot against a stone.

St. Matthew 4:3-6

Earth: Friday, April 3, 33 AD **(179 years later)**
Jerusalem

It had started out as a scientific theory, but then the Emperor had gotten the idea into his head to test it out and the next thing he knew, Hashem had broken his own rule about not interfering. And now? Azrael stared in horror as the procession wound its way through the streets of Jerusalem.

"We've got to stop this!" Azrael cried out in anguish. "This isn't right!"

"This is *your* mission, science-boy," Lucifer taunted with a malicious grin. "I don't know how my father lured such an evolved spirit down from the ascended realms, but it looks like you just got your rallying point."

Azrael stared at the adopted son of the Eternal Emperor in horror, the one he'd been forced to work with ever since he'd been sent back into this world. With white-blonde hair, white wings, and features so handsome he bordered at the brink of being too beautiful to be real, the most compelling feature about Lucifer was not his eyes that were the same remarkable shade of silver Elissar's had been, but his rabid hatred of the Eternal Emperor. Azrael wasn't certain what pleased the debauch Fallen Angelic more ... the fact a snot-nosed dweeb such as himself had enticed the Emperor to bend his rules against non-interference for a chance to stomp out Moloch worship? Or the fact they were watching that experiment *fail*?

"Not this!" Azrael fanned his trembling tentacles in the direction where the procession had stopped to let Yeshua pause and get a drink of water. "He was supposed to..."

Not this. No! Never this. Azrael had merely suggested the Emperor send someone a little less over the top than Lucifer to set a good example for these people. That was all. To do so without violating the Armistice, Yeshua had agreed to incarnate into human form with only the scantest hint of past-life memories. Not …

"Oh!" Azrael's tentacles flailed in horror as Yeshua tripped on the garish purple robe they'd made him wear and stumbled. The pole fell on top of him.

"Look!" Lucifer's wings fluttered as he rubbed Azrael's face in his own sadism. "The same people who sold him out are now helping him carry it."

Lucifer's snowy white wings picked up the fire of the noonday sun as he fluttered over to stand next to Azrael at the edge of the roof, his feathers so close they nearly brushed Azrael's deadly tentacles. Unlike most creatures, Lucifer did not pay Azrael a wide berth. In fact, if Azrael didn't know any better, he'd swear Lucifer *wanted* to get zapped, an urge the General had warned him not to succumb to no matter *how* badly Lucifer antagonized him.

"Sir," one of Lucifer's Sata'an-human hybrids hissed from beneath his cloak. "Look! Over there. We've got company."

Lucifer cursed under his breath. Azrael glanced across the roofline to see he wasn't the only Archangel who'd come investigate the barbaric crime unfolding below. Oh! Thank Haven! The General had arrived with two other archangels. Perhaps the Emperor had given them permission to intervene? Azrael made ready to teleport as far away from the slimy former Alliance Prime Minister he was forced to cooperate with as he possibly could.

"Whatsamatter, Az?" Lucifer's pale, beautiful features took on a cruel aspect as he taunted Azrael's failure. "You're not so keen on toying with the lives of mortals when you actually have to watch the results of your actions, are you?"

Lucifer stepped closer. Why did he do that? Taunt him when he knew a single zap would end his charade as the de facto Emperor of Earth? Demi-god or mortal, Lucifer's stint as Moloch's unwilling host had damaged his DNA. Although immortal, he was unable to teleport or pull his mortal shell into the upper realms to reconstitute it the way the other Archangels could and even if he died, he was barred from entering the dreamtime. Welcome neither in Haven nor Hades, Lucifer was trapped in limbo, the reluctant warden of an unearthly prison.

"They're going to nail him to a cross," Lucifer spat, gesturing towards the crowd which had started to wail. "This is some experiment you cooked up! Did you and my father sit up nights scheming how badly you had to torture the poor guy before the humans would get off their asses and react?"

Lucifer bounced forward like a circus clown, tottering at the edge of the roof where Azrael perched, his white wings pounding to keep his balance as Azrael ducked to avoid brushing against him.

"W-w-watch out!" Azrael warned. "You'll fall!"

"In case you haven't noticed," Lucifer sneered. "I'm already Fallen! You don't get any lower than this!"

The procession paused. Yeshua looked up and made eye contact with Azrael, frowning as he saw Lucifer teetering at the edge of the roof like a drunken clown. The anguish in Yeshua's brown eyes softened as his lips moved in silent prayer. Azrael could almost *hear* the words of forgiveness that Yeshua dispensed on their behalf.

"I'm sorry!" Azrael reached towards him. Black tears of primordial chaos dripped down his tentacles, dissolving tiny holes into the roof. "This wasn't what I meant to happen."

Lucifer stood, one boot perched on the edge of the roof as he drew his sword and offered it, hilt pointed at Yeshua to communicate he was willing to order his men to take up arms and slay the evil bastards leading the prophet to his execution.

Yeshua shook his head. No. He did not wish for Lucifer to interfere. An unreadable expression flashed across Lucifer's face. Contempt? Pity? Disgust? Lucifer whirled back towards Azrael, his fists clenched in fury.

"You're just another one of my father's ivory tower do-gooders," Lucifer snarled. "Come in with your lofty ideas and think you can just wave a carrot in front of these human's noses and get them to jump? Then when you get chewed up and spit out by reality, you weep like a helpless child! Only you're *not* helpless! Are you, *Death!* This is *your* rallying point. You could stop this if you really wanted to!"

Lucifer threw his head back, his white-wings shuddering with hatred as he shook his fist at the sky.

"Do you hear that, you bastard?" Lucifer shouted at the father/god who had spurned him for over 3,500 years. "This isn't another one of your stupid games of chess!"

"S-s-sir," Azrael stammered, horrified to hear the Eternal Emperor's name blasphemed. "I must protest."

"How do you think you got down here, you stupid bastard?" Lucifer snarled at Azrael. He stepped up to the spot that would be Azrael's face if he still had one. "Do you think you ended up on this world by chance? It was all just another one of my father's bets against Emperor Shay'tan!" He flapped his wings and shook his fist at the sky. "Isn't that right, Father? You sent a boy to do a man's job and didn't even have the decency to warn him this entire world is the gateway to Moloch's prison!"

Azrael felt as though he'd just been sucker-punched in the gut.

"It isn't true!"

Lucifer leaned into the swirling blackness that radiated outwards in increasing circles of disharmony. The Song of Creation which enabled Azrael's existence in this realm slipped in the face of Lucifer's lies.

"Why don't you ask him the next time you see him?" Lucifer hissed. "Or better yet, why not ask his attack dog? Everyone knows the General will not tell a lie. Not even for the Emperor!"

An Agent-infested Roman soldier shoved Yeshua forward, forcing the procession to move. Yeshua stumbled a third time. An old lame woman reached out to touch his robe and shouted she was healed. The crowd got rowdy as it dawned on them they were killing a pre-ascended being. Another Agent rammed something down around Yeshua's temples, drawing blood.

The air around Azrael roiled as he began to lose what little shape he had, his formless nothingness sparking with static as the overwhelming urge to *do something* overrode his orders from Yeshua that, no matter what happened, he must not interfere!

"Oh look," Lucifer laughed, a raucous, bitter sound as he gestured at the spectacle as though he were the emcee. "They've even crowned him king! King of the do-gooders!"

"You will be *silent!*" Azrael hissed. The rooftop beneath him trembled as he dissolved a large swath of feathers off of the bottom of one of Lucifer's wings. A warning. Be … quiet … or … else!

Lucifer stepped closer.

"Go ahead. Do it."

Azrael reached forward to yank the bastard out of his body and kill *him* instead of watching Yeshua die.

"Corporal Thanatos!" a voice bellowed. "Stand down!"

"S-s-sir!" Azrael yanked his tentacle beneath the cloak which did absolutely nothing to buffer his distressing tendency to kill or dissipate everything he touched. "I-I-I was just…"

"Oh look!" Lucifer sneered. "If it isn't my father's favorite watchdog!"

Lucifer made an exaggerated bow as though he were bowing to the Emperor himself.

"Have you come, General, to watch the show?" Lucifer taunted. "Or are you here to tell the little void creature the truth about the reason he is the way he is now?"

The General growled, his formidable self-control slipping as a murderous expression appeared upon his face. He stepped closer, his face inches from Lucifer's, and clenched his fists. Emotions warred inside Azrael's primordial nothingness as two songs battled for control. Creation? Or destruction?

A shout from the crowd below reminded Azrael of why they were all here. While heaven bickered, Yeshua faced execution. It would be even *less* desirable for his esteemed commanding officer to strangle the little weasel than if he did it himself.

"Sir?" Azrael said. "We were just discussing my ... uh ... my scientific theories."

Some scientific theory! Lucifer was right. It had been a nifty idea. The perfect religious leader. Someone to teach the humans other ways to be heard by the gods besides making sacrifice to Moloch. And it had been a great plan ... right up until the point Yeshua's own disciples had sold him out to the enemy!

The General stood poised, his hand gripped on the hilt of his sword.

"Do it." Lucifer stepped closer to the General, not backing down as any sane creature would do when facing down the greatest superhero in the universe. "Finish what you started all those years ago."

The look on Lucifer's face was not anger or disgust, but pleading.

A muscle twitched in the General's jaw. Control. Azrael had never met anyone with as much self-control as the General, but he was *this* close to ridding them of Hashem's Fallen son once and for all...

A shout of dismay went through the humans as they approached the hill at Calvary. Women wailed and men shouted. Roman soldiers rushed out and stabbed at the throng with pilum, forcing them back. Two Agents pinned Yeshua to the ground and lashed his arms outstretched across the pole they had forced him to carry to his own execution.

"We ... have ... to help him!" Azrael flinched with each strike of the hammer.

Yeshua cried out in pain, blood spurting as the spikes severed his arteries as all around him the humans wept and pleaded with the soldiers for mercy. Even the non-infested Roman soldiers questioned Pilate's decision to crucify the rabble-rousing rabbi from Galilee whose only crime had been to question the Jewish temples cozy relationship with Rome.

"Why I do believe the little science nerd was right on the money," Lucifer's mood shifted into a wolfish grin. "One minute they're selling him out and the next they're begging them to stop. Just like *him*."

The soldiers moved to Yeshua's feet, driving the spikes through the bones. Azrael wept as the soldiers heaved it upright to stand alongside the other two sacrificial victims. Crucifixions were ostensibly punishment for crimes against the state, but only the Angelics knew the reason they were so prolonged and barbaric was because the mental anguish cast off by the victim in the moments before their death was siphoned off to feed Moloch, not to appease the Eternal Emperor or any other decent god.

"Sir," Azrael wept. "Please. I didn't know ... I didn't know it would be like this! Please! We have to put a stop to it!"

"Forgive them, Father," Yeshua shouted from his cross as he made eye contact with the three angels standing on the rooftop even as he bled to death. "For they know not what they do."

"As -if- my father would get his robes dirty," Lucifer snarled. He flared his wings as he turned to Azrael. "You should know that better than anybody, little void creature. How does it feel to be a pawn?"

The crowd began to riot. Agent-infested Roman soldiers circled the hill, pikes down, stabbing anyone who dared step closer to the three sacrificial victims. The crowd went berzerk, unable to breach the Roman defenses. Some picked up stones and began throwing them at the soldiers.

"*There's* your rallying point," Lucifer said. He gave Azrael the Sata'anic gesture of respect of hands to forehead, lips and heart. "Now all we have to do is see if it lasts."

The General turned towards Azrael. Only his fist poised above the pommel of his sword let Azrael know he might still smite Lucifer with a single stroke. It was then Azrael noticed the General's unearthly blue eyes had filled with tears.

"I don't like it either." The General's expression turned from hatred to sorrow. "But it does seem you were right. Yeshua's martyrdom is making the humans wake up and question what the temple power brokers are teaching them."

The crowd began to scream. People ripped the weapons out of the Roman soldier's hands, using their own pikes against them.

"C'mon," Azrael shouted. "Cut him down!"

The Romans fought back, not caring who they killed. Women. Children. The humans circled angrily, but they did not dare breach the wall of pilum. Nobody was willing to die for the stranger they'd only moments before sentenced to death.

Yeshua's sacrifice would be in vain...

The molecules in the air began to vibrate as Azrael's agitation finally reached the point he was no longer able to control the Song of Destruction. The General stepped forward, understanding that Azrael had reached the limit of his ability to follow orders.

"Offer Yeshua the choice," the General said. "Please. Let him choose if he wishes for you to end his suffering."

In a flash, Azrael hovered invisibly at Yeshua's side. Yeshua's blood poured out of the torn flesh where the spikes had been driven through his arteries and dripped down the coarse, wooden trunk they used as a Moloch feeding pole, siphoning away his life's energy.

"I'm so sorry," Azrael wept. "It would be a great honor if you would let me end your pain."

"No," Yeshua clung to his mortal shell with every ounce of will he had. "You must not interfere! My wife. My children. I must complete the mission for *all* their sakes."

Azrael wrung his tentacles as he weighed his obligation to honor Yeshua's free will versus his overwhelming guilt. He had no ability to heal his wounds, only to sever his spirit from his dying mortal shell. The light began to fade from Yeshua's eyes. Despite his pain, he gave Azrael a victorious smile.

"They need a body to mourn," Yeshua said. "I knew when I came into Jerusalem they might kill me. It's what I..."

Yeshua never got to complete his sentence. One of Moloch's squatters decided to eliminate the cause of the riot by running Yeshua through with his pilum, straight up through his gut into his heart.

The crowd went ballistic, picking up rocks and bludgeoning the Agent-infested Roman soldiers. A rock passing through Azrael's incorporeal form momentarily distracted him as he made a mental note to track data on the way the excessively cruel actions of the soldier had overshot the mark and had the opposite effect.

"Yeshua?"

Azrael reached out to grab Yeshua's spirit at the moment of his death and found nothing. Nothing at all. Yeshua's mortal shell was empty.

"Yeshua!!!" Azrael frantically snaked billions of tentacles into the air, trying to grab Yeshua before he got sucked into the portal which had opened up between the hill at Calvary and Gehenna.

Nothing.

"No!" Azrael's tentacles came up empty. A quick perusal of the dreamtime confirmed Yeshua had not made it there, either. He had just lost the most evolved spirit to descend back down into mortal form in millions of years!

The air turned black with power. Electricity shot out as Azrael's roiling black thundercloud form became fully visible to the masses rioting below. The humans wailed in terror as the sky turned black with unfathomable power. The Song of Destruction vibrated through the city like the aftershocks of an earthquake, loosening the tiles on roofs and causing rubble to tumble from the hill at Calvary. The sky erupted with lightning as Azrael slipped between the dimensions to search for the spirit he'd just misplaced before he inadvertently destroyed all of Jerusalem.

Chapter 8

Now upon the first day of the week…
They found the stone rolled away from the sepulcher.
And they entered in, and found not the body…

St. Luke 24:2-3

Earth: Sunday, April 5, 33 AD
Jerusalem **(three days later)**

Azrael dragged the squirming wraith he'd just pried out of the mortal shell of a Roman soldier into the processing room. The underground cavern was not much to look, far too functional to be a *real* throne room, but just a bit too garish with the raised dais at its center where normally sat the self-proclaimed *Emperor of Earth*. At the moment, the 'throne' was empty.

"Where is he?" Azrael scowled at Lucifer's second-in-command, another henchman in a long line of nameless, faceless part-Sata'anic lizard/part-human scum who leaped at Lucifer's beck and call. Demons, the humans called them. It seemed as fitting a term as any.

"He's … um…"

Azrael sniffed the air. He'd learned to rely on his other senses to compensate for the lack of physical sensation. The place reeked of semen. From behind the doors to Lucifer's personal quarters, he heard giggles and a loud laugh. There had to be at least three females in there being 'serviced' at the same time.

"Take this *thing*," Azrael snorted with contempt, "off of my hands."

"Y-y-yes s-s-sir," the half-lizard demon stuttered. He motioned for his compatriots to push over a containment canister.

The demons skittered nervously at each twitch of Azrael's tentacles, fearful of his deadly touch. He rammed the low-ranking Agent into the canister which would hold him until Lucifer unlocked the blast door so the demons could roll it down into the lower levels. The blast doors were some sort of failsafe, a device which operated by a physical key, but also a non-

45

physical one as well, for only a *Morning Star* could open and shut the doors. Azrael could punch through on his own, of course; it was the sole benefit of being a creature of the void charged with accessing that realm by none other than the goddess who had created it, but the General had asked him not to. Each time something breached Ki's defenses, which were more like a 'net' than a true wall, it set off the sensors they used to tell when someone tried to help Moloch escape.

Azrael shoved the wraith he'd reaped only moments ago into the containment canister. Which was worse? Having to actually *touch* the Agents, whose souls were so filthy it made him feel as though he were covered in excrement afterwards? Or having to play nicely with the demons, creatures even Shay'tan's full-blooded Sata'anic armies scorned.

"Th-th-thank you, S-s-sir," the demons stuttered.

If anyone had told Azrael as a young man that someday people would fear him, he would have laughed. *Him?* A science nerd? Now … not only had his scientific theory blown up in his face, but the insurrection Yeshua's death had sparked had already been put down. The city-dwellers who had murdered their best chance of being led into modernity had disappeared back down into their rat-holes.

The demons rolled the canister towards the heavy blast doors that separated Gehenna from the material realm. Azrael turned to get the hell out of this accursed place. He cringed as the ornate double-doors leading into Lucifer's personal quarters slammed open and the debauch son of the Eternal Emperor came staggering out.

"Azrael!" Lucifer called, a glass of champagne upraised in one hand. "A celebration is in order!"

Lucifer's bare feet slapped against the polished granite floor as he staggered out wearing nothing but a pair of hastily donned breeches that were not even fastened shut. Behind him, a gaggle of semi-clad women followed, patting his wings and begging him to come back and finish whatever lude acts they were performing. Azrael didn't want to know!

"I don't see anything worth celebrating," Azrael scowled. His voice caused static electricity to fill the air as his incorporeal form roiled with displeasure. A warning. *Stay away from me.* Whatever shred of idealism he'd still possessed after Elissar's murder had died three days ago on the cross along with Yeshua.

The women screamed as they sobered up enough to recognize a black, tentacled creature of nightmare hovered in the middle of the throne room and disappeared back into Lucifer's bedroom. Lucifer stepped closer, swaying from the effects of too much alcohol, one misstep away from getting zapped out of his body.

In other words, it was a typical day in hell…

"You're … uh … test subject … whoops! Excuse me!" Lucifer slurred. "I mean … your rallying point … just came back and reclaimed his body. The entire city's in an uproar. They have no idea three days is an unusually long time to … um … hiccup … leave your body hanging around before you pull it up into the upper realms. Kind of gross if you ask me. Decomp an all. 'hic. Though it shouldn't be too bad this time of year. If I'd known, I would have put the body on ice or something for him."

Lucifer's slurred words finally cut through Azrael's sour mood as he realized what Lucifer was trying to tell him.

"You mean he made it?" Azrael exclaimed. "He beat death and ascended into the upper realms?"

"Of course he did," Lucifer said. "Too bad he didn't want to stay and take my place here. But … c'mon! A toast!"

Lucifer grabbed a second glass of champagne off a tray brought out by one of his demons and held it out for Azrael to take, nearly stepping on a stray tentacle and getting himself killed.

"To Azrael," Lucifer straightened and moved his wings into the eloquent dress-wings position of respect. "May all your scientific theories be verified through the peer-review process."

Just for a moment, Lucifer regained the echo of the brilliant politician who'd once captivated the imagination of a vast empire. The Morning Star, destined to lead the way through the darkest times, and brilliant enough to understand just which compliment would soften Azrael's dark mood. Peer-review. It was the highest level of affirmation a scientist could receive.

Lucifer staggered, nearly landing face-down in Azrael's tentacles. Falling. The echo faded. Lucifer went back to being the Fallen son of the Eternal Emperor once more. Azrael wasn't sure whether to be disgusted, or to pity him. *'How art thou fallen from heaven, oh Lucifer. Son of the morning.'*

"Mpf. S'cuse me."

Azrael had no mouth to drink, no stomach to digest, and no way to touch the glass without dissolving it. And anyway, he wasn't sure it was appropriate to toast Yeshua's resurrection given how gruesomely the man had died. But still … success. His suffering had not been in vain.

"You drink it for me." Azrael solidified his form into the soft, fine-tentacled one that made him look like a gigantic black fur ball, the most innocuous-looking form he'd learned to shape thus far. "I'm glad he's going to be all right."

"All right," Lucifer hiccupped. He practically whacked Azrael with his snowy white wings as he turned and staggered back into his personal quarters. He raised the glass he'd offered Azrael to his lips as he sucked it down in a single draught.

The door slammed shut behind him. Squeals of delight welcomed the Fallen angelic back to his earthy pleasures. The demons shook their heads, puzzled at how someone as emotionally unstable as Lucifer had ended up in charge of this hellish place.

Azrael practically skipped out of there. He'd been right! His scientific theory had been right! Now it was up to *him* to track data on how the causality of the rallying point rippled through the general population. If only he could hold a pen and paper without dissipating it! He'd find a way. Given how much Yeshua had suffered to make his 'point,' Azrael owed him much.

Chapter 9

What we commonly call death does not destroy the body,
It only causes a separation of spirit and body.

Brigham Young

Galactic Standard Date: 156,523.10 AE **(994 years later)**
Haven-2 — Cherubim Monastery

Through the garden lay a courtyard, and past the courtyard sat a magnificent, yet simple palace which rose from its square stone pillars like a pagoda. Enormous rough-hewn timbers, each carved from a single tree, imparted a sense of strength and permanence as Azrael moved past the guards into the winding halls. The powerful vibration of Angelic voices chanting the low, sing-song meditations of the Cherubim tugged at Azrael's grief, urging him to let it go and become one with the song.

Sound. The force which underlay All-that-is…

He closed his eyes and drank in the soothing vibration caused by thousands of novitiates chanting 'ohm' in an evening prayer. Even solid matter could be moved by the application of the Song; to create or, in Azrael's case, destroy. Life itself existed in that vibration … and death … though Azrael knew better than anyone that death was merely a change in phase and not the end of everything as mortals feared it to be. A higher voice rose above the choir, tinkling like a silver bell.

The Regent sat surrounded by her children, grand-children, great-grandchildren, and others who had taken refuge here, all creatures who held the promise of one day evolving into Archangels. Her voice rose above the choir as she sang an epic saga that was a tale about morality. The novitiates sang the 'ohm' to provide a soothing backdrop for the tale, adding their voices to the legend, but only the Regent could give voice to not only the song, but also *The Song,* for mortal ears to hear.

Azrael hung back in the shadows, listening to the Regent sing. It was hard to believe the most secretive goddess in the universe, sister and heir to the power of He-who's-not, had been nicknamed *'The Destroyer'* as she told her progeny a favorite tale. It was a story Azrael knew well, for when the General had first brought him here to learn how to contain his power, the Regent had told him this story.

"How long did Pinochiel's nose grow, *Seanmháthair*?" one dark-winged Angelic child asked, perhaps five cycles old.

"It was not his nose, silly!" a Centauri filly scoffed. "But the karmic spider web cast out by his tangle of lies!"

"It is a metaphor," the Regent smiled, her fangs not threatening. Wing-spikes rustled like the sharpening of a sword against a whetstone as she spread the appendages like a bird of prey, enhancing the lesson with their bat-like visage. "When you tell a lie, it multiplies many times over and comes back to haunt you."

"I knew that!" the Centauri filly sniffed. She was a pretty pre-adolescent who would soon be tested for entrance into the Order.

"But you are older!" the little Angelic's lip trembled at being scorned.

The Regent picked up the child and sat him upon her lap. "Arrogance can come back to haunt you every bit as much as Pinochiel's lies."

"Like happened with Lucifer," a strapping Leonid boy chipped in. "He rebelled and the Emperor cast him down!"

Azrael shuddered with revulsion. The Regent had asked him to treat the debauch gatekeeper to the fires of Gehenna with compassion, but that didn't mean he had to like it!

"The truth is much more complicated than the myth, *leon beag*," the Regent said. "Lucifer's role is every bit as important to keep the balance as yours, or mine, or even the Eternal Emperor. Never forget, archangels-to-be, that all chess pieces have a role to play. Even the lowly Fallen."

'More like a non-stop orgy,' Azrael thought to himself with disgust.

"Remember this lesson when you leave these walls," the Regent chastised the filly. "As the first Archangel novitiate amongst your species, you will be held to a higher standard than the other Centauri."

The filly looked mollified. The other children moved closer, vying for a place at the feet of the most feared goddess in the universe. Even Azrael's power paled in comparison to that wielded by the Regent, or her missing brother, He-who's-not, Lord of Chaos, the Dark Lord.

"Tell us about the Blue Fairy!" the children clamored.

"Ki understood Pinochiel was more than he appeared," the Regent said. "No matter how many times he fell, she whispered he had a choice to make, and in the end, he sacrificed his life for the good of the Alliance."

"And she rewarded him by making him real!" the children finished the story.

"Pinochiel made *himself* real," the Regent said. "He just had help making better decisions. Just as someday *you* shall all be charged with helping the mortals in this galaxy make better choices by the example you all set. Remember this, *réaltaí beag* [little stars]."

'If only the Blue Fairy would make -me- real,' Azrael thought to himself. *'I didn't do bad things. All I did was disobey a direct order from the Emperor to never interfere.'*

The children's tutors summoned them from their bedtime story to get into their pajamas, wash, and sleep in the great dormitories where genetically promising children from all species dwelt together as a single race, *archangelei*, heirs to the duty once carried by the Cherubim. Not all would become full-fledged Archangels. Few possessed the advanced genetics necessary to cast off their mortal shells and exist in a semi-ascended state, but the Regent herself was living proof that *all* species contained the seed of greatness.

The Regent waited until the room was clear before she fixed her bottomless black eyes, so much like Azrael's, upon the shadows where he lurked.

"Come, *fear faire beag* [little watchman]," the Regent said gently. "I fear I have bad news." Those black eyes were filled with pity, as though somehow she understood his pain. How could a creature so powerful know what it was like to lose the only living creature he still had left to love?

"Lucifer told me," Azrael whispered. "My sister is dying."

"You must go to her," the Regent said. "Do not let her pass into the Dreamtime thinking even your spirit was destroyed."

"I am hideous." Azrael touched the ever-present ache within his own chest. "It is better she continues to think I am dead."

"Eternity is a long time to grieve."

"I want her to remember me the way I was," Azrael said. "A beautiful, guileless boy. Not a creature of the void."

Had it really been nearly a thousand years since he'd died? It hurt Azrael's brain to contemplate what it meant to be immortal. He was still, after all, existing within the potential lifespan of his former species. His little sister's impending death from old age, however, dragged him kicking and screaming out his denial about his current condition being a permanent one.

"For every evildoer the Cherubim killed," the Regent said. "They redeemed the lives of ten good men. It prevented them from becoming as soulless as the malefactors they reaped."

"How can I redeem anyone?" Azrael asked, his voice filled with woe, "when everything I touch dies?"

The Regent gestured for him to come closer, the only living creature who dared risk his touch, for she was a void creature, too, only her brush with power had left her stronger, not condemned to exist without shape or form. Azrael tried to hide his pleasure at being touched as she coaxed an ant-like pincher that kept erupting from the crude face he'd learned to shape back into a cheek.

Touch! What mortals took for granted, Azrael would give up the rest of his immortal existence to experience one last time without killing someone.

"Death is not the end, *fear faire beag*," the Regent said. "You know that better than anyone. Sometimes, death is a mercy."

Azrael bowed his head so the Regent wouldn't see him weep. Black tears left holes in her favorite silk robe. The Regent wiped his cheek, her flesh oblivious to his power, and adjusted his cloak.

"I think this newest containment shield will do the trick." The Regent gave his shoulder a reassuring squeeze. "I know it's uncomfortable, but it will allow you to walk amongst the mortals without dissipating them."

"Thank you, my Queen," Azrael bowed. The Emperor, himself, had fashioned this latest design, an apology, he supposed, for making him the butt of Shay'tan's wager.

The Regent's tutelage had improved his appearance, but not by much. To a casual observer, he now appeared to be a tall, slender humanoid enveloped in a hooded black cloak. Beneath the cloak, however, depending upon his emotional state, he might be anything from vaguely humanoid to a billowy black thundercloud.

"Go! Go guide your little sister into the Dreamtime."

Azrael exited through the courtyard, pretending not to notice the way even full-fledged Archangels dove off the neatly tended pathway to avoid him. Even to an ascended being his touch was death, although not a permanent end as they could pull their broken shells into the upper realms and reconstitute them; a tedious, inconvenient task that could take anywhere from hours to years. Closing his eyes and focusing on the mental connection the General had taught him to form with the other Archangels, Azrael punched through the fabric of time and space to teleport himself to his sister's hospital.

"Sir," Azrael saluted.

"Sergeant Thanatos," the General greeted. "She is asking for you."

"She knows?"

"She has been apprised of your condition."

The whir of life support equipment filled the air. Azrael glanced at the curtain which separated him from the last vestige of his former life as a real Angelic; the baby sister he'd spent the past millennium remaining invisible to because the Emperor had felt it kinder to allow her to believe he was still dead rather than explain 160 years after she'd grieved his death that her brother now existed as a creature of the void.

"The Emperor himself tried to teach her how to ascend into the higher realms." The General's stoic expression softened as he delivered the bad news. "She's not genetically evolved enough to do so. He used a different sire's DNA when he helped your mother conceive her."

"Please convey my gratitude to the Emperor."

"Gazardiel wishes to see her brother before she passes into the next realm." The General's stern visage was filled with compassion. "It doesn't matter what your current physical form looks like. She will recognize you."

He stepped back and gestured towards the curtain. Azrael used the sleeve of his cloak to push it aside so he didn't dissolve it. With trepidation, he stepped into the room and waited for his sister to notice him.

"Azrael?" Gazardiel whispered through wrinkled lips, her once-blonde hair now white with age. "Is it really you?"

Blue veins showed through paper-thin skin. Her feathers had become sparse upon the white wings splayed beneath her on her bed, having years ago lost the ability to fly. Rheumy blue eyes fixed upon where he stood.

"Yes." Azrael stepped out of the shadows, standing so the light would not expose what lay hidden beneath his hood. "I had an accident. It disfigured me."

"So the Emperor told me," Gazardiel said. "Your mission must be very important for the Emperor himself to come and make excuses for you. Why did you wait until I was on my deathbed?"

"I did not wish you to see me as I am now," Azrael said. "But I have watched over you for nearly a thousand years."

"I thought many times I sensed your presence, only to find the room was empty." The heart monitor hiccupped, then resumed its weak sinus rhythm.

"I am hideous," Azrael cried. "Mortals scream in terror and run when they see me. Even the gods are repulsed by the sight of me."

"Oh … Az!" Tears welled in Gazardiel's eyes. "Don't you know I love you no matter what your appearance?"

"I know," Azrael said. "I just …"

"The Emperor said this happened because you tried to save a little girl? Did she like my old doll?"

"She died before I had a chance to give it to her," Azrael stepped closer to her deathbed. "But I think she would have liked it. She reminded me so much of you it made my heart ache for missing you."

"They said you defeated Moloch," Gazardiel said. "I had not believed the legends until the Emperor assured me it was true. He said you saved us all from destruction."

Azrael evaded talking about just how horrific and painful his own death had been. It was a good thing he didn't need sleep or he'd be plagued by nightmares. As it was, the flashbacks alone were enough to drive a less balanced individual to madness.

Mama. Gazardiel. Elissar. Agape. Unconditional love. So long as he kept the memory of just how much he'd loved each one of them, he was able to keep the horror at bay and push it out of his mind.

"The Emperor asked me to be brave and not recoil from your injuries." Gazardiel reached towards his hand.

"The accident changed me," Azrael stepped back. "I can't touch anyone. Not even a blade of grass. Every living thing withers beneath my touch. Even an inadvertent brush brings death, which is why I wear this cloak."

"So cruel!" A cough shook Gazardiel's failing body. Azrael held his breath, believing she would leave him and journey where he could not follow, but she held on. "You loved nothing more than to crawl into Mama's lap and be read stories, even when you grew too big and the other children made fun of you."

Tears streamed down Azrael's face at the truth of her words. Deadly black tears that dissolved everything they dripped upon and left tiny holes in the sheets.

"They send me to eradicate Agents of Moloch from whatever mortal host they've hijacked," Azrael said. "One touch and your spirit steps out of your mortal shell. The Emperor said I can escort you to the gateway of the Dreamtime so you don't have to make the journey there alone."

"Will there be any pain?"

"No," Azrael said. "My touch has no effect upon your spirit. Those I capture complain they didn't realize their spirits had been severed from their bodies until they looked down and saw their bodies crumpled upon the floor. But I may only touch you once. I have never been able to un-kill somebody once I've taken their hand."

Gazardiel coughed. The heart monitor beeping frantically for a half a second, then returned to normal.

"Then we will speak a little while," Gazardiel said. "You must fill me in on your adventures so I can tell Mama when I see her again. And then you shall kiss me goodbye."

They conversed until Azrael felt almost like a normal person as he told his sister about his little friend on Earth, his work for the Eternal Emperor, and the data he'd been collecting between assignments to quantify his theories of 'rallying points' as a means to encourage social evolution. His work was the only thing he had left to keep him sane. At some point, he realized she was tiring. Whether he touched her or not, Gazardiel was ready to leave this realm and she only lingered because of him. Her spirit had already begun the process of pulling itself away from her mortal shell, only tendrils of spirit keeping her here.

"I am tired," Gazardiel whispered. "I have led a good life, with a good husband and children. A life that I am proud of."

"You're all I have left," Azrael wept. "I wish there was some way for you to stay."

"I can see Mama and my husband waiting for me." Gazardiel's eyes were no longer focused on this realm. "Just but on the other side. Will you take me to them?"

"It would be my honor."

"Take down your hood," Gazardiel said. "I wish to recognize my brother when I cross paths with you again."

Azrael's hands trembled as he slid back the hood. To her credit, Gazardiel did not flinch. The Emperor had prepared her for what to expect.

"Kiss me goodbye, brother." Gazardiel reached one shaky IV-laden hand towards the sleeve of his robe. "As you used to do whenever you went off on one of your grand adventures when we were both still young."

Hastily wiping his tears lest a destructive black drop cause her mortal shell to dissolve before he'd finished what he'd come here to do, Azrael pressed his lips to her forehead. Touch. He relished the simple physical sensation of touch as he gave his beloved sister the kiss of death. Gazardiel's soul slid from her body, still bearing the form of an elderly woman, but free of the infirmary which had been the cause of her passing.

"You were right!" Gazardiel rose from the bed, only glancing once at the body she was leaving behind. "There was no pain. Only that lovely song."

Gazardiel danced a joyous waltz around him, her sparse feathers filling out and visage growing younger until she appeared as she had when she'd still been a young mother raising kids. It was the form she wished her loved ones to see once she was reunited with them.

"It's the Song of Creation," Azrael said. "Not even Gehenna can hold me so long as I hold that song in my heart."

Gazardiel traced the outline of cheekbones the Regent had spent all afternoon coaching him to hold. She closed her eyes and ran her fingers across his face, remembering what he had once looked like, and stood on tiptoes to kiss his forehead. Her touch was as wispy and insubstantial as the kiss of fog, a life-spark without physical form.

"It's not the shell which defines a soul," Gazardiel opened her eyes. "But the measure of the man who dwells within. You're as beautiful to me now as you ever were. Now take me to see Mama so I can share the good news."

Holding his sister's hand, he carried her to the gateway of the realm She-who-is had created to shelter life-sparks between the physical and higher realms, the Dreamtime, the place the humans called heaven. Only spirits of the dead could go there, not an undead creature such as himself.

"I cannot enter," Azrael said mournfully as he stood on the threshold. "But know I shall always remember you."

"The Emperor promised I could be one of the first souls to come back," Gazardiel said excitedly. "I shall be a pioneer in one of his new scientific experiments. She-who-is will allow our entire family to come back close in time and place so we can find one another, although our memories of our past lifetime will be erased so we have a chance to start over. Perhaps someday my spirit will jump out of some strange, alien creature and shout boo?"

"I would like that." Azrael kissed his sister goodbye.

Gazardiel paused, one foot over the threshold.

"Perhaps you should consider doing *this* for work? Your touch is much more pleasant than gasping for each breath until your body finally grows too exhausted to breathe!"

"I'll consider it." Her suggestion brought a smile to Azrael's face. Gazardiel still knew him better than any creature in the universe.

For the first time in nearly a thousand years, his heart felt light as his sister stepped across the threshold. Although he could not see the loved ones she reunited with, he could sense them. He knew she related word to their heartbroken mother that he still existed and that news of his continued research would bring her joy.

"Goodbye," Azrael said, wishing not for the first time he'd died the day he'd taken on Moloch. Although then his spirit would have been trapped in the fiery purgatory of Gehenna until it had either become too damaged to exist or food for a malignant god. Not a pleasant prospect.

He had a new job to do. New scientific theories to test. And a cloak that, thus far, appeared to effectively dampen his destructive tendencies. It was time to return to Earth.

Part III

My soul waitith for the Lord,
More than they that watch for morning,
More than Watchmen wait for morning..."

Psalm 130

Chapter 10

Son of Man,
I have made thee a watchman …
Therefore hear the word at my mouth,
And give them warning from me.

Ezekiel 3:17

Earth: AD 1992
Karaman House, Foca, Bosnia **(Modern era)**

Azrael…

Azrael's head jerked up from his latest scientific journal where he furiously jotted down notes about the wolf pack, the void-reinforced tally sheet slipping from his fingers. It dissolved before it hit the ground as it brushed against his deadly wings.

"Drat!"

Azrael!

Azrael closed his eyes, listening to the faint song which sang beneath the mortal wind which blew through this high, desolate forest. Ki's voice was the softest whisper of butterfly wings against his mind, but the Song grew stronger whenever she communicated with him. The Song eased the hunger growing within his spirit, forever clamoring to be fed. Azrael needed the Song to survive the way others required oxygen, or he'd have no choice but to feed upon matter to fill the aching void.

Women. Injured. No … violated! Agents were trying to breed genetically suitable host-bodies again to facilitate the escape of Moloch's larger Agents.

"Yip!"

Azrael's attention was drawn back to the wolf-pack he'd spent the past seven generations studying to collect data on non-human social structure. The creatures did not fear him, having gotten used to his observations, but they had enough sense to avoid brushing up against the black-winged Angelic who perpetually shadowed them, furiously scribbling scientific data into his great black book. The alpha-male cocked his head to one side as though he was listening to the Song of Creation as well. Perhaps he *could* hear it? Wolves were relatively evolved social animals for not-quite-sentient creatures. Aha! A topic for future study. Azrael scribbled a quick note in his ever-growing list of future scientific experiments and snapped shut his journal.

"Time to go!" He tucked his journal into his cloak pocket and wrapped the hated garment around his non-physical form.

The alpha whined as he flared his wings, a most dog-like sound as though the wolf regretted the master leaving him behind while he went off to work. Azrael had shadowed the pack for so long they considered him to be one of them, the closest thing to family Azrael possessed now that everyone he'd ever loved was dead and gone. Behind the alpha-male its mate and several 'aunties' also whined, a wolf-farewell to another wolf going out on a hunt. Azrael whined in answer, the closest he could approximate the beast's crude, not-quite-sentient language, that he'd be back as soon as he could.

With a flash of darkness, Azrael teleported between the dimensions to the scene of the crime.

Martial-sounding music blared from a speaker connected to an ancient turntable, *Mars na Drinu,* March on the Drina: a Serbian fighting song. Oblivious to his presence, an Agent-infested Serbian soldier raped a Bosnian-Muslim female. Janko was a particularly nasty Agent who Azrael had been trying to corral; one of several dozen responsible for inciting genocide against thousands of innocent Bosnian-Serbs. The woman's damaged spirit floated above her cigarette-burned body, trying to escape the violation of her flesh.

'Her name is Kadima,' Ki whispered into Azrael's mind. 'I wish for her to bear witness...'

Kadima spotted the tall, black-cloaked reaper which had suddenly appeared in the room.

"Our Lord," Kadima reached towards him as though welcoming his presence. "Grant me death."

"Who the fuck are you?" Janko hissed, realizing he had an audience. "Guards!!! Who let this asshole into the room!" Janko leaped to his feet, shoving his cock back into his pants.

Kadima curled into a fetal position and clutched her clothing to cover her shame. Human legend often depicted Azrael as being a tall, silent creature, incapable of speech, but the truth was, he rarely possessed words adequate to express his disgust. Why speak at all when the mere sight of the Angel of Death appearing into a room conveyed all that needed to be said?

Azrael lifted one arm and pointed at the Agent he'd been sent to reap, slipping his hand from the cloak which prevented him from accidentally killing someone with an inadvertent brush of a feather. He waited for Janko to do what stupid Agents of Moloch *always* did whenever they were confronted by the Angel of Death; try to collect the bounty which Moloch had placed on Azrael's head.

"Moloch has promised a seat at his table for any Agent who can defeat you!" Janko leaped at Azrael.

Azrael grabbed Janko by the throat. The bodies Agents inhabited were little more than articles of clothing, meat-puppets seized to facilitate their movement through a realm which was otherwise hostile to their existence. The human host-body fell to the ground as the now-disembodied wraith struggled to get the better of him. Light-energy to dark-energy, Janko clawed at Azrael and failed to get a grip on a spirit comprised entirely of silt-fine dark matter. In a flash, Azrael deposited Janko into Lucifer's care before teleporting back to where Ki wished him to recruit her newest Watchman.

"Allah be praised." Kadima tugged against her violated body, trying her hardest to will herself to die.

Azrael paused to tuck an ace of spades into Janko's pocket, a message to Moloch that yet another bounty hunter had failed. He liked to remind the malignant god who had murdered Elissar that he was still here. Settling his ebony wings against his back so the cloak covered them once more, he slid back his hood. Kadima gasped as Azrael revealed the face he only showed to the purest of the pure. Not the grim expression he donned when reaping Agents of Moloch, but an ebony-black version of his own original face, deliberately aged ten years so people would stop mistaking him for a boy.

"I'm sorry I didn't get here soon enough to spare you this indignity," Azrael's black eyes glittered with compassion above his high, chiseled cheekbones, "but you must bear witness to this wrong. You must let others know what happened so these men are brought to justice."

"Malak-al-Maut," Kadima wept. "Please shepherd my spirit into the bosom of Allah."

"It is not your time, Watchman," Azrael nudged her spirit back towards her body. "But you have my word no seed shall take root from this violation."

Azrael averted his eyes and pulled her torn skirt down to cover her bloodied lower body, careful to avoid touching her skin. Lately he'd developed the ability to touch inanimate matter without dissolving it, though the gift was erratic depending upon his emotional state. He lay his hand over the fabric and focused, his concentration intense as he accomplished one of the few helpful uses he'd discovered he could put his talent for destruction. Kadima gasped as he absorbed the foreign life energy Janko had implanted into her body before it could take root.

"Allahu akhbar," Kadima whispered. "God is great."

Others. Village. Safety. U.N. patrol. Images touched upon Azrael's mind as Ki communicated what she wished for him to do.

"Sleep," Azrael said. "When you awaken, lead the other women to the next village. There's a woman in a house with a thatched roof barn who will shelter you until Peacekeepers come through. Within the year, a war crimes council will be convened to prosecute those who did this to you. It would please Allah greatly if you would testify."

"Yes," Kadima agreed. "I will facilitate Allah's will."

Azrael held his hand above her face, careful not to touch her flesh. *Sleep, Watchman. Ki has chosen you to bear witness.* Kadima's eyes fluttered shut as merciful sleep overcame her. The Regent had taught him to convey images into another's mind to encourage a desired emotional state, an ability which pleased her to no end although Azrael could never understand why.

"Thank you," Kadima whispered as she drifted off. A peaceful sleep restored her as a faint, distant melody permeated her dreams and made her smile in spite of all that had happened. The Song of Creation. So long as Kadima did as Ki asked, she'd be able to hear the same beautiful song which kept *him* here. It was Ki's carrot to entice her Watchmen to forever strive to become more.

Azrael covered her with a blanket, careful not to dissolve non-living matter so long as he kept his emotions in check. He moved through the rest of the house, dispatching the other Agents. Agent-infected Serbians weren't the only ones committing atrocities, but those he left to human justice. Still … he couldn't leave them to pursue his now-free charges. Herding terrified soldiers into a room, Azrael devolved into his more versatile black tentacled form and melted shut the door.

After Kadima testified, the international community was finally horrified enough to get off its ass and intervene…

Chapter 11

And I saw an angel come down from heaven,
Having the key of the bottomless pit,
And a great chain in his hand.

Revelations 20:1

Gehenna: Earth AD 1992

It was a typical day in hell…

Azrael flung back the hated cloak as soon as he finished materializing. Two Sata'an-human soldiers nodded greeting as he stepped towards the enormous carved doors. Someone had spray painted the words *'abandon all hope, ye who enter here'* across the lintel in garish, red paint. It was a fitting epitaph for those forced to do the dirty work of keeping the worst of the worst interred here. Azrael's passing was silent, his corporeal shell nothing but an illusion, but the footsteps of the guards who escorted him echoed in the enormous, empty hallway. Azrael paused before the second set of doors to enter the main processing chamber as they were opened for him.

Things were exactly as he expected…

"Take this scum off my hands." Azrael held out the squirming wraith he'd just reaped. He pretended not to notice the sexual foreplay taking place upon the raised dais.

"You should pay more respect to the Emperor of Earth!" Lucifer waved one arm in an overstated display of showmanship. "Shouldn't he, ladies?"

The females twittered as Lucifer spoke, reaching up to caress his snowy wings, his perfect body, his handsome face. One ran her hand up his inner thigh, earning a hiss of pleasure. Touch. While Azrael hadn't experienced mortal touch without killing someone for 2,300 years, Lucifer reveled in an excess of it every single day.

"Naughty, naughty!" Lucifer's voice indicated he wished to reward the female's bad behavior, not chastise it. "Can't you see my brother is too uptight to appreciate three such splendid roses in my garden?"

The females murmured and sighed, reaching towards Azrael in an open invitation to join them.

"No, no, my sweets," Lucifer took first one's hand, then the other, and then the third to kiss the back of each hand and, in one instance, place ones finger into his mouth to suck on it. "Don't you know who this is? This is Azrael. The Angel of Death."

The females backed away from where he stood, arm outstretched, his latest quarry dangling by the throat as he prevented the squirming soul from escaping. Azrael knew such un-evolved creatures could not see the incorporeal wraith dangling from his fist, only the dark Angelic standing before them with outstretched arm as though pointing in judgment ... but Lucifer could.

"You wouldn't want to invite *him* into your bed," Lucifer told the women with a knowing smirk. "It would be a sexual experience to *die* for."

"But he's so beautiful," one whispered to the other. "Almost as beautiful as *him*."

Humph! If only they knew it was fake! After 2,300 years of trial and error, he'd finally learned to shape a facsimile of his former physical form. Beautiful, or not, he was still a creature of the void. His ebony skin sucked the light, the energy, the life force from everything it touched and composted it back into its base elements. Dark energy and dark matter. Leptons. Quarks. Higgs-bosons. And the ever-smaller particles which made up 96% of the mass of the universe.

"Off you go now!" Lucifer playfully slapped one in the ass. He stood, causing the female parked upon his lap to tumble onto the floor in a fit of giggles, and flared his snowy white wings as though he were a bird of prey.

"Rargh!!! We'll finish this later!"

The women squealed and scurried down a side-hall to Lucifer's personal quarters, where Azrael knew he had a bed large enough to entertain a small army of females. The one who had whispered she found him beautiful paused, dropping her robe to give an uninhibited view of her breasts. She ran her hand down her abdomen and mouthed an invitation before disappearing after the others.

Angel-groupies! Even if Azrael *could* mate with such creatures, he wouldn't touch one with a ten-foot pole!

Azrael looked at Lucifer with disgust. Lucifer had let slip during one of his all-too-frequent benders that he hadn't merely been Elissar's ancestor, but her actual sire.

The Fallen son of the Eternal Emperor felt it was his goddess-given duty to exercise his 'power of persuasion' to impregnate every female he chose to 'honor' with his DNA. Like a cuckoo bird, Lucifer sought the wives of movers and shakers, including General Hanno's wife, to give his offspring the best possible chance of achieving positions of influence. His mortal progeny numbered in the millions, but in all that time, not a single one had ever been born with his quasi-ascended powers ... or his wings.

"What?" Lucifer's demeanor changed as he assumed the persona Azrael had come to realize was his true one.

"Why do you do that?" Azrael asked. "Debase yourself?"

"Because we were supposed to improve their species through intermarriage," Lucifer's shoulders slumped as though he were carrying the weight of the universe upon them. "My Father refused to help these people finish evolving as soon as he'd harvested enough of their DNA to fix our inbreeding problem. There's no one else left alive to finish the job."

Out of 200 Angelics who'd rebelled against the Eternal Emperor to remain on Earth, only Lucifer had been genetically evolved enough to cheat death. The rest had cast their souls into the Dreamtime as soon as the short-lived humans they'd rebelled to marry had reached the end of their mortal lives.

"Our species was meant to take one mate," Azrael chastised. "For life. Not ... this."

"Blah blah blah," Lucifer gave a dismissive wave, his demeanor changing to yet another of the many false personalities he projected to the world. He pointed to the terrified, squirming wraith. "So what do you have for me?"

"East Turkestan Islamic Movement," Azrael said. "Caught him detonating two bus bombs in Urumqi, China to open a portal to feed Moloch. Killed three people and injured 29."

"Yup," Lucifer slapped his hands upon his thighs. "Looks like you brought him to the right place."

He pushed a button. Sata'an-human hybrid soldiers rolled in a portable containment canister.

"Take this scumbag downstairs," Lucifer ordered, waving his hand at the squatter posing as a terrorist. He slipped the key worn around his neck into a pedestal next his chair, sticking his hand into a scanner on the podium before pulling down a lever. It was some sort of failsafe. A guarantee that only *he* could open the gateway to hell even if he got falling down drunk and somebody liberated him of the key.

"Yes, Sir!" The soldiers snapped a crisp salute, accentuated by the lizard-like tail tucked up along one side of their bodies. They waited for Azrael to shove his quarry into the canister so he didn't accidentally kill them, and then dragged the screaming terrorist out of Lucifer's throne room. Heat radiated into the room as the soldiers opened the next set of inner doors, the first of many descending layers into the alternate dimension, each more terrible than the one before. Slamming doors muffled the sound of the prisoner's screams.

"It is done." Lucifer gave him a smile that would power the electrical needs of three Earth cities. "Another scumbag off the planet."

Lucifer's mercurial mood swings never ceased to amaze the even-tempered Azrael. Lucifer could, quite literally, be all things to all people. Or so he pretended. Azrael knew otherwise.

"Thank you." Azrael turned to go.

"Why won't you shake my hand in friendship?" Lucifer asked softly, stepping forward to stand behind him. "You know it is what I want more than anything in the world."

Azrael kept his back turned to the Morning Star as Lucifer projected the image into his mind. It was not friendship Lucifer sought, but death. To be freed from the burden of living life as a quasi-ascended being, appointed warden of an unearthly prison when what he wanted more than anything in the world was to join his mate in the Dreamtime.

Lucifer was as much a prisoner here as Moloch.

"Your gift doesn't work on me." Azrael picked an image carved into the doors of the General crushing Moloch beneath his boot to focus upon as he resisted the compulsion to do as Lucifer asked. "You know the terms of the Armistice. Until a new Morning Star has risen, you are not free to leave. As his former host, only *you* understand the way the bastard thinks."

"Elissar was so close." Lucifer's voice was almost a whisper. "Hezekiah was certain she was the one. Were you even aware she was using her budding power of persuasion to hold your interest?"

"No." Azrael noted the curious sensation of his heart breaking even though he hadn't needed a heart for 2,300 years. "But she didn't have to. I found her to be the most interesting, delightful child I had ever met. The fact she led me to believe she had traits in common with my little sister because she sensed how much I missed her was irrelevant."

"Was it?" Lucifer asked. "Would you have followed her into the fires of Gehenna had she not reminded you so strongly of Gazardiel?"

Azrael refused to turn around as tears of black chaos welled in the corners of his eyes.

"I'd like to think so." Emotion caused his voice to break. "Perhaps she first sparked my interest because she sensed my longing for my family. But towards the end, it was *her* I saw. Not the images she thought I needed to see to continue studying her. I saw her. And I loved her. Enough to die trying to save her."

Lucifer sighed.

"I do love them, you know," Lucifer said. "My children. Each and every one of them. I keep watch over them as best I can, given my current limitations. It brings me joy to see them achieve positions of influence, and when they die because none inherit my long lifespan, I grieve. It's why I sent a tutor to prepare Elissar to one day assume her rightful place."

"She thought highly of Hezekiah," Azrael said. "I think she would have accepted him if she'd found out who he really was."

Elissar's tutor had worn a long, loose-fitting robe to hide the tail of a descendant of a Sata'anic Fallen. Perhaps that's why Azrael found it easy to work with the 'demons' despite his fiercely loyal service to the Eternal Emperor. They were all monsters, damaged by Moloch and trapped in this hell.

"Hezekiah reported good things about my daughter's invisible friend," Lucifer said. "He urged her to keep the information from her mother. He feared seeing you would restore her mother's memories of the night I visited her. It would have pleased me had she chosen you to be her consort once she became old enough to take a mate."

"You should set a better example for your children, then," Azrael said, his back still turned so Lucifer wouldn't see him cry.

"It was the only gift my mate was unable to give me," Lucifer said. "A child who was ours. Together. Elissar's mother was descended from one of his offspring. I had such hope for her."

The tears were obvious in Lucifer's voice. The brightest and most beautiful of all the angels. The most genetically advanced creature in the universe until the Regent had surprised them all by suddenly developing the ability to channel void-matter.

Lucifer ... who himself had been conceived through deceit...

Lucifer, who loved not the women he slept with, but another man. A *human* man...

Azrael turned then.

"Ki promised I would see her again," Azrael said. "When that day comes, I shall take your hand in friendship."

"Thank you," Lucifer said, the beauty that was the Morning Star shining unblemished through his eerie silver eyes. The real person Lucifer allowed very few people to ever see because, from the moment he'd been conceived, everyone, including the god he'd been raised to believe was his father, had exploited him.

After 2,300 years of being pinged between the factions which divided Earth as though he were *their* asset and not Ki's, Azrael had gradually come to understand why the Regent had a soft spot for Lucifer. The stern expression Azrael used to hide the tender heart which bled for every innocent he reaped softened, allowing Lucifer to see he bore some sympathy for his plight.

The moment passed.

"And now I have ladies desirous of pleasure," Lucifer said, the mask slipping back into place. The persona of the ladies' man. The stud stallion. The politician. The clown took over as he clapped his hands and leaped lightly off the dais. He strutted like a peacock down the hallway where three willing females were splayed naked upon his bed, waiting for a first-hand demonstration of his legendary sexual prowess. "You should try it sometime. Highly recommended. Nothing like a little va-va-voom to alleviate the stress."

The door to Lucifer's personal chambers slid shut behind him, leaving Azrael alone in the processing chamber with two of Lucifer's Sata'an-human agents. Demons, the humans called them. Azrael knew better. They were just people. Hoping to catch the eye of a few cast-offs from Lucifer's sexual escapades so the next generation would have hope of ascending to the general population, where an armistice prohibiting interference prevented Earth's inhabitants from knowing the legends of angels and demons, and an ancient evil which had been cast down into a fiery hell, were all true.

The humans had enough problems…

Azrael nodded to the two Sata'an-hybrids who, except for their serpentine eyes and long tails, otherwise appeared human. "Sam … Emmett … until next time."

"Until next time," the two lizard-men replied. They glanced up from their chessboard to give him a knowing look, empathizing with his bafflement in dealing with the de facto emperor of Earth.

The Angel of Death had harvested his malefactor for the day. It was time to go further his scientific studies and find ten 'good people' to assist with a painless passing so he didn't become as cynical and damaged as Lucifer.

Chapter 12

Thither Death, coming like Love
Takes all things in the morn of tenderest life
And being a delicate god,
In his own garden takes each delicate thing
Unstained, unmellowed, immature, untrod

The Garden of Death, by Lord Alfred Douglas

Earth - AD December, 1992
Chicago, Illinois

"We're going to be late, Elisabeth!!!" Mama yelled. "Hurry up and get your coat!"

"Awww… Mom…" nine-year-old Elisabeth Kaiser shouted, pausing in front of the mirror to put the final touches on her angel wings. She straightened the halo jutting crookedly out of her golden curls for the Christmas pageant. She'd been chosen to play the Angel of the Lord who gives Mary the good news she'd be mother to the Savior.

"It's *your* play!!!" Mama shouted. "Franz! Tell Opa and Oma it's time to go!"

"Ze child vishes to make a stage entrance, *ja*?" Opa gave Elisabeth a wink as she came down the stairs. "I recall her *mater* [mother] primping in front of ze mirror to make such an entrance before a certain young man as a teenager."

"Oh … Papa!" Mama smiled. "She's too young to be so obsessed with her appearance!"

Elisabeth bounded down the stairs in a most un-angel like manner and did a stage pose, one hand upraised like the Statue of Liberty as she practiced delivering her line.

"Hail Mary, full of grace! The Lord is with thee."

"You're supposed to be telling Mary she's knocked up," sixteen-year-old brother Franz said scornfully, "not doing a gymnastics pose." He poked at her robe with a shepherd's hook.

"You're just mad because you're the only shepherd without a line," Elisabeth taunted, sticking out her tongue when Mama wasn't looking.

"Franz!!!" Mama barked. "Inappropriate language. In the car. Now. And not another word or I'll tell Santa to leave your presents in the sleigh."

Elisabeth glanced over to where the Christmas tree awaited gifts, colorful light bulbs making any other form of light unnecessary. When they got back from midnight mass, including her Christmas pageant, underneath the tree would be loaded with presents. The dining room table was heavily laden with sweets carefully wrapped in plastic wrap. Cake. Cookies. Fruitcake and strudel. All for Christmas dinner tomorrow when her family would invite the neighbors over for a traditional German Christmas feast.

"Only babies believe in Santa Claus," Franz taunted just loud enough so only *she* could hear it.

"Mommmm!" Elisabeth cried. "Franz says I'm a baby for believing in Santa Claus!!!"

"Only children who believe in Sankt Nicholas get presents," Oma bustled out of the kitchen balancing yet another tray of sweets for tomorrow's feast in her plump hands. "How do you suppose the presents get under the tree with all of us at church? Here, *enig engel* [little angel]. Put these on the buffet for me like a good girl. Ja?"

"Ja, Oma!" Elisabeth carried the tray of intricately iced heart-shaped lebkuchen cookies into the dining room. She had her suspicions about the presents. Papa always disappeared midway through the lengthy sermon and reappeared just in time for them to put on their annual Christmas pageant, but if she didn't believe in Santa, she wouldn't get any presents, so she ignored her brother's taunts and believed anyway.

She and Oma had pierced the lebkuchen before baking and strung a ribbon through each one to hang them on the tree after they opened their presents. Each family member had decorated a different cookie, but Elisabeth thought her cookie was the prettiest. She picked it up and watched it twist on its pretty red ribbon, showing off the angel she'd painstakingly iced onto her cookie.

"I don't think it looks like a dogs paw print!" Elisabeth carried it over to the Christmas tree and stared up at the angel who'd been her inspiration. "Do you?"

The beautiful porcelain angel which had been in the family for three generations smiled down at her, not answering. The lace had yellowed over the years with one wing glued back together after a mishap involving the cat, but it was still the most beautiful angel she had ever seen. She looked forward to it being pulled from storage each December as though she were welcoming back an old friend.

"I didn't think so," Elisabeth answered the silent decoration. "Here. I made this for you. I hope you enjoy eating it up in heaven."

She carefully strung the cookie over the highest branch she could reach of the fake plastic Christmas tree and arranged the cookie so it would be the first thing the others saw when they got back from midnight mass. She'd tell Franz that Santa must have hung it on the tree. So there!

"I hope you come see our play," Elisabeth spoke to the treetop angel. "There's lots of room in the rafters for you to fly up and watch the service. I'll be watching for you!"

Elisabeth had always adored angels the way that her friends loved unicorns and kittens. A statue of one graced the lounge of First Saint Paul's with the words 'fear god, and give glory to him' carved into the pedestal beneath it. Each Sunday after mass, she loved to sneak over to it and whisper secrets as the adults socialized about things that happened at school or home with her family. According to her CCD teacher, the angel had been the only item to survive the destruction of the original Saint Paul's church during the Great Chicago Fire in 1871.

"Elisabeth!" Mama called. "What's taking you so long? We're running behind!"

"She's probably eating all the cookies," Franz grumbled.

"Was not!" Elisabeth protested. She gave the angel a quick curtsy, almost tripping over the white sheet Mama had wrapped around her to create a makeshift angel dress, and hurried out of the living room. Oma helped her slip her arms into her coat, pushing the collar beneath her angel wings like a stole so it wouldn't crush them. She shoved her out the door to where Papa sat warming up the car on this frigid Chicago night.

"It's snowing!" Elisabeth circled joyfully in the walk, her face upturned to the air. She relished the feel of the large, fluffy snowflakes which landed delicately on her face.

"It's always snowing," Mama grumbled. "Papa will be shoveling the walk first thing in the morning for sure."

"I will help," Opa said with his heavy German accent, leaning on his cane. "I am not invalid."

"You will not!" Oma chastised him. "You have a bad heart. Franz is old enough to help his father."

"Oh … joy," Franz grumbled, holding out his arm to help his frail grandfather down the short steps to the street where Papa had the car waiting. "Ten to one I'll be out there shoveling all by myself. Heaven forbid *she* should help!" Franz jutted an accusatory finger into Elisabeth's face.

"Elisabeth must help me set the table for our guests tomorrow morning," Mama said. "It is *your* job to make sure they arrive up our walk without meeting their death!"

Elisabeth stuck out her tongue when Mama wasn't looking. Franz did it right back, just in time for Opa to catch him in the act.

Going.

"It is honor to help your Papa," Opa said. "You should be thankful for what you have. My Papa was taken from me as boy to Russian front. You are lucky you have a father."

"Yes, Opa," Franz rolled his eyes. It was a source of continued embarrassment for Franz that his grandfather was proud of his great-grandfather's service in the Third Reich against the Russians. It didn't matter that Opa condemned what the Nazi's had done to the Jews or that his father had been faced with the same choice all German young men had been faced with at that time. Join. Or be shot. All Franz cared about was his great-grandfather had fought on the 'wrong' side of the war.

"Get in, get in, get in, get in," Mama chanted, bustling all of them into the car. "And buckle up." She herded Elisabeth into the front seat to sit between she and Papa, while Franz sat in the middle of the back.

"Don't crush my wings," Elisabeth warned as Papa crammed his tall frame into the car, giving him a fetching smile.

Papa smiled back. He was a great big bear of a man, but also very gentle. He drove a garbage truck for the city, effortlessly lifting the heavy barrels into its great, orange maw. Sometimes, Elisabeth wondered if Papa turned in the great orange truck on Christmas for a red sleigh. All he needed was a white beard.

"It's slippery tonight." Papa edged the car out of the parking space and drove to the end of the street. The windshield wipers swish-swish-swished the gigantic snowflakes, which were coming down so fast Elisabeth could see the shape of each giant snowflake as it passed in front of the headlights.

"Just drive slow," Mama said. "If we're late, everyone will be late. They can't start the Christmas pageant without the Angel of the Lord, now. Can they?"

"No they won't," Oma chipped in from the back of the car. "They can't start the play without Elisabeth."

Papa slowed as they approached the red light, grumbling as the car fishtailed. He breathed a sigh of relief when the light changed green well before they'd gotten to the intersection.

"The lights are with us tonight." Papa winked as he took his foot off the brake and allowed the car to glide through the intersection.

Through the window beside him, Elisabeth saw the headlights speeding straight at them, not slowing down.

She screamed.

Pain crushed her chest as Papa got shoved into her, and then the both of them shoved Mama into the passenger side door, right into the truck waiting patiently at the other side of the red light. Her head rammed against the roof as the car folded in half lengthwise like a tent.

"My wings..." Elisabeth lamented as she lost consciousness.

Chapter 13

Abraham asked …"O Angel of Death!
What do you do if one man dies in the east and another in the west?
Or if a land is stricken by the plague?
Or if two armies meet in the field?"

The angel said: "O Messenger of God!
The names of these people are inscribed on the lawh al-mahfuz:
It is the 'Preserved Tablet' on which all human destinies are engraved.
I gaze at it incessantly."

Naqshbandi Sufi Tale

Earth - AD December, 1992
Chicago, Illinois

'The ringing of the bell has a jarring effect upon the human psyche,' Azrael wrote. *'The bell ringer stands at a public place, in this instance the exit to a busy public transportation station, and rings the bell, summoning the attention of his quarry to the small, red kettle he bears suspended from a tripod.'*

He noted a tally mark as a middle-aged woman dressed in a simple mass-produced coat smiled and tucked what appeared to be a dollar bill into the red kettle.

"Merry Christmas," the woman said.

"Thank you," the bell-ringer replied. "Merry Christmas to you, too!"

While this was occurring, a well-dressed woman wearing high heels and a mink coat exited the subway, avoided contact with the bell ringer, and haughtily made her way across the street.

'It never ceases to amaze me how humans who appear to have the least,' Azrael scribbled, *'are often the ones who give the most. Several theories have been propounded to explain this paradox. Those who've lived closest to the line between having enough, and not enough, appear to feel greater empathy for those less fortunate.'*

It pleased him that humans celebrated the birthday of the research subject who'd provided the catalyst to stamp out Moloch-worship once and for all. Azrael liked Christmas, especially in Chicago where people had emigrated from all over the world, bringing their traditions with them. For ten years now, he'd had been inexplicably drawn to this city, spending his spare time easing the critically ill into the Dreamtime. Christmas provided an opportunity to observe the positive side of human nature and restore his faith in what he did.

The humans ignored him sitting on the second-story ledge of a department store, an even darker shadow against the early winter dusk. People rarely saw him unless he wanted them to see him, for who wanted to see Death except the dying and the already dead? Or those too innocent to understand what Azrael had come to represent. A little African-American boy pulled against his mother's hand, pointing up to where Azrael sat collecting data.

"Look Mommy," the boy said. "An angel."

"There's angels all over the place today," the frazzled mother groused, juggling far more packages than was sensible. "Pasty-faced honky angels to sell pasty-faced honky dolls to pasty-faced white people. They come out earlier and earlier each year. Next thing you know, they'll be taking out Christmas decorations for the Fourth of July."

The little boy waved to Azrael.

Azrael waved back. He enjoyed studying humans, at least the ones who weren't evil, but he liked children most of all. They reminded him of a time when he had still been innocent enough to believe he might change this world for the better instead of shoveling excrement against the tide of Moloch's malevolence. Watchman? More like Trashman! He needed days like today to remind him why the mysterious goddess felt it necessary to protect her realms.

"But this angel is black," the little boy said. "Just like me. See?"

"Humpf!" Packages slipped out of the mother's hand as she glanced in the general direction her son pointed and saw nothing. "Now look! I hope nothing didn't break!"

The bell ringer stepped forward to help pick up the dropped packages, leaving his kettle unattended. Azrael put a tally mark in the plus side of his checklist and started to write once more. A rough-looking man stepped out of the shadows and edged towards the kettle. Azrael watched the exchange, suppressing the urge to pop in front of the thief and shout 'boo.'

'Overall incidents of good will increase this time of year,' Azrael scribbled. 'But those who prey on the weak never seem to go away.' He made a tally mark in the negative column of his checklist.

"Hey!" the African-American woman spied the thief trying to take the bell ringer's kettle. "Get outta there, you hoodlum! I know who you are!" She threw one of her packages, whacking the thief off the head. Azrael heard the sound of breaking glass.

Would throwing the package be considered a positive act? Or a negative one? Azrael weighed the matter carefully, then put a tally in the positive column along with a scribbled note. *'Defense of another is generally a positive trait.'*

Snowflakes began to tumble out of the sky like miniature fallen angels. One by one, the shops beneath the ledge where Azrael sat with his legs dangling over the edge like a lanky boy began to close. Pedestrian traffic became so light that finally even the bell ringer packed up his kettle and went home. A few last commuters made their way through the streets to get to wherever they would spend Christmas Eve. Even the ever-present traffic died down. Chicago became almost … peaceful.

Azrael closed his eyes and tilted his face up towards the enormous falling snowflakes, imagining the graceful crystalline structures were melting upon his flesh instead of simply ceasing to exist. He couldn't feel them, of course. Only *living* tissue held any real sensation; but to touch anything alive meant to instantly kill it. He flared his nostrils, inhaling the scent of cold, icy moisture, and listened for the crackle of the icy crystals as tiny changes in temperature caused them to contract and expand. It wasn't the touch he craved, but compensating for his inability to touch by using his other senses kept him from going insane.

Mama. Gazardiel. Elissar. For thousands of years he'd visited hospitals and the scenes of car accidents, hoping one of the spirits he eased into the Dreamtime would recognize him upon leaving their mortal shell, and for thousands of years he'd been disappointed. He was sure the goddess had sent them back into physical form many times by now, but it was unlikely they were sent to Earth. Christmas was a day to spend with family. He'd never been able to fill the aching void left by the loss of his family and friend.

A crash disturbed his musings, followed immediately by a second crash and the sound of breaking glass.

A horn blared nonstop.

A car accident? Yes. About six blocks from here. Azrael leaped off the ledge and was immediately airborne, flying to his destination instead of teleporting as he wasn't sure exactly where he was going.

"Watch wherf yurf goin, jerk…" a man in a souped-up vintage Chevelle slurred, opening the door to his smashed car and instantly slipping and falling upon the snow. Beer bottles dropped out onto the street, the snow muffling the sound of falling glass so they only made a dull thud.

The car he'd hit broadside had been rammed all the way across the intersection into an oncoming delivery truck. Azrael clenched his fists and reminded himself he was only here to reap the souls of the truly evil, not stupid drunks like the idiot who staggered away from the wrecked cars, attempting to flee the scene. Humans had their own laws to deal with situations such as this. It was not his place to judge.

The elderly Dodge Dart which had been hit looked bad. The V8 engine of the muscle car had taken the brunt of the impact, sparing its driver. The smaller car, on the other hand, had been shoved up into a tent-shape between the two larger, heavier vehicles.

It was time to go to work.

The driver of the delivery truck slumped over his steering wheel, unconscious. Azrael listened, using senses beyond the normal five to scan for injury. The driver had been stopped at the red light when the Dodge was rammed into the front of his truck by the Chevelle. According to Azrael's scan, the driver suffered whiplash and a broken clavicle, but he would live.

Azrael scanned the occupants of the car. He got nothing. Nothing at all. Not even a heartbeat.

"Senseless!" Azrael hissed, glancing down the street where the drunk had staggered. It was not his place to interfere in the affairs of mortals. All he could do was make sure these people safely found their way into the Dreamtime so they could be reunited as a family there.

He reached in the window to the back seat. A bloodied elderly man sat crushed in his seatbelt, his mouth twisted in a scream, eyes open. His spirit was already gone. Azrael closed the man's eyes. He scanned the other three adults in the car, but they were also gone. Like most creatures in existence, the victims had instinctively made their own way to where they needed to go. The consciousness of the boy in the center, however, still lingered. His body had been shoved upwards towards the roof when the car had folded like a tent. He was just a teenager, not sure what his spirit was supposed to do.

"Come with me," Azrael reached out his hand. "I will escort you where you need to go."

"But we'll be late," Franz said. "Everyone is expecting us."

"I think they'll understand," Azrael said. He double-checked to verify the boy's skull had shattered on the ceiling of the car before touching his mortal shell to complete the process of severance. The advancing state of human medicine meant Azrael had to be certain death was inevitable before he rendered assistance, but not even the Eternal Emperor could have healed such a horrific head-injury.

The boy's spirit took his hand. In an instant, Azrael teleported the boy to the gateway to the Dreamtime. He could sense the boy's parents and grandparents were already there, anxiously milling about, looking for him. The boy stepped through the threshold. Azrael turned to leave. Franz then did something Azrael had never seen before.

Franz stepped back out again!

"Where is Elisabeth?" Franz stood with one foot inside the threshold of the Dreamtime.

"That was all I sensed in the car," Azrael said, not certain he'd just seen what he'd just seen. "Perhaps she is already inside the Dreamtime?"

"Mama and Papa say Elisabeth is not there," Franz said. "She didn't make it. Please! You must take me back to find her. I promised I'd watch out for her."

"Your mortal shell is damaged beyond repair," Azrael said with a feeling of dread. "I can't bring you back. Your injuries were too severe to survive. If you go back, you risk your spirit becoming lost."

He was a strong one, this human. The boy tugged at Azrael'd hand with surprising strength. Yes. He *had* seen the boy do something impossible.

"Please!" Franz looked much older than his fourteen years. "I promised my parents I would always look out for her."

Azrael searched for signs the young man had evolved enough for his spirit to pull his mortal shell into the upper realms and reconstitute it the way an archangel did. The boy's will was formidable, but already Azrael could see the edges of his spirit-light begin to fray, early signs of dissipation. Although he was evolved, Franz had not quite reached perfection. If he lingered, not only would his life be lost, but also his soul.

"I'll go back and find her," Azrael said. "If she still lives, I'll make sure she gets into the hands of those who will protect her in your stead. If she's left her mortal shell and become lost, I will find her and bring her to you. Alright?"

Franz looked at his hand which had begun to lose its shape.

"What's happening to me?"

"You must get to the other side or you'll be lost, too." Azrael used the voice of reason he'd heard so many parents successfully use to coax their offspring into making wise choices over the centuries. "Your parents will be distraught if they lose the both of you. I'll find her. You have my word."

Franz hesitated, and then nodded.

"I'll hold you to that promise," Franz said, surprisingly adult for one so young. He was a recycled spirit. Azrael was certain of it.

He could almost see the echo of past-life memories returning as She-who-is's veil of memory loss began to slip away, restoring the knowledge accumulated over countless lifetimes. The boy stepped through the veil into the Dreamtime, leaving Azrael standing at the gateway he visited several times per day, but could never cross.

In a flash, he teleported himself back to the car accident to search for the missing girl. The driver of the delivery truck was now conscious, calling into his two-way radio for help. Several people had come out of apartments on either side of the intersection, not sure what to do. Azrael softened the edges of his physical form so he couldn't be seen and scanned the area around the car wreck for signs of a disembodied spirit.

Nothing.

He'd only detected five bodies in the car. Was it possible he'd missed something? The bloodied truck driver screamed at the bystanders standing idly by wringing their hands to go call 9-1-1. At last a man moved forward and got into the driver's seat of the truck, backing it far enough from the mangled car to get at the other door. It was stuck.

The truck driver looked in the smashed window and saw the ground meat that had once been Franz's mother. He fell to the ground and vomited.

"I'm so sorry," the truck driver wept as he clutched at the snow as though it were a child's blanket. "I couldn't get out of the way."

"Dude," the young man who'd moved the truck said. "This wasn't your fault. That other guy blew the red light and rammed them right into you."

A tiny moan drifted from the center of the car, so quiet that only Azrael could hear it. Someone was still alive?

"They're all dead," the truck driver wept.

No. They weren't. Someone was still alive. Franz's sister, he presumed. How had he missed the sixth spirit?

Sirens became audible in the distance. Police cars. Slow! Too slow! Now that Azrael knew it was there, he could sense the child's life force fading by the second. So weak. He could sense the jagged energy of fear. Panic. Pain. It was unlikely anyone could survive such a horrific accident, but Azrael couldn't bear to leave a child to suffer when one touch from *him* would alleviate her pain. If he shoved past the two men blocking the way, the child wouldn't be the only person whose spirit he'd be escorting into the Dreamtime.

'Damn! Damn! Damn!' Azrael silently screamed at them in his own mind, his wings flared, ready for action. 'She's suffering. Get out of the way!'

The police car arrived, blue lights reflecting off the falling snow which had become a heavy shroud of white covering the tomb of the family just killed. Two police officers got out. Azrael tucked his wings into his back, flicking his cloak around himself so he didn't inadvertently kill anybody.

"They're all dead!" the truck driver wailed. "It's all my fault!"

The police officer reached in and felt the pulses of the five people visible in the car. Only Azrael knew that somewhere in the middle was a sixth victim. A child. Small enough to escape notice.

"Looks like there's nothing we can do for these folks," the police officer said to his partner. "Damn! On Christmas Eve!"

"It wasn't his fault," several bystanders said simultaneously. "That yellow car ran the red light and plowed them right into the delivery truck. The driver took off."

"A drunk," the second police officer nudged one of the beer bottles nearly covered with snow with one shiny black oxford shoe.

Azrael could sense the life force panic inside the car. His sensitive ears picked up another moan, louder this time, drowned out by the sound of the approaching fire truck. An overwhelming image of someone being smothered intruded into his mind. The girl was fighting to live!

"Anything we can do?" the paramedic asked, rushing over to the car.

"Go ahead and try," the first police officer said. "We couldn't find any sign of a pulse. But maybe you can zap 'em with a defibrillator or something." He herded the distraught truck driver out of the way for questioning.

"He's right," the paramedic shouted after checking all five pulses. "I got nothing. Better send for the coroner. And the Jaws-of-Life. The front door is twisted shut."

"I hate Christmas Eve," the second paramedic grumbled as he trudged back to the fire truck, shoulders slumped with resignation. "Every drunk in the city decides now would be a good time to get behind a wheel and go a-wassailing."

'Dammit!' Azrael whispered, leaning towards the second police officer, a woman cop. 'There's a little girl in that car. She's still alive. And she can't breathe!'

The police officer paused what she was doing, and then resumed putting flares around the crash scene.

Two more police cruisers arrived, as well as an ambulance. More gawkers came out of surrounding apartments and other cars. The scene got noisier and noisier, so noisy that there was no chance someone would hear a faint moan from a dying child wedged between her dead parents.

Azrael vacillated, not sure what to do. How could these people be so stupid???

They weren't stupid. He had missed her, too, until her brother had pointed it out. He wasn't supposed to interfere ... but ...

The first police officer had stepped away from the truck driver to speak to one of the police officers arriving at the scene. The truck driver sat on the curb, distraught and wracked with guilt. For two thousand years Azrael had studied the science of creating 'rallying points,' the point where an ascended being might push to facilitate an event some would term a 'miracle,' but others would remain skeptical enough about that neither the Armistice nor the strict rules prohibiting the use of ascended power were violated. The truck driver was his most likely target.

Azrael moved to stand before the man huddled on the curb so he would be visible when he rematerialized, checked to make sure nobody was within range of his wings, and extended them just far enough so the man would know what creature stood before him now. He pushed back his hood and solidified his physical form just enough so someone in an altered state of grief might perceive him.

"Listen," Azrael said softly to the man who sat with his face in his hands, weeping. "There's a little girl still trapped inside that car. She is dying. It's too late to help her family, but it's not too late to help *her*. Even if she doesn't make it, at least you can make sure she doesn't die alone. This accident was not your fault."

The truck driver looked up and blinked, hastily wiping his eyes as he recognized the Angel of Death stood before him, black wings, black flesh, black cloak, and the kindest, most beautiful face he had ever seen. He reached towards Azael.

"Don't touch me," Azrael warned. "For my touch is death. I need *you* to make the others listen. Make them search the car one more time. The girl is trapped in the front seat between her dead parents."

"O-o-o-okay," the truck driver stuttered, placing one hand behind him to lurch shakily to his feet.

Azrael stepped back and dissipated so he was impossible to see. Only another ascended being or genetically evolved human could see him in this state. The truck driver blinked and looked around.

"Hey..." the truck driver asked. "Where'd he go?"

"You should sit down, sir," a female police officer said. "You have a concussion."

"There's someone in the car."

"We know, Sir," the female police officer said gently. "There isn't anything we can do for them. We need to make sure you aren't critically injured as well."

"No," the truck driver pushed past her and moved back towards the car. "The angel. He said there's a little girl trapped in the car. In the front seat. Between her dead parents. We need to help her."

The female officer hesitated, unsure what to do. A lifetime of seeing wacky things happen while out on patrol inclined her to not discount the claim of a witness.

"Hey ... Fred!" she called. "He said there's another victim in the car. Still alive."

"We checked already," the first police officer on the scene said. "No pulses. They're all dead."

"Was there a little girl? In the front seat between the parents?"

"No," Officer Fred glanced in and grimaced at the gruesome scene. "I see nothing."

"The angel said there's a little girl trapped in the car and she's going to die if we don't help her." The truck pushed past Officer Fred and rushing to the window of the car. "Little girl? Are you okay?"

Not a sound. Not even a whimper. Not even for Azrael's sensitive hearing. It was as though her spirit had completely disappeared. Invisible. Even to him.

"You're distraught, Sir." Officer Fred placed his hand on the truck driver's shoulder. "And you've been badly injured. There's no little girl in there. See?"

"The angel said she's in there and I'm going to get her out!" The truck driver grabbed the door handle. "Little girl! Little girl! Can you hear me? We're coming for you!"

"Sir?" Officer Fred called over to the other police officers. "I need backup here. This guy's going off the deep end."

The truck driver fruitlessly yanked the mangled door, trying to force the tangle of steel to open. It wouldn't budge.

Azrael shifted into his more versatile void-creature form and ran a tentacle along the hinges. The metal dissolved beneath his touch as though it were being cut by a blow torch, only unlike a welder's torch, his touch left no melted iron in its wake, only a clean line where matter had once existed and now did not. Metal groaned as the door came off the hinges. The truck driver fell backwards onto the snow, door and all. The bloodied, mangled mass of what had once been a human female fell out, making a sickening 'plop' as it hit the snowy pavement.

With a tiny tinkling sound, a small golden halo fell out on top of the bloody mess, the tinsel shining brightly in the flashing blue police lights.

"Oh my god," Officer Fred glanced into the mangled interior of the car. "He's right. There *is* someone else in there."

The truck driver began to weep, but this time it wasn't guilt that made him cry, but the intense emotion of knowing he'd been right.

"It wasn't my fault!" the truck driver cried aloud, reaching towards the sky. "The angel said it wasn't my fault."

Azrael made a mental note to come back and study the truck driver's reaction as soon as he'd cleaned up this mess. Activity exploded around him as the police shoved back the onlookers, giving the paramedics room to extricate the unconscious child from the wreckage.

"Her pulse is weak." The paramedic gently laid her out upon the ground. "Very erratic. I don't know how she's still alive."

"Look at her neck," the second paramedic said. "It looks broken. Hey Janice! Get the backboard!"

The female officer rushed over to the ambulance and came running back with the backboard. "Here."

"We got a Caucasian female," the first paramedic called into the radio pinned to his shoulder. "Neck appears to be broken. Both arms … broken. Both legs … broken. Pelvis … broken."

"Lung appears to be punctured," the second paramedic called, slipping an oxygen mask over her face. "At least seven broken ribs. We got a lot of blood here. I think we've got a punctured brachial artery."

"Blood pressure is barely readable," the first paramedic said. "How is this kid even still alive?"

Yes. How was this child still alive? Normally the spirit would float above their mortal shell, trying to escape the pain. A tendril of consciousness would tether the spirit until it decided whether to stay or go. This child, however, was firmly entrenched in her body and refused to budge. It was how Azrael had missed her in the first place. He hadn't seen a spirit cling so fervently to its mortal shell since the day Agent-infested Romans had nailed Yeshua to a cross and publicly executed him…

Azrael solidified his physical form to appear 'normal' and pulled his black cloak around himself before stepping forward to get a closer look. The child lay unconscious upon the snow, only a stray golden curl indicating her coloring amongst her blood-matted hair. Splayed beneath her, fake dime-store angel wings were affixed to her back, covered in blood. His awareness of the chaos which bustled around him retreated as his nostrils flared, listening for signs of whether this child would live or if he should alleviate her suffering.

"There's no way this kid is going to make it," one of the paramedics said. "I've never seen injuries this severe."

Her eyes slid open. Unearthly silver eyes, so pale they glistened like the moon, met his. Despite her pain, the little girl smiled. She reached towards him like an infant reaching towards a bauble, delighted by its spin. Azrael reached over the bustling paramedics to take her hand.

"I see you…" the little girl chimed. Her small hand closed trustingly around his.

Warmth flooded his hand as her life force flowed straight up into his heart, making it skip a beat in a way it hadn't done since he'd been rendered without form. The perpetual song that always played in the background of his spirit grew louder, other instruments joining the cello in a symphony of joy, making him choke with emotion. Azrael tugged, wishing to carry her away from her pain, but she did not follow. His black eyes grew wide with surprise as, for the first time since the day he'd become a creature of the void, a mortal touched the Angel of Death and lived.

"Wh-wh-who…" Azrael stuttered. "Who are you?"

"I'm the Angel of the Lord, silly!" The little girl's eyes glowed silver as she gave him a weak smile. "You can't start without me."

Her eyes slid shut.

Azrael felt panic out of fear he'd lost her, but her spirit still clung to her mortal shell, refusing to so much as peek a single tendril out of the body the child refused to abandon, so formidable was her will to live.

No wonder he hadn't been able to detect her spirit…

Azrael stood like some tall, dumb statue of an angel and trailed behind the paramedics as they lifted the broken child, bloodied wings and all, onto a stretcher and wheeled her over to the ambulance. Who was this child?

As the ambulance sped away, Azrael looked over to where the truck driver had stopped to pick up the bloody halo which had dropped out when he'd torn the door off the hinges with a little help from Azrael. The man crouched on his knees, hands clasped together in prayer, weeping with joy.

"Um … would you mind if I … um … took … that?" Azrael pointed to the halo.

The truck driver looked at him through tear-stained eyes and shakily extended his hand. Azrael took the fragile halo between his forefinger and thumb so as not to accidentally dissolve it or brush the fingers of the mortal who was as perplexed by what had just happened as the Angel of Death was.

"It really wasn't my fault, was it?"

"No," Azrael said. "It wasn't."

Leaping into the air, Azrael flapped his great black wings and sped after the ambulance.

Chapter 14

Then I saw another angel come up from where the sun rises in the east,
And he was ready to put the mark of the living God on people.
He shouted to the four angels,
"...Wait until I have marked the foreheads of the servants of our God."

Revelation 7:2-3

Earth - AD December, 1992
Chicago, Illinois

Azrael felt their presence. He peeked out the doorway of the hospital room, where the little girl who'd just defied death lay hooked up to every piece of medical equipment currently known to humankind, before signaling the coast was clear. Not only were the doctors scratching their heads wondering how the child was still alive, but so was Azrael.

"Who is she?" Azrael stared down at the cheap tinsel halo he still held in his hand.

"We don't know," the General said. "Not only does Hashem not know, but She-who-is doesn't know either. If she's a recycled consciousness, she didn't come from the Dreamtime."

"Is she one of yours?" Azrael gave Lucifer a pointed look. He knew enough about Lucifer's 'power of persuasion' to not assume the mother's marriage to another human at the time of the child's conception disqualified the Fallen Angelic from being the sire.

"I wish," Lucifer stared down at the child. "She looks like one of mine. But I have no recollection of servicing her mother."

The General snorted with disgust.

"We all know how reliable *your* memory is!" A scornful expression caused the General's unearthly blue eyes to glow even bluer with a hint of the Cherubim energies he wielded.

"Hey!" Lucifer protested. "I haven't had a blackout for 5,500 years. It's not *my* fault Moloch got his hands on me as a teenager!"

"Hmpf!" The General's arms crossed across his powerfully muscled chest to indicate his closed mind.

Azrael noted the exchange with detached interest, making a mental note to track data on the ongoing hostility between the two Archangels in the expanding file of scientific theories he used to occupy his mind whenever he wasn't busy reaping Agents of Moloch.

"Is she a step-in from a higher realm?" Lucifer asked. He moved to the child's bedside and took her hand.

"Nobody knows." The General moved to the opposite side. "Perhaps?"

Physical touch. Oh! How Azrael envied them. The memory of the feel of the child's hand in his; the sensation of warmth he'd felt as she had touched him, but refused to allow her spirit to become severed from her body, made his hand tingle even now as though it were alive.

Azrael glanced down at his hand, the one that was a figment of his imagination. Not real. An artificial construct shaped by his consciousness so the mortals of this realm wouldn't run screaming every time they saw him. It didn't look any different than it normally did, but it sure *felt* different. *He* felt different. As though the child had somehow transferred a tiny portion of her ... *being* ... to him?

Was that even possible? Should he ask the General to mention it to the Emperor? No. The experience had merely shaken him. He was too unimportant to waste the Emperor's time, especially now that She-who-is had put Hashem in charge of prodding species towards evolution in other galaxies besides this one. At the moment, Shay'tan was essentially in charge of the Milky Way.

The two Archangels closed their eyes and focused, each giving the little girl what Azrael could not, the gift of healing. It humbled him that the two enemies had come together to heal this child simply because he had asked them to. A look of peace came upon the General's face as he focused on the Song of Creation. Tears rolled down Lucifer's cheeks as the Song enabled him to feel the connection which still existed with the mate he had lost.

The heart monitor evened out. The little girl's coloring improved. Bruises faded.

"We must stop." The General released her hand and placed it gently back upon the covers. "She's already a miracle child. We must leave some infirmary in place to mark her struggle."

"Please," Azrael begged. "She's still in pain. She's just a little girl."

"You allowed one amongst them to see you," the General chastised. "News of this story is already being circulated in the media as a Christmas miracle. If she survived your touch, she may be evolved enough to be a host. Exposure puts her at risk of drawing Moloch's attention."

"She's a child who just lost her entire family!" Lucifer argued. "She'll struggle enough without physical limitations exacerbating her problems."

"We cannot give definitive proof of our existence," the General warned. "They must continue to evolve naturally. If we push them any faster, we'll inhibit the very traits the gods wish to foster."

"Just a little more?" Lucifer looked at his adversary through tear-stained eyes. "Please. Her spine is still damaged. If we leave scars, at least leave her with ones that won't prevent her from making her own way through this world. You, better than anyone, should understand how hard it can be to live amongst the humans."

It never ceased to amaze Azrael that, despite all of Lucifer's significant shortcomings, for some reason he'd inherited an almost human capacity to experience empathy, including compassion and hatred; conflicting moral codes that left even the studious Azrael constantly perplexed. Little did Lucifer realize his stoic Seraphim adversary was little different than *he* was in his capacity to feel, only less outwardly expressive thanks to his early years being reared amongst the Cherubim.

"Sir?" Azrael pleaded, his nostrils flaring as he inhaled the scent of pheromones that remained out of balance. "Please."

He wasn't supposed to interfere in the life-choices of mortals, but this child had made it clear by the way she clung to her mortal shell that she wished to live. Would it be wrong to make sure she didn't live as a quadriplegic? His ears heard the painful wheeze of lungs where they'd been punctured and constrictions where blood couldn't flow due to permanent physical injuries. Although the two had reconnected the severed nerves in her broken neck, she'd still spend the rest of her life disabled.

"She sure looks like one of mine," Lucifer caressed the child's cheek. "Perhaps she'll be the one who sets me free?"

The General relented, and not simply out of his desire to be rid of Lucifer once and for all. The General had *earned* his nickname, Angel of Mercy. Beneath his stoic exterior lay a tender heart.

"We shall focus on the injuries which would impede her progress through this world," the General said. "Leaving ones likely to heal through natural forces over a period of time. And a scar. There. That gash on her face. We'll leave her with a visible reminder she shouldn't be alive."

"It's not right to disfigure her!" Lucifer protested.

"It's not to punish her," the General said. "But a reminder this child defeated the Angel of Death. As –I- choose to keep a scar over my heart to remind me how blessed I am to have found my true mate."

Lucifer looked away, shame filling his eyes. The General referred to the scar where the then Moloch-possessed Lucifer had used his 'power of persuasion' to induce a disturbed young woman to plunge a venomous blade into Mikhail's heart, the source of the General's hatred. The General and Lucifer touched the child once more. The energy in the room vibrated to the song all three of them could hear thanks to their connection to Ki.

"There," the General said. "It is done. She shall struggle just long enough to cause doubt it was divine intervention which saved her."

Lucifer brushed a curl out of the child's eye before gently kissing her on the forehead. "Maybe she's a descendant? It's not often I get to interact with the children I sire." He paused, looking at his old adversary with rare vulnerability in his eyes. "Perhaps Azrael is right? Maybe I could set a better example?"

The General snorted in disgust.

Lucifer's eerie silver eyes hardened as the moment of vulnerability gone. Azrael winced at the missed opportunity for the General to reach out and encourage Lucifer to change. The two adversaries stared across the hospital bed of the child who had, just for a moment, united them with a common purpose. Both stepped back to assume their habitual, hostile stances.

Azrael made another mental note to study the opposing Archangel's hostility. It so closely echoed the ancient hostility between Hashem and Shay'tan that it amazed him the two gods had eventually become friends. Sort of friends. Friends most of the time except for when they were at war and accusing the other of being the devil? Perhaps, given enough time…?

"I have ties amongst the community who can ensure this child finds her way into a good family," Lucifer said coldly. "Doors will open and financial resources will appear at the right time to shepherd her in whatever direction the child shows a natural inclination to follow."

"She's here for a purpose," the General warned. "Interference may impede her growth."

"Her family is gone and you've left her crippled and scarred!" Lucifer accused. "Now you want to leave her destitute, as well?"

"Not … destitute," the General said. "Just … we don't know why she's here. If she's an old soul from another realm, altering her circumstances from the ones she placed herself into may interfere. We must allow her to find her own path."

"Slumming on Earth amongst the humans," Lucifer sniped. "Now that's a surprise."

The Fallen Angelic, of course, referred to himself.

"I'll watch out for her," Azrael stepped between the two before things devolved into one of their all-too-frequent physical altercations. The General possessed incredible self-control, but Lucifer knew how to push all of the General's buttons. Keeping the two of them together in the same room was never wise.

"Let me know if she needs anything," Lucifer said. "But I'm not going to rely on *him*. My own men will watch, as well." Lucifer pointed to the General, not Azrael, when he indicated who he wouldn't rely upon.

Although Azrael and Lucifer weren't friends, they weren't enemies, either. More ... he disapproved of Lucifer's debauch lifestyle. He understood Ki wished the Fallen to promulgate a certain percentage of hybrid DNA back into the human populace, a burden that had fallen entirely to Lucifer once the others had died out without ascending. But ... damn! Did he have to be so ... so ... blatant about it?

Hmmm... Perhaps that might make an interesting collection of behavioral characteristics to study? He'd seen many humans exhibit self-destructive tendencies, though none were more over-the-top than Lucifer. Azrael could almost feel his hand itching to pick up his void-reinforced pencil and start scribbling notes.

In fact ... he could almost *feel* his hand. Period...

Azrael glanced down, wondering at the curious sensation of actually *feeling* something for real, not just imagining in his consciousness the echo of what physical sensation had once felt like back when he'd still been mortal. The urge to reach out and take the hand of the child lying helpless in the hospital bed and feel connected to her was nearly overwhelming. Perhaps he should bother the Emperor with the question after all?

"I've got to get back," the General said. "She-who-is has the Emperor juggling so many galaxies in the air right now it's a wonder the poor deity knows which end of the universe is which."

He gave Azrael a rare grin. It was no secret that, just as She-who-is had kept her former husband He-who's-not jumping through hoops for her by plying him with sexual favors, the goddess now kept Hashem happily busy spending hours on end in his genetics laboratory, cheerfully splicing new life forms together from the old ones. The Architect of the Universe was nothing if not resourceful about how she enticed others to do her dirty work.

Azrael scratched all thoughts of bothering the Emperor from his mind. He was an eminent scientist in his own right. He would study the child and see if she exhibited any further curious traits.

Both visitors exited, leaving Azrael as he'd been when they'd first arrived, standing over the child's bed, listening to the beep-beep-beep of the heart monitor. He'd be glad when the doctors discovered her neck was no longer broken and removed the painful-looking Halo they'd bolted into her skull.

A raven-haired nurse carrying a clipboard barged into the room, making her rounds of the intensive care unit. Azrael faded into the shadows, tucking his wings tightly against his back and drawing his cloak around himself to guard against an inadvertent brush with death. Azrael glanced at her name tag. 'Nancy Gonzalves, R.N.' noted the child's vital signs and then ran out of the room, her step so light for a moment it appeared as though *she* might be an angel.

"Doctor! Quick! Somebody page the doctor!" nurse Nancy shouted.

Azrael smiled, true joy making his heart feel lighter. Boy. Were they in for a surprise!

Chapter 15

Ye shall not afflict any ... fatherless child.
If thou afflict them in any wise,
And they cry at all unto me,
I will surely hear their cry;
And my wrath shall wax hot,
And I will kill you with the sword;

Exodus 22:22-24

Earth: June 1993
South Side, Chicago, Illinois

Broken glass crunched beneath the slender tires of Elisabeth's wheelchair as the social worker pushed her towards the sixteen-story Robert Taylor Home. Plywood covered the windows of the two lower floors. Between the junkies and the all-too-common stray bullets from gang rivalry, it was impossible to keep the lower floors habitable. A rough-looking group of mostly African-American kids loitered at the entrance smoking cigarettes, their expensive gangsta-rap clothing and designer sneakers belying the poverty of their surroundings.

"I want to go home!" Elisabeth pleaded. "Why can't I go home? I don't like being in a foster home."

"There's nobody left to take care of you, honey child." The social worker spoke with the cadence of an African-American woman transplanted from the Deep South. "I just can't understand why your last four foster-families were so anxious to get rid of you. You're well-behaved, and you don't eat hardly nothing at all!"

Elisabeth bit her tongue. The reason she'd lost weight was because the foster families kept locks on the cupboards. She got exactly one packet of oatmeal with a cup of reconstituted powdered milk for breakfast, whatever the school cafeteria served for free lunch, and one-quarter of a package of fluorescent orange store-brand macaroni and cheese and a hotdog for supper. She'd been kicked out of the first foster home for complaining the foster mother refused to feed her lunch on the weekends.

As for the second? How could she explain the *real* reason she'd been kicked out was because her black man had gotten sick of watching her foster siblings pick on her and let them catch a glimpse of him? He rarely let her see him, but sometimes, like when the foster mother's boyfriend at the third foster home had snuck into her room at night to slip his hand under the covers to touch her pee-pee, he'd made himself visible to scare them off.

She'd told the nurses at the hospital about the black man, but it had been a mistake. They'd promptly sent her to speak to a psychologist who'd told her it was her imagination. Once you got labeled crazy, the social workers didn't believe a word you said. Six months in the system and already she'd figured out it was better to keep her mouth shut.

As for the last foster home? The foster mother had just gotten divorced. She'd taken her in to help meet the mortgage payment and her real kids weren't too mean, but along with the end of the school year had come the end of free school lunch. The state didn't pay enough to lose days out of work to run her around to all her physical therapy appointments and feed her. So … here she was. Going into her fifth foster home.

One of the gang-kids stepped in front of the graffiti-painted steel door and blew a smoke-ring in the social workers face.

"Step aside, Jimmie!" the social worker snapped. "Or I'll call your juvie probation officer and you'll be right back in that group-home!"

"Ain't be no worse than here," the ruffian said. His cohorts twittered beside him. "Whatcha got? A little vanilla ice cream?" Jimmie touched Elisabeth's pale, blonde hair. Elisabeth recoiled.

"Little white bitch thinks she's too good for us," a mulatto-skinned female twittered. She had short, nappy hair with the gangsta-rap band initials 'NWA' shaved into it. The girl shoved Elisabeth's wheelchair back a few inches with her foot.

Elisabeth was smart enough to figure out a new situation. Their old neighborhood hadn't been great, but Franz had taught her how to avoid trouble. Don't make eye contact. Pretend to focus on something else. Don't let them push you around, but don't get riled up at their taunts, either. Keep to yourself. Only now Franz was gone, too.

Why couldn't her black man have let Franz live? At least then they could've gone through all these foster homes together? Or maybe that's why the black man hung around? Did he feel guilty she didn't have anyone left? She'd love to see the look on the gangsta-kids' faces when he showed up with that black cloak of his and pointed at them like the Ghost of Christmas Future.

"Step aside," the social worker said. "Or I'll call the police. I know each and every one of you and will have you all back in juvie faster than you can sneeze."

"Yeah, yeah," the kids grumbled, stepping aside.

The social worker wheeled Elisabeth inside the building. The light bulb was missing from the lobby. A junkie leaned against one wall, humming happily to himself as the smack he'd just injected into his track-marked arm propelled him into his own happy little world. The stench of urine was so thick it made Elisabeth retch.

"I don't like it here," Elisabeth said. "Can't I just go home? Please?"

A bottle rolled across the floor. A drunk shouted something unintelligible and stumbled towards them. Elisabeth realized the social worker was scared, too. Her brusque manner to the gang kids at the front door had been an act.

'Black man? Where are you? Please! I'm scared...'

"You don't have a home left to go back to," the social worker said more bluntly than was necessary. "Your parents are dead and nobody stepped forward to take you in. Your house and everything that was in it was sold to pay their bills. This is the best I can do for you."

Tears welled in Elisabeth's eyes. The drunk fell to the floor and passed out. The social worker pushed her wheelchair through the trash-strewn floor to get to the elevator. A piece of cardboard was taped across the doors with scrawled black letters. 'Elevator broken. Use stairs.'

"How am I supposed to get you up to the twelfth floor?" The social worker stormed over to a door marked 'building manager' and pounded on it like a SWAT team about to initiate a raid. An overweight Hispanic man wearing a stained wifebeater came ambling out scratching his armpit.

"Elevator's broken," the building manager said.

"When they going to fix it?"

"Been after the city for seven months now to get that thing fixed," the building manager said. "They send someone out to get it going for a couple of days, and then it breaks again. Something wrong with the electrical system. If you ask me, the entire thing needs to be replaced."

"This kid's in a wheelchair!" the social worker said. "How the heck am I supposed to get her up to the twelfth floor?"

"I dunno. Carry her?" The building manager made eye contact with Elisabeth. His expression softened. "Or call the city. Every time I call, they tell me the city ain't got no money to go fixing no housing projects. Maybe you'll have better luck, being connected with the government and all."

'Yes ... I'm in luck,' Elisabeth thought. *'Bring me someplace else. —Please-bring me someplace else!'*

The hair stood up on the back of her neck. She glanced real surreptitious-like out of the corner of her eye, hoping to see her black man. He only let her see him when he thought she wasn't looking. There. She could detect a distortion amongst the shadows; a darker shadow where even the darkness appeared to be swallowed by midnight.

The elevator suddenly dinged.

"Well I'll be damned!" the building manager exclaimed as the doors slid open. "That thing's been broken for weeks. City musta sent somebody out to fix it and didn't tell me."

'Darn! Why'd you have to go fix the elevator?' Elisabeth glowered at the darkness amongst the shadows. *'Now they're going to make me live here!'*

The social worker wheeled her in backwards. There was a sign over the buttons that said 'out of order.' She pushed the button for the twelfth floor anyway. The elevator sprang to life. They rode up in silence

"We're in luck," the social worker said. "This is the last foster home on my list. If we can't place you here, there's no place left to go except a group home."

Group home as in ...what? A bigger group than the first three foster homes you sent me to where there were five kids sharing a bedroom?

The elevator doors slid open. A well-dressed white man had a garishly dressed black woman pressed up against the wall. Her skirt was shoved up and her legs were wrapped around his waist. He repeatedly shoved against her and grunted like a dog.

"Get out of here!" the social worker shouted. "Go find a room."

The man froze.

"Fuck off!" the woman laughed. She nipped the man in the neck. "You paid for five minutes. All you get is five minutes, whether you finish or not."

The man resumed his grunting. The woman grunted along with him.

"Is he carrying her like that because her back is broken like mine?" Elisabeth asked.

The social worker's mouth fell open. She pushed the wheelchair past the couple as quickly as she could to a gouged doorway at the end of the hall. A television blared through the door. Across the hallway, a baby squalled through a second door. The social worker knocked and then turned to her.

"Sometimes I need a little angel like you to remind me why I got into this line of work in the first place," the social worker tousled her hair. "This place will be better than the last four. I promise."

The door opened. A morbidly obese white woman with a cigarette in one hand gave Elisabeth an appraising stare. Elisabeth glanced down the woman's tree-trunk thick polyester slacks to the fat-rolls which squished over the tops of her loafers like a Pillsbury dough-woman. Behind her, an assortment of kids in every color of the rainbow hung out in front of the television, their expressions blank and mouths open as if they were hypnotized into a stupor.

"This the one nobody wanted?" the fat woman said through puckered lips. She took a drag of her cigarette and blew it off to one side.

Elisabeth glanced through to the tiny kitchenette. Even from here she could see the cupboards and fridge had locks.

"She's a good girl," the social worker said. "No back-talk. Don't give nobody any trouble."

"You didn't tell me she was no cripple," the fat woman interrupted. She jabbed an index finger as short and fat as a sausage at Elisabeth's wheelchair. "How's she gonna get up to the top bunk?"

The fat woman and the social worker began to argue. Elisabeth bit back her tears. She'd cried at the last four foster homes and it had gotten her nowhere. Two of the foster kids pointed to her wheelchair and twittered about the scar running down her face and bolt-holes the Halo had left in her forehead.

"Why can't I go back to the hospital?" Elisabeth pleaded. "If my neck breaks again, maybe they'll take me back? The nurses were real nice to me there. Maybe one of them will take me in?"

"Sorry, honey," the social worker said. "The only one who expressed an interest had … issues."

The fat woman and the social worker argued some more, and then they reached an agreement.

"You're going stay here a few days," the social worker said. "And then I'll be back. I promise. We'll work something out."

Elisabeth closed her eyes and focused on that vague sensation she'd learned to pay attention to. Yes. He was still here. Her black man. So long as he was here, she knew she wasn't truly alone.

"Okay." Elisabeth plastered a tough expression on her face so the other kids wouldn't think she was a wuss. If she showed weakness, the others would target her. Every time she got sent to a new foster home or school, a pecking order was established. She'd learned pretty fast the kid in the wheelchair was always low man on the totem pole.

The social worker left her with the fat woman with the locks on her cupboard and six rainbow-colored foster-siblings. She wished the black man would talk to her. Never once had she heard him speak. Not since the night he'd taken her entire family. Why hadn't he taken her, too? She wished, now, that she had gone with him.

Chapter 16

For the Angel of Death spread his wings on the blast,
And breathed in the face of the foe as he passed;
And the eyes of the sleepers waxed deadly and chill,
And their hearts but once heaved, and for ever grew still!

Lord Byron

Earth - AD June 1996
Kizlyar, Republic of Dagestan, Russia

"*Privyet* [hello]," Azrael greeted, watching the Russian army move into position around the hospital. "*Kakova situatsiya* [what's the situation]?"

"350 Chechen rebels seize hospital," Mansur Al-Hallaj said in heavily accented Russian, the linga franca of ethnically diverse Dagestan. "Over 3,000 hostages."

Azrael scrutinized the colorfully dressed local Sata'an-human agent. Like many of the Sata'anic Fallen, Mansur's family had retreated into a geographically isolated area to intermarry with humans and secretly raise their families. Dagestan's traditional long Circassian coat, tall boots and furred hat could hide a plethora of undesirable genetic traits.

Although in theory the elders of these remote Sata'anic families reported to Lucifer, the offspring had generations ago 'gone native.' The tolerant, Sufi-based religion practiced by Mansur's people had been passed down virtually unchanged from the religion modern full-blooded lizard-people practiced to this day in the Sata'an Empire. Tall, dark-haired, and with Caucasoid features, the only thing which differentiated Mansur, named for a Sufi mystic brutally murdered by mainstream Islamicists for preaching the heresy of equality, from the full-blooded humans his family had intermarried with, was his serpentine gold-green eyes and lizard-like tail.

Azrael eyed the other Dagestani hybrids, bristling with the traditional hand-cast knives and sabers this region was famous for manufacturing in addition to handguns and rifles; another throwback to Sata'anic culture.

"Why are we intervening in a purely human conflict?" Azrael was cautious about getting dragged into something he had no business meddling in. "You know the terms of the Armistice."

"Doctor in hospital is my brother," Mansur said. "Tail not docked. If Chechens take look under hood…"

Mansur trailed off. It didn't matter whether the rebels were Moloch's Agents or run-of-the-mill fanatical Wahhabi Islamicists from neighboring Chechnya. Having a Sata'anic descendent exposed was bad no matter *who* did the exposing.

"What does this have to do with me?" Azrael asked. "I'm only called in for Agents. Not to crack skulls. Let the Russians deal with their own mess!"

"We no fan of Russia," Mansur said. "But they not our enemy, either. Since communism collapse, they leave us alone. They educate our kids, we send them caviar. We have no interest in getting dragged into Chechnya's war."

"Chechen rebels fight Russia the wrong way," Azrael said. "But their anger is not without cause. I refuse to interfere in a civil war."

"Moloch's Agent one pulling strings," Mansur gave him an appraising stare. "He seize Chechen warlord … Salman Raduyev … as host."

"Do you have proof of this?"

"He been acting crazy," Mansur said. "Even by Chechen standards. We have intelligence he gather three, four lesser Agents inside building. Small fry. Kind of souls you reap, Malak al-Maut, without breaking sweat."

Azrael's wings perked up with interest. Reaping squatters was always a rewarding exercise, especially when he got there in time to actually make a difference. Moloch and his priests hadn't stopped sacrificing humans to their god, only changed tactics so the mass genocide of spirit necessary to open a portal appeared to be terrorist acts or casualties of war.

Living consciousness was the most powerful … and elusive … power source in all the known universes. Cause enough suffering during the death-event of a single spirit, or enough mass casualties of multiple spirits in a single place, and the energy they released could open portals into parallel realms, including Gehenna, the place where Ki only *barely* managed to keep Moloch interred.

"The Russian army is already lining up to storm the hospital," Azrael pointed out. "What do you want me to do?"

"You ever see Russian army do anything discreet?" Mansur asked. "It like using RPG to swat fly."

"That's for sure," Azrael said. "Don't you have hybrid agents amongst their numbers?" He reached into his cloak and absent-mindedly fingered the void-reinforced pencil he used to tally human behavior. He'd studied the Russian tendency to overreact.

"Not anymore," Mansur said. "Ever since communist party lose grip, things unstable. Many purges. Best we able do is keep few soldiers in low ranks of army."

"I'm not going to kill Chechens just for being here," Azrael reiterated. "Not unless I see they're infected by an Agent. But I will help you locate your brother so you can figure out how to get him out. It's the best I can do."

Mansur spoke to his fellow Fallen-hybrid agents in a rare local dialect that was neither Russian nor Arabic, but some third language whose roots stretched back into the language spoken in the Sata'an Empire. *Tser*. One of the agents came forward at Mansur's urging.

"This is Abu," Mansur said. "My cousin. He in Russian army. Abu very … precious."

Azrael studied the wiry, dark-haired young man, barely more than a teenager. He dressed like the other Russian soldiers buzzing like angry bees around the hospital, preparing for their clumsy assault. He wasn't wearing a long Circassian coat. Docked at birth?

"Abu first child born in clan without tail for as long as our people hide in mountains," Mansur said as though reading Azrael's thoughts. "He free of curse of Shay'tan that keep our people enslaved. Only blood mark him as ours."

Azrael scrutinized the young man. Sata'anic night vision and their tail were survival traits which bred true no matter *how* many generations the lizard-people intermarried with humans. It prevented, to this day, descendants of Shay'tan's rebellious 'Fallen' from disappearing, as the Alliance Fallen had done, into Earth's population. Eliminating Sata'anic genetic features was the holy grail of Fallen forced to serve Lucifer generation after generation due to an unfortunate dominant gene.

"You wish me to shadow him?" Azrael asked. "And make sure he doesn't get himself killed as he storms the building?"

"We be grateful," Mansur said. "Nobody see you if you don't wish, Malak al-Maut. Lead Abu to my brother. Get out before either side can frisk and find more than weapons under doctor coat."

"I can't interfere in Russia's civil war with Chechnya," Azrael said. "But … perhaps I'll find those Agents while I'm in there. If so, it will make this mission legitimate."

"We positive Salman Raduyev mid-level Agent," Mansur pulled out some grainy black-and-white surveillance photographs. "These three are rebels we suspect low-level squatters. Fourth one … we not confirm whether squatter or radical Wahhabist."

Azrael watched shadows move into position on the tops of buildings. Russian snipers. This raid was about to go down with or without him. It had been a while since Moloch's priests had attempted to open a portal via a mass human sacrifice, but sometimes during clusterfucks such as this, enough civilians died that a clever Agent could punch a portal through to Gehenna. Perhaps following along, just to observe, might be a good idea?

"Deal," Azrael said. "I'll find your brother … what's his name?"

"Abdullah Fa'azi," Mansur said. "Here photograph."

Azrael committed it to memory along with the four suspected Agents of Moloch. Shots were fired from the nearby buildings. Return fire shot back from inside the hospital and from a nearby tall building where the Chechen rebels had holed up with the hostages.

"C'mon, Abu," Azrael called. "It's showtime."

"Da, Sir!" Abu gave a perfect Russian military salute. The young man jogged back to the unit he was embedded in while his brethren moved into position, their own sniper rifles aimed to provide cover should it be needed.

Azrael faded from view, shadowing the young man long enough to determine what his unit's plans were before entering the hospital. Fearful hostages were jammed into several large rooms. Chechen guards with vintage AK-47 Kalashnikov automatic rifles guarded each group clustered on the floor. It would be so easy to intervene…

No! It was forbidden. As much as Azrael loathed hostage-taking, so far the Chechens had avoided civilian deaths. This was a natural Earth civil war. Several of the terrorists he moved past were reassuring terrified civilians that negotiations were underway to release them in exchange for safe passage back to Chechnya.

"It as if Raduyev deliberately botch taking of military base," one Chechen rebel complained to another. "Then he lead us here. Claim taking hospital will gain concessions."

"Raiding hospital work in Budyonnovsk," the second rebel said. "It force Russians to negotiate."

"No sooner ink dry on treaty," the first Chechen groused, "then Yeltsin back to old tricks. It buy us … what? Six months peace?"

"Don't matter what I think," the second rebel said. "Israpilov he just relieve Raduyev of his duties. Say Raduyev act like crazy man. Possessed by demons or something."

Azrael's ears perked up. Now that sounded like a squatter.

"No matter now," the first Chechen said with a shrug. "Raduyev head for hills and leave us holding bag." The rebel casually waved his machine-gun towards the cowering hostages. "We all about to be ground up and spit out by Russian army. Even them."

Azrael suppressed a sigh of disappointment. The suspected squatter was no longer in the area. Unless he stumbled across one of the suspected lesser-agents, Azrael had no authorization to be here.

"Russian government no give a shit about own people," the second rebel complained. "Much less ours. Should have never seize hospital. Kill hostages not what I sign up for."

"I don't care what Israpilov order," the first Chechen said. "I shoot Russians. No shoot civilians. In hospital, no less! That not kind of jihad Prophet Muhammad speak of, peace be upon him!"

"Yeah, yeah," the second rebel said. He turned to the hostages and waved his AK-47 in their direction.

Azrael paused, contemplating whether he should 'accidentally' brush against the rebel with one of his deadly feathers.

"Listen up!" the second rebel shouted at the hostages. "Russian army about to invade. You all lay flat on floor, put hands over back of head so they see you no armed. It lessen chance you get killed by accident."

The sobbing hostages did as the terrorist ordered. Azrael reconsidered his earlier, forbidden, contemplation. Scumbag terrorist or not, the Chechen had enough scruples to attempt to lessen the loss of life. Outside, the amount of gunfire increased, as well as explosions that were either mortars or grenades. The so-called 'rescuers' were here. It was ironic the hostages were more afraid of the Russian army sent to free them than the terrorists.

Azrael made a mental note to jot down this entire observation in one of his scientific journals. So many potential studies. So little time. Remorse. From terrorists. A reminder of why he was not supposed to interfere. His fingers itched with the urge to pick up his pencil and start writing; the fingers he could feel ever since the girl had touched them. Gunfire peppered against the concrete-and-brick exterior of the hospital. Debris fell from the ceiling as a grenade rocked the building. The hostages screamed. The Russians were coming.

Azrael moved into the next room.

"We kill hostages and show we mean it!" a different Chechen rebel shouted, the muzzle of his rifle pointed at the head of a pale, wan-looking man wearing nothing but a hospital johnnie. "Like we do in Budyonnovsk."

The prickling sensation at the edge of his consciousness clued Azrael he had found his squatters.

"This no what we sign up for," a second rebel said, holding out his hand as though to calm his comrade. "These people Muslim. Prophet say is sin to kill fellow Muslim. We wait … kill Russian nonbelievers!"

Azrael recognized the second rebel as the one Mansur had been unsure about. Not a squatter.

"We serve much older god," a third Chechen standing behind him said. "Moloch. Father-god of Whore of Babylon. He come to devour all blasphemy she create. Including you."

"Wh-what?" the second rebel asked.

BANG

The third Chechen shot the second one in the back of the head. The hostages sobbed, terrified, on the floor.

"Get to work!" the first squatter said. "We only got few minutes before Russians storm hospital."

"Save me tall guy over there for next host," the second squatter who'd shot the non-squatter rebel said, pointing to a handsome Dagestani orderly. "I want to get laid this time. This host body too ugly to attract female."

"Who says they need to be willing?" the third squatter jibed. "It's better when they fight!"

The pale, wan patient with the muzzle of an AK-47 pressing directly against his forehead made the sign of the cross. Not Muslim. Orthodox Christian, most likely an ethnic Russian. Probably why he'd been targeted first.

"Saint George, deliver me from evil," the patient prayed, trembling with fear.

Azrael winced as the terrorist fired at point-blank range, grey matter exploding out the exit wound onto the faces of the other hostages lying prone upon the floor. The hostages screamed as the now-dead patient fell dead.

Azrael felt the subtle tear caused in the fabric of the universe whenever a sentient spirit was tortured or murdered. The Chechen rebel from the other room was right. Moloch's Agents had deliberately screwed the pooch on the air base as an excuse to commit mass slaughter. By the time the Russian army stormed the building, the squatters would have opened a hole large enough for several low- or mid-level Agents of Moloch to escape and shoved their victims into the hole to feed deities with host-needs too specific to escape. The Agents would simply jump bodies into a hostage injured badly enough to weaken their resistance to possession and walk right out of here.

"Please ... you must not do this!" a doctor said, his body positioned so that he shielded one of his patients. "We are not your enemy."

"That one's next," the first squatter pointed to the doctor who had spoken up.

The other two grabbed the doctor and hauled him in front of the one who'd shot the patient. Azrael recognized him as Mansur's brother, Abdullah. Drat!

There were too many hostages! If he took out one of the squatters, the others would start shooting to open a portal, determined to complete their mission no matter what because agents who failed often found *themselves* on Moloch's menu. Lucifer segregated larger Agents from the small fry, but it was quite literally dog-eat-dog in Gehenna.

Azrael dissipated the edges of his physical form into his more versatile void-creature shapelessness and cautiously moved tentacles into position to strike host-bodies without killing Abdullah or the other hostages. Only Abdullah wasn't about to take his own death gracefully.

"Allahu akhbar [god is great]!" Abdullah cried. His tail slipped from beneath his long doctor's coat and thwacked one of the squatters as he grabbed at the machine gun of the leader.

"Shit!" The gun fired into the air.

The hostages screamed.

Squatter number three stepped backwards, right into Azrael's waiting tentacle. The host-body dropped to the ground, dead. The consciousness of a very puzzled-looking Chechen man stepped aside from a curious, angular-looking creature that wasn't even from this universe, much less this planet.

"Oh ... crap," the squatting wraith said as he realized the Angel of Death had just knocked his consciousness out of his host body. Azrael grabbed the disembodied wraith with a sturdy tentacle and wrapped it around his throat.

"Go," Azrael whispered to the owner of the host body he'd just killed. "Follow the light into the Dreamtime before you get sucked into Gehenna."

Abdullah thwacked squatter number two with his tail just in time to prevent him from getting his AK-47 aimed. The gun went off, hitting one of the hostages in the shoulder. The hostages scrambled to their feet and rushed towards the door, preventing Azrael from zapping the other two. He twisted his form out of the way so none brushed against him.

"Our Lord, I rely upon you for strength and courage," Abdullah prayed as he kicked squatter number one in the knee cap and wrestled to get the gun out of his hand.

Azrael tapped squatter number two just as he was about to pull the trigger into Abdullah's head. The host fell to the ground as the consciousness of a strange, furry pink creature stood, suddenly realizing another player had been in the room all along.

"Moloch's foot!" the wraith shouted, attempting to disappear before Azrael could get his hands on it.

"Why, that's no ordinary rabbit," Azrael grabbed the pink fuzzy creature. "That's the most foul, cruel and bad-tempered rodent you ever set eyes upon!"

The pink fuzzy wraith gave a strangled squeak as Azrael wrapped a sturdy tentacle around its throat to immobilize it.

"And no matter what," Azrael continued, dragging the two squirming wraiths in his wake as though they were toilet paper stuck to his shoe as he moved back to help Mansur's brother. "Never, ever, feed them after midnight!"

The lead squatter kicked Abdullah in the crotch. As Abdullah crouched in pain, it brought the butt of the rifle down upon his head, knocking the dazed Sata'an-human hybrid to his knees.

"One of Lucifer's scum," the lead squatter growled. "Moloch will be pleased to dine upon your spirit."

Azrael reshaped his form into a black Angelic, except for the two tentacles holding the squatters, and visibly materialized just far enough behind Abdullah so he didn't accidentally touch the hybrid as he struggled to his feet.

"Boo!" Azrael tapped the squatter in the forehead.

The host body dropped to the ground, dead. Before the squatter could even open his mouth to sneer, Azrael had it by the throat.

"Be back in a moment," Azrael said to Abdullah and three grievously ill hospital patients who'd been too sick to run when the other hostages had made a break for it. He disappeared in a flash, dragging the squatters to the processing chamber.

"Thanks, Az," Samuel Adams, Lucifer's current lead intelligence officer said as he summoned guards to haul the three squatters back to Gehenna. "All in a day's work?"

"Where is he?" Azrael asked, referring to Lucifer, who was nowhere to be seen.

"Do you really want to know?" Sam gave a wolfish grin and made a lascivious gesture with his tail. Lucifer. Out. Seducing the wife of some billionaire, president, or general. Another half-Angelic offspring carrying Lucifer's DNA to 'improve' the human species.

"No." Azrael gave Sam a disgusted look as he handed over the squatters to the guards.

The squatters were hauled through the stifling heat of the gates to a higher security-level of Gehenna than the one they'd escaped from. Unless they won over whatever disembodied deity ruled the new ring of the hell-dimension, the squatters would end up, themselves, consumed by a 'bigger fish.'

"Got to get back," Azrael said. "I saw three people who could use my help."

"Why do you do that?" Sam asked. "Reap the souls of the innocent?"

"Their bodies are failing." Azrael adjusted the hated cloak so he wouldn't zap the wrong person when he rematerialized back inside the Dagestani hospital. "Helping them leave without pain reminds me my gift has a purpose other than to kill bad guys."

"For every evildoer you assassinate," Sam recited the ancient Cherubim meditation of the Shinobi Masters.

"You must grant redemption to ten good men," Azrael finished. "Lest you lose your own soul to evil."

"Wise people, those Cherubim," Sam said. "Too bad there aren't any of them around anymore."

"The General teaches his Archangels their ways," Azrael said. "Only since I can't heal them, or interfere, all I can do is ease their passage into the Dreamtime."

"Until next time," Sam tucked his tail along his right side and giving Azrael a perfect Alliance salute.

Azrael teleported back to the Dagestani hospital, where Abdullah checked the pulse of the dead Chechens. The Sata'anic-hybrid looked up, not too surprised to see him.

"I sensed your presence when you entered the room, Malak al-Maut," Abdullah said, making the Sata'anic sign of respect of hands to forehead, lips and heart. "It was my wish to create a diversion and enable these people to escape."

As much as Mansur was more Dagestani than the Dagestan people, his brother Abdullah appeared to go to the opposite extreme. The imposition of the Russian educational system and values upon this populace had caused some, such as Mansur, to drift towards isolationism, while others such as Abdullah embraced modern values. Abdullah would not be out of place in a modern American hospital.

"What of these three?" Azrael pointed to the three ghastly pale patients the Agents had dumped on the floor without concern for the technology which kept them alive. Two were elderly. The third was the young woman Abdullah had shielded with his own body.

"Why don't you ask them yourself?" Abdullah said. "Perhaps they are ready to leave? Perhaps not? It is their choice."

The old woman waved Azrael away. Senile or not, she was not ready to leave. The man with emphysema, however, reached eagerly towards Azrael, the effort of merely lifting his hand causing him to gasp for breath.

"Take me please," the old man said, "Angel of the Lord, to meet my Beloved Allah."

"Peace be with you." Azrael relished the feel of a mortal touching his hand willingly. It only lasted an instant, and then the physical sensation was gone, only the tickle of incorporeal consciousness brushing against his remaining as the old man's spirit was severed from his mortal shell.

"Thank you, Malak al-Maut." The old man transformed into a younger, stronger man, his favorite physical form during his time on Earth. "Oh ... I remember now. I've been here before. I'm supposed to wait for my wife at the entrance to the Dreamtime until she joins me."

"Then I shall bring you there."

Azrael transported the old man to the gateway and bid him farewell before teleporting back to the hospital. Abdullah kneeled over the young woman, who coughed up blood.

"Aisha is human," Abdullah helped her sit up. "My mother's second cousin. Dido clan. Not Hinukh as we are. My father married outside the tribe in the hopes of freeing his offspring from the curse of Shay'tan."

"Had you not possessed a third fighting limb," Azrael pointed out. "You would not have prevailed."

"I prevailed because you reaped the souls of our enemies," Abdullah said. "I only provided a distraction."

Aisha stared, her eyes round at the sight of her cousin's long, striped tail and the black-winged Angel of Death standing in front of her. Abdullah answered her questions in one of the Tser-language dialects until the young woman appeared satisfied.

"Aisha has been kept in the dark about her aunt's heritage," Abdullah said. "Our village is in a remote mountain pass. Our young do not understand the risk we take living so far from Jehoshaphat. Children forget to keep their tails hidden and there is no hiding their eyes until they are old enough to wear contact lenses."

Aisha coughed, raising a handkerchief to her mouth to dab at the blood. Azrael could hear the odd crackling sound indicative of advanced tuberculosis, the wheeze of destroyed lung tissue, and the scent of decay with every exhalation she made. End-stage TB. Mycobacteria which ate the lung tissue until it was so scarred it could no longer filter oxygen. It ran rampant in this part of the world ... and had developed resistance to all known antibiotics.

"Malak al-Maut has come to take me?" Aisha eyed Azrael with curiosity, but not fear.

"Only if you wish to be taken now," Abdullah reassured her, his expression tender as he touched her cheek. "But I hoped something could still be done to save you."

"You know there is no hope, Abdullah." A smile lit up Aisha's skeletal features which had once been beautiful. "It's time to let me go."

Abdullah took her hand and pressed it to his cheek, tears welling in the corners of his eyes. Marriage amongst cousins was common in this part of the world, especially second-cousins. It was obvious Abdullah's interest in Aisha was more than as her physician or relative.

"Mama always went home to visit her family and left us behind until we were responsible enough to hide our tails," Abdullah explained to Azrael. "But now Aisha has seen me, and you, for what we are, isn't there something you can do to heal her?"

"The other Archangels possess the gift to heal in varying degrees," Azrael said regretfully. "But alas … I do not. The only gift I can offer Aisha is a painless end to her suffering."

"Grandpapa and great-grandmother beckon from the other side," Aisha coughed up more blood. "I am not afraid."

"I had hoped you would stay, vozlyublennyi [beloved]," Abdullah kissed her forehead, "and become my wife."

"My body is too ill to bear your children," Aisha gasped for breath until she finally caught it again. "This is a terrible way to die … to fight for each and every breath."

"Perhaps if I take you to the West?" Abdullah said. "The doctors there might be able to cure you?"

"You tried every medicine the West has to offer," Aisha sighed. "Do you think I do not know you bartered everything you own to purchase the medicine to heal me? My illness is Allah's will."

Outside, the rude intrusion of the Russian army storming the hospital interrupted their goodbye. Shouts erupted from the hallway as escaped hostages announced they were not Chechen rebels and surrendered. Azrael recognized one of the voices. Abu … Azrael had been charged with helping Abdullah find his way to Abu and making sure neither one of them got killed. At least the young man wouldn't be facing an Agent.

"You'd best lay down on the floor so they don't shoot you," Azrael said; ready to fade the minute the Russian army kicked down the door.

Abdullah gathered Aisha's emaciated mortal shell into his arms and protectively wrapped his tail around her body. His tribe had adopted the Sufi-Muslim customs of the Dagestani people. Although Dagestani women did not take the veil, Abdullah took a liberty only a betrothed dare take.

"I will go with you, then," Abdullah kissed her hair. "Azrael can escort us together."

"No," Aisha said before Azrael, himself, was forced to refuse. He would not reap the souls of the healthy no matter how grief-stricken they were. "I wish for you to stay. Live your life. Find a healthy wife who can bear you many fine sons. Perhaps you could name one of your daughters in my memory?" She stroked the warm, striped tail which had curled around onto her lap. "So beautiful, your tail. I wish you'd felt confident enough to reveal it before Azrael come to take me."

Tears streamed down Abdullah's cheeks.

"Can I hold her while you take her?" Abdullah asked.

"It puts you at risk," Azrael said. "But I sense you have enough Angelic DNA to sense her spirit after she casts off her mortal shell."

Shouts and the loud thud of boots attempting to kick down the door interrupted them. The Russian army was here.

"I am ready," Aisha pushed Abdullah away. "It is great honor to have Malak al-Maut personally escort my soul into Paradise."

"Come with me, then," Azrael took her hand and gave her forehead the kiss of death. He relished the warmth of her flesh touching his as her life-energy was jolted from its mortal shell. Aisha's hand slipped gracefully to the ground.

Abdullah began to keen the high-pitched, ululating zaghareet Muslim people used to wail at the funerals of martyrs.

"There's no pain?" Aisha rose to her feet and took the deep breaths denied to her in life. Her spirit filled out so she lost her emaciated, sickly appearance, beautiful once more. "I must comfort my beloved."

"Abdullah," Azrael interrupted his mourning. "Please … close your eyes and focus. Aisha is still here. She wishes you to know she is well. I sense you can feel her."

Hiccoughing, Abdullah rubbed his tears as he gathered Aisha's empty mortal shell into his arms and did as Azrael said. It was difficult to concentrate with the sound of the battering ram bashing at the door.

"Goodbye, my love!" Aisha gave him the kiss she had never dared give him in life because to do so would have been her own tuberculosis-laden kiss of death. She lingered, her incorporeal lips touching Abdullah's like a butterfly sipping nectar from a flower in the summer sun.

"I can feel her," Abdullah reached out to touch the cheek he could not see. "I can't see her … but I can feel her."

"She is free from pain," Azrael said. "But now I must go. I strongly suggest you hit the deck."

The battering ram smashed through the door. Abu was the first to burst into the room, catching a glimpse of Azrael as he teleported Aisha to rejoin her ancestors in the Dreamtime. Abu leaped in front of the sobbing Abdullah, cradling the body of his deceased patient, just in time to prevent his Russian comrades from opening fire.

"He's a doctor!!!" Abu shouted. "Don't shoot!"

Over the next several days, Azrael monitored the Chechen rebels as they held a standoff with the Russian Army, hoping to capture the Agent who'd possessed Raduyev. All but 120 hostages were let go. They moved to a neighboring village. One-by-one, the Chechen rebels slipped away and faded into the hills. In the end, the Russians ended up killing more civilians than the Chechens did, as was usually the case in a Russian hostage crisis.

Azrael did not interfere further. Without Agents to reap, he had no legitimate reason for being there. He did, however, visit Elisabeth to silently cheer her on. Although the Armistice demanded he remain invisible and not interfere, he felt better when he checked in on her. The way she fought back against her own lousy circumstances gave him a helpful reminder that he wasn't the only person who'd ever been on the crappy side of the toilet paper when it came to the intrigues of gods. Sometimes, it was enjoyable to watch people simply because you enjoyed watching the way they interacted with their environment.

So far, he'd collected reams of data about her.

Chapter 17

Thus Allah made them taste humiliation in the life of the world,
And verily the doom of the Hereafter will be greater if they did but know.

Quran 39:26

Earth - AD June, 1996
Chicago, Illinois

"Elisabeth!!!" Nancy called. "Hurry up! You're going to be late!"

"Coming!" thirteen-year-old Elisabeth shouted loud enough for her foster mother to hear. She scowled at her reflection in the mirror.

"As if anybody's going to care if you show up or not," the cripple who stared back at her from the mirror each day answered. Elisabeth stuck out her tongue and touched the glass, using her finger to trace the hideous scar which ran from her right temple, diagonally down her cheek, to the corner of her mouth. "Nobody loves a freak."

Elisabeth reached for the two C-canes she used to get around, paused, and then put them back next to the bed.

"I'll be *damned* if I'm going to walk up onto the stage in front of all my classmates using *those* ugly things!" she said to the image in the mirror. "*You* use them. I refuse."

She stepped back, wobbling unsteadily, and reached for the cane Opa had been using the day he'd died. With no one left alive to care, the landlord had issued an eviction order and auctioned off her family's worldly goods to pay the creditors. There had been no money set aside. No life insurance. Not even a scrapbook full of pictures showing how happy her family had once been. Opa's cane was the only tie Elisabeth had to a past that was gone forever.

"You can walk on stage with me, Opa," Elisabeth said to the cane, feeling the worn smoothness of the curved wood. "At least that way somebody will be there who gives a damn."

The hair on the back of her neck stood on end. HE was here again. He thought she was stupid, that she couldn't see him. Well ... she couldn't. Not usually. But although she rarely saw him, she always could sense his presence.

Ever since the night she'd mistaken him for an angel, the black man had watched her struggle to stay alive. Watched her weep when she'd learned every person who'd ever given a rat's ass about her had died. Watched her fall on her face again and again as she relearned to walk. He'd watched her friends recoil from her injuries, the scar on her face, the wheelchair, the fact she could no longer run and play; and watched her get shuffled from foster home to foster home until, finally, Nancy had taken pity on her and applied to become her foster mother.

Nancy Gonzales was the intensive care nurse whose face had been the *second* face Elisabeth had seen upon awakening in the intensive care unit of the hospital to discover her head was, quite literally, bolted to a steel frame to fix a broken neck. Nancy had calmed her and reassured her she would be okay.

His face had been the first, staring at her, his expression troubled, as though she were a puzzle he wished to figure out. In those early days she'd thought the black man who watched over her was her friend. Her dream angel, come to heal her wounds and make everything go back to the way things were before.

But the black man had *not* healed her.

He had not made things go back to the way they were before.

He had not brought Mama and Papa back to life; or Oma and Opa and Franz. He had not brought anyone back to keep her company so that she wouldn't have to be all alone.

All he ever did was flit in and out of her life to watch her. Sometimes, if she pretended to look the other way, like she did right now, and glanced in the mirror, she could catch a glimpse of him out of the corner of her eye. He was tall and wore a black robe, with his face hidden in the voluminous hood. And every time she saw him, he was scribbling in a notebook as though she were a rat in a maze, constantly being put through her paces to see how long it would take her to find the piece of cheese.

"Go to hell," Elisabeth hissed into the mirror, glancing in the direction she knew he stood even though she couldn't see him today.

She'd tried talking about the black man to Nancy and the never-ending parade of therapists the social workers made her talk to, trying to get her to 'open up' about her feelings about having had her entire family taken from her one Christmas Eve. They thought she was nuts, imagining things; an imaginary friend her subconscious had manufactured to make sense of a senseless tragedy. It was the ultimate irony she'd been dressed as an angel the night God had taken her entire family from her.

She didn't believe in God anymore…

She turned, staring in the direction she knew the black man stood, watching her. If she stepped forward, for some reason he always stepped back. It was a game she played, making him retreat without letting him know she played it. She looked through where she knew he stood to the closet door behind him.

"It might get cold later," Elisabeth said aloud. "I should bring a sweater."

She lurched forward. Opa's cane was a poor substitute for the two walking canes, and many times as she'd moved towards him she'd deliberately fallen, hoping he would catch her and show he possessed a scrap of compassion. But he never did. He always stepped back, allowing her to fall. Perhaps that was what he wrote about in that notebook? How pathetic it was to watch her fall?

She smirked as she sensed he'd stepped to one side, cramming his tall frame into the narrow slot between her bed and the wall.

"You never know when you're going to be left out in the cold," Elisabeth said aloud so he would hear it. "It's always good to be prepared."

"Elisabeth!!!" Nancy shouted again. "C'mon! If we're any later, they'll send your commendation in the mail!"

"Coming!!!" Elisabeth shouted, grabbing the sweater and heading for the door. She held onto the rail and hobbled down the stairs towards her foster mother, Nancy, carefully placing the cane for balance so she didn't go tumbling head over heels. Having already broken her neck once in her lifetime, she had no desire to wake up a second time with bolts sticking out of her head like some modern-day Frankenstein.

Nancy helped her put her coat on and they hobbled to the corner, where a city bus would take them to her middle school. Pimps and street gangs lingered at the corner, eyeing them as Elisabeth balanced on her cane, but nobody bothered them. Not even the Saints or the Paulina Boys had any interest in rolling a cripple. She stared emotionlessly out the window as the bus made its way through rush hour traffic.

Elisabeth felt numb as she sat in the auditorium and waited for the principal to call her name, oblivious to the reassuring brown hand Nancy kept planted on her forearm. She looked up at the smooth, vaulted ceiling and wondered where HE would sit to watch her get her award. She wished they'd held the ceremony in the gymnasium. At least there she could imagine HE might be there, perched amongst the support beams and raised basketball hoops.

"And now I'd like to award our top eighth-grade student," the principal boomed over the loudspeaker. "Elisabeth Kaiser."

Elisabeth pushed herself up out of her seat and waved away Nancy's offer to help as she got her balance. The auditorium grew silent as parents of her classmates realized she was a cripple. The natural acoustics of the auditorium amplified the clack-shuffle-clack of her cane as she hobbled across the stage.

"What's wrong with her?" she overheard a parent ask.

Elisabeth stared across the sea of meaningless faces. Once upon a time she'd had many friends, but not since Death had marked her. Her classmates didn't wish to be reminded that fate could reach out and take everything away from them, as it had done to her, in an instant. Her hand tightened around the handle of Opa's cane. The wood felt warm in her hand in a way the dual aluminum walking-canes with their plastic handles could never feel. She imagined it was Opa who reached out to shake her hand and let her know how proud he was of her being the top student in her entire middle school.

The black man's hand had been cool, as though death itself resided in his touch. And yet ... his face had been so kind, and familiar. As though he were an old friend. She hadn't been afraid of him then, and she wasn't afraid of him now. But sometimes, she wished he would just butt out and leave her alone.

She wondered if he watched her now...

Naw... She was daydreaming about angels again. Imaginary friends to alleviate the pathetic joke that was her life. Whoever he was, the black man was no angel. The only time she'd ever imagined he had wings was when he'd reached down and taken her hand, urging her to come with him.

Such beautiful, glossy black wings...

The audience politely clapped once or twice as she made her way off the stage then stopped. Nobody was there to see *her*. She was just the nerd they were forced to watch before they got to their own kids. Before she'd even made her way to the steps, the principal announced awards for the basketball students. The audience stood, cheering wildly, and began to root as jocks bounded victoriously onto the stage.

She sensed his presence as she reached the bottom step. She looked up, expecting to see him there, rewarding her for working her butt off studying instead of socializing with the friends she did not have. Her cane missed the bottom step. She jerked the arm which usually contained a second cane to compensate, but the hand was empty. Elisabeth fell flat on her face. Nobody caught her, but she sensed the black man step back.

Her classmates began to laugh.

"All right, everybody," the principal announced. "That's enough!" He immediately went back to his speech lauding the jocks for winning the regional basketball championship. Elisabeth wasn't sure whether to be relieved the principal did not highlight her humiliation further by stopping the ceremony, or be offended that helping a cripple was less important than praising the athletes with perfect bodies.

Nancy hurried from her spot somewhere mid-audience to help her to her feet. Elisabeth burst into tears of frustration.

"If you're not going to help out," Elisabeth said through teary eyes, "then just go away and leave me alone!"

"I'm sorry, honey," Nancy said. She bent to retrieve Elisabeth's cane. "I warned you to use your *regular* canes."

Elisabeth squelched the urge to snap 'I wasn't talking to you' and glared at the spot where she sensed he stood. The black man who liked to watch her fall.

She hated that black man.

Elisabeth resolved that, from now on, she would do everything in her power to defeat him...

Chapter 18

Fear not them which kill the body,
But are not able to kill the soul:
But rather fear him which is able to destroy
Both soul and body in hell.

Matthew 10:28

Earth - AD August 6, 1998
Iganga, Uganda

Lucifer's current chief intelligence officer was one of many Azrael had worked with over the centuries. Taller than an average human, well-built, dark-skinned and strong, Samuel Adams had inherited the trait which cursed *all* descendants of the Sata'an-Fallen to serve Lucifer. So long as a hybrid bore a tail, the Armistice decreed they were subject to the Curse of Shay'tan, the old dragon's revenge upon the ancestors who had sided with the Fallen.

"What are we looking for?" Azrael asked.

"We've received intelligence Agents of Moloch are planning an offensive against a major target in Uganda," Sam said. "But we haven't been able to isolate the target."

"A lot of help *that* does us!" Major Hayyel gave Sam a contemptuous look. "Couldn't you have narrowed it down a little?"

Major Hayyel was the latest mortal Observer assigned from Ceres Station to perform Azrael's old job. Like most Angelics, Hayyel bore the white wings, blonde hair and fair complexion of the Emperor's genetic tinkering. Although every few years the Regent managed to elevate a new archangel, the overwhelming majority of Hashem's armies remained *mortal* soldiers, just like Azrael had once been.

Sam shrugged off Hayyel's rudeness and focused his attention on the Iganga skyline. Sam was used to being treated as a second-class human, but it still made Azrael bristle. While the two emperors' armies lived in comfort on Ceres Station, doing 99.9% of their so-called 'intelligence gathering' via remote satellite and drone, Sata'an-human hybrids rolled up their sleeves and waded through the shit humanity generated without complaint.

"Do you have any prospects?" Azrael asked.

"My bet is on the American or British embassy," Sam said. "Those are the two hottest targets."

"Does it even matter?" Hayyel's lip curled. "These petty kingdoms on this backwards planet?"

"Uganda has taken important steps towards democracy since they overthrew Idi Amin," Azrael said. "It's only natural the old guard would target supporters of the new."

"The chatter has been against both targets, Sir." Sam closed his clear inner eyelid to keep out the African dust instead of blinking using both sets of eyelids to appear human. "But if I had to pick one, I'd say they're planning on hitting the Americans.

Hayyel cringed at Sam's lizard-like gesture. "So where are the bad guys so I can get the hell off this shithole of a prison world?"

"We're forbidden to interfere unless it's a direct effort to free Moloch," Azrael reminded Hayyel. "He's been recruiting disenfranchised Muslims, riling them up to make human sacrifices under the guise of suicide bombings. My bet is the attack will come from humans connected with that movement."

"If you already know who they are and why they're causing trouble," Hayyel gave Azrael an accusatory stare, "then why do you waste my time?" Like most soldiers stationed in the most remote sector of the galaxy under complete radio silence, Hayyel resented being here.

"Because the terms of the Armistice say the two emperors have a right to appoint a mortal observer, that's why." Azrael gave Hayyel a patronizing grin. "Lucky you. You get to babysit the unicorn planet."

He *didn't* add that the lengthy debriefing all Observers underwent after each return from Earth was, in fact, an examination to ensure the Observer hadn't become infected with a squatter. All those times Azrael had thought Major Skgrll had locked him in a room and grilled him because he thought him incompetent … well, actually Skgrll *had* thought he was incompetent … but the Spiderid commanding officer had also been using monitoring equipment to register the subtle spikes in energy that occurred whenever an Agent overrode an unwilling hosts natural inclinations. Equipment that was, in Azrael's case, unnecessary since now he just *knew* when he was dealing with a squatter.

"Our men are scanning the embassies in Kampala disguised as electrical workers," Sam said. "We've got them searching for explosives or chemical weapons as we speak."

"More likely it'll be a car bomb," Azrael said. "That seems to be their M.O. lately."

"We've got feelers out for suspicious purchases," Sam said. "But if they're buying anything, its components that are innocuous in their original form. Either that or they've found a source we haven't infiltrated."

"What are we looking for, then?" Hayyel asked.

"A covered vehicle," Sam said. "Most likely a truck. Bags of ammonium nitrate fertilizer. And some sort of ignition source. C4 or TNT is the best, but propane cylinders also work. There are liquid propane tanks hooked up to every house in this town."

"That's not very helpful." Hayyel looked down from the roof of the three-story brick building they perched upon now, the tallest in the area, at the dozens of box trucks, covered pickup trucks with caps, and busses parked or driving through the light traffic of the town. "What would they even hit here? Talk about the boonies!"

"Not *here*," Sam said. "Our intelligence indicates this is where the Agents are staging the attack. We believe they're heading to Kampala where the embassies are."

"So we're looking for a needle in a haystack," Hayyel said. "And we're forbidden to fly over the city lest the primitives see us."

"We're descended from these primitives, Sir." Azrael pointed to a speckling of bronze feathers hidden in Hayyel's pale wings, indicative the Emperor had re-infused his bloodline with human DNA within the last few generations to stave off inbreeding. "Even the Regent was once a human."

A spark of anger flashed in Hayyel's eyes. Azrael noted the subtle way Hayyel twitched his wings in the opposite direction as though he feared getting them soiled. In the eyes of most mortal Angelics, Azrael was even *more* of an abomination than the Sata'anic Fallen. That ever-present hunger grew worse as Azrael felt a sensation akin to being kicked in the stomach.

His hand tingled. The hand that could feel physical sensation ever since the night Elisabeth had touched him and survived. Azrael looked at his fingers, imagining the way her small hand had curled around his as she'd told him she was the Angel of the Lord. *She* was even more alone than *he* was. He would check in on her the moment they were done.

"You can't fly without being seen," Azrael said. "Being non-corporeal has its advantages."

Azrael felt a thrill of perverse satisfaction at the expression of fear on Hayyel's face when he suddenly transformed from an otherwise normal-appearing Angelic, other than his ebony visage and heavily shielded cloak, to a creature of the void. He was tired of being treated like a second-hand citizen by his own species. Former species. Was he even still an Angelic? Nobody knew for sure. It was a rhetorical question.

'*Now I know how Lucifer feels,*' Azrael thought, noting his unusual urge to deliberately irk someone.

While Azrael glided invisibly down side streets like a wraith, stopping at any house that appeared suspicious, Sam pretended to be a farmer selling plantains, blending in with the general population with his African complexion and flawless Bantu dialect. Except for his trench coat that appeared out of place in the African heat, Sam could have passed for one of the tall, chocolate-skinned Baganda tribe. Intermarriage with humans had diluted most Sata'an traits enough for the lizard-people to commingle with only a light disguise, but all Moloch's agents had to do was peek under the coat for a tail and the hybrids would be made.

"Observer, this is Brewer," Sam called into the Alliance communications device which had been disguised to look like a cell phone. "Possible suspect in the outbuilding behind the Noor Islamic Primary School. White box truck, portable liquid propane cylinders, bags of fertilizer and sandbags. Request backup."

"Brewer, this is Observer," Hayyel answered. "I'm on my way."

"Az … we need you," Sam added.

Azrael did not answer. Although the Emperor had crafted a radio sufficiently shielded to passively monitor a frequency without shorting it out, he couldn't touch the push-to-talk button without 'killing' it the same way he jolted mortal spirits out of their bodies. Sam had worked with him long enough to trust he'd come. He raced along red dirt roads to the outbuilding abutting the railroad tracks providing a lifeline for the town.

"Shay'tan's foot!" Azrael hissed, spotting the thatched-roof garage halfway between the primary school and Victoria High School. "There are children everywhere!"

Nearly two hundred elementary-aged children ran around the tightly-packed school in their bright green school uniforms. Most African schools were taught in open-air classrooms consisting of little more than a roof to shield them from the sun unless severe weather drove them indoors. Behind the more formal concrete walls of adjacent Victoria High School came the sound of older students diligently reciting their lessons.

"How many more inside?" Hayyel pointed to the three men nonchalantly filling sandbags and carrying them over to load in a U-shaped design inside an empty truck.

"Besides those three," Sam said, "I counted two inside the outbuilding tinkering with a detonation device. There was a third one, but one of the kids came to fetch him to the high school to fix a clogged toilet."

"Probably the janitor," Azrael said. "As caretaker of the property, no one would question workmen loading supplies in the maintenance barn."

"A janitor?" Hayyel asked, contempt bleeding into his voice.

"Don't knock the janitor." Azrael's annoyance got the better of him. "He's in a position of trust with a secure government job and a pension; economic security very few Africans enjoy. It's kind of the human equivalent of being a Major assigned to monitor a remote outpost."

Hayyel's mouth tightened into a scowl. Azrael made a mental note to cut Lucifer a little slack the next time he saw him.

"The sandbags will direct the blast in a desired direction," Sam said. "If I had to hazard a guess, they don't intend for this to be a suicide bombing. It will take a few moments once they reach their target to activate the first gas canister to explode. Enough time to run away and detonate it remotely."

"What about the children?" Hayyel pointed to the kids playing perilously close to the building. "If we jump them and they detonate that thing here, anyone outside will be killed."

"We've been seeing a lot of this lately," Sam said. "Moloch's agents work close to targets we'd be reluctant to raid. Not only could innocent civilians be killed, but they know we're not supposed to allow humans to know we're watching."

"We got activity!" Azrael pointed to a second truck that pulled into the narrow dirt driveway. Two more men got out and began unloading bags of ammonium nitrate from the second truck against the sandbags in the first. Ammonium nitrate was a common fertilizer all over the world ... and also a component of most Earth explosives...

"Looks like we found the right place." Hayyel peered through a pair of binoculars.

The janitor, returning from the high school, spotted Hayyel's large, white wings. He began to shout.

"Hit the deck!" Azrael warned. "We've been made!"

The men in the outbuilding erupted like angry ants defending their hive, leaping behind bags of fertilizer and pulling out guns. Their suspicions were now confirmed.

"Shit!" Sam grabbed at his shoulder as he hit the ground. "I've been hit!" The lizard-man twisted around, his tail streaming out of the split tails of his Australian over-drovers coat for balance, and shot the janitor in the heart.

The kids screamed and ran in the other direction.

Hayyel leaped into the air, pulse rifle drawn, and headed for the five men shooting at them from the fertilizer-laden box truck. Two men came from inside the outbuilding, dragging a grill-sized gas canister laden with wires behind them.

"Watch out!!!" Azrael shouted.

Agents were disembodied wraiths that 'squatted' in the mortal shells they'd seized like a tapeworm or a tick. The shells they inhabited were expendable so long as another potential host lay close enough for them to jump ship, otherwise they risked getting sucked back into the fires of Gehenna by the very portal they had just opened. Hundreds of potential vessels milled about, screaming.

"Molechku akhbar!" The two aimed the detonation device towards the truck where Hayyel was about to land.

"The children," Sam shouted. He pointed at several who'd frozen in the playground, too terrified to do anything but cry. A brave teacher rushed forward to herd them to safety. They were all within blast range.

Hayyel would be blown to pieces, a wound a mortal Angelic might not survive.

The children would definitely die.

One Angelic.

Three children. And a teacher. Four.

The canister exploded as it rolled beneath the wheels, detonating the slower-exploding bags of fertilizer piled into the truck above and around it.

Azrael made his choice. Wings erupted from the hated black cape as he flung it off and teleported himself between the children and the explosion. Shrapnel headed in all directions. Azrael flared his wings to their full wingspan, creating a barrier between the bomb and hapless children.

The children screamed in terror at the sight of the Angel of Death standing before them, his physical appearance slipping as he concentrated on the more important task of shielding civilians from the explosion. Matter hit the back of his wings and dissolved, the energy, the motion, the very molecules and atoms which held the chunks of shrapnel and expanding gasses together simply dissipating into primordial nothingness the moment they collided with his non-corporeal form. The children gaped at him, their eyes dark with terror.

"I won't hurt you," Azrael said. "But do not touch me, for my touch is death." He stepped back, wings spread wide to provide cover for stray gunfire or after-explosions.

"Please," Azrael gestured to the teacher. "You must get them to safety."

The teacher hurried forward, her face filled with both determination and fear as she stepped between him and her students and herded them back towards the building. She didn't even thank him...

Azrael was used to it by now. People just didn't understand. Just as his Angelic colleagues...

"Hayyel!" Azrael whispered. He covered the brief distance between where he stood and the smoldering truck. There was little left of it, the five men with guns, or the two men who'd detonated the bomb. Nothing except charred chunks of body parts and the scent of cooked flesh.

"Here!" a familiar voice choked through the smoke. "He's over here."

Sam kneeled on the reddened sand, a bloody heap of white feathers in his arms as tears streamed from his gold-green serpentine eyes.

"Is he?" Azrael asked, not daring to touch either of them.

"He was airborne when it exploded," Sam said. "The explosion blew him back. But he's badly wounded. I'm barely reading a pulse."

"I can't … touch … him," Azrael cried out. "Please, Sam! You have to do something to save him!"

"I'm just a mortal creature," Sam said. "I have no ascended powers and my radio is broken. Isn't there any way for you to help him?"

Azrael listened to the sound of a weakening heart and internal organs failing, the pheromones of death, the subtle dissipation of Hayyel's spirit. Something was 'off' besides the damage to his physical shell. It felt like there were … two … wounded Angelics?

For over 2,000 years, the Regent had patiently taught Azrael to reshape the facsimile of a mortal shell from the primordial matter he harnessed. She'd taught him to control his abilities so he didn't inadvertently vaporize matter every time he got upset. But because his mortal shell had been destroyed in the same fires of Gehenna which had stripped Moloch and his Agents of their shells, Azrael couldn't simply reconstitute it as *she* did. The Regent had taught him how to use the Song of Creation to do many things Moloch's Agents could not do.

But he could not heal…

To heal, you had to touch. And to touch, well … Azrael killed everything he touched. No matter how hard he tried to do otherwise.

The sensation of a second wounded Angelic grew stronger. The Song of Creation that Azrael could always hear playing in the background picked up an instrument as though somebody quietly hummed along. Hayyel stirred.

"My mate!" Hayyel grabbed Sam's arm as he stared at Azrael with terror in his eyes. Blood spewed out of his mouth with each word he spoke. "She's trying to heal me. Please don't take me. If I die, she dies, too."

Azrael's heart sank. The second wounded he could sense? Hayyel and his mate must have possessed enough Seraphim blood to bond. It was a 'defect' Hashem had practically inbred his mortal armies into extinction trying to eradicate because, whenever one half of a mated pair died in battle, the other half died too. Hayyel's life-mate would pour every ounce of her life energy into her mate's body to keep him alive. If he died, she would cast off her mortal shell to follow him into the Dreamtime.

Azrael appraised Hayyel's injuries and gave him a slim chance of survival.

"I won't take you unless I have no choice," Azrael said. "Sam … very carefully reach over and get the radio from my pocket. Just because –I- can't touch the button to call for help doesn't mean you can't."

119

Azrael froze while Sam nervously unclipped the boxy radio from his cloak. The portable radio was enormous for what it did, little more than a walkie talkie so Azrael could listen in on mortal chatter during missions, but it had to be that large to shield the delicate electronics from his proximity. Azrael couldn't touch the thing once it was turned on as he was essentially a walking EM pulse, the power surge released during a nuclear explosion. But Sam could.

"Base … Base … this is Brewer," Sam called into the radio. "We got wounded!"

Hayyel lost consciousness again. He should be dead already. Azrael had visited enough battlefields and trauma wards to recognize when somebody's will to live tried to override their injuries, but Hayyel's injuries were severe. His mate gave him everything she had, but Azrael could feel both of them slip away. The Angelic Major's spirit slipped out of his body, precariously tethered by a thread of consciousness.

"Don't take me," Hayyel pleaded, this time his spirit pleading with the Angel of Death, not the broken mortal shell lying upon the ground. "If I die, she dies too!"

"I won't unless your mortal shell expires," Azrael said. "But there are worse things than death. The Dreamtime is a pleasant place."

"I can see my ancestors waiting for me," Hayyel said. "But I do not wish to go. We have three children who will lose both parents if I die. One is too young to be on her own."

Mated pairs. The reason Hashem had forbidden his armies to marry or rear their own children until extinction had reared its ugly head. The reason Lucifer's Fallen had rebelled in the first place; to gain the same right to marry and rear a family that every other Alliance citizen possessed. A right which bore the consequences Azrael had standing before him now.

The crackle of static meant help was on the way, but the Armistice mandated they be discreet. They couldn't simply send in a medevac shuttle. The delay caused by the need to remain hidden often resulted in more deaths than had they simply been able to take their chances in a human trauma unit.

Sam began tearing chunks off his over-drovers coat to stem the bleeding. His tail twitched nervously behind him as he made a futile attempt to administer first aid.

"Twenty minutes," Sam tore at the fabric with his slightly-pointed teeth. "Shit! I don't even know where to begin with this guy!"

Hayyel's pulse grew weaker as his life's blood poured out of his body. The life force trying to fortify his was strong, but whoever his mate was, she was only mortal. She had tasted the Song, but she could not wield it. She was not an Archangel. She was not a healer. Azrael could feel the second spirit weaken as the Major lost the battle to live.

"She won't let go," the floating Hayyel wept. "I begged her to let me go, but she does not wish to part from me."

Black tears streamed down Azrael's cheeks as he realized his choice to protect the children instead of his team-member would cost two lives today, not just the one he'd weighed when he'd made his decision. Azrael had forgotten Hashem chose mated pairs to act as observers so the humans wouldn't tempt them to 'go native' as the Fallen had done. Had Azrael chosen the children because ... well ... they were children? Or because Hayyel was an arrogant jerk? Had it been Sam about to get blown to smithereens, would he have made the same choice?

"I'm sorry," Azrael whispered. His choice would have been the same. But he was still sorry.

Hayyel's heart stopped. Sam began CPR. Azrael could hear the sound of a truck racing towards them. Help was here. Two Sata'an-human agents leaped out of a box truck carrying a first responder kit and began to work on the injured Angelic.

It was too late. The slender thread of spirit keeping Hayyel tethered to his mortal shell snapped. Azrael felt a second 'snap.' The Song ceased as the consciousness of a second Angelic materialized next to her mate.

"Why did you follow me?" Hayyel cried out. "Who will care for our offspring?"

"We always knew this might happen," the female took her mates hand and pressed it to her heart. "Our youngest will be entering the military academy in the fall. We have made provisions with our family. They will survive."

Hayyel pulled his now-deceased mate's hand up for a kiss. It was ironic that, in attempting to breed the 'defect' out of his armies, the Eternal Emperor had only impaired his Angelic's ability to heal. He'd never fully been able to eradicate the instinct to bond.

"Will you guide us into the Dreamtime?" Hayyel asked. He turned his mate to face Azrael. "Perpetiel ... this is Azrael. An Archangel. He will honor us by guiding our spirits into the Dreamtime. Together. As one soul."

Tears streamed down Azrael's cheeks, dissolving the ground where they fell. Perpetiel had drained the life from her own body in a futile attempt to save her mate.

"Don't be sad," Perpetiel reached up to touch Azrael's cheek. "The cruelest fate I can imagine is to be separated from my mate. You have no idea how badly I have missed him since the Emperor assigned him to this sector."

Her touch was like the soft whisper of wind across his flesh. Insubstantial. She no longer had a physical form.

"I can see our ancestors waiting for us just but on the other side," Hayyel said to her. "We'll wait there for our children to join us."

"Yes," Perpetiel said. "I can see my grandmother waiting for me. And your great-grandfather."

"I will guide you," Azrael said. He took their hands even though they didn't need his help. Hayyel allowed him to do it simply to alleviate his guilt.

"Grandmamma!" Perpetiel cried out with joy as she stepped across the threshold into the Dreamtime, a realm Azrael could not enter because he was neither dead … nor alive.

"You made the right choice," Hayyel paused as he was about to step across as though he were listening to another voice. "Three children. And a teacher. It was the right decision."

"Thank you," Azrael released his hand. Hayyel stepped across the threshold and was gone.

Azrael sank back to where Samuel Adams, the demon named after an American patriot, kneeled weeping over the body of the dead Angelic. His comrades solemnly placed Hayyel's body onto the stretcher, covered it with a sheet, and carried him away before the humans found it. It wouldn't do to leave proof of angels in the form of a dead one in this era of autopsies and modern communication.

News of two identical car bombs simultaneously taking out the American embassies in Kenya and Tanzania, killing 224 people and injuring 4,500, hit Lucifer's news feed while Azrael helped the Sata'anic descendants prepare the body for transport back to Ceres Station. They'd only intercepted one bomb in a coordinated attack and missed two others.

The hunger ate at him like some rabid animal gnawing on his intestines. Elisabeth. He needed to go see Elisabeth. At times like this, he needed to remind himself that some people had things even worse than *he* did. He needed to feel … connected … to something. Anything! Why not the only other person on the planet who was as alone and miserable as he was?

Azrael spent the next few weeks shadowing his favorite test subject, distracting himself from his sorrow by tracking data on how she entertained herself reading Nancy's nursing manuals. She was so smart! Only Elisabeth had no mother urging her to let her intellect guide her. How he wished it wasn't forbidden to make his presence known so he could cheer her on…

If he could, he would encourage her…

Actually … he could.

He began to leave books with the pages left open wherever he thought she might stumble across them. Her room. The bathroom. The chair by the window where she liked to sit and read. It was interference. But it was so subtle … what could it hurt?

Chapter 19

The hunger for love
Is much more difficult to remove
Than the hunger for bread.

Mother Theresa

Haven-2: Cherubim Monastery

Azrael focused on today's lesson: *'How to Pretend You're Alive When You're Really Not.'* That wasn't what *she* called it, of course. The Regent preferred more innocuous sounding names for the lessons which had started with *'How NOT to Destroy a Solar System Every Time You Get Upset.'* As he'd gained control of his power, the lessons had been fine-tuned into things like *'Holding a Shape that Isn't so Repulsive People Run Screaming'* and *'How to Sit on a Chair Without Dissipating It and Landing Flat on Your Back.'*

It was only the past few decades he'd begun to master reshaping matter. Controlled destruction, she called it. A lesson the Regent knew well, but which her brother He-who's-not had never been able to master. The Regent was determined that he, Azrael, would never be as block-headed and dependent upon the whims of a creation goddess or the genetic quirks of mortals as her older brother.

"Have you been experiencing the hunger?" the Regent asked.

Wing-spikes scraped across the floor as she settled her leathery black wings into a more comfortable position. Azrael watched her demonstrate, for the umpteenth time, how to re-form molecules out of matter she had, only moments before, dissipated into primordial soup. A delicate, crystalline structure began to take shape beneath her touch.

"It's not as you describe," Azrael said. "I feel … something. Off. Like a discordant note in that song Ki lets me hear. I've always thought of it more as loneliness than hunger."

"Loneliness?" The Regent's bottomless black eyes took on a far-away appearance. "Yes. I remember a period when I mistook the hunger for loneliness, although, at the time, I was still mortal. Mostly mortal. I suspect I was what Hashem likes to call a pre-ascended being. The General felt it too, although his ability to harness void-matter is not as evolved as mine."

The work beneath her fingers transformed into an image of the General. There was a vulnerability she captured in her sculpture of her husband; a deep, abiding sense of compassion rarely displayed in the countless Alliance sculptures of the stoic Archangel crushing Moloch beneath his boot, but which Azrael had seen in Earth depictions of the Angel of Mercy. Humans, it seemed, had been privileged to see a side of the General which the larger Alliance had never gotten to know.

"I'm not lonely anymore," the Regent gave him a rare smile. She manipulated the statute of her husband to include their offspring, thousands of Archangels, every one of them capable of balancing darkness with light. "The General gave me what my brother lacked, which is why HE placed me in charge while he searches for it for himself."

"Will I ever get to meet him?" Azrael asked. "Your brother? He-who's-not?" He suppressed the instinctual shudder of fear at the mere mention of the Dark Lord's name. Even Moloch feared the *true* Guardian of the Universe.

The Regent sighed and set aside the sculpture. She rubbed her abdomen, swollen with her latest offspring even though she'd long ago become capable of simply creating them by an act of will.

"HE is not as we are," the Regent said. "We were born mortal and evolved to harness the power of the void, but He-who's-not –is- the void. It's like the difference between a house cat and a lion. I'm just lucky I was already mated with the General when I came into my power or I'm not sure I would have been able to control it."

"What will you do?" Azrael asked. "When HE comes back? You'll be out of a job."

The Regent laughed.

"I'll heave a huge sigh of relief!" She picked up another block of wood and plopped it down upon the table. "I don't like it when I'm forced to wield my brother's power. The hunger is too difficult to control!"

There were legends about the last time the Regent had staved off an escape attempt by Moloch. The Dark Mother. Kalika. The Destroyer. Azrael didn't dare ask her if it was true.

"I'm glad Ki sent you to help." The Regent shaped the block into a creature not very different than herself. "It's a lot of responsibility safeguarding the universe. Few creatures understand the need to control growth or recycle your spent matter."

"Isn't HE afraid you'll grow more powerful than him?"

Azrael watched every nuance of the matter taking shape beneath the Regent's touch. It was rare for a creature of the void to be able to both create and destroy. Or so he'd been told. He'd only ever met one other void creature, too immature to think above the level of a five-year-old even though, technically, it was older than him. That void creature was happily paired with a creation goddess to act as its surrogate mother in the Dark Lord's absence, who was both its father and mother.

Azrael glanced at his benefactress and mentor. It was kind of what the Regent was doing for *him*. Babysit the young void creature and keep him out of mischief so he didn't accidentally wipe out any more solar systems.

The Regent gave him an indulgent smile. Belatedly, Azrael remembered the Regent could pick up on his thoughts unless he made an effort to cloak them. Another lesson she'd been trying to teach him.

"Our kind is so few and far between," the Regent focused her attention back onto her block of matter. "Nobody wants to feel the emptiness which causes the hunger; to feel so utterly alone, misunderstood, unloved. My brother was overjoyed to discover he had a sister."

A stern, muscular male with the Regent's leathery spiked wings, horns and tail stared out of the sculpture, every bit as ebony-black as Azrael. Some might mistake the Dark Lord for the devil, but Azrael knew they were different creatures. Shay'tan was simply Hashem's ideological opposite, the thorn-in-his-side who forced him to constantly re-evaluate everything he did. He-who's-not was the flip side of creation. The cosmic compost pit where all She-who-is cast off was recycled into new matter for her to create. It was the lesson the Regent was attempting to teach Azrael right now ... to dissipate matter and free up its essence to create something new.

Only Moloch was truly evil...

"Whenever I start to feel the emptiness," Azrael stared at the image of the Guardian, "I focus on my connection to the three people Ki encouraged me to cherish. Mama. Gazardiel. And Elissar. And the loneliness just goes away."

"I envy you." The Regent gave Azrael a wistful smile. "Perhaps if I'd been born into a family who loved me as much as yours loved you, it would have made the transition easier? It took every ounce of strength the General had those early years to help me subdue my brother's power."

"They have this movie," Azrael gave her a grin. "On Earth. About a scientist who turns into an angry green giant whenever he gets upset."

"I have watched this movie," the Regent said. "The General brings home souvenirs whenever he visits Earth. Yes. I know how this green man feels when he warns people they wouldn't like him when he's angry."

Azrael glanced at the thousands of photographs lining the walls of her private quarters, including one of her and the General in an ornate Sata'an wedding dress; a gift from Shay'tan, it was rumored. Whatever the Regent lacked from her family of origin, she and the General had gone out of their way to make sure it wasn't missing from their own offspring's upbringing. Azrael felt honored the secretive co-ruler of the universe had taken him under her wings, even if she only did so to keep him out of trouble.

"Focus!" The Regent pointed to a chunk of wood placed on a large stone table. "It's your turn now."

Azrael gingerly picked up the wood, focusing so he didn't simply dissipate it. In a way this lesson was like how he had learned to hold a semblance of a physical form without sporadically devolving into a tentacled black ball of primordial goo. His ability to touch non-living matter without dissolving it was a relatively new development in his evolution as a creature of a void. Not only did it require concentration, but the hunger the Regent seemed so concerned about increased whenever he caused matter to change from one form into another the way a mortal might feel hungry after smelling the aroma of a decadent meal.

"Good," the Regent said as the molecules in the wood softened and became malleable. "Clear your mind. Now shape it into something else."

Azrael ran his hands over the wood. He smiled as he recognized his favorite research subject taking shape beneath his fingers. Elisabeth. Not that anybody except someone who knew the girl well would recognize her! His ability to sculpt was like everything else he attempted … rough.

Azrael gave the Regent a victorious grin. As he did, he lost focus. With a cry of dismay, the little carving dissipated into black goo before being absorbed into Azrael's non-corporeal form.

"Oh, no! Not again!" His wings drooped towards the ground.

"It's okay." The Regent gave his hand a reassuring squeeze. "We'll just keep trying until you get it right. No matter *how* many centuries it takes."

Touch. Azrael resisted the urge to wiggle like a golden retriever puppy. The Regent was totally immune to his dark gift. She was the only person, besides Elisabeth, to touch him and survive since his death.

"You'd think after 2,300 years," Azrael complained, "I'd have gotten the hang of this."

"It took my brother fourteen billion years to hold a physical form," the Regent said, "and until recently he could only give matter to She-who-is to shape. Not shape it himself. Be patient."

Azrael grabbed another chunk of wood off the pile next to the work table. Whenever they had these lessons, the Regent came prepared for lots of failure.

"I don't feel hunger the way you do," Azrael said. "But lately, I can't seem to help absorbing everything I destroy. I do it without even thinking about it."

"It's instinctive," the Regent said. "As your spirit matures you'll gather primordial matter to someday build a universe of your own. Don't fight it or the hunger will become all-consuming. Embrace it ... and then focus on only destroying what you *wish* to destroy." There was something rather ominous about the swirl of her bottomless black eyes as she tilted her head as though looking at something which had happened in her past. "Or who deserves it."

"How long will that take?" Azrael asked.

"A few million years," the Regent shrugged as though talking about days. "Now quit chattering and focus!"

Azrael's mind turned inwards as he softened, and then began to shape the latest chunk of wood. Whenever he created, his mind accessed vague memories brought back from his time in the highest ascended realms.

'You will destroy her in your current state, sweet boy,' Ki had said. *'You must learn to control your power so you can act as her protector.'*

Who? Whose protector?

Azrael glanced down at the perfect likeness of Elissar, her sweet face smiling up at him as she held out Gazardiel's winged dolly with a bandaged leg and makeshift splint. Only the scar running down the side of the sculpture's face marred her likeness. Elisabeth's scar.

Azrael startled as his conscious mind recognized the hope his subconscious mind had been nursing. Although they differed in many ways, they had similarities, as well. Elisabeth exhibited a bitterness Elissar had not possessed, but given all she'd gone through?

The wood dissipated. Azrael managed to stop himself from absorbing it only after half of it had been uncreated.

"Damantia!"

"You did fine," the Regent said. "You stopped yourself before you completely destroyed it this time. It's an improvement."

Azrael looked at the black puddle quivering on the table like a jellyfish. It didn't look like anything *he'd* ever define as an improvement.

"How come I can shape it?" frustration gave his voice a sharp edge, "but then not stop myself from destroying it?"

"The General helps me keep my power in check," the Regent said. "And I help him keep the balance. Perhaps it's time you started searching for a life-mate?"

'You will destroy her in your current state, sweet boy,' Ki had said. *'You must learn to control your power...'*

Azrael looked up at his mentor and second-mother. Ever since she'd taught him to hold a stable enough form that women no longer ran screaming the moment they lay eyes upon him, she'd been trying to play match-maker.

"Not yet, my Queen," Azrael said regretfully. "First I must master all you have to teach me."

127

Chapter 20

Doth every man among them hope to enter the Garden of Delight?
Quran 70:38

Earth - AD December, 1999
Chicago, Illinois

"Nancy!!!" Elisabeth called, hop-walking across her bedroom without a cane to the closet. "Where's my white sweater?"

"Wherever you left it," Nancy called up from downstairs.

"But I can't find it!" Elisabeth frantically rummaged through the closet. "We're going to be late!!!"

Azrael suppressed a smile, the glittering blackness of his eyes glowing even darker as he spied the errant sweater peeking out from underneath the bed. Elisabeth looked lovely in a vintage red ankle-length Laura Ashley tea dress with a full skirt and plunging V-neck bust line which the teenager didn't quite fill out ... yet. Elisabeth had argued with her foster mother that the thrift-shop gown had gone out of style with the 1980's, but Azrael thought it showed off her slender figure and blonde hair beautifully, so much classier than the tacky 'hip-hop' attire common amongst young people these days.

"We've got plenty of time!" Nancy's voice filled with laughter. "You'd think you had a hot date or something!"

"I wish!" Elisabeth muttered under her breath, hop-walking over to her bureau to rummage through the drawers even though she never put her sweater in there. "I'll be standing next to Tommy Rodriguez and I want to look presentable!"

Azrael glanced at the errant sweater, taunting him with its snowy whiteness from beneath the bed. At the rate she was going, she *would* be late. When Elisabeth hurried, she took unnecessary risks, and whenever she took unnecessary risks, the leg which still resisted fully healing reminded her who was boss ... her fragile mortal shell. *Not* her formidable, slave-driving will which refused to take 'no' for an answer.

The last thing Azrael wanted to see was his favorite research subject fall flat on her face in front of the young man she had a hopeless crush on. The young man had flirted with her during last week's rehearsal for tonight's high school Christmas recital. Elisabeth usually sank into a deep depression this time of year, but her infatuation over the young male had caused her to forget her usual aversion to the holiday season and the tragic memories it invoked.

"Nancy!!!" Elisabeth called, panic stricken. "I can't find it!!!"

Did he dare? It was forbidden to intervene in the affairs of mortals, but it was only a sweater, little different than the *Collected Works of Emily Dickenson* he'd left open on her bureau to a poem suitable as inspiration for tonight's performance:

> *'Hope' is the thing with feathers --*
> *That perches in the soul --*
> *And sings the tune without the words --*
> *And never stops -- at all*[1]

Edging over to the edge of the bed, Azrael turned his pencil around, eraser-first so it wouldn't leave a mark and used it to fish out the sweater. Although he'd gotten better about not dissolving inanimate objects, his track record was less-than-stellar. He didn't wish to mar her favorite sweater. Elisabeth turned and spied it arranged neatly on the bed.

"Never mind!" Elisabeth shouted. "I found it."

She looked right into the corner where the invisible Azrael stood watching her every move.

"I must be going crazy or something, huh?" Elisabeth stared straight at him with her eerie silver eyes as though she could see right into his soul.

Azrael shuddered as a deep emotion he could not name made his breath hitch in his throat. The last person possessing such beautiful, silver eyes had given him honey-cakes to feed his 'doll.' His pulse sped up as he nervously stepped out of the path between her and the sweater. Even with the scar the General insisted she keep as a badge of honor, Elisabeth had grown into a beautiful young woman.

"It's not like anyone's going to be looking at me, anyway," Elisabeth no longer spoke in Azrael's direction, but her reflection in the mirror. She lifted the princess skirt and stared at the steel brace she still needed to support her left leg. Although she now only needed her grandfather's wooden cane to walk, every morning the girl who had defeated death looked in the mirror

---

[1] *Hope is the Thing with Feathers* - Emily Dickenson

and reminded herself she was scarred. Ugly. That no boy would ever give a cripple a second glance.

Oh, how he longed to take her in his arms and tell her she was the most beautiful creature he had ever seen! He stepped closer, unconsciously flaring his wings as he inhaled her scent. Her scent had begun to change this past year. The scent of a woman ready to take a mate. He closed his eyes and inhaled the subtle pheromones. It was the headiest perfume he'd ever encountered in the two thousand plus years he'd been alive. The urge to be near her had become almost … irrational.

'What is wrong with you today?' Azrael scolded himself. *'Not only is it forbidden, but your first embrace will be -her- last!'*

He hoped the young man who inspired his young subject to come out of her self-imposed shell and participate would be worthy of her. If he hurt her…

Snap

Azrael clenched his pencil so hard it broke in half.

"Time to go." Elisabeth slipped the sweater over her shoulders and grabbed her cane, sighing with resignation as she made her way across the room.

Azrael noted the peculiar feeling of disappointment when she walked straight past him as though he wasn't there. She wasn't supposed to be able to see him, but sometimes he thought she did. When he realized she didn't, it was always disappointing. She hadn't even glanced at the poem.

"Elisabeth!" Nancy yelled up the stairs.

"I'm coming!" Elisabeth shouted.

Her cane clacked rhythmically down the stairs, more 'insurance' these days than actual crutch. At the foot of the stairs stood her foster mother wearing her best dress, bright yellow against the warm tones of her swarthy complexion.

"You look beautiful!" Nancy gave her a genuinely warm hug. "If there's a heaven, your family is looking down right now and telling themselves how beautiful you look tonight."

"I wish we'd bought the red heels we saw at the Vincent de Paul Society thrift shop." Elisabeth glanced at Nancy's four-inch pumps, and then frowned at the clunky 'granny sandals' she'd borrowed from Mrs. Schroeder next door. "They were so dainty and pretty."

"They were three inch heels," Nancy scolded her. "You'd have fallen flat on your face right in front of Tommy-what's-his-name."

"But I liked them!" Elisabeth protested. "This dress is long enough to hide my brace. It would have made me look normal!"

"You *are* normal," Nancy said. "Come … I'd like to get a seat close enough to the stage to actually *see* you this year!"

Azrael trailed behind them, stepping out of the way as Nancy locked the door to their small rented row-house. The neighborhood was only slightly better than the last one, but Lucifer had greased wheels and pulled strings so the opportunity to move to a better school district had appeared to fall into Nancy's lap naturally. Azrael silently followed as they walked to the end of the street to catch the city bus.

His hand tingled. Azrael liked to include sketches with his notes, so he pulled out his notebook and began to capture the scene on the bus. His pencil moved like liquid across the page, capturing the visage of the two women, Elisabeth a bright red cardinal with her red Christmas dress peeking out from beneath her worn woolen coat, Nancy reminiscent of a Baltimore Oriole in her fancy yellow dress, raven hair and utilitarian black winter jacket with a not-too-conspicuous patch holding together the underarm.

'The subject appears to have finally accepted the love offered by her foster mother and blossomed under her care,' Azrael scribbled in the margins as he found a seat in the rear of the near-empty bus and observed their almost sister-like chatter about boys. 'Although love is not an emotion that is unique to the species Homo sapiens, it never ceases to amaze me how quickly humans whither compared to other species when they perceive an absence of love in their lives.'

Azrael paused, reflecting on the gaping void in his own heart left by the loss of his mother, his sister, and his friend. A hiss erupted from beneath where he sat crouched over his notebook. An escaping tear had just dissolved a hole in the floor of the bus. He was waxing melancholy again, allowing the all-consuming hunger of loneliness to affect his normally even temperament. He refocused his attention to the conversation going on between his favorite research subject and her foster mother.

"I'll tell you what," Nancy said. "Why don't you invite Tommy to come over for cookies tomorrow afternoon?"

"Oh, no!" Elisabeth said. "I'd be mortified to ask a boy out on a date!"

"It's not a date," Nancy elbowed her. "It's just cookies. The way to a man's heart is always through his stomach!"

"That's just a myth!" Elisabeth said.

"No it's not," Nancy said.

"No it's not," Azrael said at the exact same time, thinking of how Elissar had lured him to stay.

Elisabeth's head jerked up and looked towards the rear of the bus where he sat. Had he uttered the words aloud so mortal ears could hear it?

"Is something wrong?" Nancy asked.

"No." Elisabeth turned towards her foster mother, a puzzled expression upon her face. "I just thought I heard something. That's all. A voice that sounded … familiar."

Azrael derided himself for his stupidity. He could make himself invisible, but not inaudible if he was foolish enough to speak aloud. Whatever had come over him?

Elissar. Elissar had used honey-cakes and roast chicken. Simple meals. But it wasn't the offer of food, but friendship despite the nine-year difference in their ages which had kept Azrael coming back. Elissar had needed a friend as much as *he* had. More than two thousand years she'd been in the grave and he still missed the only real friend he'd ever had.

'Why do I keep coming back to –this- particular subject?' Azrael wrote in his notebook. 'She bears a striking resemblance to Elissar, but I suspect it's more than that. Elissar was every bit as lonely as I was then, back while I was still mortal, while Elisabeth seems every bit as lonely as I feel *now*. For some reason she perceives herself to be an outcast."

Elisabeth fell deep into discussion with her foster mother about what college she wished to attend next fall. Azrael had begged Lucifer to pull strings and line up a full scholarship to the University of Chicago so she'd still have access to Nancy, the sole stabilizing influence in her life. Lucifer had informed him that, with Elisabeth's good grades, his young subject could attend any college she liked.

'I've been lurking amongst humans so long that perhaps I am becoming like them?' Azrael wrote. 'Elisabeth believes she imagined a 'watcher' because she needs to make sense of her parent's death. Perhaps –I- imagine *her* to make sense of my own sorry fate?'

The bus stopped in front of Lincoln Park High School. Azrael flew up to perch upon the portico as they made their way inside. It was crowded tonight; girls in red dresses; boys with black pants, white dress shirts and red ties; parents, grandparents, brothers and sisters. Some were dressed as though attending a grand ball, others in jeans and T-shirts, but there was another element in attendance tonight. Gang members… A significant force in the Chicago youth community. Wherever they went, trouble always followed.

Azrael decided he would blow off the reconnaissance he'd been planning on doing in North Korea and stick around for the concert. The fact he wished to observe Elisabeth's reactions around the young man she was so enamored of had absolutely nothing to do with it!

Chapter 21

When the senses contact sense objects,
A person experiences cold or heat, pleasure or pain.
These experiences are fleeting
They come and go. Bear them patiently.

Bhagavad Gita

Earth - AD December, 1999
Chicago, Illinois

Elisabeth glanced at Tommy Rodriguez through veiled lashes as her voice anchored the tenor section for Handel's Messiah. She'd always regretted she hadn't been born a high-flying soprano whose voice could rise above the chorus like an angel, but then the choral director had paired her with Tommy, a natural tenor with a beautiful voice. Tommy lacked Oma's childhood lessons about how to read music and stick to what he was *supposed* to sing, no matter *how* off-key the chorus sang around him.

Technically Elisabeth was part of the boy's tenor section, always sparse because only dweebs and the rare, truly talented male singer ever signed up for dorky chorus. Not even for an easy three credits! Tommy was the latter. He even had his own hip-hop band!

"O death, where is thy sting?" Tommy sang, the boy next to him dragging him down into the bass clef. "O grave! Where is thy victory?"

"The sting of death is sin," Elisabeth pointed to the correct notes on Tommy's sheet music and leaned close to his ear so he could hear her sing the correct notes. "And the strength of sin is the law."

His raven-black hair tickled her nose as he came back on-key, his aftershave obfuscating any scent he may have had. An overwhelming urge to sneeze nearly overcame her, forcing her to lean back into her own space.

Elisabeth glanced out into the audience, easily spotting Nancy's bright yellow dress. She 'd been so caught up in daydreams of college and Tommy Rodriguez lately that she hadn't given much thought to her imaginary black man. Sometimes … not only did she imagine she *felt* him, but whenever she thought he was there, it smelled faintly of the ocean, a clean, slightly briny scent, brimming with life. The way her sweater had appeared neatly arranged on her bed and the voice on the bus today had reminded her of her imaginary watcher.

Was he here? Her black man? Waiting for her to fall and make an ass of herself so he could write about how clumsy she was in that notebook he always had with him? She never saw him anymore. Not since she was a little girl. But more and more she sensed he was in the room, still watching even though memory of what he looked like had long ago faded.

She was determined that nothing on heaven or earth would make her fall in front of him. Ever. Again. Maybe the therapist she'd finally refused to see anymore was right? There *was* no black man.

"Alleluia. Alleluia," Elisabeth sang. She held the final alto note, or tenor depending upon whether you were a girl or a boy, as she glanced over to see what Tommy was doing. "Alle-lu-ia."

The audience clapped. Elisabeth bent to pick up the cane she'd carefully placed behind her feet before singing. After years of trying to walk without it, she'd finally made her peace with it.

"Let me get that for you," Tommy gave her one of his heart-melting smiles that had every girl in the school swooning.

"Thanks..." Elisabeth's heart did a flip-flop as butterflies tried to escape her stomach.

"Allow me?"

Tommy put out one arm to assist her as she stepped down from the bleachers. When he did it, he appeared to be a gentleman escorting a lady. Not some chaperone assigned by the school as had been the case immediately after her accident. Of course, Tommy didn't look like a chaperone, his tight butt looking mighty fine in the black dress chinos his mother must have borrowed from a relative for tonight's concert. Elisabeth felt like she was floating on air as he escorted her up the aisle to meet up with Nancy.

'Cookies...' Nancy mouthed the words as they approached, making a small circle with the fingers of one hand while she pantomimed drinking tea with the other. 'Remember to invite him to come for cookies.'

"Uh ... Tommy," Elisabeth's cheeks turned as red as the outdated 1980's dress she wore. "My ... um ...Nancy? She ... um ... wanted to know if you'd ... um ... want to stop by for ... um ... cookies? Tomorrow?"

"Sure!" Tommy gave her that sunny grin that made her knees feel like they were about to give out. He raised his thumb and forefinger to his ear as though it were a telephone. "I'll call you."

Elisabeth nearly swooned as he disappeared up the aisle after his friends. The Latin Kings had come out in force tonight to see Tommy sing, his stint in the high school chorus penance for graffiti the music teacher had bagged him spray painting on the side of the building. Tommy liked to sing, but his usual venue was a street corner rapping with his friends and dancing fancy hip-hop for change in a bucket.

"He said yes!" Elisabeth squealed the moment he was out of earshot.

"Told you the way to men's hearts is through their stomachs," Nancy said. "They make a big deal about wanting some hot babe. But the one they really want to come home to is the gal with a good head on her shoulders and a decent supper on the table."

Elisabeth was silent as they moved towards West Armitage Avenue to catch the bus. Nancy had been through a rough childhood, first with gangs, then with drugs and being kicked out at sixteen to make her own way in the world. Nancy had never told her why it had taken her so long to get approved as a foster parent, but word on the street was Nancy had started turning tricks to support her heroin addiction before getting sent to juvie to straighten out her life. She loved her foster mother dearly, but Elisabeth took her dating advice with a grain of salt.

"Hey … Elisabeth!" Tommy called from where he also waited for the bus, surrounded by his 'homies.' "Come meet my friends."

Nancy looked apprehensive. Although her reservations about Tommy had lessened, the kids hanging off his every word dealt drugs. If there was one thing Elisabeth *did* trust Nancy's judgment on, it was avoiding tweakers.

"Maybe you shouldn't," Nancy tugged her in the other direction. "Tommy's okay. The choir director said he's going to graduate unless he really screws up. But the others? They're Latin Kings. They don't even go to school here anymore."

"They dropped out," Elisabeth broke Nancy's grip. "But they're his friends. You're always telling me it's not fair to judge a book by its cover."

"Just one minute," Nancy didn't look convinced. "And then we've got a bus to catch. We promised Mrs. Schroeder you'd come over for date-nut bread and some tea after the concert so she can get a picture of you in that dress wearing her best shoes."

"I'll be fine," Elisabeth said. Nancy's reservations were already forgotten as she made her way over to Tommy, minding her step so she didn't fall on her face in front of his friends.

"Elisabeth … meet my homies," Tommy preened. "Guys … this is Elisabeth … guardian angel of the Lincoln Park chorus." He now wore the mask of a too-cool homie. The not-quite gang kid. Talented enough with his rap music and hip-hop dance that even his gang friends were rooting for him to get the hell out of this shithole of a city and make something of his life.

"She don't look like no guardian angel," a Hispanic female with blue lipstick and long, blue painted fingernails stepped in front of Tommy with her arms crossed. "Not in that red dress of hers."

Two other Hispanic females dressed like colorful exotic birds closed ranks on either side. Standing firm with their BFF against the intruder.

"It's so … 1980," the female sniped. "You got a polyester leisure suit to match the dress, Tommy?"

Elisabeth felt stricken. She'd heard Tommy was a ladies man, but she hadn't realized he already *had* a girlfriend. What an ass she had made of herself, practically throwing herself at his feet and begging him to come over for cookies? Cookies? What a dork!

"Hey, hey, hey," Tommy parted the wall of female flesh as though they were the Red Sea and placed his arm around Elisabeth. He turned to his guy friends, ignoring the three girls. "Elisabeth can sing any note they put on those squiggly lines on the page without even hearing it on the piano first or nuthin. She saved my ass after Mr. White bagged me marking our territory."

"You's lookin' like a member of the choir!" one of the Latin Kings jibed, pretending to pull up his pants by the suspenders and then tugging up his pant-legs to floodwater stage.

"He told me it was either make an ass of myself," Tommy laughed. "Or he was calling the cops and making sure I got sent off to juvie."

"Dork-boys?" one of Tommy's gang-friends snorted, striking a gang-pose. "You sure look like one of them's dork-boys in those church-pants your Mama scrounged up from the Salvation Army!"

Tommy held up a high-five. "Right on! Here's to dork boys outnumbered ten-to-one by hot babes. The most pleasant three credits I ever earned!"

The Latin Kings twittered with laughter. Elisabeth was amazed at how jibing which would have had any other gang member foaming at the mouth just rolled off Tommy's back. She could see why he was able to walk in both worlds. The mere fact the Latin Kings had turned out in force to watch him sing tonight was testament that it was possible.

"Hey…" a second gang-friend chipped in. "I kinda like the monkey suit. All ya need is a top hat and cane and you'll look like that dude in them old movies from the fifties."

"You mean Fred Astaire?" Tommy grabbed a fedora off one of his friends, slapping it upon his head as though it were a top hat, and reached for Elisabeth's cane. "Hey … Elisabeth … you mind?"

Elisabeth relinquished her cane. Tommy did a little tap-dance around her like Fred Astaire, and then went into a perfect Charlie Chaplin routine, waddling like a penguin as he swung her cane around and around.

Elisabeth ignored Nancy's frantic waving that the bus was here. She felt like she belonged. There would be another bus in twenty minutes…

Chapter 22

Alone of gods Death has no love for gifts,
Libation helps you not, nor sacrifice.
He has no altar, and hears no hymns;
From him alone Persuasion stands apart.
Aeschylus (525-465 B.C.) "Niobe"

Earth - AD December, 1999
Chicago, Illinois

Azrael sat, unseen, perched on the entrance portico supported by four enormous Corinthian columns, not sure whether to be jealous or happy his young subject finally appeared to be fitting in with her peers. It had been a long time since he'd seen her smile. Why didn't that make him happy? Nancy waved frantically as their bus came and left without them. It was curious behavior. Azrael did what he *always* did whenever something he observed did not make sense. He pulled out his notebook and began to take notes.

'The subject is normally obedient to a fault,' Azrael wrote, 'diligently obeying the rules set down by her foster mother. But for some reason, with the addition of peers into the equation, all of a sudden the subject becomes reluctant to obey guidance from the parental authority figure.'

Out of the periphery of his vision, he noticed a fancy black SUV with tinted windows slow as it approached the bus stop. That same eerie sense of evil he often got whenever he teleported into a room where there were Agents present tickled at his subconscious, but this did not feel like an Agent. More like … a warning. He hesitated, trying to figure out what the sensation was.

Dark windows slid down. A short, black tube protruded from the window. Gunshots erupted.

The Latin Kings screamed, throwing themselves down onto the sidewalk for cover like well-trained soldiers.

Elisabeth stood in shock, a tall red target amongst a sea of gang kids writhing on the ground.

Azrael's heart beat once.

An arm stuck out the window, taking aim. Without thinking, Azrael teleported himself to stand between Elisabeth and the drive-by shooters, not caring who he smote with the spread of his deadly wings or whether they saw him.

His heart beat twice.

The bullet hit him in the back of the wings, dissolving harmlessly into primordial nothingness. Elisabeth looked up, her beautiful, silver eyes locking with his as recognition dawned upon her face.

His heart beat a third time.

On the sidewalk around their feet, gang kids pulled knives and guns as they recovered and began to shoot back.

"It's you?" Elisabeth's words were lost in the screams, but her expression as she looked into his eyes said it all.

His heart beat a fourth time.

Parents screamed in terror as more gunshots erupted from the car. Azrael looked just in time to see a puzzled expression cross Nancy's face. A dark red stain spread on the front of her bright yellow dress. Elisabeth's look of horror as Nancy crumpled to the ground was the *same* look he'd seen on Elissar's face as she'd sunk down into the flames of Gehenna.

His heart beat a fifth time.

Anguish overrode reason as Azrael erupted into his true form, the Grim Reaper arriving to harvest the souls of the damned. A writhing black thundercloud of tentacles and jolts of electricity clawed into the car, shorting out the motor and dissolving fenders and doors. Without hesitation, he tore the souls of the five rival gang-members out of their mortal shells, punched a hole into Gehenna, and fed them straight into Moloch's grinning maw.

It only took a two minutes.

It took too long.

He returned, invisible once more. Elisabeth's hands were covered in blood as she pressed her hands into the gunshot wound in her foster mother's heart.

"Hang on, Nancy!" Elisabeth cried. "Please! Don't leave me here alone!"

"The ambulance is on its way!" one of the other parents shouted, holding out their cell phone.

In the distance, police sirens could be heard. The gang kids had all disappeared, including Tommy. So had the parents and children, none wishing to take any chances with the mangled SUV stopped dead in the middle of the road. Two gang kids lay dead upon the ground, victims of senseless gang rivalry. Azrael listened for the viability of Nancy's body, nostrils flaring as he recognized the scent of death.

"Elisabeth," Nancy choked as her heart attempted to beat and could not.

Azrael could hear the bullet lodged in her heart, the severed artery causing blood to gurgle in the chamber, but not beat. How was Nancy even still alive? And conscious? Did Elisabeth possess latent healing ability? Azrael began to hope, against hope, that Nancy would beat the odds.

"Stay with me!" Elisabeth cried. "Nancy! Please stay with me! You're going to be okay!"

Azrael knew Nancy saw him. Her spirit fought to separate from her body and escape into the Dreamtime.

"Please ..." Azrael said inside Nancy's mind. "Hang on. Elisabeth needs you."

"Elisabeth," Nancy said. "I see him, your black man. He's come for me."

"Stay away from him!" Elisabeth shouted. "Do you hear me? Don't you even look at him! You don't have to go with him! Tell him no!"

"My grandmother waits for me," Nancy said. "I can see her standing in a white room. She said it's time to stop running away and come home."

Azrael stepped closer, watching Elisabeth battle to keep her foster mother in this realm even as Nancy stretched her spirit towards the Dreamtime. He'd seen humans refuse to leave their bodies or hover, unsure what to do once their mortal shells expired. He'd even seen a mated pair of Angelics cling to life together and then expire as one soul. But never had he witnessed one person hold another's spirit in a broken body against their will.

"Please Nancy," Azrael pleaded. "Don't leave her. I won't take you if you don't want to go. I'll ask the angels to come help you heal. Please! You're all she has."

"Let me go," Nancy gasped in pain. She reached towards Azrael. "Please. Let me go with him. My grandmother wants me to come home."

Azrael hadn't detected a heartbeat in more than three minutes. He didn't know what Elisabeth was doing, but somehow she was reanimating a dead body and forcing Nancy's spirit to inhabit it. Even if the ambulance came and shocked her heart, Azrael could hear the gurgle where the bullet had shattered two chambers and the aorta. The chances of Nancy getting a spur-of-the-moment heart transplant were zero and none.

"Take me home," Nancy pleaded, her hand outstretched.

Azrael closed his eyes, trembling with the terrible choice he faced. The only thing keeping Nancy here was her foster daughter's will to make her stay. Azrael had seen this happen once before ... when Hayyel's mate had drained the life from her own body trying to save him. *Both* had died.

"So beautiful, your watcher," Nancy whispered to Elisabeth, her body shuddering with pain. "He's the most beautiful man I've ever seen."

Elisabeth was only human. If Azrael didn't intervene, Nancy would pull Elisabeth into the Dreamtime along with her just as Hayyel had pulled his mate. Elisabeth wasn't the only one who'd ever lost everyone she'd ever loved. After all these years shadowing her, hoping...

She would never forgive him!

He couldn't bear to lose her, too. Even if it meant she hated him for the rest of her painfully short human life.

A sob escaping his throat, Azrael reached down. Nancy's hand clasped around his, her empty mortal arm falling limply to the ground the moment it made contact with his flesh.

"No!!!" Elisabeth screamed. She struck out with bloodied hands to grab the air where Nancy now stood between them, trying to grab her and hit him at the same time.

"I never believed her when she said you watched over her," Nancy gave the body she left behind a cursory glance. "Will you keep protecting her?"

"No! No! No! Nooo!" Elisabeth keened, grabbing Nancy's lifeless hand as she lifted her head into the air and screamed like a wounded panther.

"Yes," Azrael said, his heart breaking along with his young subject's at what fate had just forced him to do. "I never ... I had no idea this would happen. I would have tried to protect you, too."

"I hate you!!!" Elisabeth screamed into the air, striking the empty air around her to hit him. "Do you hear me? I hate you!!!"

Tears sprang to Azrael's eyes. He'd protected her life, but he'd failed to protect the one person who cared about her. For the second time in her young life, Elisabeth had just had him take everyone away from her.

"Come," Nancy tugged his hand. "My grandmother calls to me. She's the only one who ever really cared about me. Will you bring me to her?"

Azrael looked at Elisabeth, screaming that she hated him as the police and ambulance drivers finally arrived and attempted to resuscitate her foster mother and the other two victims. Police swarmed the black SUV, tearing open the mangled doors to arrest the gunmen and scratching their heads in puzzlement as they realized all five gangbangers were dead without a scratch.

Azrael's wings flared with indecision, nearly zapping one of the paramedics. He didn't want to leave Elisabeth here alone. Not even for a second...

A non-corporeal hand reached up to touch his cheek.

"I'm glad she has you in her life," Nancy said. "I can find my own way. It would make me feel better if you stay with her."

"Thank you," Azrael replied.

He stepped closer to Elisabeth as a police officer pried her off her foster mother's body. The officer tried to make sense of her wailing keens about black men and monsters, asking her to repeat it several times. They thought she screamed she hated the gangbangers. Only Azrael knew she hated *him*.

Nancy stepped into a white light and was gone, having found her own path into the Dreamtime as most sentient creatures had done since time immemorial. Elisabeth had only prolonged the inevitable.

Tucking his wings against his back and wrapping his cloak so he didn't inadvertently kill anybody else today, Azrael followed her. Paramedics verified none of the blood was hers. Police questioned her. There were police reports. Calls to social services agencies too busy to care about a seventeen-year-old girl whose foster mother had just died. Queries about relatives who were all dead. Finally, a police officer simply put her in the back of his cruiser and drove her home to her empty house.

"I hate you, I hate you, I hate you..." Elisabeth keened, lobbing whatever object she could lay her hands on at wherever he stood, invisible, until she finally cried herself to sleep.

Azrael stood watch, but he did not dare comfort her. Not because he feared violating the prohibitions against making himself seen, or interfering, or even displeasing the two emperors, but because she would claw his eyes out and, in doing so, the curse that was his deadly existence would kill her.

Azrael pressed his black wings against the wall of the hallway just outside her tiny room and slid down to a squat, weeping at the horribleness of what he'd been forced to do.

"I'm so sorry..."

As long as she lived, he knew she would never forgive him...

Before he left, he changed the page on the *Collected Works of Emily Dickenson* he'd left on her bureau this morning to inspire her singing to a poem more suited to the circumstances. It was the only way he could communicate how sorry he was.

> *I measure every grief I meet*
> *With analytic eyes;*
> *I wonder if it weighs like mine,*
> *Or has an easier size.*
> *I wonder if they bore it long,*
> *Or did it just begin?*
> *I could not tell the date of mine,*
> *It feels so old a pain.*

Azrael failed to notice his wings had dissipated the wall where he'd sat. No matter how many coats of gypsum the landlord piled onto the wall, nothing would ever remove the imprint of wings where the Angel of Death had wept.

Chapter 23

As I look upon Thy mouths terrible with many tusks of destruction.
Thy faces like the fires of Death and Time,
I lose sense of the directions and find no peace.
Turn Thy heart to grace, O God of gods!
Refuge of all the worlds!

Bhagavad Gita 11:25

Earth: January 5, 2000
Colombo, Sri Lanka

Azrael stood just far enough back from the window of the Sri Lankan Prime Minister's residence so he was out of sight, watching Sata'an-human hybrids scurry around in police uniforms and trench coats. Six security guards, one of them a Sata'an-human agent embedded with their security force, and some unfortunate woman who'd been seized as a host by one of Moloch's squatters under the guise of 'recruitment' for the Tamil Tigers, were dead.

The Sri Lankan leader had been whisked off to safety, claims leaked to the media that he hadn't even been home. Truth was, today's operation had been a failure, just like everything else Azrael attempted to do lately. Fail! Fail! Fail! Everything he touched just withered and died!

A potted palm grew at the side of the window; a magnificent, pampered specimen. He concentrated, willing with every ounce of his being to, just once, not kill a living thing as he touched one leaf between his thumb and forefinger. The leaves wilted, turned black and disintegrated. Azrael's wings drooped to the ground, the white marble also turning into a puddle of black nothingness at his feet.

"Ahem," Special Agent Emmett Till coughed, making his presence known. "Major Thanatos. Are you okay?"

Emmett Till, named after the murdered African American boy who'd sparked off the civil rights movement, was second in command to Samuel Adams. Ironically, *this* Emmett Till was as pale and white as any other Eastern European human, but it hadn't stopped his parents from idealizing the oppression the original Emmett had come to symbolize amongst their species, forced to lurk in the shadows by a 5,500 year old war humanity had no idea was still being fought to this day. Azrael had worked with Special Agent Till many times.

"We should have seen this coming," Azrael's voice was lackluster. "When the suffragists began demanding equal rights for women, I don't think this is what they had in mind."

"The Tamil Tigers are actively recruiting women to act as suicide bombers," Emmett said. "They knew we'd be looking for a man."

"Why are Moloch's agents suddenly able to seize women?" Azrael pondered. "They've never been successful before. Not on this scale. The way the two hemispheres of their brains are wired makes them too difficult to control as hosts."

"This is a Muslim country," Emmett repeated. "The Tamil Tigers dangle the promise of equality, including the right to fight alongside the men, and recruit their fighters when they're still children, eight or nine years old. Their brains are still malleable. Moloch is simply replicating his success with Lucifer."

Azrael sighed. Lucifer. The longer he was forced to serve alongside the estranged son of the Eternal Emperor, the more he sympathized with him … and the so-called 'demons' who served under him. With the exception of the General, who made a point of personally checking in on Earth from time to time, the others of his species, both ascended and mortal, just didn't get it.

"I didn't spot the squatter until she'd already detonated her vest," Azrael said. "His control of his host was nearly seamless."

"Hashem never noticed anything amiss with Lucifer, either," Emmett reminded him. "And Lucifer was infected with Moloch himself. Not just some lesser Agent."

Azrael glanced out the window and watched Sata'an-hybrid agents use shovels and buckets to remove body parts off the ground because the remains were too shattered to simply put into a body bag.

"Is there enough left to perform an autopsy?" Azrael asked.

"Already on it," Emmett said. "Lucifer is taking a personal interest in this case. He's got us checking for technological implants."

"As if Lucifer would get his hands dirty," Azrael snorted.

Emmett blinked with his clear, protective inner eyelid, giving away an otherwise flawless disguise as a full-blooded human.

"In case you haven't noticed," Emmett said. "Lucifer has been doing nothing *but* getting his hands dirty for the past 5,500 years. You sound like one of *them*."

Azrael paused. Emmett was right. Every time he made a trip back to Ceres Station, his fellow Alliance citizen's condescending attitude towards humans and the Fallen who babysat them rubbed off. It was easy to criticize the goings-on of Earth from the comfort of space when you didn't actually have to live here, on Earth, with Moloch destabilizing every accomplishment the humans made. He was behaving unfairly.

"I apologize." Azrael turned back towards the window. "It's just ... Lucifer's extracurricular activities have a way of making you forget just how much of a sacrifice he's made by staying here."

"His 1,000 year sentence was up 4,500 years ago," Emmett said. "The only reason he's still here is because She-who-is won't let him enter the Dreamtime. He promised his mate he'd protect his people until he could join him there."

Azrael's thoughts drifted to his young friend ... and her tragic demise so many years before. Elissar. Although all of Lucifer's prodigious offspring inherited his intellect and a modicum of his 'power of persuasion,' only Elissar had ever shown true pre-ascended abilities. Abilities he'd scrutinized the teenaged Elisabeth for ... hoping.

Usually he knew when he dealt with a recycled spirit because he'd get echoes of past life memories, but with Elisabeth he got nothing. It was as though she wished to remain hidden.

These days, she just wished him gone. Now that she knew he was more than a figment of her imagination, she flew at him, screaming, whenever he checked in on her. Even attempts to lift her mood by leaving inspirational readings were met with hostility. He'd had more than one book dissipate into primordial nothingness when she'd lobbed it at his head, her ability to sense his location no matter how well he kept himself hidden uncanny.

The last thing he wished was to cause her any more pain. He'd finally retreated so far away to make his observations that he could barely sense her anymore.

Touch. He'd been so focused on *physical* touch that he hadn't been aware that for the past eight years he'd been wallowing in the pleasure of Elisabeth's *non-physical* touch. Her spirit was larger than most humans, large enough that she could sense him from quite a distance. And him ... her. It wasn't until he'd suddenly been shut off that he realized he'd been touching her the only way he could.

His wings drooped further as he deliberately dissipated the tie-back for one of the garishly ornate drapes. He then attempted to reshape it back the way it was before, as the Regent had been trying to teach him, and had no luck. He sighed, his dark mood weighing upon the room like a fog.

"I wish he'd just stop doing ... you know," Azrael mumbled, staring out the window at the gruesome spectacle below. "So things wouldn't be so murky."

"He's the most misunderstood Angelic in the universe," Emmett's tail twitched with exasperation as he defended his Fallen leader. "His *real* father, who desperately wanted a child, never knew he existed because his adopted father stole him before he was even born. And then his adopted father abandoned him when his mother died. And then Moloch grabs him for a host and nobody gave a crap enough about him to even notice. And then, to top it off, Hashem let Moloch's agents kill his mate, the only person who ever really cared, because he was pissed off!"

"Yeah," Azrael watched them finish shovel entrails off the sidewalk. "I guess you're right."

"He's the only person who's got an even shittier deal than *you* do," Emmett said.

A second tier of otherwise human-looking agents began sweeping the area with magnifying glasses, a metal detector, and tweezers. Beyond the compound, a large crowd of local civilians had gathered, rubber-necking to see the carnage. Azrael's thoughts turned from self-pity to the reason he was here. Something was going on. He just couldn't put his finger on it.

"If the Tamil Tigers really wanted casualties," Azrael's wings twitched with thought. "They should have waited until now to detonate a bomb."

"Already got special agents dressed as civilians sweeping the crowd," Emmett said. "Just in case."

"Good." Azrael stared at the crowd of gawkers, focusing on the subtle body language of the people below. Some stared with horror, hands over their mouths or weeping as they pointed to the blood-stained ground. But others ... others lauded praises upon the woman who'd turned her body into a bomb to get at an unpopular elected official.

Human nature ... forever see-sawing between hope and violence. If Azrael, himself, hadn't grabbed the squatter within seconds of the bomb exploding, this could easily be mistaken for a random act of violence.

"Is it just me?" Azrael asked, "or have the terrorist acts Moloch's Agents have been pulling lately changed?"

"I haven't been around as long as you have, Sir," Emmett said. "But ... yes. The older Fallen have the same complaint as you do. Moloch has always allied with shadow-corporations and puppet governments, but now he's coming at us sideways with these random acts of violence and we can't figure out why."

"Sideways," Azrael pondered. "Moloch has always cultivated potential enemies. But this ... yes. I agree. Sideways is an apt verb to describe that vague feeling I keep having that we're missing something important."

The two of them stared out the window, together, at the grim specter being hosed off the sidewalk below.

"Sometimes I feel as though it is the end of days," Azrael softly. "As though we're in the middle of war, only we're so blind none of us have woken up yet to realize we're even fighting it yet."

"We've always known this is a war, Sir," Emmett said. His cheek twitched with suppressed anger. "How could we *not* know we're all condemned to fight it? *We're* the ones being used as cannon fodder."

"This is different," Azrael fingered his cloak pocket where he kept his scientific journal. "I can feel it. I just haven't tracked the data yet to quantify it."

"Why Moloch is suddenly so interested in this part of the world," Emmett asked. "Sri Lanka isn't on a major geological fault line, so there's no easy way to punch a hole into Gehenna. If we hadn't received intelligence from an ally there was suspicious activity, we wouldn't even be here."

Azrael absent-mindedly curled one wing forward as he stared out the window, twirling a tendril of consciousness shaped to resemble a long primary feather as he mulled over the latest pattern of suspicious activity. Emmett gave a polite cough, his grin revealing the slightly pointed shape of his teeth. Azrael looked down and realized he'd twirled that portion of his wing into something resembling an enormous pig's tail. Azrael reshaped the limb back into a wing.

"As much as I hate to admit this," Azrael surreptitiously rustled his feathers to make sure he hadn't let any other part of his appearance slip. "No matter how long I police his Agents, I just don't have a devious enough mind to foresee some of the stunts Moloch pulls."

"Lucifer really *is* the only person who can outthink the bastard," Emmett said. "And even *he* has a hard time keeping a lid on things. Did you ever stop and think there's a good reason She-who-is forces him to babysit this planet?"

"Harumpf!" Azrael snorted. "Now that's a scary thought! The humans have this saying. It takes a thief to catch one…"

"That's Lucifer," Emmett laughed. "He's like … a cross between Robin Hood and King Arthur."

"More like the fox assigned to guard the hen-house!" Azrael's dark mood lifted for the first time in weeks. "Sure … he guards it. But every time you see him, he's got a mouth full of feathers."

"And how that fox does love those lovely hens," Emmett said.

"Yes … he does," Azrael's hand tingled. His smile disappeared at the perpetual sense of urgency which had niggled his subconscious since the day he'd first met the source of that sensation. Elisabeth. He fell silent, staring out the window at the agents now hosing down the blood off the sidewalk.

"Sir?" Emmett asked. His tail twitched with concern. "I ... um ... we all kind of noticed you ain't been too happy lately. Is there anything we can do to help?"

The part-Sata'an human tucked his tail up one side as full-blooded Sata'anic soldiers still did in the Sata'an Empire, not sure if he crossed a magical line subordinates should never cross with a superior officer. 5,500 years amongst humans and the Sata'an-human hybrids had never fully lost their strict Sata'anic adherence to chains of command and rigid social structure. It was only the past few centuries, with the rise of democratic experiments in the America's, the French Revolution, and Ghandi in India, that the hybrids had begun idealizing notions of freedom and casting off Sata'anic mores. It was why so many Sata'an-human hybrids were named after freedom fighters.

"No," Azrael sighed. "I guess I've been off my game."

Emmett shifted from one foot to the other as he treaded further onto delicate ground.

"Sam ... um ..." Emmett said. "He um ... said ... someone caught your interest. But they ... um ... I just want you to understand that ... um ... we all know what it's like when a human rejects you for something that ain't your fault! Sir!"

Azrael scrutinized Emmett's uneasy demeanor. Lucifer demanded they keep him up to date on Elisabeth's progress so he could nudge open doors and put bees in ears to help the young woman along. He wasn't being entirely altruistic, though she wasn't the first human the Fallen Angelic had lavished resources upon simply because they'd sparked his interest. His 'pets' Lucifer called them, fluffing off inquiries about why he sometimes chose random humans to help for no reason other than it suited his mood.

In Elisabeth's case, Lucifer had originally taken an interest hoping she'd develop pre-ascended abilities so he could leave this world. She hadn't. At least that's what they'd all thought until the day she'd forced Nancy to linger in a body with a shattered heart. Now ... Azrael suspected Lucifer kept tabs on Elisabeth because she was the only leverage the Fallen Angelic had to get into *his* good graces. She was the only person, besides Elissar, who'd ever inspired him to break Hashem's strict rules about non-interference.

"First I took away her entire family," Azrael said. "And then I took the only person left in this world who cared about her. I don't blame her for hating me."

"We ... um ..." Emmett said. "We ... ah ... we all think you should just make yourself visible and talk to her. See what happens."

"The Emperor forbids it," Azrael said. "You know that. I'm no more permitted to make myself known than you are."

"She's already seen you twice," Emmett said. "The damage is done. What could it hurt?"

"She keeps throwing things at me," Azrael said. "I'm afraid she might touch me and die."

"I think if you help her understand," Emmett said, "it will make her ... I dunno ... feel better?"

"It's forbidden," Azrael said. "Besides ... what am I supposed to say? Hi ... I'm the Archangel who follows you around with a tally sheet and kills your loved ones?"

Emmett's mouth opened as though he wished to say more, and then shut it. Azrael glanced out the window, noting all traces of the carnage which had occurred mere hours ago had been erased. Life for the Sri Lanka Prime Minister would go on, untouched except for, perhaps, tighter security around his residence. Only the grieving families of the five human security guards and single Sata'an-human agent killed would remember this incident tomorrow.

"Very well, Sir," Emmett said, his tone back to the formal second-in-command of Lucifer's intelligence wing. "Good day, then, Sir."

"Thank you, Special Agent Till." Azrael forced his wings to stiffen out of the dejected slump they'd been in since the day Nancy had died. He gave Emmett a salute goodbye. He was done here. It was time to pour over his notes and figure out what the hell Moloch was up to.

Chapter 24

Come away, come away, death,
And in sad cypress let me be laid.
Fly away, fly away, breath;
I am slain by a fair cruel maid.

William Shakespeare

Earth - AD May, 2000
Chicago, Illinois

"Let me take a picture, dear," Mrs. Schroeder said. "You two make such a beautiful couple."

Elisabeth posed, lackluster, in front of the mantle while Mrs. Schroeder adjusted the fancy corsage Tommy had brought like a broody hen picking over a nice, fat bug. She went through the motions for Mrs. Schroeder's sake, but she just wasn't feeling the love. Since Nancy's death, Elisabeth hadn't felt happy about anything. Not even the fact Tommy Rodriguez followed her around like a love-sick puppy.

After six refusals, Tommy had circumvented her resistance to the senior prom by showing up at her new foster mother's house, the elderly neighbor who'd loaned her the shoes the night Nancy had died, with some potted tulips and offered to help the frail widow plant them, weeding out her entire bed of daylilies. By the time he was through, not only had Mrs. Schroeder twisted her arm to go with him, but was already talking about what a fine husband the former gangbanger-turned-college-aspirant would make.

Not!

"I wore this the night I met Harold at the CSO dance," Mrs. Schroeder adjusted the hem of the ancient, circa World War II sheath she'd scrounged out of a trunk in the attic of her Chicago row-house. "It was always his favorite."

"Isn't that you wearing this exact same dress over there?" Tommy pointed to a picture of a young Mrs. Schroeder posed next to a smiling man wearing an air force uniform on the mantle.

"That's me," Mrs. Schroeder's hazel eyes twinkled with happy memories. "I was quite the catch in my younger days. I used to love to go dancing every Saturday night with my girlfriends. My dance card was always full."

"I can believe that, Mrs. Schroeder," Tommy put his arm around her shoulders and did a tap-dance. "If you were a few years younger, it would be you I'd be asking to my senior prom." He gave her wink.

Mrs. Schroeder giggled like a teenager. She enjoyed the attention Tommy piled upon her whenever he came around. And Mrs. Schroeder knew how to keep the attractive young man coming around. With cookies. And banana bread. And invitations to supper, lunch, tea, or just about any other excuse she could find to match-make the persistent young man and point out to Elisabeth how lucky she was to have a talented, City College-bound aspiring music major so interested in her.

Elisabeth, on the other hand, had never forgiven Tommy for abandoning her to stand alone in the crowd while his 'homies' opposing gangbangers had shot at her and killed Nancy. If –HE- hadn't stepped between her and the bullet, she'd have joined her.

He was the most beautiful man she had ever seen…

He was the most hideous monster that had ever haunted her nightmares…

He was an angel…

He was the devil…

How could her watcher be both at the same time? Was he what they called a fallen angel? Or something else? Never, in her life had she heard of angels erupting into that … thing … he had turned into when he'd torn into the car to kill everyone inside. Not even fallen angels did things like that. And since that night, she searched through the bible and every other book she could get her hands on to try to figure out what the hell he was!

She hated him! Hated him! Hated him! Hated him! Hated him for taking Nancy and her entire family away from her! Nancy had been so eager to go. Why hadn't he taken her with him, too? It would have been a lot kinder.

She missed his reassuring visits…

"Elisabeth?" Mrs. Schroeder asked. "You didn't answer, dear."

"Huh?" Elisabeth had no idea what part of the endless chatter between the charming Tommy and the all-too-easy to bullshit Mrs. Schroeder she had missed. "I'm sorry."

"You were a million miles away." Tommy put his arm around her in a gesture of familiarity she did not feel, but she tolerated it because, at one time, she'd dreamed of what it would be like to have the dashing Tommy Rodriguez put his arm around her. She was supposed to be charmed by the attention he lavished upon her. Everyone told her how lucky she was. Honestly ... she could have cared less.

"Only Harold ever caught my eye," Mrs. Schroeder prattled on, cheerfully reminiscing about the past. "He was a gentleman. A real gentleman. Not like the boys you see on the television shows these days! Harold sure knew how to treat a lady."

"That's 'cause you *is* a lady, Mrs. Schroeder," Tommy charmed the support pantyhose off the old woman. "Just like Elisabeth, here."

"Oh ... Tommy," Mrs. Schroeder waved him away with a laugh. "You sure know all the right things to say. Elisabeth ... say cheese!"

"Cheese!" Tommy said as Mrs. Schroeder snapped the picture of them standing together in front of the mantle, he in his rented tuxedo that his mother must have traded half her monthly food-stamps allotment to procure, Elisabeth wearing the vintage dress she'd finally relented to wear only because Mrs. Schroeder had been kind enough to take her in after Nancy had died.

Elisabeth glanced with disinterest at the Polaroid as it developed before her eyes. Tommy was smiling. She looked ... grim. Her dress was nothing elaborate. Not even a prom gown. But it was pretty, complete with matching gloves, hand bag, and shoes. It made Mrs. Schroeder very happy to think of Elisabeth going to her prom in the dress she'd met her husband in. Elisabeth forced a fake smile and expressed the proper gratitude.

As for the other baggage ... the elderly widow had gotten the notion into her head that Tommy was future husband material. Husband? Elisabeth had two years of nursing school to start up in the fall and needed to find a job that would accommodate her grueling class schedule. Then she'd have a two-year internship where she'd work for zero wages in order to get her license. The pittance of a foster care check the state gave Mrs. Schroeder for taking her in would cut off in two weeks, the day she graduated high school. Elisabeth didn't wish to be a burden.

Besides ... she was afraid –HE- would take Mrs. Schroeder from her, as well, if she allowed herself to get attached to her...

"We're going to be late," Tommy tugged at her arm.

"You don't want to be late for your big night!" Mrs. Schroeder exclaimed, taking her other arm and shoving her towards the door.

-HE- used to always show up for nights like this, lurking in her room and watching her fuss over her appearance. She'd almost convinced herself he was a figment of her imagination until she'd seen his true form. But now he no longer came. Or if he did, he stayed far enough away that she couldn't sense where he stood to claw out his eyes. The bastard!

Didn't he care about her anymore? She felt ... abandoned. In the end, HE had left her, too. Now she truly *was* alone.

The look of anguish in his bottomless black eyes as he had jumped between her and the bullet with her name on it haunted her. She hadn't realized how big of a void the black man had filled until, one day, he simply stopped coming. She wiped her eyes, turning her head so Tommy wouldn't see her cry as they walked to the bus stop together.

"You okay?" Tommy pulled her closer as they waited for the bus.

"Yeah … sure."

Elisabeth closed her eyes and tried to sense if HE had come to watch her tonight. Once in a while, the hair on the back of her neck would stand up while she was walking down the street or waiting for a bus. She'd try to figure out what direction the sensation was coming from and move towards it, hoping against hope he'd come back, but whenever she got there, the sensation disappeared. Not 'gone' as in 'stepped aside.' But 'gone' as in 'never there in the first place.'

"Here's our bus," Tommy said. He kept his arm firmly planted around her shoulders as they rode the bus to the fancy banquet hall where the wealthy-wannabe popular kids had insisted they hold the prom. Sixty-five dollars per ticket! Just to eat and dance for two hours? Elisabeth had balked at the price, but Tommy had come up with the money.

Elisabeth glanced around. No sign of him. Not even the black man who took everyone she loved away from her cared about her anymore.

She felt … empty.

Chapter 25

The Grieved – are many – I am told –
There is the various Cause –
Death – is but one – and comes but once –
And only nails the eyes –
There's Grief of Want – and grief of Cold –
A sort they call "Despair" –
There's Banishment from native Eyes –
In sight of Native Air

Emily Dickenson

Earth - AD May, 2000
Chicago, Illinois

'It's a curious facet of the male human psyche,' Azrael wrote in his notebook, 'that the less interested the female is in *him,* the more he appears to desire *her.*'

Azrael glanced up from his perch on the balcony of the fancy banquet hall just in time to see Tommy slide his hand down his favorite research subject's back as they slow-danced together to the band. Azrael still watched her … now more than ever … but he stayed far enough away to avoid upsetting the fragile equilibrium she'd pasted back together from her twice-shattered life.

'Elisabeth appears to have come to the same conclusion that –I– did before the incident,' Azrael continued. 'The young man is not a suitably reliable protector. He *did*, after all, abandon her to be shot at while he made his *own* way to safety. Why she agreed to attend the dance with him perplexes me.'

Azrael absent-mindedly chewed upon the pencil, causing the containment field that kept it intact to dissolve. Drat! He reached into his void-reinforced satchel to pull out another one.

'It's difficult ascertaining what motivates the subject now that I dare not enter her living quarters to listen to her conversations with herself in the mirror,' Azrael wrote. 'My presence upsets her, even though she cannot see me with her eyes. Allowing her to see my true form was a mistake. I just … I just couldn't bear the thought of losing her.'

Lucifer had been highly amused when Azrael had burst -out- the front gate of Gehenna without first walking -in- to deposit the five scumbags he'd mercilessly executed. The Emperor, on the other hand, had been quite upset. Although Azrael had the ability to punch his own way in and out of the hell dimension at will, they feared doing so would destabilize it. He'd earned a stern lecture from the Regent … and also a knowing smile. As though she and the General knew something Azrael hadn't quite figured out.

'The young man is taking inappropriate liberties with the subject,' Azrael noted, suppressing the urge to burst into the middle of the dance floor. 'If he slides his hand down to caress her buttocks one more time, I swear I'm going to tap on his shoulder and ask him if I can have this dance just to see the look on his face when his body drops dead on the floor.'

Azrael's wings twitched with agitation. He'd studied countless couples engage in mating rituals over the centuries, but he'd never cared about the outcome before. He wanted Elisabeth to find a suitable mate so she'd be happy, but Tommy had come up short. She deserved better!

The music picked up. Tommy wanted to dance, but Elisabeth didn't wish to jump around a dance floor with a leg that gave out whenever she moved too fast. Although her cane was insurance, never once had Azrael seen his favorite subject cut loose. Tommy danced around her, but Elisabeth seemed unmoved. Although he couldn't hear what they said above the obnoxious rap music, he could read their lips.

"Let's go," Elisabeth said.

"But I don't want to leave yet," Tommy said. "Things are just getting warmed up."

"I'm tired," Elisabeth said. "My leg hurts."

Azrael expected Tommy would act selfishly and insist upon staying. He hoped Elisabeth would storm out of there.

"Okay," Tommy said. "I … um … expected this much time on your feet might wear you out. I … uh … took the liberty of renting a room upstairs. In the hotel."

Azrael drew back, horrified. Tell him to go to hell, Elisabeth! Who does he think he is? Assuming you're going to…

"That sounds like a good idea," Elisabeth gave him a grateful smile. "Maybe I'll feel up to dancing later."

"Come," Tommy gave her the crook of his elbow as she limped off the dance floor, leaning on his arm as she made her way through the lobby to the elevators.

What?

Azrael was so stupefied he almost forgot to watch what floor the elevator stopped at as he didn't dare step into the crowded elevator with them. Not only would she sense him standing there, but he'd accidentally kill a half-dozen teenage prom-goers who appeared to have the exact same plans. His favorite subject was going into a hotel room with a boy? Didn't she realize what fast boys like Tommy Rodriguez expected on prom night?

Floor? What floor had the elevator stopped on? If he had to, he'd search every room in this hotel so he could protect her when she realized what Tommy was up to! Floor 7 ... Azrael dissipated his form enough to pass through matter and flew up to the floor in question, staring down the long hallway trying to figure out what room they'd gone into. He invisibly filtered through rooms filled with drunken, fornicating prom couples until at last he found the right one. He lingered as far as he could from his favorite research subject and the boy attempting to seduce her, undecided whether to follow proper scientific procedure and stay far enough back to be an impartial observer, or to make himself visible and put a stop to this?

He decided upon a middle road, to linger close enough she'd sense his presence and attempt to claw his eyes out, breaking the mood. Yes ... that was it. He sank into the shadows against one wall the approximate distance he'd often stood when he'd watched her as a little girl. She'd often turn and speak to him, even though he never answered because it was forbidden. He stood there now, ready to flit out of the room at a moment's notice before Elisabeth could actually touch him and get herself killed. He decided jotting notes down at this point was impractical. He might need to take action and ... he wasn't sure. He felt agitated and was having a hard time keeping a grip on his physical form.

"You know I love you, Elisabeth?" Tommy led her over to the bed. "Don't you?" He sat down on the edge with practiced ease, drawing her down to sit beside him.

"Do you?" Elisabeth asked, her expression skeptical. "Really?"

Hah! Azrael noted she didn't say the words in return. Any moment Elisabeth would sense his presence and lob something at his head, ruining the mood when she started ranting about invisible death angels following her around. 'C'mon ... Elisabeth. Show that German temper of yours!'

"I do." Tommy tilted up her chin. "You have the most beautiful, silver eyes I've ever seen. From the first moment I saw you, all I've wanted to do was see what those eyes would look like filled with passion."

'Yeah, yeah, yeah...' Azrael muttered, waiting for the inevitable slap. 'C'mon c'mon c'mon ... I'm standing right here. Slap him so we can blow this joint. I've got your back. I've *always* got your back.'

"Do you love me at all, Elisabeth?" Tommy asked. "Even a little? I know you think I'm beneath you because my family is Hispanic, but I'd be a good provider. My mother adores you. And so does my grandmother."

"I don't know," Elisabeth said softly. "I don't care where your family comes from. It's just … I don't know *what* I feel anymore. Ever since Nancy died, I feel empty inside."

"I can fill that emptiness for you," Tommy said. "Let me show you what it feels like to be loved."

'What a godsdamned player!' Azrael sneered. 'Elisabeth isn't stupid enough to fall for –that- old line.' Anger he usually reserved for Agents of Moloch made the room shudder, but to someone who didn't understand he was in the room, it could be mistaken for the high-rise swaying in the wind.

"It hurts," Elisabeth started to cry. "I feel so empty inside it hurts. Nobody understands the way I feel. And I don't think anyone can ever make that feeling go away."

Oh...

Truth rippled through Azrael's incorporeal form. Elisabeth had just described exactly the way *he'd* felt for the past 2,300 years. Empty. Only the occasional kind word from someone whose suffering he alleviated as he freed them from their mortal shell prevented him from going insane. And her. *She* had been filling up the terrible hunger in his heart since the first time he'd laid eyes upon her. Those same beautiful, silver eyes that captivated Tommy had captivated *him*, as well.

"I can make the emptiness go away," Tommy murmured, his mouth descending down upon hers.

No! Azrael's heart felt like someone squeezed it in a vice. Instead of slapping him, Elisabeth allowed the kiss, her hands pausing before sliding around the back of his neck.

Azrael's wings twitched in panic, inadvertently dissolving the draperies behind him. The lights were so dim they didn't notice his heightened emotional state caused them to flicker and go out, the entire building and the prom still going on floors below suddenly cast into the dark. He hoped Elisabeth would sense he was close so it would distract her from what Tommy tried to do, but she did not. She didn't notice him at all!

"Yes," Elisabeth whispered, pulling back to look into Tommy's eyes as she touched his lips. "I've never … um … I'm a … I mean … I want you to teach me."

'No!!!' Azrael wanted to scream as Tommy groaned, his erection straining at the fancy black tuxedo pants as he lost all semblance of the gentle tempter and turned into a hot-blooded Latin panther moving in for the kill.

I'm not supposed to interfere

I'm not supposed to interfere
I'm not supposed to interfere
I'M NOT SUPPOSED TO INTERFERE!!!

Azrael screamed silently into his own mind as Elisabeth passively allowed Tommy to undress her and lay her down upon the bed like a sacrificial offering on one of Moloch's alters, her small, pale breasts shining like an offering to the gods as Tommy bent his head to first suckle one nipple, and then the other. Azrael's wings dissolved a hole into the plaster behind him.

He wanted to kill him.
He wanted to kill him.
He wanted to KILL him!!!

"Touch me, Tommy," Elisabeth pleaded as she trembled beneath his touch. "I need you to touch me so the emptiness will go away."

Touch. It was the one thing Azrael could never give his beautiful Elisabeth. The one thing Azrael, himself, craved more than anything in the world. She needed to be touched, and he could never, ever touch her because his first touch would also be his last.

He was in love with her. He'd been in love with her for a very long time. He wasn't sure when his feelings had transformed from curiosity to caring to something more profound, but he was losing her because he could never give her what she needed. It cut through his heart like a knife.

Tommy growled. He tore down his pants before moving into position to impale his sweet virgin and make her his.

'I'm not supposed to watch this,' Azrael choked, his heart breaking at her betrayal even though she had absolutely no idea he felt betrayed. 'She has chosen her mate and I am not supposed to interfere.'

Angelics descended from the Seraphim bloodline took one mate, for life. Once they had chosen their mate and consummated their relationship, not even death would keep them apart. He was in love with her. He wanted her to be his mate…

…And he had dropped the ball by being too chicken to speak to her…

With a whimper, he teleported his sorry ass to the darkest, most remote corner of the universe to prevent himself from killing the man she had chosen over *him*.

For the first time since Ki had coaxed him back to the material realms, Azrael recognized the hunger the Regent had warned him about. The hunger to be loved. Without Elisabeth to fill the void, the emptiness threatened to consume him. Azrael screamed, unleashing the destructive power he kept so carefully under control. The Song of Destruction. His primal howl was so anguished he swallowed three nascent galaxies and a few dozen stars from parallel universes in harmonic resonance with the galaxies here.

And then he wept.

How could he have been so blind to his own emotion? How could he have been so blind to her need? Touch. The one thing he could never, ever give her. Humans needed to be touched or they withered and died. The same way everything he touched died.

Stupid! Stupid! Stupid! Stupid!

Elisabeth was not his to love.

Part III

And next ... Moloch, Scepter'd King
Stood up ...and these words thereafter spake.
My sentence is for open Warr: Of Wiles
For while they sit contriving, shall the rest,
Millions that stand in Arms, and longing wait
The Signal to ascend, sit lingring here
Heav'ns fugitives ... Let us rather choose
Arm'd with Hell flames and fury all at once
O're Heav'ns high Towrs to force resistless way,
Turning our Tortures into horrid Arms
Against the Torturer ...
Which if not Victory is yet Revenge.

John Milton – Paradise Lost

Chapter 26

First MOLOCH, horrid King besmear'd with blood
Of human sacrifice, and parents tears,
Though, for the noyse of Drums and Timbrels loud,
Their children's cries unheard that passed through fire
To his grim Idol.

John Milton – Paradise Lost

Earth: September 11, 2001
New York City

"Thanks, Khalid," Susan said, an administrative assistant at one of the financial services companies in the World Trade Center. "You're a peach, bailing us out like this at the last moment."

"Yes, Ma'am," Khalid Ja'far Al-Nasiriyah politely averted his eyes as he handed her the cream cheese to go with the continental breakfast he'd just delivered to the 104th floor of the World Trade Center. "That is why we here. You need food for meeting. I make food for meeting. It's all good." He handed her the acceptance sheet signifying the meal had been delivered and was satisfactory.

"How much longer before they'll let you bring the rest of your family over?" Susan asked.

Khalid glanced up to see her genuinely interested expression and then averted his eyes, not wishing to insult her. Such forwardness was unusual amongst women of his own culture, but two years spent working for his uncle, manager for the cafeteria, had taught him to accept the ways of his new country. Susan … cared. In a building where cafeteria workers were expected to be invisible, it was an honor.

"Immigration say long wait list to bring," Khalid said. "My wife, my mother, seven children. I work many hours, send home money. Wait for government to say okay to bring."

"It's ridiculous how long they make you wait," Susan said. "My great-grandparents came over during the great potato famine. My great-grandfather had a job lined up at a factory, the staff at Ellis Island waived the entire family through. Now ... it's ridiculous."

"They no like Muslim people," Khalid said. "Make us wait long time. But Omar say you keep trying, they let you come. Four, sometimes five years. If no let come one way, under green card, let come other way, spouse of U.S. citizen. Two years, seven months from now, I apply. Become citizen. Separation only temporary."

Omar was Khalid's uncle, the cafeteria manager who'd convinced the corporation he worked for to sponsor him for a work visa. Susan gave him a sympathetic smile.

"Let me know if there's anything we can do to speed the process," Susan offered. "We need more people like you. Hardworking. Reliable. It's what America was all about. Back before the fat cats and the politicians ruined it for everyone."

Susan gestured towards the enormous wall of plate glass that overlooked New York Harbor. Towards the Statue of Liberty. The statue Khalid spent many a lunch hour sitting with his uncle contemplating the barriers his children would smash once he brought them here from Iraq. Dreams. Khalid was resigned to the fact he would never be more than a cafeteria worker. But his children? In America, a parent could work hard and make his children's' dreams come true. Even Muslim children.

Khalid's revelries froze in horror as he realized the plane he'd assumed was circling in for a landing at La Guardia was headed right for them. Raised in a country with constant sectarian violence, Khalid reacted instinctively. He yanked Susan under the enormous, sixty-foot long conference table just as the plane crashed into the floors below. The building rocked as though it were about to fall over. A sound like a freight train roared through the building.

Susan screamed.

An enormous fireball licked up the outside glass wall. Khalid prayed to Allah. Just barely audible over the noise, he could hear Susan make similar prayers to the Christian god.

"Come," Khalid helped her up. "We must get out. Fast. Take stairs. Elevator not safe."

Her teeth chattering in terror, Susan took his hand and allowed him to lead her towards the stairwell. Others in the company had the same idea, pushing against the door.

"Wait!" one of the general managers shouted at a broker ramming his shoulder against the door. "You should check first to make sure it's not..."

The man never got to finish his sentence. Just as the door opened, a backdraft sucked a wall of flame shooting up the stairwell into the room, incinerating everyone within fifteen feet of the stairwell. Susan screamed as the stench of burnt flesh assailed their nostrils. Khalid shoved her out of the way, shielding her with his body. She was only a friend. Not even that ... an acquaintance. But it was ingrained into his culture that a man's job was to protect a woman.

"Wh-wh-what's that," Susan pointed at the raging inferno shooting through the open door.

Khalid frowned. The fire burnt a sickly green color, not red. The color of infection. He'd witnessed RPG attacks and suicide bombs during the First Gulf War, but never a fire that burned ... green?

Enormous fiery arms reached out before Khalid could react and yanked them both into the putrid green portal. He shouted as fire surrounded his flesh, but did not consume it. Cold fire? The prayer he'd been about to utter giving thanks to Allah for his unusual deliverance died upon his lips as he realized he'd fallen at the feet of an enormous bull-headed beast.

"*Cena servierunt, Magister,*" a smaller creature pointed to Susan with what Khalid could only construe to be a grin.

The bull-god picked Susan up by the legs and shoved her into its gigantic maw before Khalid could even react.

"*Ego potest gustabunt Lucifers sanguine cerrit per venas,*" the bull-like demon said, chunks of what had once been Susan's arms and legs falling out of its enormous mouth as though they were chunks of spaghetti. "*Forsitan posset a militia inter hoc coetus?*"

Even though Susan's body had been chewed to pieces, Khalid could still hear her scream. No ... not hear. Feel. He could *feel* the sound her spirit made as the enormous bull-god devoured her soul. As more of Susan's co-workers got sucked into the portal, the bull-god picked them up and chewed on several more, holding an investment broker in each enormous hand as though they were French fries.

The smaller god turned suddenly towards Khalid and sniffed.

"Allah protect me," Khalid prayed as he backed towards the wall of fire. The closer he got, the hotter it burned. He stopped. Only death lay in that direction.

"*Quid iam quaeris quid ego credo,*" the smaller god grinned at Khalid as though he were an appetizer. It strode towards Khalid backed against the wall of fire.

"Don't be afraid," it spoke in Arabic now as it stalked towards him, cornering him like a farmer pursuing a chicken it was about to behead for supper. "I've been waiting a very long time to find a suitable host-body."

Khalid screamed as the creature grabbed him, its enormous hand so large his body was little more than another finger. He shut his eyes and prayed for a quick and merciful end and the safety of the family he would never see again.

"There, there," the smaller-god crooned, its voice hypnotically reasonable. "I'm not going to kill you. But I can't very well have you interfering with my use of your body, now. Can I?"

Small, slender tentacles shot out of its hand. Khalid screamed as the lesser god pinned him to the ground and shot the tentacles towards his eyes.

"Our Lord…" Khalid screamed. "Condemn us not…"

The prayer for deliverance died upon his lips as the tentacles shot up through the corners of his eye sockets, into his brain, and severed the frontal lobes. Although he was still alive and conscious, Khalid no longer had any control over what his body did other than to breathe. He couldn't even cringe in revulsion as the strange, angular god rammed its enormous body into his own as though he was a jumpsuit.

But he *could* understand now what the evil bastard was thinking. Oh! Allah! Not even the most fanatical imam preaching against the Great Satan possessed a clue about what evil was truly like.

Khalid tugged at his mortal form, trying to get away. To die. To cast himself into the fires he instinctively knew would consume his soul and destroy it. Anything other than serve the evil purpose he could sense the malevolent god wished to use his body to commit.

"Master," Khalid's body spoke of its own volition, a puppet now for the master that was Chemosh. "Would you mind giving me a lift towards the portal so I might begin engineering your escape?"

"*Utique,*" the bull-god said, dropping body parts as it stuffed more victims from the bombing into its gigantic maw and consumed their souls. With a laugh, its enormous fiery arms closed around Khalid's body without burning it and lifted it back up towards the inferno it had just escaped from.

"Allah, protect me," Khalid prayed, unable to sever his spirit that was forced to ride along with his former body and escape into Paradise.

He could feel the evil lesser-god feeding upon his spirit like a child sipping soda through a straw…

*****

"We found one alive!!!" a fireman shouted. Emergency responders crowded around the survivor.

"Sir?" the fireman pulled pieces of rubble off of the swarthy-skinned man wearing a filthy, white cafeteria worker uniform. "Are you okay?"

Chemosh compelled his host-body to open its eyes.

"Why, yes," Chemosh said, his voice reassuring and pleasant as he projected soothing images into the first responders minds. "I am okay."

"It's a miracle!!!" the firemen shouted triumphantly.

'You have no idea...' Chemosh thought to himself.

Chapter 27

If thou, Lord, shouldest mark iniquities
O Lord, who shall stand?

Psalm 130

Galactic Standard Date: 157,841.10 AE
Zulu Sector - Gliese 581g

'The research subject appears to prefer polyamorous reproduction,' Azrael wrote in his notebook, 'to monogamy. Just like the failed breeding policies of the Eternal Emperor with his hybrid armies at the time of the Fracture. Perhaps that's why this species birth rate has dropped precipitously low?'

Azrael stared at the mouse-sized primates and sighed. He'd chosen this planet because it was far enough away from Earth that he wasn't tempted to 'accidentally fly by' Elisabeth's house. He'd wanted to stay at the other end of the universe, but with He-who's-not still off to points unknown and an increase in activity by Moloch's agents, the General had asked he stay close.

He stared down at the notebook and realized his pencil had, of its own volition, sketched a drawing of Elisabeth, the lines of her face soft and ethereal as she stared back at him from the page. Every single one of Azrael's notebooks was filled with such images, scribbled amongst the data. He caressed the cheek of the drawing. The downward lines he'd drawn in the corner of her mouth gave her a wistful appearance, as though she missed him, too.

"I hope you're happy," Azrael said softly to the drawing. "What a silly little science nerd I am! I was so busy observing signs your mate was falling in love with you that I failed to notice –I- was exhibiting the same symptoms."

The girl on the page did not answer him. How could she? Even when he had been in her presence, he'd taken great pains to remain invisible. But every day he was forced to live without her made him sadder and sadder until, sometimes, he wished he could just touch *himself* and cast his *own* spirit into the void to uncreate it!

"In retrospect, of course I fell in love with you," Azrael told the drawing. "You're the closest thing I've had to a friend since Elissar died."

A soft cough sounded behind him.

"Sir!" Azrael snapped shut his notebook. He fumbled for the piece of paper with the tally marks on it and pretended to be interested in the mating habits of the tiny primates. They weren't even sentient, but it was what he'd been trained to do in the science academy. It gave him something besides chasing down murderous evil gods and mourning Elisabeth's choice of a mate to occupy his mental energy.

"The Regent asked me to speak to you," the General's unearthly blue eyes were filled with concern. "It's been more than a year since you took up residence on this planet. She's worried."

"I'm fine," Azrael said with a sigh that communicated he was *not* fine. "I've gotten my emotions back under control. I won't destroy any more galaxies. I promise."

Azrael glanced at the promiscuous mouse-sized mammals and checked off another tally mark when the female twitched her tail inviting another male to mount her. At least Elisabeth had chosen carefully from the available males and selected just *one*.

"May I?" The General carefully took the notebook, a risky venture as one brush of his hand would result in a 'vacation' in the upper realms patching his physical form back together.

Azrael averted his eyes to the ground, his guilt staring out from the pages of his scientific journal as his commanding officer flipped through sketch after sketch of her until he got to the final one.

"I was once in love with someone who didn't love me," the General said softly. "I know how you feel."

A companionable silence stretched between them, Azrael not being an especially gregarious Angelic and the General famous for being outright taciturn. The General traced the penciled rendition of the scar he'd deliberately left on the real Elisabeth with one finger.

"Elisabeth tried to hold Nancy here even though her heart was so shattered it couldn't beat," Azrael finally said. "The only reason she failed is because I released her."

"It would have killed her if you hadn't released Nancy," the General said. "It damned near killed my mate keeping *me* alive when I was that badly wounded and I didn't have shattered internal organs."

"Maybe if I'd summoned help?" Azrael said. "Perhaps Hashem would have made an exception to let you heal Nancy the way you did her?"

"The parties agreed to heal Elisabeth because she was a special case," the General said. "She survived your touch. We hoped … it's in everybody's best interests if Lucifer isn't the only Morning Star."

"She never showed any pre-ascended abilities until she tried to heal Nancy," Azrael said.

"Hashem asked me to take samples of her DNA," the General said. "She's got genetic markers from all four hybrid species, Sata'anic Fallen, and Lucifer running through her genome."

"So she's what the two emperors are hoping will evolve from this world?"

"She's also got genetic markers from Seraphim Angelics who haven't existed in this universe for thousands of years," the General said. "Angelics whose bloodline, to our knowledge, died out. She's a step-in. An ascended consciousness come back in mortal form."

"But the Seraphim were killed before they ascended as a species," Azrael said.

The General flinched. As a boy, he'd been the sole survivor of the Seraphim genocide.

"The species as a whole did not ascend as the Cherubim and Wheles did," the General said. "But they were close to perfection. Many Archangels are Seraphim come back to finish their evolution."

A tiny spark of hope lit in Azrael's breast and was extinguished. Elisabeth had chosen somebody else. Azrael's wings drooped dejectedly.

"Elisabeth carries enough of her original genome to possess pre-ascended abilities even without her memories," the General said. "It's why she survived your touch. Some Seraphim evolved the capability to tolerate void-matter."

"Like you," Azrael stated.

"Like me," the General said. "But more importantly. Like *you*. Hashem won't reveal who your sire was, but you have Seraphim DNA running through your bloodline."

"You … mean?" Azrael asked, and then stopped as the full magnitude of what the General was telling him slammed home like a sledgehammer. "You mean … there's a possibility she might …"

"Why do you think we never reassigned you after the incident with the gang-shooters?" the General said. "We hoped you'd follow your heart and make your presence known."

"It's forbidden," Azrael said. "Hashem was livid I showed myself."

"Hashem was livid you punched a hole into Gehenna to personally feed her assailants to Moloch," the General said. "Not because she saw you. You're Hashem's policeman, not his executioner."

"Elisabeth was so angry," Azrael said. "I was afraid she'd strike me and die. She can sense me no matter how invisible I make myself."

"We don't know if she'll ever be able to tolerate your touch," the General said. "But we'd like you to return to Earth and resume your mission."

"I can't!" Azrael flared his wings and inadvertently vaporized a swath of ferns. "It's cruel to ask this of me!!! The Regent doesn't understand!"

"She understands better than anybody in the universe," the General said. "We think Elisabeth may be a Seraphim who suffered a broken bond. As I once did."

"I thought the fate of a broken bond was to wander all eternity alone?" Azrael asked.

"A Seraphim with a broken bond is unable to reunite with their family in the upper realms," the General said. "Because they remain imperfectly bonded to the false mate, they suffer the same karmic injury over and over again until something breaks the cycle."

"How terribly cruel," Azrael's wings fluttered with horror. "How can you heal a wound you can't remember receiving?"

"You choose," the General said. "Free will. Every lifetime a spirit is reborn, they're given a chance to make a different choice."

"It's cruel! She-who-is should let them remember."

The General flipped through Azrael's notebook until he came to a picture that was not of Elisabeth. In one of his darker moods, he had sketched the look of terror on Elissar's face as she'd reached up from the fires of Gehenna towards his hand.

"Sometimes memory loss is a blessing." The General touched the tiny penciled hand so vividly drawn it practically reached out from the page. "My amnesia was only temporary, but much of what I accomplished was done because I couldn't remember who I was when I chose to help the people of her world."

Azrael looked at the picture of his young friend. The only real friend he'd ever had besides his sister. Oh … gods! How he wished he could forget her terrible death. His *own* death. The feeling of loss he'd felt as her small body had shuddered in his arms and died. The fact Moloch still existed and put her world at risk. What he wouldn't give to have back the carefree bliss he'd experienced when Ki had allowed him to bask in the Song of Creation without his memories!

But even there, he'd been able to sense a connection to Elissar's mind. A connection which had grown faint once he'd been coaxed back to Earth to protect her world. A connection which, even now, enabled him to keep his dark gift under control even though she'd been dead and in the grave for 2,300 years…

"I would not give up a single memory of her," Azrael said. "Not for all the power in the universe. Not Elissar. Not Mama. Not Gazardiel. And not Elisabeth! Even if she *did* break my heart."

"I'm beginning to see why Ki entrusted you to hear her song," the General said. The slight uptick of one corner of his mouth indicated he found favor with Azrael's words. "Only those capable of unselfish love can access the highest realms. It's Ki's insurance policy to make sure Moloch's agents can't escape the material realms."

The General flipped to a picture Azrael had drawn of young Elisabeth reaching up to take his hand, dime-store angel wings crushed beneath her in the bloody snow. She'd just received the wound which would become her scar. She had looked up at him, her body broken, her family gone, and yet she'd smiled and told him she was the Angel of the Lord. In the picture, they were touching. The only touch, besides the Regent's, Azrael had experienced without killing somebody since his death.

"Perhaps your despair is premature," the General said. "Elisabeth still lives."

"It's too late!" Azrael said miserably. "She chose someone else. I'll get to kiss her just once, the day she dies, and then she'll be gone."

"Lucifer sent the Regent a message," the General said. "An old friend of yours kept tabs on her after you left. Samuel Adams. Her country just went to war. She made an appointment to speak to an Army recruiter, so Sam got himself assigned to be that recruiter."

"Th-the … army?" Azrael stammered. "She'll be killed!"

"She told Sam her scholarship to the University of Chicago wasn't enough," the General said. "She doubled up her classes so she'd graduate early, but she has no money coming in to meet her living expenses. She loathes being a burden on Mrs. Schroeder."

"But … her leg!"

"The Army is willing to overlook her disability because she won't be on the front line," the General said. "They're desperate for nurses and they'll help her finish her training. She ships out to basic training in two weeks."

"B-b-but Tommy … they … I saw… um…" Azrael trailed off. He did not wish to divulge he had stayed far longer in the room than he should have stayed.

"You caught an eyeful of something you wish you'd never seen?" the General asked, one eyebrow raised in bemusement. "Sam asked her about the boy. She said she broke up with him at the beginning of the summer."

"She … broke up?" Azrael whispered. A glimmer of hope ignited in his heart.

"Although humans are *capable* of forming the Bond of Ki," the General said, "it's rare they actually do. Whereas Seraphim Angelics evolved to form the bond automatically, it takes an act of will on their part to form a bond that unbreakable. Same as the mortal Angelics who make up Hashem's armies."

"Unmated. Like my mother?" Azrael remembered how heartbroken his mother had been as she had gone through each failed mating cycle trying to conceive his little sister and finally resorted to 'help' from the Emperor a second time. "Only … Mama was never … I mean … I never saw her with any other Angelic except during a heat cycle. *We* were her world."

"You'd better keep that in mind when you go mooning after her," the General warned. "I have no idea whether or not the young woman is capable of bonding. But she did not bond with *him*."

"Oh…" Azrael whispered. "You mean … she … we … I might still have a chance with her?"

"Don't get your hopes too high," the General stood back up and stretched his wings. "You still have your original problem. Unless she's as resistant to void-matter as the Regent is, she dies. Your only option is to wait and see what develops. I suggest you observe her until you figure out what you want to do."

The General ruffled his dark black-and-brown striped wings, a twinkle of darker, warmer blue in his unearthly blue eyes. "For all I know, we could be dead wrong."

"Dead … wrong," Azrael repeated, and then realized his esteemed commanding officer had just made a joke.

"Go!" the General ordered. "It's dangerous where she'll be going. Protect her. But protect your heart, as well, until you are certain she will not break it a second time."

In a flash, Azrael was gone, forgetting to give the General the proper military salute.

Elisabeth didn't have a mate!!! Whoopie!!!

Chapter 28

Death is as sure for that which is born,
As birth is for that which is dead.
Therefore grieve not for what is inevitable.
Bhagavad Gita

Earth - AD October 7, 2001
University of Chicago Medical Center — Chicago, IL

"We've got de-fib," Elisabeth said.

"Is it me?" Chief Medical Director Abdullah Fa'azi asked in his lilting Dagestani-accented English. "Or are there more gang-related deaths in this city each year. 360 Joules, please, Elisabeth?"

Doctor Fa'azi tore open the young man's shirt and expectantly held out the paddles. For some reason, the Chief Resident continuously challenged her to do more than the other nurses.

"Charging now." Elisabeth automatically flipped the dial to the correct number and grabbed a bottle of medical gel to squeeze onto the dual paddles. "Gang-related violence is up. The Saints and Latin Kings are going at each other over turf to sell drugs."

"Why do we have to get them?" Student Nurse Maria complained as she shoved gauze into the gunshot wound in the young man's chest. Gang tattoos could be seen covering nearly every visible inch of the young man's body.

"Clear!" Doctor Fa'azi shouted. The body jerked up, and then back. "Because this is a teaching hospital. We take them so you aspiring young nurses have a human guinea pig too poor to hire a lawyer to sue if you screw up while you learn."

Doctor Fa'azi had the pleasant up-and-down cadence to his voice typical of most Indo-European doctors who flocked to the University's teaching staff. The gunshot victim, unfortunately, did not. The heart monitor screamed in alarm as the jagged up-and-down lines on the paper readout spaced out and went flat.

"Flatline," Maria said. "Do we shock him again?"

"It's not like jumpstarting a car," Doctor Fa'azi reminded her. "The defibrillator only works if the heart is in defib. It does nothing if the patient is flatlined. We have to restart the heart using chemical means. Elisabeth … start manual chest compressions. Maria … get me 50 milligrams of atropine, please."

"One-one-thousand, two-one-thousand, three-one-thousand," Elisabeth counted, wincing at the sound of rib bones cracking as she pressed the ball of her hand deep into the patients sternum. "C'mon, kid!" Her own heart raced as she tried to will the young man's heart to start pumping on its own.

Maria reached into the cabinet and shakily prepared an enormous, hollow needle with adrenaline to restart the heart. "Here, Doctor."

"Thank you, Maria," Doctor Fa'azi said. "Elisabeth … I need access, please. Step aside."

"Yes, doctor." Elisabeth cringed as Doctor Fa'azi felt along the patient's ribcage and jammed the enormous needle between two ribs to inject the adrenaline directly into the heart.

"C'mon," Doctor Fa'azi muttered, watching the monitor. They all watched the monitor, praying for the patient's heart to start beating on its own.

One minute. Two minutes. Three minutes. The monitor remained flat.

"We've lost him!" Nurse Maria said, tears coming to her eyes. "Are you going to call it, Doctor Fa'azi?"

"Time of death…" Doctor Fa'azi started to say.

The hair stood up on the back of Elisabeth's neck. It was a sensation she hadn't felt in more than a year, but she knew exactly what it was. HE was here to take this kid. Her German rose in her veins at all the stupid, senseless, meaningless deaths she'd been forced to endure since she was a little girl.

"Not so fast!" Elisabeth grabbed the gunshot victim and pulled his limp head to face her. "Hey … you … gang boy! I'm talking to you. You going to give up and just go into that dark night? Or are you going to get up and show that camel-jockey of a doctor and 'spic nurse that you're a Saint?"

She visualized grabbing the young man by the scruff of the neck and dragging him kicking and screaming back into his body.

The heart monitor beeped once. Jagged, irregular waves scratched across the paper readout and then dissipated. Defib … and then flatline again.

"Yeah… that's right," Elisabeth said. "I'm talking to you!!! Here you go getting all shot up and dripping your blood all over my emergency room. You think you're going to go to some pie-in-the-sky honky heaven where hot angel-chicks are going to fawn all over your scrawny ass and give you head all day long? Well I got news for you, Saint-boy! I've seen that angel who's come for you and, you know what? He's black. He's black as night 'cause there's only one place you're going right now. And that's straight to hell. You hear me? That black man holding out his hand and telling you to go with him? Well I've seen his true form! And let me tell you, it's ugly, ugly, ugly! You ask him to show you his true form before you take his hand. 'Cause it's the last thing you'll ever see!"

The heart monitor registered a few weak beats, and then went flat.

"Dead, huh?" Doctor Fa'azi asked the dumb-struck Maria. He rushed to the supply cabinet and pulled out a second syringe, filling it with more atropine. A second injection went directly into the gangbanger's heart.

"Nothing," Maria said with a hint of gloating.

"Give me those paddles," Elisabeth said. "400 joules."

"That's too much," Maria whined. "The training manuals said we should never give more than 360. Besides … he's flatlined again. The paddles won't work."

"He's dead," Doctor Fa'azi reminded her. "Remember? He's got nothing to lose."

The doctor jacked up the dial and handed Maria the bottle of medical gel. Maria nervously squeezed it onto the paddles as the machine charged.

"Clear!" Elisabeth shouted, her expression intense as she pictured kicking the gangbanger in the ass hard enough to knock him back into his body as she rammed the paddles down onto the center and side of his chest and felt the body jerk upwards.

The heart monitor beeped.

It beeped again.

"That's it, Saint boy," Elisabeth crooned, her voice soothing now as the monitor beeped, then paused, then beeped, then beeped again, and then paused before settling into a normal sinus rhythm. "You can do it. Tell that black man he can be the one to go to hell, taking people who never did him no wrong away from their families and leaving nothing but shattered lives in his wake. You tell him you're going to hang around here a little while longer and see if you can't straighten out of the mess you've made of your life."

Her entire body tingled. She could feel him standing so close behind her it felt like he was inches from her back. The scent of ozone-filled air after a thunderstorm had passed filled her nostrils. It was the scent she'd come to associate with him even though the nearest ocean was thousands of miles away.

He was back. Her watcher had come back. She turned to face him even though no one except maybe the gangbanger on the table could see him and crossed her arms.

"I won," she said, a tigress protecting her cub. "You can't have him. He's mine."

Nurse Maria stood in shocked silence at Elisabeth's outburst. Doctor Fa'azi, however, began to clap.

"Nurse Maria!" Doctor Fa'azi ordered. "We have a tension pneumothorax to treat. He's lost a lot of blood. Get me a pint of B-positive and a colloid drip. Elisabeth! Get a chest tube. We need to re-inflate that lung."

"Right away, Doctor Fa'azi." Elisabeth did as she was told now and handed him the tube.

"I think you should do the procedure," Doctor Fa'azi gave her a smile. "You're going to be doing a lot of these where you're headed to in three days."

"But she's only a student nurse!" Maria complained. "Like me."

"She's a natural trauma nurse," Doctor Fa'azi said. "Or more likely, a future doctor. And she doubled up classes all last winter and through the summer so she's almost ready to graduate. The Army is darned lucky to get their hands on her."

"Thanks," Elisabeth said, closing her eyes so she could reassure herself HE was really back. She could feel him. So close that if she stepped back, she might nestle into his arms.

What would it be like, to be held by an angel? Her hand tingled at the memory of the time she'd touched him. Was he back to watch her? Or had he simply come to retrieve the gang member lying on her table? Oh, how she'd missed his constant, silent presence. As if … he cared.

Did he care?

"I told the Army I want to go active duty the moment I graduate boot camp," Elisabeth said. "This time in nine weeks, I'll be getting shot at by the Taliban."

She sensed his silent form stiffen at her back. She could have sworn she heard a sharp exhalation of breath that did not belong to either of the other two people in the room. The news disturbed him. Good. For some reason, it mattered to her that it disturbed him.

Doctor Fa'azi nodded.

"Troubled part of the world," he said. "I should know. I came here to get away from trouble there. Now you're going there to find it. May Allah protect you."

"Thanks," Elisabeth said. "I have a feeling I'm going to be just fine."

Feeling lighter than she had since the day Nancy had died, she scrubbed out as soon as they'd gotten the boy settled into the ICU and practically skipped down the hall, her gimpy leg hardly slowing her down at all.

Chapter 29

"Where ye are, death will find you,
Even if ye are in towers, built up strong and tall"

Quran 4:78

Earth - AD October 7, 2001
University of Chicago Medical Center – Chicago, IL

"I'm glad you're back," Abdullah Fa'azi tucked his tail up under his white doctor's coat as he finished scribbling notes onto the patient's medical chart. "Lucifer asked me to transfer onto the teaching staff here and train her."

"She's amazing," Azrael said, not bothering to hide the shit-eating grin which lit up his face. "Isn't she?"

The former Dagestani doctor cocked a dark eyebrow at him, his expression amused.

"Yes, she is," Abdullah said. "Since I gather you're here to check in on our talented young nurse, and not to reap this chap, I'll leave you while I finish my rounds."

"Thanks, Abdullah."

Azrael sat at the foot of the bed, watching the young man sleep. He supposed he should be upset the way Elisabeth had spoken about him, but she was right. He was the black man who took people she loved away from her.

He hadn't come to take them. He came to see *her*. Her scent was like a drug, her voice a sweet, dulcimer song to his ears. The moment he'd left her presence, the yearning to be near her again made his body ache with an all-consuming hunger. Fifteen months away had been so miserable and painful, she could call him whatever names she liked and he would still worship the ground she walked upon. He was an addict, and she was his drug of choice…

He'd faded back enough so she could no longer sense him and observed her happiness as she'd finished her shift. In her mind, she'd defeated him.

Seeing her happy made him happy. Her desire to defeat him was pushing her to develop her pre-ascended abilities. Emotion. The ability to wield her gift appeared to be tied to strong emotion. If she became strong enough, perhaps someday she might even survive his touch?

"How I yearn to touch you again." Azrael reached out to caress the single carnation Nurse Maria had put in a plastic cup so it would be the first thing the patient she'd written off as dead would see when he awoke. His hand tingled at the memory of how warm her small hand had felt as her fingers had closed trustingly around his. The feeling of deep-seated recognition which had passed into his heart, as though she were someone he had been looking for his entire life.

The carnation wilted and turned black.

"Not ... yet," Azrael said with regret. He plucked the dead flower out of the cup and finished the job, dissolving it the rest of the way so the kid didn't wake up with a dead flower staring at him like an evil omen.

No evil omens today. She was headed to Afghanistan! Where he had just been assigned! Moloch's agents were crawling all over that part of the world like fleas on a dog, but Azrael would protect her. He'd protect her even if it meant he had to vaporize half the Middle East...

It was irrational for him to be so happy about something so grim, but he was. Happy. A happy grim reaper. She had beat him! She had beat him and it made him happy.

His hand itched with sensation, a sensation he quelled these days by pulling out his notebook and drawing whatever image came into his mind. Nearly always her! The feel of void-reinforced pencil scratching against the page was reassuring. Almost as though he could feel the images taking life beneath his fingers.

The young man stirred, the heart monitor beeping a little faster as he rose towards consciousness. Slowly he opened his eyes. After a moment of adjustment, he realized Azrael was sitting in the chair next to his bed, sketching.

"Am I dreaming?" The young man glanced warily at the enormous glossy black wings carefully arranged over the back of the chair; a chair comprised of dead matter which Azrael only avoided dissolving into nothingness because he had finally mastered the art of keeping his emotions stable.

"No," Azrael said, unsmiling as he glanced up from his sketch book to take in the unique slant of the young man's cheekbone, including marks tattooed on his cheeks showing his gang affiliation, and continued sketching.

Silence. There was no sound except Azrael's pencil scraping against the paper. The Emperor had spared no expense inventing a means for Azrael to document his scientific observations, since no electronic device would work for him and pens dissolved the moment he began to put any feeling into his writing. Despite his efforts, a simple pencil with a bit of shielding remained Azrael's most reliable means of collecting data.

"Are you here to take me to hell?" the young man finally asked. The heart monitor hiccupped, mirroring his agitation.

"Hmmm? Not right this moment," Azrael said, not looking up. "Maybe in a little while."

More silence. Azrael finished his sketch to go along with his notes from earlier today documenting every detail about how his favorite subject had defeated him. Nancy had been too badly broken to stay, but this young man had stood a fighting chance. It overjoyed him to see her win.

"You're an angel," the young man asked. "Right?"

"Not really." Azrael snapped his sketch book shut and rose to his feet. "Not anymore. I sever souls from their mortal shells and bring them to either heaven, or hell. It depends upon how bad you've been during your lifetime."

The young man tried to skitter back in his bed, but was tethered by a spider web of IV's, wires and other medical paraphernalia.

"Who are you?"

"Who do you think I am?" Azrael asked, black eyes glittering above grim features.

"Death."

"Ah-hah!" Azrael held out his hand so it was about a foot away from the young man's hand. "Would you like to come with me now? Or would you like a second chance to straighten up your life?"

"There was a woman," the young man said. "She was talking to me when I was in the emergency room. It was like I was floating above my body or something. She said I shouldn't go with you."

"It's not my job to judge you," Azrael said. "I just take you to one gateway, or the other. If you've done bad things, you can't escape the truth of it. There are no illusions in the Dreamtime. "

The young man cringed.

"Sounds like hell to me," he whispered.

"Then maybe you should do what she told you," Azrael shrugged. "Straighten things out so you don't end up back up here. Next time ... I'll just take you."

"I ... I ... I'll straighten up," the young man stuttered. "I ... I ... p-p-promise."

"Good," Azrael said. "Then I can go?"

"Um ... Sir ... Dude ... Er ... Angel ..." the young man said. "Um ... what did you write in the book about me."

Azrael opened his book to the page he'd drawn Elisabeth ramming the defibrillator paddles down on the young man's chest as his consciousness floated above his body, Azrael stood behind her, wings flared, reaching to take the young man until Elisabeth had ordered the him to stay.

"I didn't imagine that then, huh?"

"No," Azrael said. "You didn't. She defeated me. You're very lucky."

Snapping the book shut, he disappeared in a flash of darkness. If Elisabeth saved spirits *he* wouldn't have bothered saving, the least he could do was scare the crap out of them so they'd take advantage of the second chance she'd just given them.

It was the least he could do for her...

Chapter 30

And the recompense of evil is punishment like it,
But whoever forgives and amends,
He shall have his reward from Allah;
Surely He does not love the unjust.

Quran 42:40

Earth - AD December 17, 2001
Valley of Jehoshaphat

Azrael stormed into the processing chamber dragging a reaped human spirit, determined to have it out with Lucifer once and for all. It hadn't been squatters he'd reaped from Tora Bora valley, or even run-of-the-mill Taliban, but friends! Sata'an-human hybrid friends! Friends too badly injured to survive even if he *had* been able to get them out of the elaborate cave complex where they'd followed the Agent occupying Osama Bin Laden down the rabbit hole and been ambushed.

With thousands of Coalition forces bombing the hell out of the mountains and the place teeming with supposedly allied Afghani soldiers, how the hell had Bin Laden managed to slip his grasp? Not only had the squatter's filthy consciousness slipped the trap, but so had the genetically unique mortal shell known as Bin Laden!

"Why didn't you authorize the Alliance to send in troops to help out?" Azrael practically screamed at Lucifer. "Do you have any idea how many men we just lost?"

He didn't look bright or beautiful now, the debauch Fallen son of the Eternal Emperor. The stench of alcohol was overpowering. Lucifer sat slumped on his so-called 'throne,' Italian designer clothing smeared with dirt, wings crumbled carelessly beneath him as though he didn't care if he crushed or broke his feathers.

All around them, video screens displayed the live streaming footage of dozens of Sata'an-human hybrid operatives embedded with Coalition, Afghan allied, and even civilian village groups as they frantically searched the area for the escaped Agent they'd been trying to pin down. Easy? Tora Bora was supposed to have been a cinch!

Lucifer lifted his head from its weary slump, his eyes unfocused as he shakily lifted a glass of scotch to his lips and took a long, silent dreg.

"If I invite one emperor in," Lucifer said, a sneer coming to his lips at the mere mention of his father's name, "I have to invite the other. And then we've got a whole different set of problems to deal with."

"Then let Shay'tan send in his observers, too!" Azrael shoved the filthy consciousness of the Taliban he'd reaped in anger into Lucifer's face. The molecules in the room shuddered as emotion added force behind Azrael's words, but he was in good enough control of his anger to keep a lid on it. It wasn't really Lucifer that Azrael was mad at but … life!

This clusterfuck had just prolonged the war Elisabeth had thrown herself into!

"Those two idiots will grind this planet into dust," Lucifer slurred, swirling the amber liquid around and around his glass so that the ice cubes made a slight tinkling noise. "Or have you forgotten how you ended up here in the first place?"

The molecules in the room trembled in harmonic resonance to the discordant note Azrael broadcast below the threshold of human hearing. The human Taliban he'd reaped squeaked in terror and began to plead in Pashto for his life or … not life. He was already dead, zapped out of his mortal shell when the bastard had leaped out of the shadows and finished off Ben Franklin, a Sata'an-human hybrid Azrael had done countless missions with over the years. Azrael usually didn't reap non-squatter patsies and drag them to Gehenna, but this one had especially pissed him off, shooting the dying man while Azrael had been off dissolving matter for a rescue team to get inside without collapsing the cave.

In the end, it hadn't made any difference. Buried deep in Bin Laden's elaborate fortress of hidden caves, Azrael hadn't been able to summons help in time to save Ben Franklin's life. The pathway out had been blocked by falling rubble caused by a Coalition bomb. He couldn't teleport Ben out beyond the blockage because touching him meant instant death. He hadn't been able to teleport a medic *in* for the exact same reason. Azrael had stood by, helpless, as his friend's life blood had poured out of his bullet-ridden brain while his spirit pleaded not to take him because he had a pregnant wife and children.

The sound of Ben Franklin's human widow keening as someone broke the news of her husband's death echoed throughout the underground network of caves. Sarah Franklin was legally blind, with a terrible scar that ran across her face from a car accident that had left her disfigured. She hadn't cared that her husband with the strong Sata'an-lizard features had been different from other males, or that the home he'd made for her was really the gateway to Hell. All she knew was that Ben had worshipped the ground she'd walked upon and left her with six young children to raise without a father, a seventh on the way.

"Sir?" one of the Sata'an-hybrid guards inquired, his voice warbling with emotion at the news of the death of yet another friend. "What should I do with … um … sir? He's not a squatter."

Lucifer looked up, the drunken fog clearing for a moment as he regarded the frantic, squirming spirit wriggling from Azrael's grasp. His silver eyes locked with Azrael's, not the guards, as he gave his orders.

"It's up to *him* to decide what he wants to do with him," Lucifer said, his words measured. "He says he walks the middle pathway between the Commandments of my father and the Sharia law of the old dragon. Let *him* interpret what the law says in this situation."

Somewhere behind him, the wailing of Sarah Franklin grew to a screeching crescendo as she broke the news to her eldest son and daughter, both old enough to begin training as Lucifer's operatives. Azrael felt as though he was responsible for their pain.

If only he'd been more aggressive about dissolving the collapsed entrance to the cave so help could have gotten to Ben sooner instead of timidly dissipating one rock at a time so he didn't bring the mountain down upon his head! If only he'd watched Ben's back when the airstrike had caused an avalanche instead of flitting cavern-to-cavern like a wraith, trying to cut his way through the electromagnetic jamming device Bin Laden had deployed to make it difficult to sense the squatter's exact location. If only he'd done a better job of searching the place Ben had been injured from falling debris before leaving to summons help.

If only he hadn't left Ben alone, barely conscious and bleeding, an easy victim to be shot execution-style by the Taliban while he'd cleared a pathway for help!!!

"Go to hell!" Azrael hissed, aware of what Lucifer was trying to pull. He was making Azrael solely responsible for breaking protocol, putting the decision back on *him* as to whether this spirit got consumed by the 'guests' occupying the lower levels of Gehenna or transported to the Dreamtime to face the truth of his poor life-choices.

"Be my guest," Lucifer said. His gaze became frightfully clear as he willed away the alcoholic stupor he'd been trying his hardest to sink into and the cold, hard politician who'd once led the Galactic Alliance and kept Shay'tan at bay made a rare appearance. Without breaking Azrael's gaze, he reached into his shirt and pulled out the key, slipping it into the failsafe device that opened the enormous blast doors that led into the fiery hell-dimension. With a shudder, the doors slid open. Heat blazed into the room, giving Lucifer's snowy white wings an eerie, fiery glow.

"It's your free will…"

"Get the doctor," someone shouted behind him. "Her water just broke. She's fainted."

Sarah Franklin wasn't doing so well…

With a scowl, Azrael dragged Ben Franklin's murderer down through the descending levels of gateways until he got to the precipice overlooking the deepest level of Gehenna, the pit where he'd met his death. It was pitch black here, lit up only by the fires below as if he stared down into the throat of an active volcano. Far below, so far down it wasn't possible to see them, he could hear the squabbling Agents vying for position.

Azrael could hear the chatter grow louder as the inmates recognized the sound of the gates opening above like monkeys in a cage. It was feeding time. He hung the Taliban who had murdered his friend over the precipice and prepared to let go.

'You're Hashem's policeman,' the General had said. 'Not his executioner.'

The song which perpetually played in the background of Azrael's mind grew stronger, reinforcing his memory of the advice his mistress, Ki, wished for him to follow.

"Bah!" Azrael screeched at the terrified spirit.

He tightened his grip around the man's throat and stormed back up through the passageways, dragging the accursed spirit behind him past the seven blast doors, back into the processing chamber where Lucifer gave him a bemused stare. It wasn't usual for the even-tempered Angelic to go off the deep end like this, but ever since his cluelessness about his own feelings had nearly cost him the woman he loved, a whole *bunch* of emotions kept demanding to be noticed.

"It's not so easy being the Emperor of Earth?" Lucifer said softly, a mixture of 'I told you so' and compassion radiating out of his eerie silver eyes. "Is it?"

Without another word, Lucifer pulled the key out of the failsafe device, sank back into his chair, and grabbed his drink, downing it in a single gulp. Behind him, the sound of seven blast doors slamming shut accentuated his words like a drum solo at a rock concert. He held out the glass and another immediately appeared in his hand, his minions well trained after 5,500 years to keep their leader plied with alcohol after a mission went south.

"I do hope you sealed up the entrance to that complex so the Coalition Forces don't find it," Lucifer's eyes glazed over as the scotch hit his system. "The last thing we want is whatever technology they were building that fooled *you* getting into human hands."

With a grunt for an answer, Azrael broke protocol and teleported directly out of Lucifer's throne room, depositing the unworthy scumbag he'd reaped for murdering his wounded friend at the gateway to the Dreamtime, where all non-Agent infected sentient souls were supposed to go until She-who-is decided to send them back, whether they were worthy in his mind of rebirth or not. It was not his place to judge.

"Get in there," Azrael hissed. "Before I change my mind."

No sooner had the Taliban disappeared through the veil than Azrael teleported to where Elisabeth was getting baptized by fire her first week out of boot camp, patching together soldiers injured chasing Taliban into caves. This mission would go down as one in which there were no Coalition casualties. Because of the Armistice, the real story of how many good men had given their lives chasing a ghost through the elaborate subterranean complex Moloch's agents had been building as a staging area would never be told.

Perhaps he should have stayed on the primate planet?

Chapter 31

O death, where is thy sting?
O grave, where is thy victory?
The sting of death is sin;
And the strength of sin is the law.

1 Corinthians 15:55-56

Earth - AD March, 2002
Paktia PRT, Gardez, Afghanistan

A low shudder vibrated the flimsy tent as a slow-flying AC-130U "Spooky" flew overhead. Bottles and vials tossed onto makeshift carts rattled as the converted C-130 Hercules turned gunship moved towards the Shahi-Kot Valley where the U.S. 10th Mountain Division and Australian Special Air Service Regiment were pinned down in the 'kill box.' Or as the heavy casualties coming into the triage tent from the I-87 who'd been pinned down earlier called the long, narrow valley surrounded by Taliban and Al Quaida, "Hell's Halfpipe."

"Clamp!" Elisabeth shouted over the din, pressing down on the brachial artery spurting blood out from underneath the arm of the Afghan National Army soldier. Grabbing one from the translator, who wasn't even a nurse, Elisabeth pressed into the bullet wound and fished for pieces of the severed artery.

The man moaned something unintelligible to Elisabeth, whose Pashto after less than four months in Afghanistan was limited to 'my name is Elisabeth' and 'you're going to be okay.' She skipped the second sentence. Such reassurances were not appropriate under the circumstances.

"He said he wants a male doctor," Kadima said in English that would have been perfect except for a light accent that was neither Canadian nor Pashto. "He does not wish to die at the hands of a woman."

"Tell him too bad," Elisabeth snapped, grabbing some gauze to mop up blood on the soldiers arm. "It's me ... or my black friend whenever he decides to make his next appearance."

Kadima opened her mouth, and then shut it again. No doubt she had no idea who Elisabeth referred to. While Elisabeth refused to bow to the traditions of the country, flaunting her blonde hair, Kadima demurely wore the long sleeves and khimar expected of a Muslim woman over her Canadian uniform. Elisabeth hadn't worked with Kadima long enough to know if she even *was* Muslim, or simply took her role as translator seriously.

Kadima paraphrased something to the soldier that Elisabeth was certain was not an exact translation. The soldier closed his eyes, his expression grim, and nodded affirmation. Whatever the translator had told him, the soldier understood the not-even-yet-a-full-fledged-nurse jamming a needle full of a general anesthetic into his arm was all he would get.

Off in the distance, the AC-130U Spooky could be heard circling the valley where the 10th Mountain Division was pinned down. Unlike the faster, more powerful F-18 and F-16 jets, once darkness fell, the modified cargo plane with its four turboprops could fly in circles and repeatedly hit the same position without dropping out of the sky, giving them a chance to airlift wounded troops out of the kill box.

"I don't suppose it's too much to ask to have a *real* doctor come over and help?" Elisabeth muttered aloud, glancing up to where the trauma team frantically worked to save the lives of two U.S. soldiers from the I-87. She glanced down at the Afghan soldier who'd broken out in a cold sweat. Shock. He'd lost a lot of blood.

"I could go ask them for you?" Kadima offered. When she was nervous, her accent became heavier. Like the USA, Canada was a nation of immigrants. Elisabeth couldn't quite place where Kadima was originally from. Not Afghanistan.

"Don't bother," Elisabeth didn't bother to make eye contact. "I was 'unofficially' briefed my first day in Afghanistan. Coalition forces get top priority when triaging patients, not the locals. Why do you think they have *me* doing surgery? If we wait for *them* to get around to treating him, he'll be dead!"

"Tell me what you need me to do to help," Kadima said, her voice even and calm. "I'm a translator, not a nurse, but I've received basic medic training. I'm not totally useless."

"Talk to him," Elisabeth chewed her lower lip as she fished in the gunshot wound to figure out where, exactly, this guy's artery had been hit. "Ask him questions. Something to keep him here. Is he married? I don't even know his name!"

Kadima asked a series of questions which Elisabeth understood only a little. His name. His family. What village he was from. Even though Elisabeth couldn't comprehend much of what he said, Kadima needed to ask the same question several times to get a coherent answer, another sign of shock.

"His name is Mahboobullah," Kadima said. "He's from Herat. He has a wife and three daughters."

"Mahboobullah," Elisabeth made eye contact with the dark-skinned man. "I'll do my best to make sure you get back to your family. Okay?"

Kadima translated. Mahboobullah muttered his assent. The look he gave her now was not one of contempt, but a frightened man who simply wished to live.

"He understands," Kadima said. "I told him you are a great doctor in your country. I told him you are his best chance to save his life."

"I'm not a doctor," Elisabeth hissed, no longer looking at either of them as she fished back into the wound, searching for the severed artery so she had a prayer of stitching it back together. "Heck ... I won't even officially be licensed as a nurse until I take my exam."

"This is a war zone in a third-world country," Kadima said softly. "You are the closest thing to a real western doctor he's ever seen. Even licensed doctors from his own country don't match your training. It does no harm to let him believe you have a chance of saving his life."

The bloody artery finally came into view. "Got it! Kadima ... this thing is too fine to suture. Could you please thread those needles for me?"

"Right away!" Kadima moved to a tray with various bloody medical implements scattered on it to find the requested items.

The Afghan soldier slid into unconsciousness. Elisabeth pressed a bloodied, gloved hand upon the base of his neck and noted the presence of an erratic, weak pulse. Still alive. She heard exclamations from the adjacent gurney as the trauma surgeon pieced the American soldier back together. All around her, other nurses were doing as she was doing, trying to keep the lower-priority wounded alive until the real doctors were free to attend to them.

Elisabeth knew a thing or two about being dead last on other people's priority lists. Ever since the day she'd gotten here, it had struck Elisabeth how stoic and accepting of being on the shit end of the stick the people of Afghanistan were.

"Somebody screwed the pooch on this mission," Elisabeth grabbed a needle and began to stitch the artery she had pulled towards the surface back together. "And I thought it couldn't get any worse than the clusterfuck at Tora Bora!"

"I thought there were only supposed to be 200 Taliban in that valley?" Kadima asked. "We're way undermanned for the casualties we're getting."

"They now estimate 1,000 well-trained Al Quaida insurgents armed with mortars and RPG's," Elisabeth replied. "And they're not running away as expected. They're dug in and are fighting."

"Hell's Halfpipe," Kadima said. "Fitting name for a long, skinny valley surrounded by mountains with guns pointed at you. Somebody's going to catch hell for dropping the I-87th right into the kill box."

"Sponge?" Elisabeth nodded at the table with the bloody surgical sponges. Nurse ... or no nurse ... Kadima was all she had. She was more competent than some of the other nurses who wrung their hands in dismay, one sobbing as she pulled a sheet over the head of an Afghan soldier. Kadima dabbed the place Elisabeth stitched so she could see what she was doing.

If Kadima thought *this* was bad, she should have been at Tora Bora. Elisabeth's first week on the job straight out of boot camp and they dropped her into the middle of *that* mess. The one that would go down in infamy as the mission that let Osama Bin Laden get away!

"It appears the bleeding is slowing down," Kadima said as she dabbed. "That's a relief."

"No ... it's not," Elisabeth said. "I'm nowhere near done. Exsanguination. He's not bleeding because he's nearly bled out. Any minute now, his heart will stop because he doesn't have enough blood left in his body to pump. Pulse?"

"Oh," Kadima said softly, feeling his neck. "I see."

To her credit, Kadima didn't even pause as she dabbed at the now-trickle of blood as Elisabeth worked. Stitch-by-stitch, Elisabeth sewed the severed brachial artery back together and shoved it back into his arm, stitching the muscle and skin above and then packing it with gauze. If he lived, it would be ugly as hell and limit the mobility in his arm, a lifelong reminder that a greenhorn had patched his arm back together and not a real doctor.

"C'mon, Mahboobullah," Elisabeth crooned as she finished looking over his less life-threatening, but still serious injuries. "Stay with me here, buddy. Okay? Got to get you back to that wife and three daughters."

Mahboobullah didn't answer. He'd been unconscious for quite some time. There was no spare heart monitor available to read how he was doing, but Elisabeth could tell by the bluish cast to his lips and chalk-white skin, despite the weak, erratic heartbeat, that Mahboobullah's chances of survival were slim.

Elisabeth wasn't in the mood to lose any more patients today. She'd lost one a few hours ago, an Afghan with his guts blown open with no chance whatsoever of surviving even if the trauma surgeon got to him. Elisabeth had gotten the unpleasant task of marking a black 'X' on his forehead and then worked on him anyway, terror in his eyes as he had slowly slipped from this world.

Why the hell couldn't her black man have showed up to kill that one? A quick, painless death like he'd given to Nancy would have been a mercy! Probably too busy... God only knew how many men were out there dying right this moment? Theirs. Ours. The low rumble of a bat-winged B-1 bomber flying overhead to drop its payload into the mountains reminded her of just how many more were likely to die before Operation Anaconda was done.

Elisabeth glanced up. The AC-130U Spooky could still be heard blasting shot after shot at wherever the Taliban had dug into where *they* shot, in turn, at the 10th Mountain Division. The other patients were paired off with nurses or, in two instances, a doctor. There was no one else at the door. For now... She could stay with her patient a few more minutes.

"Maybe you should go help one of them?" Elisabeth suggested. She checked the patient's dog-tags and hooked up an IV with a pint of O-positive blood, nodding towards where two other student nurses were being yelled at by a wounded Afghani soldier for lord-only-knows-what. Probably for being female. Stupid misogynistic notions! "This guy's out cold."

"Yes," Kadima excused herself. She gave Elisabeth a grim smile which did not go all the way to her eyes and headed over to assist the others.

"Stay with me," Elisabeth wrapped her hand around Mahboobullah's. "You got that wife and kids to think of. Trust me. You don't want to leave them behind. I know a thing or two about being left behind."

She was the last person he'd wanted to have work on him, a woman in a country where females were chattel and men were gods, but at least he'd accepted her after her translator had made it clear he didn't have another option. Unlike the idiot three gurneys down who the efficient Kadima was trying to calm down. Elisabeth hummed the old German prayer Oma had taught her to make skinned knees feel better and chase away the monster-under-the-bed.

> Lord, Thy death and passion give
> Strength and comfort in my need.
> Ev'ry hour while here I live,
> On Thy love my soul shall feed.
> Thou didst death for me endure,
> And I shun all thoughts impure;
> Thinking on Thy bitter pains,
> Hushed in prayer my heart remains.[2]

The chop-chop-chop of Chinook helicopters rattled the tent as they flew overhead towards the Shahi-Koht Valley to extract the wounded. Her time

---

[2] *Oh Liebe Miener Liebe,* by Johann Heerman (1644)

with this patient was short. Within 20 minutes the trauma unit would be flooded with more wounded. She was exhausted. Protocol said she should take these few moments and get some rest. Just a catnap. God only knew when she'd get a chance to take another one? But this guy hovered betwixt and between. If she left him, he'd slip into that dark night and be gone. She'd just put in too goddamned much work stitching the guy back together to let that happen.

The minutes ticked by, her hand in his. Slowly, the blood dripped into his body, replenishing some of what he'd lost. Three gurneys down, Kadima got the situation under control with the recalcitrant Afghani soldier, coaxing him to submit to examination by two female nurses. The guy must not be that badly wounded or he'd have buckled like Mahboobullah had. They all made a big show of being big, powerful Tarzans. Right up until the point they had a boo-boo too big for Cheetah to make go away, and then they all wanted Jane to come fix it for them.

Tired. So tired. All she wanted to do was sleep…

The hair stood up on the back of her neck. HE was here.

"Malak al-Maut," Mahboobullah muttered fitfully, his hand weakly tightening on hers. "Malak al-Maut."

"Tell him no," Elisabeth bent down to her patient's ear. "Your artery has been repaired. Your blood is being replenished. You have a chance to live if your will is strong enough. Think of your daughters. What will happen to them if you leave them?"

"Malak al-Maut," Mahboobullah murmured, and then uttered a string of words which Elisabeth understood only a little. His daughters. He was worried about the same thing she was. A widow with three daughters in a country where females were viewed as burdens had dim prospects.

Elisabeth turned to where she sensed HE stood. He never spoke or showed himself, but ever since he'd reappeared after a long absence, he visited her at least twice a day. Sometimes patients would tell her they spoke to him. He appeared intrigued she could defeat him. She fought hardest to save her patient's lives when he did come, willing her own life-force into their bodies to save them, if such a thing was even possible.

"Why weren't you here earlier today when you could have done some good?" Elisabeth accused, exhaustion lacing her voice. "This guy has a chance. Please. Can't you just leave him alone?"

"Malak al-Maut?" Kadima came up beside her, gesturing to her head, her heart and her lips as she looked at the exact same spot Elisabeth looked at. "You honor us with your presence."

"You can see him?"

"I can feel him," Kadima said, unafraid. "The same as you. Although once he let me see him. We are old friends, he and I."

"You can't have him!" Elisabeth stepped between invisible black man and her patient, arms crossed in defiance. "I won't let you. He is mine!"

The trauma doctors shot curious glances in her direction from where they were finishing up the American soldier, apparently still alive. Elisabeth ignored them. Let them think she was nuts! Less than four months in the field and already her 'save' rate of the hopeless cases was four times that of the trauma surgeons.

Mahboobullah muttered behind her. Kadima rushed to his side and spoke back and forth to him. She glanced at Elisabeth, as though not sure of what the Afghani soldier was telling her, and then in the direction they knew the black man stood.

"Mahboobullah said the Angel of Death is not here for him," Kadima said, her expression puzzled. "He's here for you. Are you unwell?"

"No," Elisabeth said curtly. "He's been visiting me ever since my parents died when I was nine. He took them from me. And then he took my foster mother, too. He is the bane of my existence."

"Elisabeth," Kadima's expression was confused. "Azrael is one of the holiest archangels in Islam. He does not cause death unless you are evil. He helps the souls of the worthy depart the body when it is time to leave and safeguards them until they get to paradise. He once saved my life."

"I hate him," Elisabeth spat. "He's taken everyone I've ever loved!"

Mahboobullah muttered some more, and stirred. Kadima spoke to him and then translated.

"Mahboobullah is dangerously close to losing his grip on his body, Elisabeth," Kadima coaxed. "That's why he can see him. Please ... Azrael told him you could help him hang onto his mortal shell so he can return to his wife and daughters. For some reason, Malak al-Maut thinks you have the power to defeat him. He encourages you to do so now."

The light, clean scent of an ocean breeze lifted the cloying stench of blood and fear that gripped the tent like a fist and eased her breathing. Whenever he was close, the air felt as though a thunderstorm had scrubbed the world clean. His scent. A buzz of electricity gave her goose bumps, but not in an unpleasant way. It felt like standing next to the Tesla coil at the Chicago Museum of Science and Industry.

He was close. So close that if she reached out, she was certain she could touch him. Memory of the last time she had touched him surfaced from deep within her memories. When she had touched him before, it had felt as though she were being reunited with someone she'd waited to see for a very long time. Her hand moved of its own volition towards where he stood.

"Elisabeth!" Katima shrieked, grabbing her hand and pulling it away just as Elisabeth felt him move back. "Don't touch him! His touch is death!"

"But I touched him once before?" Elisabeth reached up. Her hand met with … nothing. He'd moved back. In fact, she could tell he was no longer in the room. The stench of sweat and blood rose up to suffocate her once more. He was gone.

For some reason, it felt like loss…

"You're going to be okay," Kadima touched Mahboobullah's forehead. "Malak al-Maut has found you worthy to live."

The thunder of Chinook helicopters carrying their wounded pounded through the air as they approached the base.

"We've got more incoming wounded!!!" an airman stuck his head inside the tent. "Some crazy Aussie signalman crawled in under fire and dragged their sorry asses into a creek bed to patch 'em back together! He's gonna get a medal for sure for this one!"

"Get him out of here!" Elisabeth gestured for a couple of assistants who had come in to move out the previous rotation of wounded into the recovery tent to make room for the new wave. "Kadima … can you go with Mahboobullah and stay with him a little while? I don't think I'm going to need a translator for this next shipment."

"Sure," Kadima stepped aside so the corpsmen could move the patient onto a litter and carry him out of the tight confines of the tent.

Elisabeth tossed bloody sponges and medical implements into the trash and hastily dumped alcohol onto everything else to sterilize it as best she could. They'd gone through their 'sterile' instruments two shipments ago and were now sterilizing things on the fly. Not an ideal situation. One of the corpsmen stripped the bloody gurney and tucked in a clean sheet. At least they had enough of those. For now.

"Elisabeth?" Kadima made eye contact just before she disappeared. "We need to talk. Later. He's not evil."

"Mahboobullah?" Elisabeth deliberately pretended not to understand who she was talking about.

"Malak al-Maut," Kadima said. "The Angel of Death. He told Mahboobullah he would spare him because you asked him to. He said you are his friend."

Elisabeth stood there stupidly as though waiting to catch flies. Any further questions were cut off as Kadima was shoved to one side by a fresh shipment of wounded. American wounded. Lots of them.

They were seriously understaffed. It was triage time. Shoving her questions out of her mind, Elisabeth buckled down to the task they had trained her to do. Sort the seriously wounded, who needed attention right away; from the less seriously wounded, who could wait; from the hopeless, who would receive no treatment at all except for comfort as they died.

Marking a big black 'X' on the forehead of a tall, skinny kid who had even less chance of surviving than the last patient, Elisabeth had to wonder just who was the angel of death now?

As technically a still-student nurse, Elisabeth's only real job was to sort, assist, and give comfort to the hopeless...

"Go to hell," Elisabeth muttered, glancing at the direction she had last sensed HIM before he'd departed. Gesturing for one of the corpsmen to assist, she heaved the lost cause onto her makeshift operating table and shoved a fresh sponge into the corpsmen's hands. Her version of 'giving comfort to the hopeless' saved lives.

The corpsman took one look at the side of the kids head and retched, nearly blowing his supper upon the floor.

"Jackson," Elisabeth snapped, reading the name off the corpsman's name badge to distract him. "What's this kid's name?"

"Basile!" The corpsman read the name off the dog tags and carefully averted his eyes to not look up to the kids grey brain tissue hanging out behind his missing ear. "Jimmy Basile."

"Listen up, Jimmy," Elisabeth reached into the kid's shattered skull and picked out pieces of shrapnel from his brain. "I already lost one kid today and I ain't in the mood to lose no more. So you're just going to have to do as I tell you and not go with that black man when he comes to take your hand or I'm going to get really pissed off. You got that, soldier?"

Her face grim, Elisabeth began to piece the wounded soldier back together.

Chapter 32

The difficulty, my friends, is not in avoiding death,
But in avoiding unrighteousness;
For that runs faster than death.

Socrates

Earth - AD March, 2002
Afghanistan

"So, tell me everything you know about our visitor," Elisabeth asked. She wrapped her hand around a cup of coffee strong enough to melt the rust off of a Humvee.

"Malak al-Maut?" Kadima grimaced as she held her lower back. "It's kind of personal."

Elisabeth wasn't in the mood to hear excuses. For three days the two had worked together in a fog. Elisabeth had done the best she could to save lives, feeling let down when she'd failed, and each of those days, usually just before a new shipment of incoming wounded arrived, HE paid her a visit.

The brain-shot eighteen year old had somehow managed to survive...

Another Afghani soldier who had come yesterday had not. Despite Elisabeth's best efforts, when Malak al-Maut had taken the poor man, even Elisabeth had been forced to admit it was for the best. The lower half of the man's body had been blown off by an RPG. Thank god her 'friend' had come before the man regained consciousness. HE had taken him the moment Kadima convinced her to step aside.

"I'm Bosnian," Kadima whispered. "Muslim Bosnian. I survived the Serbian genocide."

"Oh." Elisabeth realized she was intruding upon something deeply personal. She'd been a little girl at the time, but even *she* had heard what had been done to female Muslim survivors when they covered the class in World History.

"Malak al-Maut came for the man who ... hurt ... me," Kadima hedged. "He judged him evil and took his soul straight to hell."

"At least I'm glad he serves some purpose other than ripping apart families," Elisabeth said caustically.

"He didn't *have* to come back for me," Kadima said, a hint of anger in her eyes as she defended him. "But he did! He told me a war crimes commission would be convened and asked me to testify so the world would intervene. Then he reaped the souls of the other evildoers so we could escape. Twenty-eight of us got away because of him."

"Oh," Elisabeth said, somewhat mollified. This was different than how she was used to thinking of him. She'd suspected he was an angel, perhaps even a so-called death angel, but the … thing … she'd seen him turn into after he'd stepped between her and the bullet defied explanation.

"Sometimes he checks in on me," Kadima said. "Especially since I joined the Patricia's to be near my husband. Some of the people we've treated have been so badly wounded that it's a blessing when he takes them."

The Princess Patricia's were a light infantry division of the Canadian army. They specialized in missions where enemies needed to be cleared out of mountainous terrain.

"I'm finding that out," Elisabeth said, feeling somewhat ashamed. "It still doesn't change what he did to my parents."

"How did your parents die?" Kadima asked.

"Drunk driver," Elisabeth stated as though she were discussing statistics. "Ran a red light. Killed my parents, my brother, and both of my grandparents. They were all I had in the world. And then eight years later he took my foster-mother away from me, too."

"What happened to her?" Kadima asked.

"Drive by shooting," Elisabeth said. "Chicago. Gangs. Nancy was still alive when he came for her. She told me she wanted to go with him, and then he took her even though I begged her not to go."

"Azrael didn't kill any of those people," Kadima said softly. "His touch is a mercy to those he takes. It is said he seeks to alleviate the suffering of ten good men for every evildoer he drags to hell."

"Did he have to take Nancy?" Elisabeth shouted, and then realized the entire mess tent had heard her. She lowered her voice to an angry hiss. "She was still alive when she took his hand. They could have saved her!"

"Apparently not," Kadima said. "Or he would not have taken her. He refused to take *me*. He forced me to stay even though I pleaded with him to take me to paradise after … after …" Tears welled in her eyes.

"You don't have to say it," Elisabeth realized she was acting like an ass. She squeezed Kadima's hand and deflected the conversation into a less painful topic. "So … how did you end up in Canada?"

"The U.N. Peacekeepers who found us happened to be Canadian," Kadima got her emotions under control. "Harold was a real gentleman. Made sure we all got to safety. Kept checking up on us even after it was no longer his concern. He even came to hear us testify before the U.N. War Crimes Commission."

"He liked you?" Elisabeth said.

"I think so," Kadima said. "But he wasn't the only Canadian who came back to make sure we stayed okay. Just the one I eventually fell in love with after mourning my first husband."

"Weren't you offered asylum in the U.S. after you testified?"

"Yes," Kadima said. "But even before September 11th, Canada was a much more welcoming place than the United States. There's a decent-sized Muslim community in Edmonton. Several of us relocated there."

"My countrymen don't think too highly of people from this part of the world," Elisabeth nodded agreement. "They treated the Chief Medical Director where I went to nursing school like crap even before September 11th. But you don't look Muslim. You're almost as fair-skinned as I am."

"Eastern European Muslims look like anyone else," Kadima said with a shrug. "I've gotten less strict since I moved to Alberta, but I still wear long sleeves and cover my head." She pointed to the simple triangular kerchief she used to tie back her hair when off-duty.

"Bosnia was … what?" Elisabeth asked. "Ten years ago? Your accent is barely perceptible. How'd you learn English so fast?"

"Hard work and motivation," Kadima clasped both hands around her mug and stared into it. "The U.N. communicates to each other in English. Harold felt my testimony would be better received if I spoke English, so he taught me English."

"It sounds like he was quite taken with you?"

"He taught all of us," Kadima said. "It wasn't like I had anything better to do at the time. It took nearly a year for the international community to get off their collective rear ends and do something. By the time they did, there was no home left for any of us to go back to."

"Not having a home is something I understand," Elisabeth was remorseful for her grouchy attitude earlier. "I'm really sorry."

"I'm okay now," Kadima said. "Harold adopted my two daughters and has encouraged them to be respectful of Muslim ways, not just his own Christian ones. He has a grown son from a first marriage and my daughters are now grown. We make it work. I joined the Patricia's after the last one headed off to college so we wouldn't spend any more long deployments apart. I miss him when he's gone."

"You should have them train you to be a nurse," Elisabeth said. "You're damned good at it."

"Then I'd be assigned to a different unit than my husband," Kadima said. "As it is my being stationed with light infantry is highly irregular. Technically I'm their Muslim chaplain, translator and also a medic. Harold's got enough rank that he was able to pull some strings once I learned Pashto. They're desperate for translators."

"Understatement of the year," Elisabeth said. "Having a chaplain in your unit who's friendly with the Angel of Death?" It was a rare attempt on her part at humor.

"Harold says he'll take every advantage he can get," Kadima said. "I've told him about my angel friend. He humors me, but I don't think he really believes me."

Elisabeth stared down at the congealing coffee-mate floating in the top of her cup of coffee. Across the room, she heard somebody call her name. Coffee break was over.

"At least I'm not the only nutcase walking around talking to invisible angels." Elisabeth downed the rest of her cup in a single gulp. "Until he stopped a bullet from hitting me the day Nancy died, the counselors all had me convinced I was nuts. Especially when I told them he watched me."

"He watches me, too," Kadima said. She gave Elisabeth a smile. "Though never as much as he watches you. You must be very interesting if he checks in on you every day."

"That's me," Elisabeth said with a shrug. "A rat in a maze."

"The last time someone took that much of an interest in me," Kadima said. "They asked me to marry them. Harold. He's my angel."

"Not likely!" Elisabeth headed towards the trauma surgeon gesturing for her to come. "But it was good talking to you. Can't keep the doctor-gods waiting."

Elisabeth made the Muslim gesture of hands to forehead, lips and heart that Kadima always used to give thanks to Allah towards the pompous prick of a trauma surgeon who'd been the bane of both their existence this entire operation.

Kadima snorted coffee through her nose at Elisabeth's blatant irreverence towards the doctor who was also a superior officer. Elisabeth was glad Kadima could appreciate the humor without getting upset.

The doctor … not so much.

Chapter 33

The guards that went around the city found me,
They smote me, they wounded me;
The keepers of the walls took away my veil from me.
Song of Solomon, 5:7

Earth - AD December 24, 2002
Lashkar Gah, Helmand Province, Afghanistan

"Joy to the world," the soldiers sang at the top of their lungs in the mess tent where they had all gathered for some Christmas Eve cheer. "The Lord is come!"

"Elisabeth!!!" Kadima called over the din, her words inaudible above the cacophony but her lips clearly forming the words as she waved. "Come!!!"

Kadima was Muslim, but she appeared to enjoy the Christmas holiday as much as anyone else on the base. Harold had his wife firmly pinned against his side, one bearish arm wrapped around her shoulders.

"No..." Elisabeth shook her head as she knew there was no way Kadima would hear her above the ruckus. She used her hand to point towards herself and then the door of the mess tent. "I'm going outside."

"What?" Kadima shouted.

"Outside," Elisabeth yelled. "I'm going outside for a walk." To accentuate her words, Elisabeth made a motion with her fingers as though she were walking.

"Okay!" Kadima shouted. Harold held what appeared to be a sprig of dried mistletoe, although it was more likely a weed, over his wife's head and pulled her in for a kiss. The Princess Patricia's cheered and egged them on.

Elisabeth gave a false smile and worked her way out the door, avoiding eye contact and pretending she had someplace important to be. The last thing she wanted was to be forced to participate in the Christmas revelries. She did not wish to explain she was a Grinch because her entire family had been taken from her one Christmas Eve, and then her foster mother two weeks before another.

Elisabeth passed a contingent of British troops just returned from a mission rifling through the lucrative poppy fields irrigated by a dam funded by the United States during the 1950's. Warlords! Elisabeth didn't know which was worse. Ousting the Taliban? Or dealing with the warlords who were often the only allies the Coalition had? Lashkar Gar would be a desert town if it weren't for the Helmand River and the dam.

The city had been laid out by United States engineers in an orderly fashion like the suburbs of Los Angeles in the 1950's, with wide tree-lined streets and modern concrete houses. The Soviet invasion had ended all that. Most trees had been cut down and walls built around the houses to shield the local inhabitants from stray bullets. Now … it was just another hotspot up for grabs in the war.

"You're not s'posed to go outside the fence without an escort, Second-Lieutenant Kaiser," the British serviceman chastised her with a Cockney accent so thick it nearly bludgeoned her ears. "Who's gonna patch us all up if ye get yerself shot?"

"I'm just going down to the river, Lance-Corporal Leatherby," Elisabeth grabbed the black headscarf Kadima had finally strong-armed her into using and wrapped it around her head in a makeshift hijab. "I promise I'll be careful."

As a member of the nursing corps, she'd been promoted to the lowest level of commissioned officer the day she'd passed her nursing exam. Six months ahead of schedule! That meant she outranked most of the enlisted soldiers, something she used to feed her need for privacy. Leatherby would not stop her from going.

"Yes, Ma'am," Leatherby gave her a salute and a grin. "Merry Christmas, Ma'am." As a frequent guard at this gate, Leatherby was used to her peculiar comings and goings.

"You too, Leatherby," Elisabeth forced herself to return the smile she did not feel. She carried her grandfather's cane, but nine weeks of boot camp had strengthened her body, and her resolve, in a way that years of nonstop physical therapy never had. The drill sergeant had groused about the lax standards the military had adopted in order to recruit personnel into an active war, but towards the end, even *he* had been forced to acknowledge her will to succeed forced her fragile body to toe the mark.

Once Elisabeth set her mind to something, it was as good as done…

She tugged her service coat close to guard against the cold and made her way out past the harsh spot lights and layers of barbed wire to the pockmarked remnant of a paved road. Once out of sight she granted her leg the concession of leaning on Opa's cane, wood tapping lightly against rocky ground like a third footstep. Cautiously moving through the shadows, she wandered through abandoned neighborhoods to the river which provided a lifeline for the surrounding area.

Dry. Absent irrigation, Afghanistan more closely resembled the cold, lunar landscape which stared down at her from the waning moon than anyplace people might wish to live. In a bizarre way, both the terrain and its people, excepting the crazy ones, of course, had grown on her. Finding excuses to slip the confines of the base and mingle with the locals, binding wounds, administering vaccines, even delivering twin calves, gave her life meaning. The people of this town had come to know her and treated her with respect. Elisabeth liked it here.

She sat down on a rock, alone with her thoughts. Joining the Army had enabled her to become a registered nurse in record-breaking time and provided something she'd sorely missed in her life. If there was one thing the military fostered, it was a sense of family. Or as the C.O. called it, 'battle buddies.' In the field, you needed to depend on the soldier next to you to watch your back.

So deep was she in her thoughts that she didn't hear the rustle from the brush behind her.

"You move," the barrel of a rifle pressed between her shoulder blades. "We kill you."

Elisabeth exploded into action the way she'd been taught in basic training, swinging her elbows and the cane up behind her as she twisted around and jarred the barrel from her back milliseconds before the Taliban fired.

"Enemy insurgents!!!" Elisabeth screamed at the top of her lungs. She finished spinning the rest of the way around to slug the insurgent in the face, hoping a patrol was within earshot, and then landed the cane solidly on the insurgent's head. Three more dove at her as she reached for the service pistol clasped to her hip. The only reason she was still alive was because they hadn't expected her to be carrying a cane.

"Infidel whore," one of the Taliban snarled. He used his weight advantage to disarm her before she could pull her gun and threw her to the ground. "We teach American scum what happens when they bring their whores with them."

Two of the Taliban pinned her so she kneeled facing the AK-47 aimed directly between her eyes. The two, plus the third, picked up round river rocks from the shore while the fourth kept the gun aimed at her head.

"Go to hell!" Elisabeth hissed, expecting to be shot.

A fist-sized rock hit her off the side of the head.

"Umph!" she grunted, knocked to one side as she saw stars.

A second rock hit her in the chest.

"Help!!!" she screamed, trying to lurch to her feet so she could run away.

"This what happen to woman who wander streets at night without male escort," the Taliban with the gun sneered, kicking her behind the knee she used to get to her feet and picked up his own rock to hit her squarely in the chest. "Punishment for adultery is stoning to death!"

Elisabeth raised her arms to protect her head as a stone slammed into her jaw. The moon appeared double. What on Earth had ever convinced her that just because she wandered amongst these people during the daytime helping them, that they would treat her with the same compassion with which she treated them?

"Help?" She crawled towards the water and realized she wouldn't make it as she began to lose consciousness. No patrol heard her screams. Blood spurted from her mouth and something ejected from one side as she tried to plead for her life. A tooth?

"Ahhhh!!!" the Taliban leader screamed.

The others screamed, too. Anger?

Silence.

The scent of the river filled her nose as she lost the battle to remain conscious and keep her head above the shallow water.

"Please, Elisabeth. You must get back to the shore. I cannot help you."

Water. Freezing from the December temperatures. She tried to move and slipped on the rocks. So easy to just let go. To let the gentle whisper of the river carry her away, carrying her pain with it.

"Elisabeth!" the voice said again, his tone urgent. "Please! I won't take you unless I have no choice. But I cannot help you! You must help yourself!"

The voice was familiar. Compelling. Salt. Blood. Elisabeth's head spun with the sharp pain of bone grinding bone as she tried to move her mouth to answer. Her hands moved helplessly on the rocks, unable to push herself up to her hands and knees to crawl out of the river. She was drowning in less than a foot of water. Of all the stupid, asinine ways to die!

"Please, Elisabeth!" A frantic edge belied the speakers panic. "I'll fetch help, but you'll drown before they get here. Pull yourself closer to the shore."

"Help … me," Elisabeth whispered, reaching one hand towards the voice.

"I can't," the voice was filled with remorse. "If I touch you, you will die. You must do this thing yourself because I cannot do it for you."

She knew who spoke to her now. The invisible 'friend' Kadima had spent the past nine months trying to convince her was not evil. The black man who always allowed her to fall, stepping back as she drew near. Always watching. Was he here now to watch her flounder in the river and die? Taking notes in that great book he scribbled in the few times she'd caught a glimpse of him out of the corner of her eye? Anger motivated her to force her numb limbs to move towards the edge of the river. Anger at him!

"Good!" he urged. "Keep going! You can do it!"

His voice sounded very far away, as though he were speaking under water. The moon faded as she collapsed, face-down on the rocks.

"Go to hell," she muttered, moving her head just enough so a rock kept her nose was out of the crevasse where water still trickled.

"I'll go get help," the black man said. "Just hang on … okay? I'll be right back. I promise."

The world went black.

Voices. Thick Cockney accents and shouting. Hands picked her up and put her on a litter.

"We've got you, Elisabeth," Kadima took her hand. "Our friend told me where to find you."

Elisabeth tried to move her mouth. Pain stabbed through her jaw. It felt as though one of her teeth had been knocked out.

"They're all dead!" a thick British accent said. "Not a mark on them. Who is this gal? Special forces or something?"

"Just a nurse," a familiar voice said, Harold, Kadima's husband. "Let's get her back to the base."

"I told her not to wander out here alone," another familiar voice said. Corporal Leatherby?

"She's been spending a lot of time amongst the locals," Kadima squeezed her hand. "Trying to win their support. I warned her the Taliban would target anyone who undermined their grip on the local population, but she didn't believe me."

"She's not the first one who got taken in and screwed," Harold said. "Okay, boys! Patricia's! Get off your asses and help the Brit-boys get our star trauma nurse back to the infirmary. She's all banged up, but I think she's going to be okay!"

"Hey … Colonel … Sir!" one of the Brit-boys called to Kadima's husband. "All four of these insurgents have an ace of spades tucked into their shirt pockets!"

"That's his calling card, boys," Harold said glibly. "Just be glad it wasn't *you* he came for today."

Several of the men carrying Elisabeth laughed nervously.

"Kadima's friend," one said, his Canadian accent sounding more akin to Midwestern-America than the thick Cockney accent the British troops had, marking him as one of the Patricia's. "I saw him once. One second this guy with a gun to my head starts ranting in some strange language I never heard before. The next there's this flash of darkness and the guy just drops dead to the ground. Not a mark on him."

"Really?" another soldier said with a thick British accent. "I thought that was just a ghost story the Patricia's like to tell to spook the newbies?"

"Do they look like ghost stories to you?" Corporal Leatherby asked. "Four of them. No weapons. No blood. Not a mark on them except for his calling card. Shit! Talk about death from above!"

"I seen him once, too," another Canadian accent said. "Scariest motherfucker I ever saw. Real tall and thin. Got a black cape with a hood just like the Ghost of Christmas Future in that Christmas Carol movie. The one with George C. Scott. Only I didn't see no grim reaper scythe or nothing. Just him reach out and touch a guy and he drops dead."

"You're fucking with us!" the British-accent guy laughed nervously. "Patricia's! You guys have been hanging around with the Americans too long!"

Elisabeth slid the rest of the way into unconsciousness. Had he really finally spoken to her?

Chapter 34

I am black, but comely, O ye daughters of Jerusalem …
Look not upon me, because I am black,
Because the sun hath looked upon me.

Song of Solomon, 1:5-6

Earth - AD December 24, 2002
Lashkar Gah, Helmand Province, Afghanistan

Azrael hovered nervously in the corner, his cloak wrapped tightly so no one would bump into him. He'd been busy helping the Archangels track down Agent-possessed Al Qaida leaders in a network of caves when he'd sensed her cry for help. He wasn't sure *why* he'd sensed her need, but he had. Thank the goddess he'd been able to break away!

He almost hadn't made it in time…

Kadima tucked a blanket around Elisabeth's neck.

"I'll sit with her a while if you don't mind," Kadima said to the other nurse, Lucy. "You go get some eggnog and see if you can't call home before they use up all the minutes on those calling cards. I'll come get you if she needs anything."

"Thanks," nurse Lucy said. "She's damned lucky. We warned her the locals will thank you for fixing their kids broken leg one minute and turn you over to the Taliban the next, but it was like talking to a wall. You can help them, but you can never, ever trust them."

"We've all been burned," Kadima said. "Now … she'll listen."

"I sure hope so," Lucy said. "For a newbie straight out of nurse training, she's the closest thing we've got to a third doctor on this unit. She's saved more lives than *they* have."

"She spent a lot of time in rehab and her foster mother was a nurse," Kadima said. "From the time she was nine years old, she's been reading medical journals and volunteering at the hospital. They wanted her to stay in Chicago and continue onto medical school, even offered her a full scholarship, but she turned them down. She wanted to come here."

"Foster mother?" Lucy said. "I had no idea. We all thought, well, she's so aloof. We just assumed she thought she was better than us."

"I think it's more she's afraid to let anyone get too close," Kadima said. "First her entire family dies. And then her foster mother dies, too. Cut her a little slack. Okay?"

"Yeah," Lucy said. "I will. Nobody ever said anything to me."

"Go get some eggnog," Kadima ordered. "I have it on good authority Private Wallaby has a few nip-bottles of contraband to spike your cup if you're nice to him. Tell Harold I'll be along shortly."

The nurse left. Thankfully the infirmary was empty tonight. Kadima pulled the privacy curtain around Elisabeth's cot and looked him right in the eye, knowing that to make eye contact she needed to look up.

"Malak al-Maut," Kadima gestured to her head, her lips and her heart as a sign of respect. "You can show yourself now. There isn't anybody here to see you who hasn't already seen you before."

Azrael solidified into his preferred form. He had reshaped himself to appear the same height as the other Archangels, so tall that had this been a normal building instead of a tent his wings would have scraped against the ceiling, but he had not made himself burly the way angels were often depicted in the Christian church. If the General was a German shepherd, Azrael preferred to think of himself as looking like a greyhound.

"Her life signs appear to be stable," Azrael moved to the side of her bed, concern etching his face. "I'm glad I was able to get your attention in that crowd. My superiors would have been very upset if I'd been forced to appear in front of an entire regiment of Coalition peacekeepers."

"Thank you for saving her," Kadima said. "You left your calling card?"

"A small act of rebellion on my part." Azrael allowed a hint of humor to light up his face. "The ace of spades was the symbol of my old military unit. There's not a lot to do on long tours of duty, so we played cards."

Azrael moved within a foot of Elisabeth's bed. He listened carefully, inhaling her scent, as he ran his hands six inches above the length of her body to ascertain the strength of her life force.

"I sense no injury that won't heal," Azrael said, relieved. "Her life energy dipped so low at the riverbank I was worried we might lose her, but now it feels even. I never know with this one. She has always clung so tightly to her mortal shell."

"Why do you follow her?"

"The same reason I check in on *you* from time to time," Azrael made eye contact. "I like to make sure you're both okay."

"You're here every single day," Kadima gave him a knowing look. "Sometimes more than once per day. Even when we don't have incoming wounded. It's not me you're here to visit."

205

"Sometimes I'm here to see *you*," Azrael's mouth curved up in a guilty grin. "I visited you even *before* you crossed paths with Elisabeth."

"You should let her see you," Kadima said. "It's not right, letting that poor girl think she's responsible for everyone around her always dying."

"She hates me!" Azrael's expression was troubled. "I watch over her, but she doesn't understand."

"She said she once touched your hand?" Kadima asked. "Is that why you're so intrigued by her?"

The slight tremor of ebony feathers was his only answer. Azrael lifted his right hand and touched his fingers to his thumb, noting the faint tingle of physical sensation, asking himself the same question.

"No mortal has ever survived my touch," Azrael said. "Even the gods fear me. You have no idea what it's like ... being unable to touch the people you care about. I'd ... I'd given up hope of ever feeling the simple sensation of touch again until ... until she touched me and survived."

"You're obviously quite smitten by her."

"I am?" A guilty expression crossed his face. Although he often played poker against the Sata'anic descendants, he'd never been able to actually win. Unlike his Cherubim-trained brethren, every aspect of his body betrayed what he was feeling.

"You should speak to her," Kadima said. "Make her understand. I think it will comfort her to know she has meaning to you."

"She can be volatile when she's angry," Azrael said. "If she strikes me before she understands I have no control over my power, she'll be dead before I warn her not to touch me. Once your soul is severed from your body, that's it. There's no putting the genie back into the bottle."

"She's bedridden," Kadima said. "If she leaps at you, you have time to step away. You can't keep shadowing her like this and never speak. It's ... strange."

"I'm afraid anything I say will just make things worse," Azrael said nervously. "What if she tells me to just ... go away? Completely? I tried that once and I was miserable."

"And so was she," Kadima said. "You are the only constant she's known since her parents died. Whether she wishes to admit it or not, she finds comfort in your visits."

Azrael looked up, surprise showing in his black eyes.

"You just saved her life," Kadima continued. "Try to talk to her. Please? I can tell you want to. You need to let her know you have feelings for her."

"I ..." Azrael stammered. "I'm kind of ... not used to ... um ... I'm a little ... shy?" The combined look of pure longing and fear in his expressive dark eyes and tremor of feathers betrayed what he really meant to say to the perceptive Kadima. He was terrified if he made himself known, Elisabeth would order him to go away for good.

"The last time somebody shadowed me that much," Kadima said. "He ended up asking me to marry him. I'm not an idiot, you know?"

"I will remain corporeal until she wakes up," Azrael said. "If it appears she will hurt herself, I will dissipate again."

"I'll be in the mess tent singing out-of-tune Christmas carols," Kadima said. "Harold and I have a deal. I go with the flow for Christmas, while he doesn't eat bacon, lettuce and tomato sandwiches in front of me when I am fasting for Ramadan.

"Kadima?" Azrael asked, his expression intently curious.

"Yes, Azrael?"

"You had a husband before Harold," Azrael asked. "And yet you married again. I could never understand how humans can have more than one … mate. We're … different."

"Rahim was a good man," Kadima said. "I still miss him. But he is gone and I am still here. I had two daughters who needed a father and Harold wanted to be that father. Harold understands my first husband will always hold a place in my heart."

"What will you do when you are reunited with him?" Azrael asked. "When someday I come for you, you will rejoin Rahim in the place you call paradise."

"I guess we shall all just have to learn to share," Kadima said, a smile lighting up her face. "Harold is divorced, not a widower, so I suppose *he* will have to do the adjusting. I love both of them. Only in different ways."

"I see," Azrael said, really not seeing. The relationships Kadima described with both husbands appeared to be more like the close friendships unmated Angelics shared. Not the intensely bonded relationship between those few lucky enough to find a life-mate.

He was beginning to understand why Lucifer's Fallen had been so quick to abandon the Emperor once they'd discovered humans were capable of forming the Bond of Ki. Rediscovering humans, and then telling hybrids tottering at the brink of extinction they were forbidden to intermarry had been … stupid. The ones who'd chosen to remain behind had done so because separating them from their mates would have killed them.

"What's it like?" Kadima interrupted his thoughts. "Paradise?"

"I don't know." Regret marred his beautiful features. "I'm neither alive nor dead, so I can't cross over. But I can sense the loved ones of those I guide waiting just on the other side to greet them."

"How terrible!" Kadima exclaimed. "To spend your days escorting souls to the gates of heaven and never be allowed entry yourself!"

"It's not that I'm … barred," Azrael said. "You're only barred if you're evil. It's just … it's complicated. Let's just say I can't go there the same reason I can't touch *you*."

Kadima glanced to where Elisabeth was beginning to stir. She was not sedated. Some of what they were talking about was likely filtering in through the fog.

"I'd better go," Kadima said. "It was good talking to you. I wish you'd make yourself visible more often."

"Maybe I will," Azrael said. "I'm not supposed to converse with the ones I watch. But it gets lonely sometimes."

"Kadima?" Elisabeth moaned.

Azrael winced as Elisabeth grimaced in pain.

"Elisabeth," Kadima bent over the bed, taking her hand. "I'm just going to the mess tent for a bite to eat. I'll be back in a little while. Our friend will watch over you while I'm gone. Okay?"

"Mmmm…" Elisabeth grumbled. "Too much talk."

"For nine months you've complained he never talks to you," Kadima said. "And now that he's willing to say hello, you want me to tell him to be quiet?"

"Huh?" Elisabeth's eyes fluttered open.

"He saved your life." Kadima brushed a long strand of blonde hair out of her eyes. "Don't bite his head off. Okay? I'll be back in a little while to make sure you're all right."

Kadima glanced at Azrael nervously shifting his weight and adjusting his wings. Who would believe the most feared angel, Death, was afraid of revealing his feelings for a certain grouchy American nurse?

Kadima nodded farewell and stepped out of the tent.

Elisabeth turned her face towards the opposite curtain of the makeshift room. Away from where he stood.

"Hello?" Azrael vainly attempted to prevent his voice from cracking as he formed the words. He hung back, ready to disappear if being there upset her.

"Why are you here?" Elisabeth grimaced as she adjusted her position and registered the bruises left by rocks the Taliban had thrown at her. "Ouch."

Azrael had a theory. He believed Elisabeth went on the offensive to prevent people from pestering her with questions she didn't wish to answer. Like why she'd taken the foolish risk of being outside the safety of the gate in an active war zone. He would avoid asking that question. Perhaps it would prevent her from ordering him to leave?

So … how did he answer he'd sensed she was in danger and dropped everything without mentioning the fact she'd been alone at the river when he'd found her? Although Archangels could sense when those they were close to were in danger, the ability usually only extended to immediate family, mates, and those who specifically trained together to foster the ability. Immortality alone did not grant omniscience.

"You don't talk much," Elisabeth asked. "Do you?"

"No," Azrael said softly. "I'm not exactly someone people are dying to talk to."

Elisabeth stared at him as though he had two heads and then burst out laughing as she got his joke.

"Dying to talk to?" Elisabeth snorted, and then grimaced in pain as bruised facial muscles protested the sudden movement. "Ouch! Don't make me laugh!"

Azrael allowed a small smile to soften his otherwise harsh features, giving Elisabeth a glimpse of the shy young man he had once been. She smiled. A small, painful little gesture that disappeared as quickly as it had appeared, but it took his breath away.

His nostrils flared, quivering as he inhaled her scent. Her scent was intoxicating. Enticing him, tempting, taunting him with the promise of something he could never have. Forming a relationship when your touch was death created insurmountable logistical problems.

Who would love a creature of the void?

A small, quiet voice in his heart whispered the hope he'd been carrying since the day she'd touched him and resisted his gift. Maybe if he didn't blow it? If her pre-ascended abilities continued to develop and grow? Maybe someday she might be able to touch him and survive?

Maybe, someday, she might grow to love him as much as he was hopelessly in love with her?

"Are you just going to stand there?" Elisabeth asked, her brow furrowed in concentration as she studied her tall, silent savior. "Or will you tell me what you find so fascinating that you keep scribbling about in that notebook of yours?"

"Oh?" Azrael suddenly felt embarrassed. "I ... um ... I hadn't realized you'd seen my ... um ... notes. I ... um ... study things. And draw. I ... um ... I can't use a computer because I ... um ... short it out so I ... um ... write. To keep track of things. I'm a scientist, you know. Before I ... um ... became like ... um ... this."

The last word was spoken as a whisper. 'Like this.' How could he ever explain what 'this' was?

"Why did you kill my parents?" The question was a challenge as her soft expression disappeared and her eerie silver eyes hardened to polished steel.

"I … didn't," Azrael said. "Your parents and grandparents had already left their bodies and found their own way into the Dreamtime … um … paradise … um … heaven when I got to the scene of the car crash."

"What about Franz?" Elisabeth winced as she pushed herself up into a sitting position.

"His mortal shell was too badly damaged to stay," Azrael said. "Not even *you* could have saved him."

Elisabeth stared, hostility in her eyes. Azrael knew the foster care authorities had taken great pains to avoid revealing just how gruesome her families' injuries had been.

"Franz asked me to watch over you until it was time to rejoin your family," Azrael said. "I expected your soul had become lost. I was surprised when I discovered you were still alive, trapped in the car. The police and firefighters had overlooked you."

"That I'd heard," Elisabeth said with a sniffle, tears gathering in the corner of her eyes. "The policewoman who was at the scene recognized my name last year when I was manning the ER while you were … gone. She said the guy who pulled me out of the car insisted a black angel told him there was still a little girl in the car."

"I'm sorry for your loss," Azrael said gently. "But I do not cause death unless you are evil … like the men who hurt you. I only help those who suffer or might become lost if I happen upon them during my work."

"Then what about Nancy!!!" Elisabeth retorted, her anger making her ignore her pain. "Nancy was still alive when you took her from me!"

"*You* were keeping her alive," Azrael said. "The bullet lodged in her heart and shattered two of the chambers. The chances of survival were nonexistent without a heart transplant and we both know the chances of that were remote."

"You don't know that a heart wouldn't have been available had you let me keep her alive long enough to go to the hospital!!!" Elisabeth screamed, tears streaming down her battered cheeks. "How dare you interfere???"

"*You* were keeping her alive," Azrael said a second time. "She wanted to go and you were the one who interfered. You have a gift. The ability to loan your life energy to those who need it. You can help them hang on long enough to repair the damage so the person has a chance to heal. But you do not have the ability to cause somebody to grow a new heart. Even the Emperor has limits."

"Why didn't you let me keep her here?" Elisabeth sobbed. "She was all I had left in this world."

"I know," Azrael said. "But she told you she wanted you to let her go. She wasn't like these soldiers you save who want to fight. Nancy wanted to rejoin her grandmother. You would have drained the life energy from your own body trying to keep her here."

"I would have succeeded!" Elisabeth said.

"The Regent once did that," Azrael said. "Kept the General alive when he should have died. He survived, but it nearly killed the both of them. He wanted to live so he wouldn't leave her behind. Nancy … Nancy wanted to leave. The last thing she did as she rejoined her grandmother was ask me to continue watching over you."

Elisabeth put her face into her hands, sobbing. Azrael ached to take her into his arms and soothe her pain, the way he'd done when his little sister or Elissar wept, but he couldn't. Touch. Azrael couldn't even give the simplest, most basic comfort. All he could do was stand there like a stupid, tall tent-post and watch her cry.

"I'm sorry," Azrael whispered. Words. All he had to offer the woman he loved was hollow words as her frail human body shuddered with emotion.

The hiss of dissolving matter caused her to look up and see the next black tear hit the table he'd placed between them. Tears expressed what Azrael had never been able to convey via words or actions. That he truly was sorry he'd watched her lose everyone she ever loved.

"You're not what I expected," Elisabeth wiped her eyes and frowned at the IV poked into her hand. She reached down and began to pull off the tape.

"Please … don't." Azrael stepped forward then realized he'd come within reach. He stepped back. "It's … um … they're worried about hypothermia. You were in the river for almost 25 minutes."

Elisabeth stared at him, as though putting together a puzzle in her mind.

"I won't hurt you," Elisabeth said. "Why do you always step back whenever I get within arm's reach?" She glanced down at the small hospital table beside her bed, which now had tiny holes eaten through the surface.

"My touch is death." Regret tinged Azrael's voice.

"So I've heard," Elisabeth said. "So … just don't zap me with your mojo and we'll get along just fine."

"You don't understand," Azrael pointed to the holes in the table. "I have no control over my power. It's taken me thousands of years to learn to touch objects that aren't alive. Even an inadvertent brush of a single feather kills whoever I brush against. It's why I wear this terrible cloak."

"-I- touched you once," Elisabeth reached for his hand. "I'm not afraid of you."

"I know," Azrael stared at his own hand, the one that sometimes felt real. "But there's no guarantee you'll be so lucky a second time."

"What if I'm willing to take the risk?" Elisabeth kept her hand still held out. "It's not like I have anything to lose."

"I can encourage a spirit that hasn't become severed from its mortal shell to settle back in if it isn't too badly damaged," Azrael crossed his arms against his chest to prevent them from obeying the irrational impulse to take her hand. "But once I touch living tissue, it's dead. I've never been able to un-kill somebody I touched. Even the other Archangels fear me, although they don't *stay* dead because they know how to recreate new bodies from what's left of the old one."

"Chicken," Elisabeth said.

"Eagle, actually," Azrael ruffled his ebony feathers. "If the Emperor had used chickens when he engineered our DNA, we wouldn't be able to fly."

Elisabeth blinked in confusion before she realized he'd just made a very lame joke. Outside the infirmary, the sound of revelers pouring out of the mess tent singing Christmas carols at the top of their lungs could be heard. Half the base, by the sound of it, and largely out of tune as they split into sections singing Jingle Bells. It was obvious they were headed this way to give Elisabeth a little Christmas cheer, whether she wished to be cheered or not.

"I have to go." Azrael looked into her beautiful, silver eyes; the eyes of a pre-ascended being?

"Yes," Elisabeth said. "They wouldn't understand."

Azrael paused, inhaling her scent. It had changed. The way she viewed him, with hostility, had changed. It was an improvement. He would take it.

"You'll come back again," Elisabeth asked. "Won't you?"

"Yes," Azrael said. "I'll even talk to you again if you wish."

Before she could say no, Azrael disappeared back to the fight his Archangel brethren were still mopping up. It would take Lucifer's agents several days to lead a Coalition regiment into the caves under the guise of being a local informant to find the bodies Azrael had reaped earlier.

He tucked an ace of spades into the pocket of each one he'd been responsible for taking. The ones possessed by Agents. The worst of the worst. Since the World Trade Center genocide, the two emperors had stopped bickering long enough to work together and eradicate Moloch's latest threat.

Azrael wanted the evil bastard to know he was still here…

Chapter 35

And they built in the high places of Ba'al…
To cause their sons and their daughters to pass through the fire unto Moloch;
Which I commanded them not,
Neither came it into my mind,
That they should do this abomination.

Jeremiah 32:35

Earth - AD January 27, 2003
Royal Palace - Tikrit, Iraq

"You were right," Chemosh examined the coding sequence of the strand of DNA displayed on the computer monitor. "She *is* one of Lucifer's offspring, not merely a descendent. How in Hades did you discover her?"

"Her brother suffers from kidney failure," Saddam Hussein spoke with that almost robotic stiffness that most western media outlets ridiculed him for. "When the doctors tested the siblings for a donor, they discovered the husband had been cuckolded."

"Hmmmm…" Chemosh said. "The third strand of TNA is less complete than the sire's. I'd like to test the girl's mother to find out if it's a defect passed down from the mother, or a genetic mutation. Her DNA should be more complete than this."

"You can't." Hussein's brusque movement betrayed his incomplete control over his mortal host. "The moment the husband found out his wife had been unfaithful, he poured gasoline on her and burned her alive in front of his entire village."

Chemosh gave his subordinate Agent a fish-eyed stare. "Pity. It wasn't like she had any choice resisting Lucifer's power of persuasion. I taught that boy *myself* how to manipulate others to do his bidding. It'll set back Moloch's plans by months, possibly years, while we unravel this mystery."

"It was her husband's right." Hussein's eyes hardened in hatred at Chemosh's reappearance from Gehenna. "You've gotten soft." As a mid-level Agent who'd had free reign since the Nazi's had helped him escape Gehenna during World War II, Hussein was resentful at suddenly being a small fish in a large pond.

Chemosh had run into many Agents such as Saddam Hussein, ascended beings who purportedly served their god, but who'd grown a little too eager to seize power at Moloch's expense. Not that it hadn't happened countless times before. Agents served two masters, Moloch, and themselves. It was why he often languished for thousands of years between escapes each time Ki defeated him. But things always changed once Chemosh escaped. Chemosh was loyal, and Moloch rewarded him accordingly.

Chemosh gave the usurper an indulgent smile. His demeanor changed as he transformed himself into an obsequious, ass-kissing clerk. The one fools always underestimated.

"We'll fix this problem," Chemosh projected images of Moloch rewarding the upstart god for loyalty and giving him even more power than he had now. "It's not your fault a mortal took it upon himself to destroy the evidence. Perhaps you might be kind enough to direct your minions to exhume the mother's body so we can figure out why, in over 5,500 years, Lucifer has never sired a single pre-ascended being?"

A confused expression crossed Saddam Hussein's face, then disappeared as a sadistic grin appeared.

"Yes, of course," Hussein said. "Of course we'll exhume the body. Moloch's wish is my command!" He hurried out of the throne room of his royal palace built along the Tigris River and began barking commands at his minions to get the job done.

Chemosh turned from the computer monitor to the terrified girl shackled to an examination table in the makeshift laboratory. Because her third strand of TNA was incomplete, Moloch could not possess her as a host. And she was far too young to impregnate .... yet. However, the girl was a start. Now he just had to experiment with which male's seed would produce the desired genetic traits.

Males. Males were much more useful. They could impregnate dozens of test subjects a day, as Lucifer had kindly been doing for the past five thousand years. Unfortunately, possession by Moloch had damaged Lucifer's third strand of TNA. Perhaps it was an intentional defect engineered into all sentient life by She-who-is to prevent her malignant father-god from escaping more often? But life always found a way.

Chemosh had his first test subject.

"Don't be afraid," Chemosh projected comforting images into the girl's mind as he jabbed a needle into her arm and pushed down the plunger of the sedative. The girl's eyes slid shut.

"What will we do, Sire?" Chemosh's second-in-command, Abid Hahmed Mahmud asked. "She's too young to bear children."

Chemosh reached for his scalpel, thankful for his foresight to assign a lesser Agent hungry for his *own* place in Moloch's hierarchy to act as Presidential Secretary to the Agent who'd seized Saddam Hussein as a host. Like most who followed Moloch, Mahmud was loyal first and foremost to himself. But self-interest was easily manipulated.

"We'll artificially stimulate the ovaries to produce eggs early and harvest them each month," Chemosh sliced through the child's lower abdomen. "The normal human female produces 20 egg follicles each month, but usually only one matures enough to be released. With this, we can force her ovaries to mature and release all 20 eggs and artificially inseminate them for implantation into mature human incubators."

With a practiced hand, Chemosh implanted a microcomputer and a series of tiny injection and harvesting machines into the child's abdominal cavity.

"Won't that cause medical problems for the child, Sire?" Mahmud asked.

"What does it matter?" Chemosh said with a shrug. "We'll use her until we find a more promising option. Once we're done with her, she'll make a nice snack."

"What about Saddam Hussein?" Mahmud asked.

Chemosh silently finished wiring up the harvesting equipment and stitched the girl's abdomen back up. Only the scar and tiny collection machine protruding out of the girl's belly button gave any indication she possessed technology no Earth fertility clinic had ever dreamed of.

"That idiot American president has an Oedipus complex about his daddy's unfinished war," Chemosh said at last. "He's been blustering about coming after our dear friend, Saddam Hussein. Why don't you send him a little gift?"

"What kind of gift?" Mahmud asked.

"Why … weapons of mass destruction … of course," Chemosh said pleasantly. "I'm sure you can cook up the appropriate doctored evidence to get the neocons to invade this petty kingdom and keep our upstart Agent too busy to throw a monkey wrench into Moloch's plans. It will divert resources away from the *real* battle our brother Bin Laden wages in Afghanistan."

"I have just the evidence to get the do-nothing government keeping the American president on a leash off their asses to invade," Mahmud said with a bow. "Would materials to produce 500 tons of Sarin, mustard gas, and VX nerve agents do the trick?"

"Perfect," Chemosh said.

Chapter 36

Our fear of death is like our fear that summer will be short,
But when we have had our swing of pleasure,
Our fill of fruit,
And our swelter of heat,
We say we have had our day

Ralph Waldo Emerson

Earth - AD February, 2003
Baghram AFB, Afghanistan

The hair stood up on the back of Elisabeth's neck.

"Go!" Kadima gave her a knowing smile. "I'll finish up here."

Elisabeth smiled down at the young man who'd come to the infirmary complaining of stomach pain and gave his shoulder a reassuring squeeze. Eighteen. First tour of duty. Arrived in Afghanistan three weeks ago. Baptized by fire clearing Taliban from caves in the Adhi Ghar mountain range during Operation Mongoose. And now … cut down at the knees by an Afghani chicken. Roast chicken, that is…

"There's a reason why they tell you not to eat street-vendor food," Elisabeth said. "The stool culture came back positive. Textbook salmonella. We'll notify your C.O. you're out of commission for the next few days."

The Private nodded and clutched his stomach, ready to puke the contents of his now-empty gut into the bucket nurse Mary held for that purpose.

"Go!" Kadima glanced towards the shadow in the corner. "There's nothing going on here we can't handle."

"You'll be fine," Elisabeth reassured the young soldier. She casually scrubbed out and grabbed her coat. She did not acknowledge his presence, but knew he followed as she made her way to the first checkpoint.

"Yer not be going out and about alone, me hopes, Lieutenant Kaiser?" a British soldier asked in a lilting north-English accent that was more akin to a Scottish brogue as she passed through the first checkpoint.

"I'm not going past the second checkpoint," Elisabeth reassured him by reaching into her pocket and pulling out his calling card. "And I'm not alone."

"Ay ... very good, miss," the soldier gave her a grin. "Yer just be careful, all right? Don't wanna be hunting down no missing nurses in none of them gullies."

A legend had grown up around her. Elisabeth. The nurse who could defeat Death. In the past month, three more groups of Taliban had mysteriously appeared, dead, when so-called 'local informants' led Coalition forces into remote areas where there were rumors of Taliban feeding supplies over the border from Pakistan. The details were kept tightly under wraps, but at each site the bodies were without a mark to indicate how they had died except for the ace-of-spades neatly tucked into the neckline of their shirts.

Elisabeth found her way to a semi-secluded spot, little more than a flat rock overlooking a bit of a gully out of sight of the main area of the base, and sat down, placing her cane next to her with a satisfied sigh. Barren rock. Unless it was irrigated, Afghanistan was little more than rock.

"You can come out, now."

Azrael solidified behind her like an enormous, black-winged Cheshire cat. "Hello, Elisabeth."

"Come ... sit with me," Elisabeth patted the rock next to her. She needed to coax the reclusive angel to get close enough to even hold a conversation. He wasn't antisocial. Just ... shy.

"It's too small." Azrael moved to the rock she indicated, but did not sit down. "I don't want to bump against you."

"I'm not going to leap at you," Elisabeth said. "I trust you're not going to thwack me with one of those big chicken-wings of yours."

Azrael's stern countenance softened into a boyish smile so sweet and innocent it almost took her breath away. Chicken wings. It was a sign of the easy rapport which had begun to develop between them now that she understood who he was and why he watched her.

"I'll be careful." Azrael sat as far away as he could while still having his posterior planted on the same boulder. He carefully arranged his glossy black wings facing away from her so an inadvertent flap wouldn't brush against her and kill her.

"How go the wars in heaven?" Elisabeth asked.

"Same old same old," Azrael said. The boyish look disappeared. "Not well. We made a mistake assuming events in different nations were isolated incidents. We weren't expecting your level of technology or economic interconnectedness to jump the way it did the past twenty years."

"I still don't understand the prohibition against giving us technology!" Elisabeth groused. "Think of how many lives I could save? We're saving lives here that Nancy couldn't have dreamed of only five years ago."

"Moloch's signature was always easy to identify because he favors advanced technology," Azrael said. "He's always had the best and brightest new toys. If we found advanced technology, we could track it back to him."

"Had?" Elisabeth asked. "Past tense?"

"He's changed tactics," Azrael said. "He's learned to hide in plain sight by giving others the advanced technology and quietly manipulating things behind the scenes. It's like trying to spot somebody using sign language in a crowd full of people using bullhorns."

"So he's like a hacker or something?"

"I think so." Azrael's expression softened and a wistful look appeared on his face. "I wouldn't know. I haven't been able to touch a piece of electronic equipment for over 2,300 years."

Elisabeth stared down into the gully. The wind cut into the tiny openings in her coat and made her shiver. She should have brought her military-issue beret, but some odd impulse had made her leave it behind. She was no Abercrombie wannabe, wishing she was thin and cool enough to step foot into one of their stores without being lambasted by some tone-deaf CEO about only popular kids being welcome to shop there, but lately she wished she could dress a little nicer. Her choices were olive green. Olive drab. Khaki green. Khaki beige. Khaki drab. Black. And taupe. With a good measure of … you guessed it … army green if she had an excuse to wear her dress uniform. Even her hair had to be kept neatly tied back in a regulation army bun.

She noticed the way Azrael's interest became even more intense whenever she allowed her hair to cascade down her back. She liked the fact he noticed. Could Kadima be right? Did her ebony friend have an interest in her that was more than mere scientific curiosity?

"I'm cold," she said. Her excuse. She reached back and pulled her hair from the elastic, watching through veiled eyelashes the way his nostrils flared and chest rose as he inhaled the scent of her shampoo as she shook loose her locks. For ten years he had watched her. Now it was her turn to watch *him*.

"What was it like?" Elisabeth asked softly. "Learning to re-hold your physical form after your accident?"

Little by little, Azrael had revealed how he'd ended up in the predicament he was in now. The young friend he'd tried to save. Being shunned, even by his own kind, because he was a creature of the void. His loneliness at never being able to touch a living thing without killing it, not even a blade of grass.

"Time consuming," Azrael bent to pick up a rock and tossed it into the gully below. "It took me nearly a thousand years to hold a form you might even recognize as humanoid, and another thousand to reshape my original appearance enough that people didn't run screaming in terror whenever they saw me."

Elisabeth stared off into the February sun, closing her eyes and absorbing the weak sunlight as it warmed her skin. Needing a long time to recover from an accident was something she could understand.

"Rehabilitation," Elisabeth remembered what it had been like. "They said I would never walk again. But I did. Did you know I used to imagine you came to watch over me those first two years to help me learn to walk again?"

"I did," Azrael said. "I held my breath and prayed each painful step you took. You have no idea how much it hurt watching you fall and not being able to catch you."

"I knew you were there," Elisabeth said. "And I hated you. I hated you because I couldn't understand why you would come every day and then let me fall. I wish you had said something. Made me understand you didn't catch me because you couldn't. It would have made things easier."

"It's forbidden," Azrael picked up another rock. This time, instead of throwing it into the ditch, he simply crushed it in his hand until it dissolved into black nothingness and disappeared. "But I wish I'd disobeyed. I'm sorry I hurt you."

"You're not the one who hurt me," Elisabeth said. "A drunk driver hurt me. Why didn't you throw *him* into hell?"

"It's not my place to interfere in the affairs of mortals." Azrael's wings involuntarily twitched in anger. He hastily got his emotions back under control and aimed the traitorous appendages as far away from her as he could, tucking them behind the rock at an angle that *had* to be uncomfortable. "But know that I wanted to. Even before I knew you! I'm not brave like my Archangel cousins, but even –I- loathe that kind of cowardice!"

Elisabeth felt the peculiar shudder of the rock beneath her. She glanced down. Earthquake? She noticed the way Azrael closed his eyes and breathed as he forced himself to relax. Not an earthquake. He said it required concentration to not dissolve whatever chair he sat down upon. His dark gift must be tied to his emotions.

"You threw yourself into a fiery pit to save a friend," Elisabeth said. "Even though you knew you had little chance of surviving. That sounds pretty brave to me."

"I ..."

His words trailed off as he stared, not at the barren mountains, but events in a past so distant Elisabeth could hardly fathom it. Whenever she asked him about his young friend, he didn't want to talk about it. She could tell he still grieved her loss even after all these years. She was learning that, to get him to talk about himself, she needed to tie it to something about *her*.

"I felt like a freak," Elisabeth changed the subject back to her own rehabilitation. "All of a sudden everyone I ever cared about was gone, and the people who'd been connected to them just didn't know what to say. They avoided me like the plague because … well … I'm not sure why."

"People don't like to acknowledge bad things can happen to them," Azrael said. "I see it all the time in my work. People like Kadima. They survive. But when they tell their story, people don't want to hear it. They marginalize the victim. Blame them …even. It's why I like to check in on people I ask to bear witness."

"We don't make it easy for people to come forward and rub our noses in reality," Elisabeth sighed. "Everybody wants to live in their own perfect little world. Nobody wants to be reminded that death is around every corner. I mean …"

Azrael smiled at her slip-of-tongue.

"You know what I mean!" Elisabeth said, rolling her eyes. "I didn't mean you!"

"I'm just one person," Azrael threw his hands up into the air in a 'who me?' shrug. "I get blamed for a lot of things that I'm not there to do."

"Kind of like Santa Claus," Elisabeth laughed. "You even have a naughty list!"

Azrael reached to the pocket of his cloak and pulled out his latest scientific journal. He turned so she couldn't see as he rifled through the pages, and then flipped it open to a page full of tally marks. Doodled into one corner was scratched a remarkably good picture of an Afghani elder scolding a goat.

Elisabeth burst out laughing.

"The goat kept getting out of his enclosure and into his wife's garden," Azrael said. "The old man couldn't figure out how the goat got out of the pen because the fence was solid and the gate was always closed. The goat figured out how to jiggle the lock on the gate and open it. Because it was built out-of-plumb, gravity would make the gate shut behind him and the latch would automatically fall shut."

"And you let the poor man rip out his hair instead of just telling him what was happening?" Elisabeth asked in a mock accusatory voice.

"Shouldn't I have?" Azrael looked crushed as he misconstrued her teasing for displeasure.

"I'm sorry," Elisabeth said. "I was only teasing. How did you manage to not reveal yourself laughing your tailfeathers off as you watched?"

"He figured it out eventually," Azrael glanced at the book. "He hid around the corner of his house and watched how the goat kept getting out. He fixed the gate after that."

"And what did you learn from that little scientific study?" Elisabeth asked.

"It just reaffirmed what I already knew," Azrael said. "Your species capacity to find a way around problems is on par with some of the most advanced species in the universe. Only the ease with which your emotions can be incited to undermine your own self-interest holds you back."

Elisabeth looked down at the ground.

"That's what I used to tell Tommy," she mumbled. "We're raised to believe we want the alpha-male, and then when you get him, you realize he's a mess."

She glanced up to see the expression of jealousy dance across Azrael's face before being neatly tucked away behind a blank expression.

"Why did you choose him for a mate?" Azrael's voice was strained. "And then leave him?"

"I dunno," Elisabeth shrugged. "I was lonely, I guess. Everybody said I should be flattered the best-looking kid in school had a thing for me and ... well ... prom night. I was beginning to feel like a freak being the only ... well ... you know. I guess I just gave in. Didn't you ever have a girlfriend or anything that didn't work out? I mean ... before ... um ..."

"No," Azrael said curtly. "Our species takes one mate. For life."

"One mate?" Elisabeth noticed the stiffness in his posture. "For life? That's ... pretty romantic."

"That's the way it should be!" Azrael scolded. "Much misery in your world could be avoided if people took their interpersonal relationships more seriously."

"I wish it were that way down here," Elisabeth looked into his bottomless, black eyes that swirled with an even deeper darkness. Hurt? Had she hurt him, her immortal watcher, when she'd succumbed to her loneliness?

Elisabeth was a realist. Sex was ... well ... sex. You did it to scratch an itch. Or at least that was what she'd told herself after discovering Tommy had the sexual prowess of a grunting boar. Every time Tommy had fucked her, instead of seeing *him,* all could she imagine was the distraught look in her dark watcher's eyes the day he'd jumped in front of a bullet to save her.

It was what had finally made her break things off...

Azrael ... on the other hand? Elisabeth knew he'd be a sensitive and attentive lover. One mate. For life. What would it be like? To touch a man who'd never known intimate touch? To feel his form quiver beneath her fingers the way he sometimes did simply because she got close? Like now?

He was already obsessed with the fact she'd once touched him and survived. How would he react if she bent across the rock and kissed him?

"Tell me about the Regent," Elisabeth changed the subject. "You said she is like you?"

"She was once human." The shadow of jealousy disappeared as he discussed one of his favorite people. "Your species periodically spits out an evolutionary leap that far surpasses anything in the universe. Like the Regent. She's the only person who can touch me without fearing death."

"But she can touch others?" Elisabeth asked.

"Yes," Azrael said. "She keeps her power firmly under control. But her physical form was not destroyed as mine was when she learned to harness the power of the void. It took her brother billions of years to figure out how to do it on his own from scratch."

"Oh," Elisabeth said, disappointed. "Billions of years? So … um … how long does she think it will take you to become … solid?"

"I don't know," Azrael sighed, staring off into the jagged mountains off in the distance. He bent down to pick up a pebble and threw it into the gully. "I can hear the Song of Creation. Faintly. She doesn't understand why I haven't been able to use it to recreate my physical form."

"I thought that's what the fires in hell did?" Elisabeth asked.

"The fire alters your essence so you can't directly manipulate the atomic structure of the material realm," Azrael said. "It's some sort of safety feature. To prevent Moloch and his Agents from simply using the matter here to escape. To rebuild your physical form, you have to know how to access power that transcends the material realm."

"Like … prayer … or something?" Elisabeth asked.

"You have to love somebody so deeply that you'd be willing to sacrifice your very existence just to be with them." Azrael's expression grew intense. "Only the most worthy are chosen by Ki to hear the Song of Creation."

Memory of the anguished look on Azrael's face when he'd suddenly materialized in front of her, stopping the bullet that had been coming for her, intruded into Elisabeth's mind. The memory which had haunted her dreams ever since that day. Was Kadima right?

"Nobody's ever loved me like that."

Azrael's mouth opened and closed without speaking. Platitudes? Or had he been about to profess he had feelings for her? The intense expression disappeared behind the cautious, shy one.

"Archangels have to be very careful who they become involved with," Azrael took a stick and pretended to be interested in jamming it into the rocky soil instead of making eye contact. "If our mate's love is false, it can kill us. Most have been unable to find mates because Moloch wiped out the Seraphim home world."

"How sad," Elisabeth said. "But I can't blame this Ki-goddess for being cautious. An evil bull-god who devours children can't understand what it means to truly love somebody."

"No," Azrael's dark wings drooped dejectedly. "He can't. But sometimes I feel ... oh ... I don't know!"

Elisabeth understood.

"You feel like maybe you're not healing because somehow you're not worthy?" Elisabeth guessed.

Azrael looked up, nostrils flared as he used his other senses to make up for his inability to touch. Beautiful. Elisabeth had never met a more breathtakingly beautiful creature than the chiseled angel who had shadowed her since she was a child. A plethora of emotions danced across his obsidian features. Angst. Remorse. Anger. Sorrow. Like a fine Grecian statue. Too beautiful to be real.

"You're not the only one who's ever had to pick yourself up off the ground and start from scratch, you know?" Elisabeth said. She reached towards him and stopped when he pulled away. She neatly laced her fingers together in her lap lest he jump up to maintain a safe distance.

"I know," Azrael said. "Watching you struggle has reminded me I'm not the only one who suffers because of somebody else's actions."

His black eyes were so full of sorrow that Elisabeth wanted to take him in her arms and give him a hug. How she longed to give him the simple reassuring hand on his shoulder like she'd given the sick Private back at the infirmary. Comfort she could never give. Elisabeth touched the scar which ran from her temple to her lips.

"I begged the General to remove that when he healed your spine," Azrael traced it in the air, a foot from her face. "He said it is a badge of honor. That you met Death and defeated it. Not a punishment."

"I hate it," Elisabeth said. "It makes me ugly."

"The one you call Saint Michael wished the world to see how special you are inside," Azrael said. "He, himself, keeps the scar over his heart healed by his mate even though it is within his power to remove it. He said he likes to look in the mirror each morning and be reminded every single day is a gift."

"He sounds very wise," Elisabeth touched the gnarled pink flesh that sank into her cheek. "I had no idea the scar had significance."

They sat there together, staring off at the distant craggy peaks, in a companionable silence. Azrael's notebook sat between them, still open to the page with the goat until an errant gust of wind blew it to another page. Elisabeth stared down at a sketch of herself staring back from the page. Scarred. But the scar had an ethereal quality about it. As though it were a beauty mark. Was this how he really saw her?

Azrael looked mortified. He silently grabbed the book and tucked it back into his cloak. Elisabeth stared off into the distance, pretending she hadn't seen. Her dark watcher was a man of deep emotion and few words. Pressing the reclusive angel about his art would cause him to recede back into the woodwork.

"Tell me about heaven?" Elisabeth asked, picking a neutral topic.

Chapter 37

Their associate-gods have made the killing of their children
Seem fair to many idolaters,

Quran 6:137

Earth - AD March 18, 2003
Dora Farms, Baghdad, Iraq

Azrael peered uneasily through the binoculars at what otherwise appeared to be another henchman's palatial home tucked into one of the most densely populated neighborhoods in Baghdad. He'd sent in tendrils of his consciousness, trying to ascertain the position of the squatter, but some sort of force field surrounded the compound. Although several species had developed dampening technology, humans had not yet progressed that far. Unauthorized technology was worrisome.

The rustle of somebody moving through the tree-lined walls, muttering curses under his breath, clued Azrael that Samuel Adams was on time for their rendezvous.

"Our intelligence says he's in there," Sam grunted as he shook leaves out of his collar. "There are guard vehicles hidden amongst the trees so they can't be spotted by satellite."

"Saddam Hussein?"

"No," Sam said. "Chemosh. Moloch's highest ranking Agent. We don't know how the fuck he did it, but he escaped from Gehenna."

"Chemosh?" Azrael asked. "I'm afraid I'm not up on my prehistoric Moloch history. Which one was he?"

"A really, really bad one," Sam said. "Another god. Big. Like Shay'tan. Not just a run-of-the-mill ascended bad guy. Chemosh needs a fairly evolved host to interact with this realm. But he's not as limited as Moloch."

"Still not ringing a bell," Azrael said. "I thought you had the worst ones sequestered into their own level of Gehenna so they can't interact."

"This one's clever," Sam said. "The General knew him by the name of the host he seized. Zepar. The technological genius who wired up Lucifer's brain to make him compliant enough to use as a host for Moloch without tipping off Hashem he had a squatter in the palace."

"Oh." Azrael felt a sinking feeling in his gut as he put two and two together and realized why he was unable to pierce the compound. "That one. Does Lucifer know?"

"Oh, yeah," Sam twitched his tail. "And he's pissed. We still haven't figured how the hell he got out. It takes a power surge big enough to fry all of Europe to open up a portal large enough for the big ones like him to escape. The two emperors haven't registered anything that massive from Ceres station."

"That's not good," Azrael furrowed his brow. "That means they tampered with Shay'tan's monitoring equipment. It wouldn't be the first time."

"The last time Chemosh got loose," Sam said. "He helped Moloch waste one universe and then punched a hole into ours. If it wasn't for the General's partial immunity to void-matter, we'd all be on the sacrificial altar."

"Oh … joy," Azrael muttered. "Perfect timing … the Regent is with child again and the Dark Lord is still on sabbatical. Why do –I- always have to be the void-creature du jour?"

"Because you're so good at it, my boy," Sam said. "The mere mention of your name gets them quaking in their boots."

"All hype," Azrael snorted. "Few teeth. Compared to the Regent or He-who's-not, I'm just a baby."

"A baby who can take out an entire platoon of bad guys without breaking a sweat," Sam said with a wolfish grin. "Waah! I'd sure be crying if I saw you coming for me when you do that black thundercloud thing."

Azrael gave Sam his sternest 'knock off the dark humor' look. "So … who's Chemosh using for a host? Some scumbag with delusions of devil-worshipping grandeur?"

"Just some civilian!" Sam threw his arms up in exasperation. "Our intelligence says he stumbled across a genetically compatible host a year and a half ago. Chemosh performed a frontal lobotomy to kill his higher brain functions. They seized the guy's entire family as potential hosts."

Azrael noted the agitated thump-thump-thump of Sam's tail escaping his trench coat as he spoke. Sam was usually pretty careful about not revealing his … differences … while out on the field. He must be really upset to be so careless.

"So what do you need me to do?" Azrael asked. "Take out the squatter before the Americans and Brits get here? They're about to invade this country."

"Yes." Sam pointed to the lights gleaming even in the middle of the night at the farm. Men with guns herded several women, children, and an

elderly man towards the guard vehicles tucked under the tree line. "Look …
they're getting ready to flee. If Chemosh goes underground, we'll never find
him. We need you to ensure that doesn't happen."

"You said the host he's using is an innocent," Azrael said. "If I take
Chemosh, the host will die as well."

"He's already as good as dead," Sam said. "It's not like Lucifer where
he was more useful to them as himself than as a permanent host because the
Emperor can spot a squatter. The poor guy is trapped. He can't cross into the
Dreamtime because he's not dead. But what kind of life will he lead without
his higher brain functions? Word has it the guy is a vegetable whenever
Chemosh steps out. Can't even feed himself."

Trapped betwixt and between? Like him? Azrael struggled with what
Sam asked him to do. It wasn't Sam he was wary of trusting, but Lucifer.
Lucifer had a grudge against the Agent who'd recruited him as a teenager to
be Moloch's meat-puppet.

"I want to see for myself when we go in," Azrael said. "Then I'll decide.
Elisabeth has shown me many injured we once wrote off for dead are
capable of surviving. I refuse to kill an innocent man just to get at a guilty
one."

Only *one* creature could knock an Agent out of its mortal shell without
killing it if the host-spirit wasn't powerful enough on its own to evict the
monster. The Eternal Emperor. Unfortunately, the Emperor had not stepped
foot on Earth in over 5,500 years.

"Chemosh will get away…" Sam warned.

"The Coalition is about to bomb the crap out of this entire country,"
Azrael flapped his wings with annoyance. "How far can he go? Elisabeth's
staging a medevac unit in Kuwait."

"Elisabeth, huh?" Sam gave him a knowing grin. "So that's where
you've been off to lately. Somebody's got it bad!"

Azrael didn't justify the comment with an answer. He'd been warned
the Sata'an-hybrids enjoyed a good wager. Especially when it revolved
around relationships. For all he knew, he was the hottest betting topic in the
Valley of Jehoshaphat right now and Sam was fishing for insider
information.

"Whatever," Sam said with an indifferent shrug. "Go ahead. Don't talk
to me. In case you forget, it was *me* who watched over your girlfriend while
you took your little sabbatical to study … what was it … pond scum? On
some remote planet … where? East Buttfuck?"

"Pre-sentient primate-like mammals," Azrael ruffled his feathers with
feigned indignation. "And it was a solar system too close to Earth for anyone
else to study them without violating the terms of the Armistice. It was
worthy work that needed to be done!"

"*This* is worthy work needing to be done," Sam flashed his slightly pointy teeth that otherwise looked normal. "That was you getting dope-slapped by reality! Human females are a lot more earthy than the frigid Angelic chicks Hashem has cruising around the galaxy in his cushy command carriers."

"They shouldn't waste time on the wrong person!"

"Whose fault was that, Mister Silent Lurker?" Sam jaunted. "If you don't let them know you're interested, they go looking for affection elsewhere."

Azrael studied the compound, ignoring Sam's knowing look. His appraisal of the situation was accurate. Both situations, actually. Elisabeth had gotten involved with Tommy hoping it would ease her loneliness. Loneliness caused, in large part, because *he* had backed off so far she couldn't sense him anymore. She'd thought he was gone for good.

"The quarry is getting ready to move out ahead of the expected American invasion," Azrael neatly deflected the topic of conversation. "We need to move or we'll lose them. How many men do you have with you?"

"Just me and two others," Sam said. "There … and there. See?"

"Just two?"

"Been a stretched a bit thin since human medicine advanced to the point our young people can pay some hack doctor to cut off their tails against their parent's wishes," Sam said. "We don't have the manpower to babysit everything Moloch's agents do anymore. Pretty soon, you guys will be on your own!

"That's a scary thought," Azrael said. "The two emperors are so busy proving the other one is wrong that they'd sacrifice this world to one-up the other in a heartbeat. Ki knew what she was doing when she had her Agent entice Lucifer into caring."

"Lucifer may be an ass," Sam said. "But he's an ass who loves humanity in all of its flawed, fucked-up glory. Absolutely adores them. Especially their vices!!!"

"That's for sure," Azrael said. "Their self-destructive nature has both emperors scratching their heads. Lucifer is the only one who understands them.

"What'cha guys going to do when there's no more demons to guard the gates to the underworld?" Sam taunted. "Roll up your sleeves and get your pretty wings all dirty?"

"I'll be happy for you," Azrael looked at his old friend. "It's not right, your people having to hide because some dominant gene keeps cropping up in your offspring to make you just a little bit different than humans."

It wasn't so far in the past that he'd viewed the Sata'an-human hybrids with contempt. Demons. When had that perception begun to change? More importantly, why had that warped perception even started in the first place? Propaganda? Yes. Propaganda. Neither emperor wished their armies to be lured into rebellion by Lucifer a second time. Dehumanizing the descendants of the soldiers who'd rebelled discouraged others from Falling.

Was that what was happening to him? Falling? Was Azrael one of the Fallen because he'd fallen in love with a human? Or did it take more to arouse Hashem's eternal condemnation? Yes … it took more. The General's mate had once been human and it was reported most Leonids were descended from a single human male.

"Heck … you're more human than I am!" Azrael added. "You're like, what? Fifty-five generations removed from the Sata'anic Fallen who rebelled against Shay'tan?"

"Fifty-nine," Sam said, exasperation in his voice. "And every single generation of my family since then has made damned sure they intermarried with humans, not other Sata'an-Fallen, trying to eradicate the gene."

"The humans would accept you, I think," Azrael said. "Especially now. They're big on affirmative action in the western nations."

"I know they would," Sam said. "Their ancestors accepted our great-grandsires once they stopped exploiting this planet for Shay'tan and started protecting it against Moloch. And those guys really *were* lizards!"

Sam shuddered at the mention of his own lizard ancestors. Sata'an descendants divided themselves socially according to who appeared most human. 'Demons' who could blend in simply by donning a trench coat and contact lenses, such as Sam, were at the top of the hierarchy. On the other end, those unfortunate enough to inherit more lizard-like characteristics were shunned. The poor things existed in the shadows, never daring to walk amongst humans lest an inadvertent sighting give the two emperors cause to pounce on this planet like a tasty morsel.

Azrael had studied such visual pecking orders amongst Anglo-Indo populations in India and African-Americans in the United States. What a Sata'an descendent wouldn't give to be born with Sam's handsome chocolate complexion and tightly curled afro! Amongst Sata'anic Fallen females, Sam was the alpha male. The golden boy. It was too bad Sam wouldn't have them. He was holding out, waiting to find that 'right' human female who would accept him for who he was.

"One day," Azrael said. "Your species will finish assimilating into humanity as the Fallen Alliance hybrids did."

"Scary thought," Sam said. "Then Lucifer will be the only one left to safeguard them. Do you trust Hashem to not screw things up? At least Shay'tan has a history of upholding his bargains."

Azrael didn't answer. He loved the Eternal Emperor with all of his heart, but he suspected when that day came, Earth would be in trouble…

"Lucifer in charge of humanity," Azrael said. "It still makes my brain hurt just thinking about how that even happened! He's so … so … so …"

"Over the top?" Sam said with a grin. "Flamboyant? In-your-face anything-goes debauchery? He gives Shay'tan conniption fits over his lifestyle. Doesn't want Lucifer giving the Sata'an full-bloods ideas. Although at least the old dragon seems to trust him to keep his end of the bargain so far as the Armistice is concerned. Lucifer forced the Fallen Alliance hybrids to treat the Fallen Sata'anic citizens fairly back when our species were first forced to work together. Wouldn't tolerate one snooting down their noses at the other."

"Full-blooded lizards aren't so bad," Azrael said. "They're just people. No different than you or I. I'd gladly grow a tail if it meant I could touch somebody without killing them!"

"You think that gal of yours would be so interested in you if you had one of these instead of them fancy wings?" Sam thwacked his tail against the ground. "Every time I seen one of us depicted in one of their religious icons, it's us getting crushed beneath the boot of one of yours."

"I served time with the full-bloods on Ceres station before my accident," Azrael said. "They were a lot more affable than my own citizens. I was kind of a nerd back then."

"-Was- a nerd?" Sam teased with a grin. "As in … past tense?"

"Hey," Azrael feigned indignation. "Watch it! I'm supposed to be the most feared Angelic in the galaxy! Whooooooo! One touch and the boogey man will get you!" Azrael did his best Hollywood-movie impersonation of himself, reaching up one arm to silently point at Sam as though he were being singled out to be dragged to hell.

"Every time I see you," Sam laughed. "You've either got your nose buried in a book, or you start spouting some obscure scientific theory that nobody else is smart enough to even understand! Much less discuss it with you! It's like … you start talking and it's nappy time!"

"Okay…" Sam's levity alleviated the vague sense of unease he'd felt ever since he'd teleported into the Baghdad suburb. "So I'm still a nerd. In a perfect world, I'd follow humans around all day studying their behavior and figuring out what makes them tick instead of doing this stuff."

"Especially one particular human," Sam guffawed. "A certain pretty blonde nurse, perhaps?"

Azrael hid his guilty smile and looked back to the compound they were supposed to be getting ready to raid, not making small talk about wooing human females. Sam's radio crackled. He put in his earpiece and answered in the Sata'anic language.

"My guys are now in position," Sam said. "The only target Lucifer really cares about is Chemosh. Anyone else is gravy."

"I'll grab the squatter," Azrael said. "You and your guys secure the perimeter. As soon as you hear shooting, you'll know they've seen me. Move in and grab the hostages so they don't kill them."

"Or abscond with them," Sam reminded him. "Granny and the kids are potential hosts as well."

"Got it," Azrael said. "Ready? Three. Two. One…"

He flashed between the dimensions into the room where a larger-than-ordinary wraith dominated the humans. The room had several adult males all meeting the description Sam had given of the host. Which one was Chemosh? The dampening field inhibited his ability to tell one from the other!

"Malak al-Maut!" The agents dove for their weapons.

"Our esteemed guest has arrived at last," a man wearing a white ghutrah said, holding up one hand to indicate he wished for his men to hold their fire. "Tell me, young void creature. Do you feel up to the task of taking on a god?"

Azrael froze. This wasn't how things usually went down.

"I don't see any gods in this room," Azrael replied, carefully sending out tiny, invisible tendrils of spirit into the room to get a gauge for just how big this Agent's consciousness was before he made a grab for it. He could sense the lesser agents moving into position. Hostages were pushed to the forefront. Human shields. No matter which way he extended tendrils of spirit, all he could feel was that damned dampening field Chemosh must have deployed to mask his presence.

"Let's not play games, little one," Chemosh said pleasantly, projecting a sense of calmness and ease along with his words. "You're a cute little void creature. I'd really like to study you."

Azrael felt the compulsion in Chemosh's voice. Powerful. Much more powerful than Lucifer, although these days Lucifer usually only used his gift to seduce women.

"No," Azrael resisted the image Chemosh projected into his mind of the two of them conducting fascinating scientific experiments together. "I prefer to work alone. But if you'd like to validate my research, you're welcome to look up any of the non-classified studies I've published in the Journal of Galactic Sociology. You can peer-review any one you wish."

Shit … this guy could read him like a book! The Regent had taught him to shield his thoughts, but he'd never really had to do it against such a powerful being before. Lucifer was a cake-walk next to this … thing! Chemosh's body movements were deliberate and slow as he moved towards the human shields.

ANNA ERISHKIGAL

"Pity," Chemosh said. "I do so enjoy picking things apart and figuring out how they work. I rather looked forward to working with you. We could really use somebody like you."

Azrael felt Chemosh's consciousness sizing him up even as he did the same thing. Shit! This … thing … was huge. It extended beyond the walls of the compound and out into the city beyond. No wonder he'd felt uneasy the moment he'd teleported into Baghdad! That was no dampening field! That was Chemosh cramming his enormous consciousness into a human host! How the hell had he not put two and two together?

Because, until now, the only full-fledged god he'd ever encountered up-close-and-personal was Hashem and the Regent, and *she* kept tabs on him no matter where he was in the universe. It hadn't occurred to him to even look!

Azrael moved into position to make a grab. "I've heard stories about the kind of experiments you like to conduct on the species you enslave. I think I'll pass."

"But Moloch insists," Chemosh projected an overwhelming urge to trust him into Azrael's mind. "You're exactly the kind of ally our beloved god has been looking for if you ever figure out how to piece your body back together. Let us help you."

For the first time since the day he'd taken on Moloch to save his friend, Azrael remembered what it felt like to fear for his own existence. Moloch had wanted him then, and he *still* wanted him now. There was a reason the Regent insisted Archangel novitiates exist within the safety of the Cherubim monastery until they became powerful enough to resist Moloch and his agents.

"It's better to be consumed by the fires of Gehenna," Azrael said. "Than to spend a single day being possessed by filth such as Moloch."

"Ahh…" Chemosh purred, projecting images of a reasonable, sycophantic friend who only wished to help. "But being without form is so lonely. Isn't it, young void creature? Especially for you, poor thing. Such a sensitive soul to be so feared! How terrible it must be, to never know the touch of another creature."

Chemosh was right. He was a young void creature, still learning to control his own power and not at all comfortable wielding it. This monster, on the other hand, was nearly as old as Moloch himself. Older than this universe. This wasn't going to be an easy grab.

"We are alike," Chemosh's voice was hypnotically reasonable. "Victimized by Ki. Why … I didn't ask to be stripped of my body any more than you asked to be stripped of yours."

Chemosh stepped up to one of the hostages, a teenage boy, and caressed the fearful child's cheek. Tears welled up in the boys eyes.

"You're not a creature of the void," Azrael said. "And neither is Moloch. Just because you lost your body doesn't make us alike."

"Don't be afraid, my son," Chemosh crooned in Arabic to the son of the host he currently occupied. "Papa will make everything all right." He turned to Azrael. "Isn't that true, my young void creature? Oh … I forgot. You don't have a father!"

Chemosh plucked the image of an old childhood fear out of Azrael's mind, amplified it, and shoved it back into his mind, insinuating the reason he didn't have a sire was because he'd been rejected at birth.

"That's it!" Azrael launched himself at the malignant old god. He was reasonable, not unfeeling. Innocent host or not … nothing could host that filth and remain untainted.

He realized his mistake too late…

Chemosh stepped to one side and pulled the boy in front of him, right into Azrael's flight path. Azrael twisted mid-air and frantically flapped his wings, trying to land somewhere, anywhere, but where he was aimed. He almost made it. Almost. But not quite. A single feather brushed the boy's arm. His eyes locked with Azrael's even as his mortal shell fell to the ground.

"Nooo!" Azrael tucked his body into a roll as the boy dropped dead from his touch.

Chemosh laughed. "So gullible, little void creature!"

Azrael exploded into his true form, the tentacled creature of nightmare. Static electricity electrocuted those agents he didn't actually touch as he bolted after Chemosh. The malignant agent didn't even bother trying to run.

"You can't drag me back to Gehenna!" Chemosh laughed. "You're too small!"

Azrael wrapped his consciousness around the physical form of the host, jolting Chemosh out of the former cafeteria worker's body. The body dropped to the floor. Khalid's spirit stood, perplexed, as he looked around the room.

"What did you do to my boy?" Khalid wailed. "He was innocent!!!"

"He killed him!" Chemosh accused, his consciousness assuming his original form of some type of angular, slug-like creature. "Not me! -I- wanted to keep the boy safe!"

Khalid wept as he reached towards his son. Azrael wrapped thousands of tentacles around Chemosh to drag the bastard back to Gehenna. The old god didn't budge. He was too large. Azrael couldn't even wrap his spirit around the evil thing, much less teleport it anywhere.

But Chemosh was big enough to wrap his consciousness around *Azrael*!

Oh … crap!

"Come, little void creature," Chemosh laughed, clawing at Azrael's spirit. "Moloch is very anxious to meet you. It's too bad you have no physical shell. You'd make such a fine host."

"Screw you!" Azrael hissed, reshaping his form so that he had the thick, powerful tentacles of an octopus instead of the millions of microvilli he normally used to sense the world around him. He worked one tentacle into the clawed ones Chemosh was using to pin Azrael against him.

"Whatsamatter, little void creature," Chemosh taunted. "Bite off more than you can chew?"

'Yes,' Azrael thought silently in his own mind.

"No!" Azrael shouted aloud. Bolts of static electricity shot off of him as he gave up trying to hold any semblance of a form. He allowed himself to become one with the void. Thought did not exist in this state. Only … hunger. An absence of love unlike any he'd ever felt before.

An absence of light.

Darkness.

Pure … void.

He hungered to fill the gaping absence of love with … something. With … Chemosh. The molecules in the room began to vibrate as Azrael lost control.

"He's summoned the Guardian!!!" one of the other agents in the room screamed, believing him to be He-who's-not.

"Not so fast," Chemosh crooned. "This isn't the Guardian. He's a spunky little devil? Isn't he? But this one is still a baby. Too small to destroy the likes of me!"

Chemosh rammed an image into Azrael's mind of being picked up by the scruff of the neck like a kitten and carried off to Gehenna to be devoured by Moloch. The Agent's main power seemed to be his 'power of persuasion.' Well … the Regent had taught *him* how to resist that gift.

'Wanna bet?' Azrael allowed his anger to increase the instability of the molecular structure of everything around him.

The walls of the compound begin to dissipate.

Hunger. So hungry. He drew the primordial nothingness which underlay all matter into his own spirit as he destroyed the housing compound, making himself grow larger. Neutrinos. Quarks. Higgs-bosons. Leptons. His power grew. The hunger grew. The malignant consciousness in front of him began to resemble a tasty snack.

"Uh-oh!" Chemosh said. "Looks like the little guy's finally feeling his oats. Everybody … out! It's time to go!"

Azrael grabbed at the fleeing mortal agents, not just jolting their consciousness out of their physical form, but dissipating their bodies completely. He sought not just to reap, but to destroy them.

"Sayonara, little void creature!!!" Chemosh taunted as he teleported between the dimensions.

The building collapsed, dissolving into primordial nothingness as Azrael used it to feed his hunger. His rage. He fed ... indiscriminately. There was matter beyond the walls. He would consume that as well.

A small voice cried out in terror.

The boy.

His spirit was still here.

Azrael had killed an innocent boy ... and then left the terrified spirit here to fend for itself while he destroyed everything around it.

This is wrong!

Azrael fought to regain control of the hunger consuming his reason. Hunger. Why hadn't the Regent warned him the hunger was all-consuming?

"Please don't hurt me!" the boy cried.

"I can't ... control it!" Azrael gasped. "Please ... go!"

The Regent hadn't warned him because he hadn't told her he'd begun having trouble with the molecules in the room vibrating whenever he got angry, that's why. He'd meant to. But he'd been so busy he'd never gotten around to it. Control. How did the Regent regain control of her dark gift when it began to spiral out of control?

An image of the General opening the palm of Regent's hand and giving it a kiss popped into Azrael's mind. The General helped her subdue her gift. But Azrael had no mate.

But he did have a friend who he wished could be more. He pictured her as she had been the day he had first met her. Dime store wings splayed on the snow beneath her. Golden curls darkened with blood, curling endearingly around her face. Her beautiful, silver eyes as she'd looked up and curled her small hand around his. Touch. He could feel, even now, what it had felt like when she'd touched his hand. The only touch he had felt in 2,300 years.

She had smiled at him and told him she was the Angel of the Lord.

The hunger began to abate.

Sanity prevailed as Azrael got his dark gift under control.

Azrael looked around as he reshaped his physical form into that of an Archangel once more. The compound looked like it had been bombed, only shattered walls remaining where he'd indiscriminately lashed out and fed. The Agent's bodies were gone. Absorbed into his own essence which Azrael could sense had grown larger from the feeding. The host's body was gone as well. His spirit was nowhere to be found.

And neither was the boy's...

"Aban?" Azrael called, using the name which had leaped into his mind when he had brushed against the boy.

There was no answer. "Khalid? Aban?" Azrael called again, feeling sick to his stomach. "Are you okay? I'm not going to hurt you."

Nothing. The boy was gone. And so was the father.

Although the heart Azrael had learned to fashion to go along with his preferred shape wasn't real, he had taught it to beat like a real heart. It indicated emotion like a real heart. And right now, that heart raced in panic as he realized the boy had gone missing and he couldn't remember whether the boy had escaped along with his father, or been consumed along with the agents. He darted between the dimensions, to the gateway to the Dreamtime where he usually guided the souls of the deceased until they crossed over.

Nothing.

Not a peep from the other side. The room was dark and empty. There was no indication the boy's loved ones had gathered there to welcome him. Or that he'd even found his way there at all.

"What have I done?" Azrael choked.

With a cry of grief, he threw himself between the dimensions to search for the spirit of the child he'd just murdered.

Chapter 38

I opened to my beloved,
but my beloved had withdrawn himself; and was gone.
My soul failed when he spake:
I sought him, but I could not find him.
I called him, but he gave me no answer.
Song of Solomon, 5:6

Earth - AD March 24, 2003
Nasiriyah, Iraq

Fiery arms reached up to tear her out of her bed and pull her down through the mattress. Pain. The sensation of being shoved inside a gigantic maw and eaten alive. Shattered. Darkness. Light. Terror. She was falling. Falling faster and faster as the flames consumed her. She looked up and saw a black-winged blur speed into the fire after her.

"Azrael!!!" she screamed and reached up for his hand.

He grabbed her and refused to let her go as she pulled him down along with her into the fire. He pulled her against his body and tried to shield her as it solidified into molten lava.

'I've got you,' he whispered, wrapping his wings around her. Protecting her with his life.

With his very soul…

The bull-god tried to rip her from his arms and failed. A cello sounded, mournful and beautiful as the fires of Gehenna exterminated the shell she'd assumed for this lifetime. He hadn't abandoned her!!! The connection they'd formed, although tenuous and new, was strong. Stronger than the other, broken bond she'd hoped to repair. She could hear the Song, faint, but clear. It was too bad she'd been taken before this shell had matured enough to consummate it. She had a choice to make. She strengthened the connection to the one who hadn't abandoned her.

"Eosphorus…"

Hands reached down to grab her, urging Azrael to expend his lifespark so he could push her to safety. She fought, not wishing to leave him behind.

She'd searched too many lifetimes to find him! He pushed her up out of the fire, sacrificing himself to save her.

'Let me go!!!' she screamed as hands lifted her out of the fiery hell. "I won't let you take him from me!!!"

'You must find him,' Ki whispered into her mind. *'He needs you.'*

"Azrael," Elisabeth cried.

"Elisabeth?" Susan, one of the other nurses said, gently shaking her awake. "Elisabeth … you're having a nightmare."

'He needs you. You have to find him.'

Elisabeth shot straight up, banging her head on the bunk above as she hyperventilated in a cold sweat. Standing around her were three of her barracks-mates, bleary-eyed and grouchy at having been awoken by her shouting in her sleep.

"And I thought –I- had bad dreams," Mary said, the nurse who slept in the bunk above her.

"Musta been the chili they served for supper," Lucy said, another barracks mate. "Talk about your acid reflux!"

"We don't need to invade Iraq to steal their gas," Mary said with her southern drawl. "This platoon here's got enough of its own after that chili!"

The other nurses giggled at the joke.

Dream. It was just a dream. This was reality…

"Green mossy skeletons," Susan said, the engineering specialist who'd shaken her awake. "That's what –I- always dream of after eating five-alarm chili. Nasty bony hands clawing up through the earth to pull me into their graves." She reached towards Elizabeth with clawed hands. "RARGH!!!"

Elisabeth shuddered. It felt a little too close to what she'd just been dreaming of.

'He needs you,' the voice echoed again.

"Huh?"

"I ain't said nothing," Mary drawled. "Gal … you been burning the candle at both ends too long. You been having nightmares every night this week, talking in some strange language I ain't never heard before."

"German?" Opa had taught her German, but she was not fluent. More like … tourist German.

"Will you guys shut up?!!" someone shouted from further down the portable housing unit. "Some of us need to get some sleep!"

The nurses had lucked out by being assigned a portable housing unit, which had air conditioning and slept sixteen, instead of a tent, which didn't have air conditioning and slept fifty. Chatter after-hours was cause to be banished back to the sweltering, bug-infested tents.

"No," Lucy whispered low enough so the ones complaining wouldn't hear. "I did two tours of duty at Ramstein Air Force Base. It wasn't German."

"Who cares?" Susan said with a shrug, yawning loudly in everyone's faces. "You heard the girl! Let's get back to bed."

"You!" Mary chastised her. "Next time! No chili before bed! Ya hear?"

The other nurses crawled back into their bunks. Elisabeth lay awake, unable to sleep. One by one, her barracks-mates breathing became rhythmic and shallow. The dream stayed with her long after her racing heart began to slow.

She hadn't seen him for six days. It was unlike him not to check in on her, especially now that he'd shown himself and she had started to coax him out of his shell. The first day she hadn't thought too much of it. She'd been busy herself packing up and moving the medevac unit forward at the rear of the advancing troops and it was entirely possible he'd only been able to flit in so briefly that she'd failed to recognize his proximity. Azrael had his own war to wage and it wasn't the first time something had come up.

By the second day, she'd begun to worry. It wasn't like him not to pop in for a few seconds ... just long enough for her to sense his presence. But she was busy and, anyway, who would she call? 1-800-Dial-a-Death?

By day three she'd started looking over her shoulder, hoping every sand-flea and bead of sweat crawling down her back was really her nerves sensing he was there. Either he was really busy reaping his own bad guys, or something was wrong. Azrael was conscientious to a fault. He wouldn't simply abandon her. Especially after she'd told him how empty she'd felt when he'd vanished after Nancy had died.

Day four they'd pulled up the base in Kuwait and moved forward to stay close to the advancing front lines. She'd wandered the outskirts of the base, calling into the shadows and frequenting the few secluded places on the teeming Forward Operating Base she could find, hoping he would materialize.

He hadn't.

Yesterday she'd asked Harold to discreetly put out feelers as to whether there'd been any incidents involving unexplained enemy deaths with aces of spades tucked into their breast pocket. As far as he knew, there hadn't been. The dream was most likely her subconscious spewing forth her own insecurities. It was foolish to worry about him. He was the Angel of Death, for chrissakes! What could possibly happen to him?

More likely, she'd said something to offend him...

Elisabeth lay in the bunk, the gentle whir of the air conditioner humming as she ran over everything in her mind they'd said to one another the last time he'd visited. She'd been exhausted and grumpy from having to suddenly rip up roots in Afghanistan and plop them down again at the border of Iraq, but Azrael had been in a good mood. She'd teased him about his appearance, insinuating without actually saying the words that she found him attractive. He'd fluttered his wings like a puppy waiting for his master to throw him a bone. It was cute, the way the most feared angel in the universe followed her around.

'He needs you,' the voice came back in her mind.

"Aw … crap," Elisabeth groaned. Obviously, she wasn't going to get back to sleep! She pulled on her combat boots, even though she was technically supposed to always be far enough back from the front line that she wouldn't have to see combat, and took off her sweatshirt before shuffling out the door into the sweltering night.

Dust. And she'd thought Afghanistan had been bad! The moon had an eerie orange tint, lingering effects of a rainy sand-storm which had passed through, dropping orange sludge on everything. She'd always thought rain in the desert would be a blessing until she'd actually gotten it.

"Azrael?" Elisabeth called softly into the night. Something bit her bare legs. Sand fleas? She should have pulled on her pants instead of wandering out in the boxer shorts she wore off duty. She sat down on a crate, the whine of overloaded supply trucks coming back from points forward to be reloaded and shipped right back out again cutting through the silence.

Nothing.

In the dream, the voice had called her a different name. Not Elisabeth. Nor Elissar, the name of the child Azrael had tried to save. She'd finally been able to coax bits and pieces of the story out of him. He'd looked like he would break down and cry when he'd finally spoken about the loss of his young friend. So sensitive... Why couldn't he have been born a normal guy and sat next to her in chemistry class in high school? They'd have been the happiest dweeb-couple to walk the halls of Lincoln Park High School since Romeo and Juliet!

Was her subconscious trying to tell her something her conscious mind had missed the last time she'd seen him? Perhaps... Oma had possessed the second-sight. Mama disapproved of Oma's talk of the gift, but Oma had taught her anyway.

She closed her eyes and tried to sense where he might be. She had a small picture he'd drawn of her bandaging up the leg of a GI tucked into her T-shirt pocket. Oma had taught to use a personal belonging to focus on another person. Azrael was not on the base, but he wasn't far. To get off-base, she would need authorization.

"Kadima!!!" Elisabeth pounded on the door to the tiny private room of a portable unit her friend shared with her commander husband. "Kadima!!! I need your help."

Kadima shuffled to the door and opened it, not pleased.

"It's three a.m.," Kadima groused.

"I need Harold to pull some strings to let me use a jeep," Elisabeth said. "Alone."

"We're in the middle of an active war zone," Kadima grumbled. "Harold's a bear when he's woken up."

"I think Azrael is in some sort of trouble," Elisabeth whispered. "Please … he needs me. I can feel it."

Kadima's mouth opened, and then shut again. Her own dealings with the Angel of Death had taught her he was not the invulnerable purveyor of death legend painted him to be. Kadima jokingly referred to Azrael as 'marshmallow angel.'

"Give me a few minutes," Kadima grumbled. "This will take some convincing."

Forty minutes later, Elisabeth had her jeep and sped down a pock-marked road following nothing but a feeling. She didn't need to go far. A farm. Floodlights were everywhere. Jeeps crawled all over the compound, men going through the buildings with plastic baggies and tweezers. Spooky sorts of men wearing long black trench coats, the kind who reported directly to the CIA. Looking for something.

"Probably searching for something to save their ass for fucking up at al-Dura," Elisabeth muttered, remembering the opening volley of bombings to behead the snake five days ago. Why randomly bomb an ordinary house in a crowded Baghdad suburb even before the invasion had begun without at least verifying the target was there?

Elisabeth smelled a cover up...

World-wide live broadcasts of B-1 bombers delivering 'shock and awe' to kill Saddam Hussein and his two sons at some compound outside the city had turned into a debacle about how gullible the superpowers were when given bad intelligence. Elisabeth, herself, had been forced to learn damned quickly in Afghanistan to be wary when a local announced they had intelligence about some bad guy holed up someplace and offered to show you where they were. More often than not, such 'invitations' turned out to be live beheadings on YouTube.

But they were still weeks out from Baghdad. Nasiriyah had just been declared 'secure,' with only sporadic resistance. What was going on? She parked the jeep and killed the lights, fishing for her military ID so they wouldn't shoot her on sight as a spy. If they found her here, it would take quite a bit of explaining. But whatever had happened, it had involved Azrael. She could feel it. In fact, she could feel him.

Elisabeth froze at the sound of the safety being slipped off an M-16.

"Stop!" an American accent shouted in Arabic. "Or I'll shoot!"

Elisabeth didn't speak much Arabic, but that was the first phrase they'd made sure everyone knew how to say as they'd flown them here.

"I'm an American," Elisabeth took care to hiss her 's' and elongate her 'ah' sounds to accentuate her Chicago accent. "I'm … looking for somebody."

"You're out of uniform, soldier!" the man said in English this time.

"I'm a nurse," Elisabeth said carefully. "I'm going to turn around, okay? And then you can check my ID. I have permission from Major Harold Steiner to come off the Forward Operating Base in Nasiriyah to look for an … um … an informant."

"What informant?"

She guessed he was a CIA operative by the long black trench coat and fedora he had pulled over his eyes. And tinted glasses even though it was nighttime. Spooks. That's what they called the CIA guys. Spooks.

"It's top secret," she said glibly. "I could tell you. But then I'd have to kill you."

"I'm not amused, Lieutenant Kaiser," the operative read her name off her military ID. "Spit it out or face court martial."

"Um … either you know what this is and so I'm not spilling the beans," Elisabeth reached back into her pocket. "Or you don't know, in which case good luck getting a disciplinary action to stick against me."

She was bluffing. She knew she was bluffing. But he didn't. The last thing she wanted was Harold to get in trouble for finagling things so she could slither off the base in the middle of a not-very-secure 'secure' zone.

She pulled out the Ace of Spades.

"Shit," the operative said. He touched a button attached to a communications device stuck into his ear and spoke into a tiny microphone. "Deputy-Director Adams? This is Agent Washington. I got something here that might interest you."

"What?" a voice crackled from the tiny earpiece in the operative's ear.

"Some American gal just walked right in," Agent Washington said, "and gave me your friend's calling card."

Elisabeth heard the earpiece crackle, but couldn't make out the words.

"It's dark but …" Agent Washington said, "yes … I think so. Blonde."

More unintelligible crackling.

"Roger," Agent Washington said, then turned his attention back to Elisabeth. "Come with me. The Deputy-Director wants to see you."

Elisabeth obediently followed the CIA operative. There was no point in running. They'd seen her ID and discovered the Jeep. They walked past a half-dozen agents with guns guarding the simple mud-brick farmhouse. The agent led her inside the modest shelter. Carpets adorned the rammed-dirt floor, cushions largely sufficing for chairs. Around the room, a fearful elderly woman, several children ranging from infancy to just barely teenagers, and a second woman who had to be their mother eyed her warily. One of the CIA operatives took blood samples and DNA swabs.

"Salam alaikam," Elisabeth murmured in greeting, trying to put the homeowners at ease.

The homeowners stared at her long blonde hair trailing down her back and bare legs exposed by the man's boxer shorts she'd worn to bed. Agent Washington led her to a back room in the farmhouse and gestured for her to go inside.

"Elisabeth," a voice greeted warmly in a perfect Midwestern accent. "We meet again."

"Sergeant ... Adams?" Elisabeth recognized the tall African-American man who'd recruited her into the nursing corps and pulled all kinds of strings to get her accepted in spite of the physical limitation posed by her leg. "You're in charge here?"

"For now," Samuel Adams said. "And please ... it's Sam. What are you doing here?"

"I'm ... um ..." Elisabeth hedged.

"Looking for Azrael?"

"H-h-how did you know?" Elisabeth stammered. "I mean ... how do you know ... Az?"

"Azrael and I have been working together a long time," Sam said. "But I don't suppose he's told you about us. He's not supposed to, you know. Actually ... he's not supposed to talk to you at all. But who's going to tell him no? I mean ... it's not like we can do anything to him for disobeying!"

"I ... um ... you have me at a bit of a disadvantage," Elisabeth said. "Is he ... um ... here?"

"He is." Concern etched Sam's brow. "But I'm not sure he's in any condition to talk to anybody right now. He ... um ... we had a mission head south on us and he's ... well ... you know how Az is. He's beside himself."

"Is he okay?" Fear gnawed a hole in the pit of her stomach.

"Physically?" Sam said. "Who knows? Nobody knows how he even exists on this plain. Much less what he is or is not supposed to be like on any given day. But I think he's okay. Emotionally, on the other hand..."

Sam trailed off, his implication clear. Something had happened during a mission to upset him. Elisabeth had treated enough soldiers suffering from post-traumatic stress that she knew what Sam referred to.

"Bring me to him right away," Elisabeth said. "He needs me." If Sam really was a Sergeant, which she doubted, she now outranked him. If he was some sort of Deputy-Director of the CIA, then he outranked her, but Sam didn't appear to be stonewalling her. In fact ... he seemed as concerned about Azrael as she was.

"C'mon," Sam said. "I can't promise he'll even let you in. But I'll give it a try. Maybe you can talk some sense into him."

"What happened?" Elisabeth asked.

"He killed somebody he didn't mean to kill," Sam said. "Or at least I think that's what happened."

"A friendly fire type incident?" Elisabeth asked. "Who died?"

"All he'll tell me is someone died," Sam said. "Although … with him … dead usually doesn't mean dead as in like … dead. As in when you and me are dead. Technically … Azrael's dead, too. But as you know … he's not … really … dead. He's just …"

"The Angel of Death," Elisabeth said. "Neither here nor there."

"Yeah … well …" Sam brought her to a tiny mud-brick shed with a ramshackle roof. "I don't know what the hell to call any of them. They're not like regular angels, Azrael and his kin. Though he's pretty far out on left field, even for an Archangel. But … I'm rambling. He's the one you should be asking questions."

Elisabeth stared at the tiny shed, barely large enough to fit a couple of goats, much less the tall, slender Azrael. He was hiding in there? How could he fit those big wings of his?

"Hey … Az," Sam called. "You got a visitor."

"Go away," Azrael called from behind the door. "Before I kill you, too!"

A threat? Elisabeth looked with surprise at Sam, whose facial expression was one of concern, not worry or anger. Not a threat.

"Oh…" Elisabeth's mouth dropped into an 'O' as she realized what had probably happened. Azrael was adamant he only reap the souls of those who were either evil and slated for hell, a place he called Gehenna, or escort the spirits of good people to heaven. He must have jumped the gun on somebody.

"Azrael," Elisabeth made her voice as warm and welcoming as possible. "It's me. Elisabeth. I was worried about you."

"Sam shouldn't have called you," Azrael said, a catch in his voice. "I'm too dangerous to be around you anymore."

"Sam isn't the one who called me," Elisabeth said. "I found you on my own. I was worried about you."

"Did you hear what happened?" Azrael said, his voice hoarse.

"Not exactly," Elisabeth said. "You … um … you took somebody you didn't mean to take?"

"I'm not fit to be around living creatures," Azrael choked from behind the door, obviously crying. "I'm too deadly!"

Sam gave her an 'I told you so' look.

"Azrael," Elisabeth coaxed. "I'm not leaving until you come out and talk to me. And I'm definitely not going in there. It's too small and it reeks of goat shit! So you're just going to have to come out."

"No!"

"Then I'll just wait," Elisabeth said. "You have to come out sometime."

"No … I don't," Azrael said. "I'm not … real. I'm not even alive! I can sit in here until this planet's sun turns into a red giant."

"Fine," Elisabeth said. "Then I'll just sit out here until I'm reported absent without leave and they come to court martial me. The battle is going badly just north of here. Soldiers will die because I'm not there to save them. It will be all your fault."

Silence.

She looked at Sam. Sam looked at her and shrugged.

"I've got to get back to work guarding the other potential hosts," Sam said loudly enough so Azrael could hear it through the door. "When the MP's come, I'll tell them where to find you."

"Thanks, Sam," Elisabeth said just as loudly. "Hopefully they won't take me away in handcuffs and throw me in a jail cell with rats. I hate rats."

"Good thing we're not in Saudi Arabia," Sam said loudly. "The morality police would definitely arrest you in that getup. I don't think you're supposed to go wandering around an active war zone wearing nothing but boxer shorts."

Elisabeth suppressed a smile as Sam stomped his boots on the hard soil so Azrael could hear him move away. Sam had obviously spent considerable time 'handling' their sensitive friend. Angel of Death her foot! Azrael did what he did because there was no one else who could do his job. Not because he enjoyed it!

She waited.

And waited.

And waited some more.

Silence.

Was he even still in there? She knew he could flash from one place to another simply by thinking about it. But she could sense he was still crammed into the too-tight shed, probably concentrating with all his might to not accidentally dissolve the walls of his hideout.

What might coax him out of his stinky bower? Hmmm… She knew what he craved most in the world. Staring at the ground until she found what she wanted, she picked up a rounded pebble, clutched it to her chest, and gave it a kiss.

"I've got something for you," Elisabeth slipped the pebble beneath the uneven wooden door.

"What?" Azrael said, a sniffle in his voice.

"A hug and a kiss."

"My touch is death," Azrael said. "In case you didn't get the memo."

"I know," Elisabeth said. "So I put it in that pebble I just slid under the door. You can pick it up and do that thing you do to make it disappear into your hand, and then you can have it. A hug. And a kiss. From me. 'Cause you really seem like you need one right about now."

Silence.

She heard the slight scrape of wings against the wall of the shed. They didn't dissolve, so he must be in control enough of his emotions to remain solid. She heard him find the pebble in the dark.

Silence.

He fumbled with the latch. With a squeal like a haunted house, Azrael swung open the rickety door and peered outside.

"Thanks," he said. "I ... um ... kind of needed that."

"I know."

Silence.

She waited.

He stood there. Not moving. His expression anxious. Although he'd explained his physical form was not 'real,' a figment of his imagination, his imagination told him it would be appropriate to manifest his appearance as having puffy eyes from crying because it was obvious he was seriously upset.

"I ... um ..." Elisabeth said. "I forgot to bring my cane. Can we go someplace we can sit down to talk? Please? My leg hurts."

Azrael hesitated.

"I don't want to hurt you," he said mournfully.

"Then you can sit out of wing-whack range," Elisabeth said.

"That might not be far enough," Azrael said, his eyes haunted.

"Then we'll sit far enough apart that I can run away if you turn into the boogey man," Elisabeth said.

Azrael froze. It was the wrong thing to say.

"Listen," Elisabeth said. "I don't know what happened. And I'm not going to know unless you tell me. So either you come tell me like a big person. Or I'm going to have to wrestle your friend to the ground using one of those Canadian Special Forces holds Kadima's husband taught me and force Sam to tell me at gunpoint."

"Sam's a lot ... bigger ... than he looks," Azrael said.

"Then it will be your fault if I get hurt," Elisabeth said sweetly, using every feminine wile she possessed to appeal to Azrael's overdeveloped sense of chivalry.

Silence.

"Okay," Azrael said. "We can ... um ... go over here to talk. But I ... um ... I want you to stay at least fifteen feet away from me at all times in case ... in case I lose control."

"I highly doubt that," Elisabeth hobbled over to a strategically placed boulder. She groaned with not-too exaggerated pain as she sat down upon the rock.

Azrael stood exactly fifteen feet away, his wings poised as though ready to take flight and clutched his cloak around his physical form. She waited. After months of almost daily conversations, she knew he would talk when he was ready.

Elisabeth picked up another pebble and pretended to stare at it. She watched Azrael's reaction, the way his nostrils flared as he gauged her mood from her scent the way a dog might gauge the mood of its owner. Azrael claimed he didn't need to breathe anymore, but his spirit automatically recreated the illusion of physiological processes he'd once possessed when he'd still been mortal. She suspected it was a trait he fostered within himself so he would feel alive. Azrael obsessed over the difference between being dead ... or alive ... and all the millions of shades of grey which lay somewhere in between those two states.

"I made ... a mistake," Azrael finally said, his voice almost a whisper.

Elisabeth waited, her expression sympathetic and interested as she waited for him to tell her more.

"I ... killed ... somebody," Azrael said. "An ... innocent."

Elisabeth had already figured that much out on her own. This wasn't the first time she'd seen a soldier come in all freaked out because he'd thought he was killing an insurgent and had either killed or wounded a civilian. Dealing with this kind of thing was part of her training.

"It happens sometimes," Elisabeth said, filling her voice with understanding. "This is a war zone. Accidents happen."

"He was just a boy," Azrael suppressed a sob. "The squatter pulled him right in front of him when I went to take him. I should have known better. I should have known better than to try to take him with a hostage that close. It was so ... obvious ... that was what he meant to do! What kind of person uses a child as a human shield?"

Azrael turned his back to her so she wouldn't see him cry. His wings drooped to the ground in despair, glossy black feathers trailing lines of dissolved matter in the dusty soil as his shoulders dry-heaved the sobs he kept from escaping his throat.

"Oh ... Az." She'd counseled soldiers before with almost identical incidents, but this was the first time she'd been friends with the soldier who was freaked out. "Listen. You only go after the worst of the worst bad guys. This is what they do. This is what they do so people like us won't go after them. They know we feel despair when an innocent person gets in our way and dies. But you can't just not go after them! If you give up … they win!"

"Never!" Azrael hissed, his back straightening ramrod straight. He turned, his eyes black with anger as his wings flared as though stabbing someone. "Moloch will never win so long as there's a single subatomic particle of my spirit still in existence!"

Elisabeth smiled. Anger. She had a whole lifetime's worth of experience in harnessing anger to overcome adversity. Azrael might be a tender and sweet like a peach. But beneath that tenderness lay a stony pit that would break your teeth if you made the mistake of thinking you could bite off a chunk and spit it out.

"We have a saying in my country," Elisabeth said. "Payback's a bitch. If you can't undo what you've done, then all you can do is get even."

Azrael took one step forward, his mouth opening as though to agree with her, and then stepped back.

"You don't understand," he said quietly. "I lost control. I lost control of my gift."

"I've seen you lose control once before," Elisabeth said gently. "Remember? The day Nancy died?"

"That was … intentional," Azrael said cautiously. "They tried to shoot you and they *did* shoot Nancy. It was … justified. This was different. I've gotten upset and destroyed things before. But not … this. This was bad."

"Then you need to train yourself to keep control so it doesn't happen again," Elisabeth said. "Do you think you're the only person who ever screwed up?"

"I … don't…" Azrael said, unsure of his answer.

"Do you think you're the only person who ever bought a shiny new car and then got in an accident?" Elisabeth asked. "Or put their heart and soul into building some new project? A dream house? A company? A railroad bridge? And then had it all come tumbling down around your ears for reasons that might or might not have anything to do with you?"

"No," Azrael's voice trembled with emotion.

"You get right back behind the wheel of the car and you be more careful next time," Elisabeth said. "You look up the building code next time you put a hammer to wood so your house doesn't fall down around your ears. Or you ask for help if something is beyond your expertise so you learn to do it right next time so you don't fuck up. That's what it means to be human!"

Azrael's wings quivered with indecision as he absorbed her words.

"What happened, Az?" Elisabeth asked softly. "I can't help you fix the problem if you don't talk about it."

Azrael began to cry for real this time, not bothering to hide it. Elisabeth waited, allowing him his grief. Whatever had happened, it had upset him enough to hide knee-deep in goat shit for the past six days so he'd be close enough to protect the people Sam's men were guarding inside the house from whatever evil bad dude Azrael had tried, and failed, to reap. Azrael was a peculiar mixture of sensitivity and courage, but he was no wilting wallflower.

"I can't find him," Azrael finally said between hiccoughs.

"Find who?" Elisabeth asked.

"The boy," Azrael said. "I searched and searched for him. He never made it into the Dreamtime."

"Oh," Elisabeth said, not sure what to say. "Where else might he have gone?"

Azrael sat down on a low stone wall and clutched his knees to his chest, pulling his wings around himself so Elisabeth couldn't see his face.

"I think I ate him," Azrael mumbled from behind the feathers.

"You ... what?"

"She said I would feel hunger," Azrael's wings muffled his words and making them sound as though he were speaking through a wall. "When I got big enough. But I ... um ... the bad guys. I ... uh ... you know that thing I do with the rocks. Like you just had me do to the pebble?"

"Dissipation," Elisabeth said. "You call it dissipation."

"I fear that's what happened to the boy," Azrael said. "When I tried to get away from the squatter."

"Wait ... get *away* from the squatter?" Elisabeth asked. "I thought ... you said you just touch them and they drop dead."

"This one didn't," Azrael said. "I mean ... the shell he squatted on did. But his consciousness ... he's too powerful."

"Who is he?" Elisabeth wished she knew more about the inner workings of the world Azrael lived in instead of bits and pieces coaxed out of him. Until now, she'd thought the other celestial creatures were afraid of Azrael.

"His name is Chemosh," Azrael said. "He's a god. Like Moloch. A really, really bad god. He's a lot bigger than I am."

"Oh," Elisabeth was beginning to get an idea of what had happened. "So ... this guy ... Shamoo."

"Chemosh," Azrael corrected.

"Chemosh," Elisabeth repeated. "So this evil bad dude, Chemosh, used this kid as a human shield? And then he was winning, because he's a lot bigger than you. And you were trying to defend yourself, right?"

"Right," Azrael wrapped his wings even more tightly around himself.

"So you had to ... what?" Elisabeth said. "Use your gift in a way you never had to do before? To stay ... alive?"

"I think so," Azrael said. "I haven't felt that frightened since tangling with Moloch."

"So it was you," Elisabeth said. "Or this evil Chemosh guy. And you defended yourself. And the kid got in the way?"

"Um … yes," Azrael said.

"So you … what? Dissolved everything around you into … goo … like you do with the rocks … and this kid … who was still around … got in the way somehow?"

"Yes," Azrael said. "No? I don't know!!! All I know is he was there and I told him to get the hell out of there because I couldn't control it. And then he disappeared and I couldn't find him."

"Did you check that gateway you sometimes tell me about? Maybe he found his own way there? You said that's what usually happens, anyway."

"He wasn't there," Azrael said. "I checked. I could find no sign of him."

"Isn't there some way you could find out for sure?" Elisabeth asked. "I mean … isn't God supposed to be in charge of who gets past the pearly gates? Or Saint Peter, maybe?"

"There is no Saint Peter," Azrael said. "At least … not guarding the pathway mortals take to enter the Dreamtime."

"Isn't there somebody you could just ask? I mean … the answer might be 'no.' The kid never found his way. But if you're going to beat yourself up over this for the rest of eternity, at least be sure about it."

"There might be somebody I can ask," Azrael's wings finally parted as he peeked through, his brow furrowed in thought. "Through certain channels."

"Then I suggest you do that," Elisabeth raised both eyebrows. "And figure out who might be able to help you learn to control your gift better so you don't accidentally vaporize the wrong person the next time you're put into that situation. It makes a lot more sense than hiding in a goat shed in the middle of a war zone."

"Oh," Azrael said. "Yes. Of course. The Regent … I'll ask her to … she can ask … and maybe … yes … SHE might talk … to him."

Elisabeth had no idea who Azrael would ask to do what, but the idea put him at ease. She prayed, for his sake, that the missing boy had made it into the afterlife or, failing that, that this goddess Azrael told her about, the one who'd purportedly once been human, knew where to send him for some obi-wan Zen training so he didn't become a hermit. That would make her unhappy. Elisabeth had made a lot of friends since joining the Army, but her closest friend of all was the one who'd been silently shadowing her for the past ten years. Now that she'd finally gotten to know him, she didn't want to lose him.

She noticed Azrael intently watched her. Studying her. Trying to discern the train of her thoughts from her body language, scent pheromones, and heart rate, which she knew he could hear every tiny nuance. Let him discern this…

Elisabeth took the pebble she'd been tossing in her hand, clutched to her chest as she had the first one, and gave the pebble a kiss. Stepping forward to middle ground, she placed the pebble down upon the ground.

"That's for you." Her eyes met his bottomless black ones that swirled darker whenever he felt strong emotion. "A hug for the next time you need one."

His nostrils flared as he inhaled her scent. His wary expression gave way to pure longing as he stepped forward and picked up the pebble, quivering like a dog. He stepped back. Quickly. As though afraid she'd leap forward to touch him and then he'd be responsible for her death as well.

"Thank you." He clutched the pebble to his heart.

It was the closest, she knew, he'd come to touching another non-ascended living creature without reaping them since the day she'd had her car accident.

"Consider yourself kissed," Elisabeth said.

Chapter 39

If hundreds of thousands of suns rose up at once into the sky,
They might resemble the effulgence of the Supreme Person
In that universal form.

Bhagavad Gita 11:12

Galactic Standard Date: 157,731.03 AE
Haven-1

Down a long and featureless white corridor, the only thing which marked the door which led to the Emperor's genetics laboratory as a *special* door was the tall, dark-featured Archangel whose wings were so black they appeared to be almost bluish-purple in color. Like most of the Regent's offspring, Jeremiel bore a strong resemblance to the general, but unlike either parent, the gatekeeper to the Emperor possessed eyes so dark blue they appeared to be the color of a field of violets.

"He'll see you now," Jeremiel nodded towards the double doors. "Go ahead in. They shouldn't be too hard to find."

"Thank you," Azrael gulped. "Usually we meet in the throne room. This is the first time the Emperor has invited me into his genetics laboratory."

"Then you have moved up in his estimation," Jeremiel said. His stern expression softened into one which was the spitting image of his mother except for the fact his eyes were violet instead of black.

Azrael noted the way his Archangel brethren stepped much further away from the door than normal to avoid a brush of one of Azrael's deadly wings and twitched his purplish-black appendages out of the way so he didn't accidentally dissipate a wide swarth of feathers. Although a full-fledged Archangel like Jeremiel could survive a 'brush with death' by pulling his damaged physical form into the upper realms to reconstitute it, it was an unpleasant, time-consuming experience which most ascended creatures preferred to avoid.

That sense of despondency Azrael had felt ever since he'd tangled with Chemosh, the feeling that no matter *how* hard he tried he'd never fit in even amongst his own kind, settled into his non-corporeal center like a fist gripping at his heart.

"I'm not exactly a welcome guest," Azrael tucked his wings against his back. "Too many delicate pieces of equipment I might short out."

As though in reply, the lights in the hallway dimmed and brightened to reflect his nervousness. It wasn't a question of *would* he disrupt the electromagnetic field of everything he was near, but how badly. It all depended upon his emotional state. Right now, he was nervous as hell.

"Go." Jeremiel's violet eyes crinkled with compassion. "The Emperor doesn't bite. Much. Well … sometimes he does. But I hear Lucifer deserved what he got. What's he really like?"

"Arrogant," Azrael gave Jeremiel a salute, "contradictory, unpredictable, and debauch." He *didn't* add that after personally tangling with the evil bastard who'd snatched him out from under Hashem's nose at fifteen years old and manipulated him into being a host for Moloch, he'd found the Fallen Angelic rather hard to hate.

Since the incident with Chemosh, Azrael had become cautious about sensing the differences between mortals, quasi-ascended beings such as Archangels and the other old races, and the larger consciousnesses humans called gods. Even before he'd finished teleporting onto Haven-1, Azrael could feel an enormous, overpowering spirit permeating everything on the planet. The Regent, of course, had the same over-arching consciousness, but this felt different. Another dampening field? Ever since the botched raid at al-Dura, he no longer assumed his inability to penetrate an area and size up another spirit was simply mechanical interference.

Squeaks, grunts, purrs and growls assailed his ears as the scent of tens of thousands of creations wafted up to his nostrils as he stepped into the Emperor's cavernous genetics laboratory.

He reached into his pocket to feel the reassuring lump. The 'hug' Elisabeth had given him in case he needed one after meeting with the Emperor about the boy's fate. Little did she realize how much that small gesture had warmed his heart! It was silly, really. Falling in love with a woman you'd only touched once as a child! Like Prince Charming falling for Cinderella based on one dance and a discarded glass slipper!

Azrael's 'glass slipper' itched, reminding him why he'd always been so obsessed with her. Unlike Prince Charming, there wasn't an abundance of 'feet' who could survive the testing of the shoe.

He hurried down the cluttered aisle, avoiding brushing against the thousands of cages of living creatures which were piled floor-to-ceiling, hissing and chirping as he went. A humanoid male with wild 'mad scientist' hair was engrossed in something on a table. The Emperor. Out of his robes of state and into the laboratory coat of a scientist … like him. Across the table sat the Emperor's laboratory assistant perched upon a high stool. She was an ethereal creature with gossamer wings, pointed facial features and ears humans would describe as 'elfish.'

"Why GC GC AT GC and not GC AT AT GC?" the Emperor asked.

"You're looking to balance the creature's survival instinct with its social capacity," the assistant said. "What better way to become more sociable than increasing its sex drive?" She batted her eyelashes in a flirtatious manner, reaching across the table to touch his hand.

Azrael saw what had the two so engrossed. Some poor mammal lay dead upon the table, its internal organs splayed as the two picked through its reproductive system with medical instruments. To one side a souped-up electron microscope displayed what appeared to be a male gamete cell, while on the other side a gene sequencer crunched numbers.

The laboratory assistant didn't need the equipment to know what she examined. She picked up a chunk of flesh and rattled off an unintelligible sequence of amino acids. The Emperor placed the sample into the gene sequencer to document her results.

The woman only appeared proper at first glance. Upon closer scrutiny, Azrael couldn't help but notice the designer cut of the lab coat, the proper pencil-skirt had a slit that went just a little too high up the thigh. Tendrils which had escaped her prim bun were too artfully arranged around her chiseled features to be accidental. Modest cleavage scooped just a little too enticingly over the swell of breasts, accentuating what was hidden rather than concealing it. She was like a fashion-magazine centerfold version of a laboratory assistant, right down to the discreet glitter of diamonds embedded in the corners of her eyeglasses.

They didn't smell like a mated pair, but pheromones of the female's sexual interest flooded through the laboratory so headily that even Azrael found himself affected. Rumor claimed the Emperor was asexual, but Azrael figured he'd better make his presence known before he interrupted something.

"Ahem," Azrael coughed, tucking his wings tightly against his back in the formal 'dress wings' formation the Regent had taught him to use when addressing the Emperor. "Your Majesty? I'm here at your request."

"Ahh!" the Emperor turned and gave Azrael a benign smile. "Our little void creature is here. Innana! There's somebody I want you to meet!"

The laboratory assistant gave him a fearful look from behind her thin-framed black eyeglasses, allowing him to see, for the first time, that her eyes were golden.

"Hashem!!!" she snapped. "You know I can't stand void creatures! They're always breaking my toys!"

Azrael almost choked as he realized who poked amongst the entrails of some failed genetics experiment they were autopsying together as though it were a hot date. She-who-is. Moloch ... and Ki's ... daughter. Architect of the Universe.

"Temperance, my dearest goddess," the Emperor took her hand and give it a squeeze. "Azrael apologized for that little misunderstanding. He'd had a bad letdown that day, that's all. Haven't you ever had one of those days?"

Words were not said, but Azrael could almost *hear* the mental conversation which passed between the two deities as SHE demanded he leave and the Emperor urged her to give him a chance. She-who-is had the answer to Azrael's question. The Emperor used this as an excuse to get the two of them into the same room together. For what purpose, he didn't know.

"The boy you killed is fine," She-who-is snapped with a dismissive waive of her hand. "His father found him and escorted him into the Dreamtime. Now leave!"

"Was that so hard?" The Emperor kissed her knuckles like a knight kissing the hand of his queen. "If you want the boy to serve you, you have to be nice to him once in a while. That's all. There's no need to avoid him."

"Nice?" The goddess gave Azrael an up-and-down appraisal which made him feel like a prize bull going up for auction at a meat market. He could sense the goddess's enormous consciousness reach out and appraise the size of his, the same as Chemosh had done. Whatever it she looked for, it put her at ease. She gave him a coy smile.

"Such a ... beautiful ... boy," She-who-is accentuated the word 'boy.' "One of our better collaborations, Hashem. Your Angelic hybrids. Pity there's nothing left of this one to grab hold of and enjoy."

Azrael realized the goddess had both praised his desirability, and then cut him down at the knees. Oof! No wonder Emperor Shay'tan had all sorts of prohibitions against love goddesses. Only Hashem appeared to be capable of navigating that fine line between flattering the goddess' need to be desired while simultaneously encouraging the most formidable intellect in the universe. Hashem had found his intellectual equal, packaged in a pretty container with a bow. He could enjoy his cake only so long as he encouraged her to keep her ... frosting ... under control.

"Thank you, your majesties," Azrael bowed deeply. "It is my pleasure to serve you both."

She-who-is stepped from behind the laboratory table, the click-click-click of her high heels resounding against the white marble floor as she boldly strode to stand in front of him, mere inches from his body, no longer afraid.

"So beautiful." She-who-is moved her hand millimeters from his cheek, a feral glint coming into her eyes as she noticed the way he trembled. "The Regent taught him to hold his shape well. I wish she'd been around the first thirteen billion years HE was still here. It would have made creating the universe so much less ... repugnant!"

Azrael held his breath, afraid to breathe lest he brush against her. He knew SHE could survive his touch, but didn't know whether she was immune to getting jolted out of her current shell. Azrael could think of no better way to piss off the Architect of the Universe than to find out!

This was a creature who'd once been lovers with someone like *him*. Okay ... not quite like him. He'd been born mortal and become a void creature. He was tiny compared to the vast consciousness the goddess simply referred to as HIM. Even the Regent was petite compared to HIM. The Dark Lord had finally left because She-who-is had never loved him. After fourteen billion years of being used, HE had finally had enough.

Was this what Azrael had to look forward to once Elisabeth reached the end of her mortal life? Being needed? Being used? But never loved? Someday, she would become mated to somebody else for real and, as her 'friend,' Azrael would hide his broken heart and pretend to be happy for her. The emotion associated with that thought caused him to sharply inhale. The rise of his chest caused his head to jerk and brush against the hand the goddess held millimeters from his cheek. Warmth from her hand permeated his face as he felt her power flow into his body and be absorbed.

"Dammit!" She-who-is shrieked. "He zapped me!"

Her mortal shell dropped to the ground. A brilliant white light shone in front of him. Immediately, the molecules of the mortal shell dissipated into stardust and swirled back into the spirit before him. She would not be inconvenienced for long.

"So ... beautiful ... your majesty," Azrael stared at her naked spirit. Stripped of her physical form, she was an opposite version of *him*. What they called 'tentacles of darkness' in a void creature were 'rays of light' in her. But otherwise, she looked exactly the same as *he* did. What the Regent had told him was true. The base element of all life was spirit. She-who-is's was just larger than most.

She reached out with a ray-of-light tentacle and slapped him on the face. Not hard enough to hurt. Just enough to communicate her annoyance at being unexpectedly jolted. And he could feel it. It felt ... good. Not as good as when Elisabeth had touched him, but good nonetheless.

"Well?" She-who-is asked. Toying with him. Punishing and issuing a sexual invitation at the same time. She waited, the beautiful white tentacle of starlight millimeters from his face where her hand had been only moments before. Waiting. Waiting for him to reach up and take the hand she offered.

Touch. Touch she must have known from her former husband that void-creatures hungered for more than anything in the universe. The pheromones of attraction were nearly overwhelming. A heady drug…

A drug for the unwary…

The General had warned the Archangels to avoid falling prey to the goddess' 'affections.' Woe be the male that became her favorite! That male's downfall was usually even more meteoric than his rise to glory.

"Thank you, your Majesty for blessing me with the sight of your true form," Azrael deflected the blatant sexual invitation in a way least likely to offend her. He bowed deeply. "I am your most loyal servant."

"Hmpf!" She-who-is snorted, annoyed Azrael had not taken the bait. "Hashem! We'll discuss this later!"

And with that, the goddess who ruled the universe finished dissipating her physical form out of the teeny-tiny space she'd crammed it into in order to fiddle with dead things in Hashem's laboratory and disappeared. Almost immediately, the overwhelming consciousness Azrael had sensed since his arrival dissipated with her. Hashem's spirit was large and imposing, but not like that.

"I'm sorry I displeased her," Azrael bowed and remained bowed.

"Stand straight, young man," the Emperor ordered. He gestured to the poor dead creature whose entrails were splayed across the laboratory table. "I had to entice her to come with something she found fascinating. For all her provocative demeanor, she really is quite brilliant. I think she does that … other … thing she does out of boredom. It's lonely when there's nobody around intelligent enough to cater to your vast intellect."

"Yes, Sir," Azrael said, not sure what else to say. He'd just zapped the ruler of the universe out of her temporary shell and annoyed the heck out of her. He was relieved the Emperor didn't seem concerned.

"Despite her foibles," the Emperor said, pushing a button at the base of the table, "she has a good heart. She's sacrificed so much to keep this universe safe from her father, but it's a tough job. Sometimes she lets her blind spots get the better of her."

Azrael was silent as two laboratory assistants came in and rolled away the remains of a predator from one of the protected seed planets. Who was *he* to criticize the gods?

"I shouldn't throw stones about blind spots," the Emperor added. "That's the Regent's job. She tells me when I'm out-of-line, while the General makes sure my backside stays covered no matter what missteps I make."

"Yes, Sir." Azrael waited. He sensed the Emperor had called him here today to do more than pass along information about whether the boy had made it safely into the Dreamtime. The Emperor stared at him, his golden eyes glowing as though lit by internal suns as he weighed how he wished to present what he had to say. Eyes like … Elisabeth's. Only gold instead of silver.

"She-who-is informed me your mother was released from the Dreamtime," the Emperor said. "About thirty-seven years ago. She chose Earth in the hopes she might cross paths with you. She's in a new physical form and without memory of who she was before. Not that young research subject you seem to be so interested in, mind you! Obviously. Wrong age. I just wanted you to know."

"Thank you, your Majesty," Azrael said excitedly. Mom? Reborn? On Earth? Of course, she wouldn't recognize him until she was already dead again, but at least it gave him something to look forward to every time he did his ten good deeds. Perhaps … maybe she'd been attracted to work similar to what she'd been doing before for the Emperor? It gave him someplace to begin looking.

"Very well then," the Emperor said absent-mindedly. "Back to work. I'm glad She-who-is finally got over her little … phobia."

"Sir?" Azrael's brow furrowed in confusion. "I jolted her and she slapped me!"

"Oh … that?" the Emperor waved his hand. "She fully intended to get jolted. Ever since the Regent put her back into her place a few thousand years ago, she's been like a little kid who suddenly developed a fear of dogs. I've been bugging her for centuries to systematically desensitize herself, but until *you* were standing right in front of her, she didn't have to force herself out of her comfort zone. It was time for her to get over her fear and pat the dog."

"Oh," Azrael said. All of a sudden, her peculiar behavior made sense. Hashem had granted him an audience when SHE would be here in the more 'natural' setting of the genetics laboratory so it would be less threatening.

And he was the 'dog.'

"That will be all, Colonel Thanatos."

"But … sir," Azrael said. "I'm only a Major."

"You are what I say you are," the Emperor said. "Dismissed."

Azrael bowed deeply, and then backed up one row of tables before turning and making his way out of the Emperor's laboratory. He touched the cheek where SHE had slapped him. He couldn't feel an echo of sensation the way he did where Elisabeth had touched him. But … wow! There were creatures out there other than the Regent capable of touching him! Non-void creatures!

"A colonel…" Azrael exclaimed to Jeremiel as he burst through the double-doors to the hall. Wings flared with excitement, he practically skipped down the hall to the Garden beyond. A colonel! He couldn't wait to tell Elisabeth!

Chapter 40

For he will command his angels concerning you
To guard you in all your ways.

Psalm 91:11

Earth - AD March 25, 2003
Najaf, Iraq

"I can't see more than 25 yards in front of us in this soup," Tank Driver Vasquez shouted into his headset. Vasquez stared with dismay at the controls between his knees, not even sure whether they were even on the road any longer. "This sandstorm has visibility down to nothing! You've got to be my eyes and ears, Jaworsky!"

The M1 Abrams tank was part of a 7th Cavalry Regiment headed north after securing the bridge over the Euphrates River code-named 'Objective Floyd' to secure a second bridge which would isolate the city of Najaf. They had come under heavy fire at the bridge after crossing it, but had prevailed. Or so they had thought. Now ... not so much. The sound of dozens of automatic rifles came at them from close range.

"The bastards must have snuck up on us during the sandstorm!" Tank Gunner Jaworsky shouted into his headset as he peered through his gun sights into an orange haze of blinding sand. "This place is crawling with Iraqi forces!"

"Bradford!" Tank Commander Silva shouted from the turret. "Get this baby reloaded!"

"Come to Papa!" Gun Loader Bradford coaxed, choking on the air thick with blown sand. He kissed the enormous shell before loading it into the firing chamber of the boxy gun. "This one's for my sister Susan who died on the 104th floor of the World Trade Center."

"Ready?" Gunner Jaworsky asked.

"Ready!" Gun Loader Bradford called back.

"I'm detecting heat signatures on the infra-red at ten o'clock, Sir," Gunner Jaworsky shouted. "Request permission to engage?"

"Engage," Commander Silva yelled.

More small arms fire came at them, pinging harmlessly off the side of the tank as the hum of the turret swinging around shuddered through the heavily armored vehicle. Gun Loader Bradford dove into the belly of the tank to avoid being hit.

"Shit!" Loader Bradford shouted. "There's got to be hundreds of them out there! They're like fleas in the sand!"

"Request permission to show them who's top dog, Sir!" Gunner Jaworsky shouted, pointing at dozens of heat signatures swarming towards them in his sights.

"Permission granted!" Commander Silva shouted. "Fire!"

The ear-splitting thunder of the main gun firing shook the tank ... even through the radio headsets the crew wore to drown out the ruckus created by the tank.

"We got a direct hit, Sir," Gunner Jaworsky shouted.

"Bradford!" Commander Silva yelled. "Get up there and tell me what's going on. We're flying blind here!"

"Yes, Sir!" Gun Loader Bradford popped open the hatch.

The whistle of an incoming anti-tank missile cut through the air

"We've got incoming!!!" Gun Loader Bradford shouted. He dove back into the belly of the tank and slamming the hatch shut just in time.

The tank rocked as a deafening explosion shook the tank. Seconds later, a secondary explosion rocked them. The ammunition which, luckily, had been modified to sit outside the hardened belly of the tank or they'd all be toast, exploded.

"Fuck!!!" Driver Vasquez screamed as the vehicle lurched and then stopped, knocked off its tracks.

Smoke poured into the turret, causing the crew to choke.

"We're on fire, Sir," Driver Vasquez stated the obvious.

"Oh god oh god oh god oh GOD!!!" Gun Loader Bradford shouted, his eyes clenched shut as he thanked god for giving him the time to slam shut the hatch or they'd all be dead right now.

"Shit!" Commander Silva shouted. "We're dead in the water! We need to get out of here. Jaworsky! Any more heat signatures?"

"Can't tell, Sir," Gunner Jaworsky said, peering through the sights of the infra-red scanner. "We're on fire. We're the hottest thing around right now. Not the Iraqi's."

Black smoke filled the cabin with its toxic mixture.

"We've got to get out of here!" Gun Loader Bradford coughed. "Or we're all going to die of smoke inhalation!"

"This thing is supposed to be hardened against chemical, nuclear, and mortar fire," Commander Silva said.

"Well Old Betsy here didn't get the memo!" Gunner Jaworsky shouted. He called into his radio for help. "Papa Bear! Papa Bear! This is Red Fox! We're hit! We're hit! We're dead in the water and under enemy fire!"

His radio sputtered out as the power died inside the tank.

"Sir?" one of the soldiers said in the dark between gasps for air.

"The rubber gasket must have breached," Commander Silva said. "We need to get out of here. If we can."

There was a light tap on the hatch of the tank. Two taps. A pause. And then three rapid taps. The all clear signal.

The four soldiers glanced nervously at each other in the dark even though they couldn't see one another. The signal tapped a second time.

"That's the all clear, Sir," Driver Vasquez whispered.

"Bradford," Commander Silva ordered. "Open the hatch. The rest of you ... take aim."

Bradford opened the hatch and poked his M-16 through the crack.

"The fire's out," a voice with a perfect Midwestern accent said reassuringly. "But there's nothing I can do about your engine. I'm afraid it went along with the ammo."

"What the hell was that that hit us?" Tank Gunner Bradford called up through the crack.

"Russian 9M133 Kornet anti-tank missile," the voice said. "You're the third tank they took out before I was able to neutralize the squatter."

"The ... Russians ... are in on this?" Tank Commander Silva asked.

"Not really," the voice said. "Just a rogue element doing a little free trade agreement. Let's just say the Ba'ath Party has friends in very low places."

"What's your name, rank and unit, soldier?" Commander Silva nodded to Bradford to get ready to burst open the hatch at the signal. He hissed in a low voice ... "three ... two ..."

"Um ..." the voice said. "I'm really not supposed to say but ... some within your chain of command know me."

The slight rustle of an object passing into the crack permeated the thunder of the tank crews beating hearts.

"Now!!!" Commander Silva shouted.

Bradford burst through the hatch just in time to come face to face with...

"Hello!" Azrael gave Bradford a boyish grin.

Bradford stood there, mouth hanging open at the sight of an enormous black angel standing on top of his tank. His body blocked the hatch so the others could neither see, nor get out.

"Bradford ... MOVE!!!" Commander Silva screamed.

Bradford's mouth moved to make words but his brain couldn't get his vocal cords to cooperate at getting out any more than a surprised squeak.

"Whoops!" Azrael stretched one wingtip to where an errant tongue of fire licked at the sole undetonated shell in the ammunition chamber. As soon as the feather touched the fire, it died. "Missed one."

"Bradford!!!" Silva pushed at his rear end from inside the tank.

"Uh ... thanks?" Bradford finally managed to squeeze out.

"Gotta go now," Azrael made a 'V' with two fingers. "There's still Iraqi Army crawling around in the dust. You're going to have to deal with them on your own. I only reap squatters!"

The coal-black angel leaped into air with a rustle of enormous black wings and disappeared in a blinding dark flash.

"Bradford!!!" Commander Silva screamed, shoving him in the ass to get him to move it out of the only exit they had out of the ruined tank.

Bradford climbed out onto the top of the tank and reached down to help Silva, Jaworsky, and Vasquez climb out of the smoky cockpit.

"Who was that?" Jaworsky asked.

"You ain't gonna believe me if I tell you," Bradford said. "They'll Section 8 me for sure." The Gunner made a motion with his hand over his mouth as though he were closing a zipper and refused to speak of the matter any further.

"Whoever he was," Vasquez clutched something in his hand. "He left his calling card."

"Give me that," Silva ordered. He grabbed the playing card Vasquez had fished out of the tank on his way out. "An ace of spades?"

The four members of the tank crew stared down at the 'Bicycle' playing card their mystery helper had left behind which depicted Lady Liberty standing in the middle of the black ace.

"Thanks ... friend," Bradford said softly, staring at the spot where the angel had disappeared and giving it a thumbs-up.

Chapter 41

Will the Lord be pleased with thousands of rams,
With ten thousands of rivers of oil?
Shall I give my first-born for my transgression,
The fruit of my body for the sin of my soul?

Tanakh, Micah 6:7

Earth - March 26, 2003
Imam Ali Mosque, Najaf, Iraq

"Allah wishes you to order your followers to conduct suicide bombings against the infidels, your holiness," the local Baathist Party leader said, his voice soothing and reasonable. "Our Beloved has provided your holy warriors with the latest weaponry to resist their incursion into this holy place."

The Grand Ayatollah clutched his holy beads and prayed. The demon tempted him with images of being carried to Paradise by a chariot of fire drawn by angels to meet Allah. He resisted. His lips moved silently, the deeply ingrained ritual fortifying his mind as the compulsion the Angel of Mercy had warned him would follow such tempting images also jumped into his mind. The illusion that the rusted, broken AK-47 Kalashnikov rifle with a broken firing pin was really a cutting-edge Russian AN-94 Abakan assault rifle.

"Shi'a do not support the Saddam Fedayeen," the Ayatollah said with a calmness that did not betray his inner turmoil. "We will deal with the Americans on our own terms."

The Baathist leader gave him a benign smile.

"Num occidere te, domine?" Saddam Hussein's henchman Mahmud asked in what the demon thought was a language the Ayatollah could not understand. The demon was mistaken. This was an ancient land, with ruins dating back to a time when the Angel of Mercy had walked the Earth as one of them. The Ayatollah had studied more than the Quran during his reign as spiritual leader. He understood Mahmud wished to kill him, and that the Baathist leader was really possessed by a demon named Chemosh.

"Not yet, dear friend," Chemosh said in the ancient language. "The host-bodies we occupy now command the loyalty of the Saddam Fedayeen, elite warriors, while the good Ayatollah only controls the Al-Quds army. They are many in number, but largely civilians and old men who haven't fought since the First Gulf War. The Al-Quds are hostile to both host bodies we currently occupy."

"We don't need them," Mahmud scoffed. "The Fedayeen are enough."

"Ahh, dear friend," Chemosh purred. "Such decisiveness! You sound like our dear brother, Saddam Hussein. Hit the nail on the head and be done with it! But sometimes, it is wiser to come at your enemy sideways. Don't you agree?"

"Sideways?" Mahmud asked. "I don't understand."

"I can sense him," Chemosh said. "Ki's lapdog. Just outside the city. His consciousness has grown larger since his last feeding. He's now large enough that I can sense him whenever he gets close. Lucifer and his minions plan to use the invasion as cover to storm the city."

"Our Agents reported the 101st Airborne Division just relieved the 3rd Infantry," Mahmud said. "They appear to be supported by a battalion from the 1st Armored Division."

"Tanks?" Chemosh raised one eyebrow in surprise. "No ... the Americans would never agree to anything so ... low-tech ... as an old-fashioned tank charge into the city. Why it's ... un-American!"

Mahmud burst out laughing, an evil, almost cackling sound. The Ayatollah schooled a stone-faced expression, careful not to let the tiniest hint of emotion register as he strained to translate the demons' battle-plans. It did not behoove him to let on just how much he knew about the two demons standing before him now. There was a reason holy men grew such great, bushy beards. You could hide many physiological symptoms of emotion beneath such a beard ... such as the nearly overwhelming urge to gulp in fear or the subtle twitch of one cheek hidden beneath his greying moustache. The beard was to a devout Muslim male what hijab was to a female ... their shield against a hostile world.

"They haven't had a real tank battle since World War II," Mahmud laughed. "The tanks must simply be there to make these old geezers quake in their boots. We've been giving them a run for their money in the sandstorm."

Chemosh addressed the Al-Quds army he'd summoned in the Grand Ayatollah's name. The men were largely retired veterans who'd ostensibly been recruited by Saddam Hussein to reclaim Jerusalem during the 1990's. A fool's errand to give the Shi'ite majority the illusion of a role in the Ba'athist government. They were men with families, businesses, and strong ties to the community. Devout Shi'ite Muslims who would die for their country and their faith, but who, unlike their Iranian counterparts who went by the same name, balked at outright terrorism. The Al-Quds watched Chemosh's Baathist host-body warily, decades of distrust over being targeted by Saddam Hussein tempering their inclinations to side with their former adversaries henchmen.

"Bring them in," Chemosh ordered.

Dread sank into the pit of his stomach as the Saddam Fedayeen dragged in the wives, elderly parents, and children of the Al-Quds army. Cries of dismay went out amongst the aging fighting force as the Saddam Fedayeen soldiers cocked their rifles. Targeting families was a common tactic amongst both the Saddam Fedayeen … and also the fanatical jihadists who descended upon this country like locusts to 'free' them from the Great Satan advancing upon their city in tanks. Caught between the devil's anvil and Satan's hammer, the people the Ayatollah was charged with guiding were mere cannon fodder to the interests targeting al-Najaf as their latest battle ground.

"Our beloved country has been invaded by infidels," Chemosh said. "And some cowards amongst you refuse to fight. This is how all cowards will be dealt with."

The Ayatollah schooled his face into a stone-faced expression meant to signify his disapproval, the same accusing glower that posters of him throughout the city bore. The Al-Quds murmured nervously. Although the men were by no means cowards, decades of being at the wrong end of Saddam Hussein's rifles for the mere reason of being Shi'ite, not Sunni, had instilled caution. Good! They were skeptical their Grand Ayatollah would really cooperate with the Sunnis. The Ayatollah sent up a silent prayer to the Beloved, praying his people would give the surface illusion of just going along until a better situation presented itself.

"That one there," Chemosh pointed to one of the civilians who'd just been dragged in. "And yes … that one. The young one. I do so like them when they're young."

An elderly woman and young boy were dragged forward, sobbing in terror. Innocents! Would the demons really slay innocents to make their point? Usually an example was selected from amongst the men gathered as a first example! Innocents were only slain for those who didn't fall into line.

"This is what we want you to do to the Americans," Chemosh mercilessly shot first the old woman, and then the boy through the head. "Or we will kill every family member of every man gathered in this courtyard. Do you understand?"

The Ayatollah clamped down on his urge to order the Al-Quds to attack, an action which would only lead to massive slaughter. The tactics of terror were something he knew well. These demons needed something from them or they would have just killed them outright. Cries of anger went out through the courtyard, but the Al-Quds were unarmed. They could do nothing to defend themselves or their families. They must endure. All the Ayatollah could do was deepen his trademark glower and reassure them with his calmness that he would lead his people to exact revenge later, when the Al-Quds weren't surrounded by guns in a concrete courtyard with no escape.

"Allah has provided manna from heaven to make victory a certainty," Chemosh said. He nodded to his men. "Line up ... and accept your gift from our Beloved."

The Ayatollah gave the leaders of the Al-Quds a subtle nod, signaling them by the way his fingers danced over his holy beads that already he had composed a Fatwa calling for the deaths of these demons in his mind. They were to obey until a more fortuitous situation presented itself. One by men, the Al-Quds army lined up to take the aging, rusty, and largely broken Kalashnikov AK-47 rifles left over from the cold war and gathered into units manning cars, pickup trucks, and strategic houses along the route they anticipated the American push into the city. They weren't given any bullets, of course. Why give bullets to cannon fodder? The demon used the Al-Quds to attract air strikes so the real militia could sneak around behind the advancing tanks and drop grenades down the hatch.

"It's a pleasure serving such genius, my Lord," Mahmud said, still not realizing the Ayatollah could understand his ancient language. "I have much to learn from your example. What do you call this tactic?"

Pickup trucks rolled out filled with aging veterans carrying empty rifles to make their suicide runs against the American tanks. The demon known as Chemosh knew what he was doing. Whether or not the Grand Ayatollah urged temperance, the residents of this city would not welcome the invaders after their Al-Quds patriarchs were killed. The Grand Ayatollah inwardly wept as cars clogged the road. Cars dying to do battle against a tank.

"We call this strategy Iraqi Rush Hour," Chemosh said with an indulgent smile one might give a naughty child. "These men are just *dying* to get home to their families."

"Allah will send you straight to hell where you belong," the Grand Ayatollah hissed.

"Been there, done that," Chemosh said with a bored wave of his hand. "Sequester the Ayatollah in his mosque to pray for the freedom of his people. Give his holiness every comfort, but keep him inside. I sense he's genetically complete enough to be a backup host if this one fails. The rest of you ... come with me."

'Our Lord ...' the Grand Ayatollah prayed, his fingers dancing over the holy beads as he focused his prayers the way he had been taught by the Angel of Mercy to plead divine intervention. 'Grant me deliverance from these demons so I may reap justice in your name.'

Chapter 42

They will say: Our Lord, twice have You given us death
and twice have You given us life…
Quran Al Mumin 40:11

Earth - March 26, 2003
30 miles south of Najaf, Iraq

"Sponge!" Elisabeth shouted, forceps buried up to the hilt in the soldier's brain as the coppery scent of blood filled her nostrils.

"This don't look good," Nurse Mary drawled, dabbing at the exposed grey matter. "Half his face is missing."

A large black 'X' adorned the man's forehead. In a triage situation, they were forced to make split-second decisions as to who got treated first. This soldier had been deemed too badly injured to survive. With other seriously wounded, potentially treatable soldiers in the queue who could also die, this soldier would only be treated after the surgeon finished up the 'urgent' cases. –If- this soldier happened to still be alive.

"You hang on!" Elisabeth ordered, frantically trying to find the 'bleeder.' A mortar had torn off chunks of the kid's cheek, ear and neck. "You hear me, soldier? You hang on to that body of yours with everything you got!"

They avoided looking at the blood dripping down the torn white plastic onto their boots. Hypothermia-induced shock was the second-biggest threat to wounded soldiers after blood loss. 'Hot pockets,' body bags improvised with a cutout for the face so they could breathe, helped keep wounded soldier's body heat in close to their bodies. But … dang! The fact Elisabeth's patient had already been wearing a body bag even before she'd started working on him was morbid as hell.

"Heart rate is falling," Nurse Lucy said. "Elisabeth … we're losing him."

"He's not going until I say he can go," Elisabeth snapped. "You hear that, Sergeant? I outrank you! You don't get to leave until I say you're dismissed."

Elisabeth used a combination of prayers Oma had taught her as a child and Archangel focusing meditations taught by Azrael, but this was the

Army. Hallelujah and praise the lord went over like a fart in church. Soldiers expected to be given orders, so she gave them.

"That … um … friend of yours … stop in yet?" Mary nervously looked over her shoulder.

"You know that's classified," Elisabeth grunted, gently pushing aside a bit of grey matter, fishing for the source of the blood pouring down the white plastic onto her boots. "Besides, if I talk about it they'll Section 8 me for sure."

Mary turned grey at the sight of the kid's brain tissue, exposed by the mortar which had taken a chunk of his skull along with it.

"Goddang reject flack helmets," Mary mumbled, her hand over her mouth to prevent herself from succumbing to the urge to vomit. "When's them Pentagon bean counters gonna acknowledge them two-piece chin straps are a piece of crap? This kid's helmet should've protected him better!"

"Maybe your friend can help?" Lucy pulled a bloody photograph out of the soldier's breast pocket and held it under Elisabeth's nose. "Look … this guy's got five kids stateside."

"Not his job to save lives," Elisabeth said. "That's my job. Hey! Soldier! You going to abandon those five kids of yours when you can hang on a little longer? Just give me some time! Ain't nothing wrong with you that can't be fixed if you just give me a little more time!"

"Blood pressure is fifty over ten," Mary said. "We're losing him."

"Doing the best I can." Elisabeth spotted the bleeder. "Got it!!!" she shouted victoriously as she dug in with the forceps and clamped it off. "Middle temporal artery. Lucy … jot that down on his chart … it will affect the eye."

"Sixty-five over fifteen!" Mary said hopefully.

"Adding another pint of blood," Lucy said. "He's losing it faster than I can get it into him."

"Seventy over forty!" Mary practically jumped up and down.

"C'mon … c'mon … c'mon…" Elisabeth muttered, squinting through the eyepiece of the surgical binoculars she wore as she began the painstaking process of piecing the two ends of the severed artery back together. "Tick tock … race the clock … get you stable and send you off."

The hair on the back of her neck stood on end. Azrael … stopping in. She no longer felt the need to fight him. This patient was nearly out of danger. Azrael only took those who wished to leave their mortal shells behind. In a way, his presence had become reassuring. More than one surviving patient had told her they'd been floating above their bodies, able to see into a white room filled with deceased loved ones when Azrael had urged them to give her a chance to save their lives.

"Be with you in a few, Az," Elisabeth was too busy to speak to him right now. "This guy's almost out of danger. You'll have to find somebody else to be your good deed for the day."

The other two nurses looked at each other and glanced nervously around the tent. They'd learned to humor their colleague's peculiar ramblings into empty air ... not sure whether the rumors of a death-angel were true ... but too awe-struck by Elisabeth's 'save' rate to question it.

"At least we don't have to worry about insurance companies or lawsuits," Mary quipped as she watched Elisabeth fearlessly dive into the folds of the soldier's exposed brain. "So long as we save lives, they give us free reign."

"Stabilize the patient," Lucy said. "Keep him alive. Ship him off to someplace more qualified to treat him. If he survives the first 36 hours, his chances of recovery are good."

"They never let me do this kind of thing back home," Mary lamented. "Why do you think I keep re-enlisting? I can't adjust to being treated like a stateside nurse."

"All we have to do is keep them alive," Elisabeth muttered. "Let the doctors pretty things up and wrap a ribbon around it."

"We're sure doing a surgeons job!" Mary poured on her southern accent as thick as maple syrup. "They figure they ain't got nothin' to lose by letting us pretty little gals comfort the black-X triage cases while the big boys are busy."

"Yeah," Lucy said. "Only Elisabeth's brand of 'comfort' is kicking the trauma surgeon's asses and making them look bad."

"Medics out in the field do the same thing we're doing," Elisabeth reminded them, breathing a sigh of relief as she made the last stitch and searched for signs of other damage. "They're the real heroes. That first hour after they're hit is critical. At least we're not getting shot at while we're working."

"Usually," Mary added with a wry grin. "If you discount the RPG's shot over the wall at the compound."

"Or the grenade someone threw into the tent last week," Lucy added.

"Hey ... Lucy!" Elisabeth interrupted. "Quit gabbing and get me some more blood!" Blood continued to seep out of the soldiers head wound, but it no longer spurted like a lawn sprinkler. He now had a chance. –If- they were able to airlift him to Germany fast enough so a real neurosurgeon could repair the damage. Speed. Saving lives was about quick, decisive action.

"Okey-dokey, boss-woman Sir," Lucy said good-naturedly, omitting the salute as both hands were occupied at the moment doing other things. "Fill 'er up, AB-positive."

Both Lucy and Mary outranked Elisabeth, but when it came to trauma cases, they followed her lead. Although it wasn't unheard of for nurses, or even medics, to suddenly be deputized 'de facto surgeon' when the need was great, it was unusual for Elisabeth to consistently be given such free-reign in the more formal setting of a mobile combat trauma unit. Elizabeth suspected Azrael's friends in high places had passed down instructions to humor her so long as she got results.

"One-ten over sixty-five," Mary breathed a sigh of relief. "I think you got him."

"And here is …" Elisabeth pushed a fragment of shattered bone back into place, "your … piece of … skull … back … Sergeant. Next time, keep your helmet securely on your head. That's why they make you wear it in the first place."

"Pressure bandage?" Lucy held out a special bandage used when a patient had extensive skin damage and burns such as this one did.

"Roger." Elisabeth painstakingly pulled what tissue she could back into place before applying the bandage. "Careful … this guy's skull is like Humpty Dumpty right now."

"Lieutenant Kaiser?" the trauma surgeon stepped behind her. "I'll take over now."

Elisabeth could sense Azrael move so he didn't zap her boss. In close quarters such as this, his wings would be tucked into his cloak so he didn't accidentally kill someone. Especially after the incident with the boy. Elisabeth was slowly, but surely, getting used to the idea Azrael didn't view leaving your mortal shell behind and journeying into heaven with the same … finality … that those around her did. But he still believed life was too precious to just casually throw away.

"Your sandbox, Major Devens," Elisabeth said to the surgeon, stepping aside. "Male … twenty-seven years old … mortar damage to the left side of the cheek, ear, and neck … skull fractured with fragments imbedded in the grey matter … severed middle temporal artery … pieced it back together … likely damage to the left occipital nerve due to oxygen deprivation."

"Thank you, Lieutenant Kaiser," Major Devens said. "That will be all. You can scrub out and grab a bite to eat."

"Yes, Sir," Elisabeth glanced down at his clean, blood-free boots and wrinkled her nose with disgust. Bloodied boots were a badge of honor in this unit. The fact Major Devens didn't like to get his hands gory spoke volumes about his level of dedication. Elisabeth gave him the obligatory salute. "Thank you … Sir."

"Unless you'd like to wait until I get off shift," Major Devens added, giving her his most charming 'nurses throw themselves at my feet and suck my dick' smile. "We could do lunch together. I've been wanting to talk to you about your career possibilities."

"I've already got lunch plans," Elisabeth glanced over to where Azrael observed from the shadows. For the hell of it, she gave Major Devens a coy smile, hoping it aroused a twang of jealousy in her invisible friend. "But thank you, Sir. Maybe some other time?"

Elisabeth knew damned well the only reason Devens was taking over was because the upper ranks had noticed she was kicking his ass. Devens claimed the credit. It was the same shit Nancy had complained of while she'd still been alive.

"I'll just clean up and go get some fresh air, Sir," Elisabeth gave Devens her sweetest 'fuck you and die' smile.

She held up her hands. Blood had travelled beyond her latex gloves, down her arm, all over the front of her shirt, her neck, her cheek, and down her pants to her boots. Devens backed off, his expression one of disgust. Except for a few stray spatters of blood on his pale blue doctor's scrubs, Devens was clean. He turned to the patient and pompously rattled off his 'diagnosis,' the exact same diagnosis Elisabeth had just told him.

'Prick!' she silently mouthed the moment Devens turned his back so that Mary and Lucy saw it.

Mary, who was in the direct line-of-sight of the surgeon snorted as she suppressed a laugh, while Lucy, who was at his back, pointed to her crotch and made a motion like she was jerking off. Elisabeth smiled. She wasn't the only nurse Devens hit on. Fraternization was against Army regulations, but a dire shortage of competent doctors willing to put themselves in an active war zone forced the military to overlook Deven's extracurricular activities. It was the same shortage which had caused them to deputize three nurses as a de facto trauma team.

Azrael disappeared through the walls rather than risk weaving his way through the crowded trauma ward. Their meetings had developed a pattern. Azrael manifested just enough of his spirit for her to sense his presence. Sometimes he could only stay long enough for her to sense him. Other times he stayed and observed.

Elisabeth scrubbed out, automatically clipping spare surgical clamps to her clothing and tucking medical tape and syringes in her pockets … just in case. She grabbed something from the canteen and hobbled beyond a small rise at the far end of the makeshift heliport, leaning on her cane. She'd been on her feet nonstop for days.

"Come out, come out, wherever you are," Elisabeth called into the shadows, groaning as she lowered her aching body to a convenient boulder.

"Olly olly oxen free!" Azrael faded into view like an enormous black-winged Cheshire cat.

"Did you see that?" Elisabeth groused. "Devens stole my 'save' again."

"I could brush up against him if you like?" Azrael gave her a look of such pure innocence that she burst out laughing.

"You wouldn't!" Elisabeth laughed. "But thanks for offering."

"No … I wouldn't," Azrael said. His smile disappeared.

"You've got something on your mind." Elisabeth took a bite of her soggy tuna salad sandwich and grimaced as tuna juice dribbled down her chin onto her last clean shirt. Blech! Now she'd smell like tuna fish until she had a chance to take a shower. How romantic! But if she didn't snarf down her sandwich as they talked, she wouldn't get to eat. The 2nd Battalion was meeting fierce resistance over Objective Jenkins, a bridge over the Euphrates River just north of Najaf. It was only a matter of time before the next medevac chopper came roaring in with more wounded.

"Chemosh and a bunch of squatters are in Najaf posing as Saddam Fedayeen fighters," Azrael said. "He's been gathering up local al-Quds militia, putting outdated Kalashnikov rifles in their hands, and sending them up against your troops. That's why casualties on both sides have been so high."

"Then they'll be shot," Elisabeth said dispassionately, thinking of the soldier she'd just pieced back together. "They were ordered to put down their weapons or face the consequences."

"Chemosh lined up their families and threatened to shoot them if they didn't do suicide runs against your troops," Azrael said. "They're not even giving them any bullets."

"Why would our guys shoot back if they're not shooting in the first place?" Elisabeth asked.

"They're calling it 'Iraqi Rush Hour.'" Azrael said. "The al-Qud irregulars are being sent against tanks at the same time real insurgents are doing the same thing. The tank drivers have no way of knowing which of the guys coming at them are which."

"How many of these al-Qud militiamen have been lost so far?" Elisabeth asked.

"We think over 800," Azrael said. "And climbing. There can only be one outcome when a pickup truck meets a tank."

"Why don't they just walk up with their hands above their heads and surrender?" Elisabeth asked. "That's what half the official regular Iraqi army has been doing."

"The men are doing suicide runs in the hopes of saving their families," Azrael said. "Civilians who've managed to escape are meeting your troops on the road and begging them to take the city, but your troops are so spooked right now that they're shooting anything even remotely hostile. A lot of civilians are getting killed."

"I'm out of the loop," Elisabeth said. "How close are our troops to securing that city?"

"Too far out," Azrael assumed the grave facial features most people thought of when they pictured the Angel of Death. "Chemosh has gone crazy ... shooting old ladies and children. We ... um ... I could use your help."

"*My* help?" Elisabeth asked. "I'm not a soldier ... well ... technically I am. But I'm ... not ... really. My combat training is a mile wide and a half-inch deep."

"Sam's got men imbedded with the 101st Airborne Division," Azrael said. "They're getting ready to thrust into the city."

"I thought you weren't supposed to choose sides?"

"We're not," Azrael said. "We're only going in because Chemosh is slaughtering civilians. He's killing children."

The nightmares about clawed hands reaching at her through fire leaped into her mind. She'd had such nightmares her entire life, but they hadn't started becoming ... well ... real ... until Azrael had told her followers of those he fought to keep imprisoned sacrificed humans trying to engineer an escape.

"You're worried Chemosh might open a portal to this Moloch-god?" Elisabeth asked.

"It would be the perfect cover." Azrael face grew angular and stern as hatred swirled through his midnight black eyes. "You've got air strikes. The most advanced military equipment from all over the world. And enough electronics chatter to drown out even the most sensitive monitoring equipment. We now suspect the World Trade Center bombing was cover for Chemosh to escape."

"How can I help?"

"The al-Quds?" Azrael said. "A lot of them are just old men with medals from past wars. Don't get me wrong ... they're radical Shiite Muslims fighting to protect their faith. But they have more in common with the veterans who come out to march in your parades back home than Al Qaida."

"Opa's father was a veteran of World War II." Elisabeth frowned. Franz had been embarrassed at the fact their great-grandfather had fought on the 'wrong' side of the Great War. "Opa said his father hated what Hitler and the Nazi's did to his country, but he earnestly believed he was fighting to protect it. He was an honorable man."

"We're going in to eradicate the squatters and cover it up with a US airstrike," Azrael said. "With conditions on the ground the way they are, there's no way we can do that without significant civilian deaths. I was hoping..."

"You want me to see if I can save some of them?"

"I won't let you go in until it's secure," Azrael said softly, his face grave. "But the al-Quds are not the only ones being slaughtered and not being given medical treatment. We, um … Sam's men. They … um … you know how black ops are. Cover your tailfeathers first. Worry about the guy you sent in to do sneak-and-peak last."

"They won't let me go in," Elisabeth said. "My leg means I'm a liability in a firefight. I'm too valuable to them here."

"Sam has connections," Azrael said. "They're going to move some of you up closer to the action. Your team will be put in charge of the hopeless cases. All I ask is when you triage the wounded, you remain color-blind as best you can without getting into trouble."

"You know I will." Elisabeth looked into his bottomless black eyes and noticed the way his nostrils flared, the slight hitch of his breath, the way he unconsciously curled his wings forward. Her breathing slowed. Her heart beat faster as the urge to touch him became almost overwhelming.

"Thank you," Azrael's expression softened. He fished inside a pocket of the hated cloak he'd tossed over his shoulders to free his wings and pulled out a small pendant. "I … um … thought you might like this. I made it myself."

He held out one hand, fist clenched, until she put her hand underneath to catch it. Trust. He trusted her not to bump against his hand. She trusted him to not bump against her. It was a dangerous game they'd been playing lately without speaking about it, to see how close one could get to one another without touching. She could feel his expanded consciousness nestle against hers.

"Thank you," Elisabeth admired a tiny wooden twig looped into an infinity symbol enclosed in an intricate platinum wire cage. "I didn't know you were an artisan." She pulled off her dog tags and slipped the chain through the loop.

"It's from the Eternal Emperor's garden on Haven-1," Azrael said. "The wood is from the tree Hashem planted the day he assumed rule of the Alliance. Your legends call it the Tree of Eternal Life."

"Oh!" Elisabeth lifted the chain to stare at the tiny fragment of wood. No wonder he'd fashioned such a beautiful cage to protect such a simple object of nature. "Was it okay for you to take this?"

"I have no idea." A guilty grin appeared on his face. "It's forbidden to touch the tree. Especially me! It's said so long as the tree thrives, so shall the Alliance. But the wind blew loose a few leaves and that small twig was attached. I figured if I didn't ask, they couldn't say no."

"I will cherish it always," Elisabeth clutched it to her chest. "I have to keep it under my uniform but … see … I'll wear it right next to my heart."

Azrael stepped closer. If she reached up, she could touch him. She wanted to touch him. She stared up into obsidian eyes, blacker than the darkest night, into the hunger which swirled beneath the surface he had fashioned to walk in this world. Azrael's bottomless black eyes were the mirror to his soul.

Her hand reached up and stopped just inches from his cheek.

"Elisabeth," Azrael whispered, his voice husky with emotion.

They both froze, understanding that to touch would mean death. Elisabeth did not fear death. But she did fear losing him. The angel who'd always been a part of her life, even before her accident. The smoke-darkened angel she'd spoken to in the lobby of First Saint Paul's church as a child. The angel with the yellowed robe and glued wing who'd graced their Christmas tree. The invisible friend she'd imagined sitting across the table as she'd played dolls and tied bandages around her dolls arms and head. Long before Azrael had found her, she'd been calling to him. And he had come. He'd come when she had needed him most.

If she touched him, she would go where he could not follow. Memory of the nightmare came back to her. The abandonment she'd felt when he'd disappeared. No. She would not lose him a second time. Her lip twitching wistfully with regret, she slid her hand into her pants pocket.

"I have a present for you, as well," Elisabeth said. "Not as meaningful as your gift, but I thought you might like it."

She pulled out a fragment of clay with symbols pressed into it. She held out her hand, waiting, while he placed his only inches beneath hers for her to drop it in. Azrael closed his eyes and paused, relishing the feel of the small gift in his hand as though she had touched him herself.

"One of the local Iraqi's gave it to me after I stitched up a gash on his little boy's foot," Elisabeth said. "He found it at the ruins of the Great Ziggurat at Ur."

"It's a family seal," Azrael read the cuneiform off the fragment. "It says 'Nanna bless our...' The missing word is probably 'harvest'. Nanna was an Ubaid lunar god who ruled the planting of the grain."

"You can read it?"

"What you call cuneiform is a grossly simplified form of our language," Azrael said. "Ur was one of the villages which banded together under the General to defeat Moloch. This seal appears to originate from shortly after that time as it's our language, but before they started calling their god 'Sin' after the son of the Fallen Angelic who'd settled there died."

"Died?" Elisabeth said, looking up quickly. "I thought..."

"Archangels are quasi-immortal by virtue of their advanced genome," Azrael said. "Angelics are mortal. They're stronger than humans and can live a thousand years. But they're as mortal as any human."

"Fallen angels?"

"The Fallen intermarried with your species and died out," Azrael studied her face as he spoke. "You carry their DNA."

"How can you tell?" Elisabeth smiled. "Do I have tiny wings tattooed across my back?"

"The General took a sample after you survived my touch," Azrael retreated behind an unreadable expression. "You carry genetic markers from all four Alliance hybrid races as well as Sata'anic DNA, which is curious because you don't have a tail."

"A ... what?"

"A tail," Azrael said. "Why do you think Samuel Adams and his men always wear trench coats? They're 59th generation human, but the genetic marker for the Sata'anic tail is a dominant gene. It's nearly impossible to eradicate."

"A ... tail?" Elisabeth asked again. "I ... I ... I didn't ... see..."

"They're good at disguising it," Azrael said. "Many parents cut off their child's tail at birth in the hopes they can integrate with humans, but that pesky tail keeps cropping up in their offspring. If they have a tail, the armistice says they're forbidden to make their presence known to your species."

"That's ... awful!" Elisabeth exclaimed.

"That descendants of the lizard-people walk the earth?"

"No!" Elisabeth said. "That they're ... outcasts!!! How could your emperor tolerate such an abomination?!!"

"Why do you think they name their children after civil rights activists and patriots?" Azrael said. "You've already met Samuel Adams, George Washington, Malcolm Little, which was Malcolm X's real name, and Mahatma Ghandi."

"I ... noticed ... it was odd," Elisabeth said. "I assumed they were using code names because they were under cover."

"Those are their real names," Azrael's expression was serious. "If you're going to work with them, then you should know who they really are. They're stronger and their lifespan is a bit longer than pureblooded humans, but they're as mortal as you are. If they become wounded in this battle ... you need to make sure their differences don't come to the wrong person's attention."

"You know I'll be discreet," Elisabeth stared up at her changeable friend who shifted personas from stern soldier to egg-headed scientist to the most feared angel on Earth in a matter of seconds. All these facets of his personality were real, but she suspected the sensitive, artistic side of his nature was a side he guarded from all but his closest friends.

There was a pause, more awkward than the companionable silence they normally shared. Elisabeth had been around the block once before. When a male gave you jewelry, it was usually because they wished to 'mark' you as theirs. She meant more to him than some freak curiosity.

"Thank you for the gift," Elisabeth clutched the tiny lump beneath her shirt. "I'll cherish it … always."

Although Azrael's ebony complexion was too dark to show when he blushed, his wings were his 'tell.' The dip to one side and way the tiny pin-feathers flared as though sensing wind currents gave him away. Her own heart leaped as she wondered what it would be like to kiss him?

"You're welcome," Azrael's enormous raven-black wings curled forward, encircling her with his deadly feathers.

Elisabeth froze, not out of fear, but because she understood this was the closest he could come to embracing her. It was a strange sensation, being enclosed in a wall of darkness. She could feel the compulsion radiating from his form. The sensation was … pleasant. As though a thunderstorm had passed and cleansed the air. Not at all what one would expect when surrounded by death.

She could sense tendrils delicately caress the outer shell of the expanded consciousness Oma had explained surrounded every living creature. It was how she'd always been able to sense he was there. Even as a little girl. All those times she'd cursed him for letting her fall, he'd been reaching out to her, trying to comfort her the only way he could without killing her. The touch he gave her now, however, was not the sympathetic touch of a curious scientist, but the intimate caress of a lover. Her heart sped up as she looked into his bottomless velvet eyes.

Elisabeth pictured reaching up to touch his cheek, mindful that her real hand did not follow the example of her mind. She felt his spirit tenderly grasp the 'fingers' she'd just used and gently intertwine with hers, her heart leaping with a joy. It was as though she were a musical instrument and he the musician who could make her heart sing.

"You're learning." Azrael's voice was husky with emotion. He trembled with the need to touch her, his breath jagged and raw as control over his emotions slipped. His wings sprang back, slapping against the air as he disappeared without so much as a goodbye.

Elisabeth sighed. She was falling in love with an angel she could never, ever touch. Impossible! Why should love be any easier than anything else in her life had ever been? Bending for her cane, she picked up the wrapper from the soggy tuna sandwich and what was left of her apple and hobbled back to the combat trauma unit to make sure Major 'Doc' Devens didn't fuck up and kill the patient she'd just worked so hard to save.

Chapter 43

Say: the Angel of Death, put in charge of you,
Will (duly) take your souls,
Then shall you be brought back to your Lord.

Quran 32:11

Earth - March 30, 2003
Al-Najaf Airstrip, Iraq

Elisabeth held onto her seat for dear life. Eyes scrunched shut, she swallowed the bile which had regurgitated into one sinus cavity, burning as it went. The ear-splitting whump whump whump whump of the blades was not loud enough to drown out the sound of small-arms fire peppering their ride with bullets.

"I thought they weren't supposed to shoot at vehicles with the Red Cross on it?" Mary shouted into the mouthpiece of her headphones. "This is a hospital evac chopper!"

"Last I heard," Lucy answered, "Saddam Hussein and his cronies weren't exactly choirboys for the Geneva Convention."

"Aren't we going to shoot back, or something?" Mary asked.

"Sorry 'bout that, ladies," the chopper pilot said calmly as though he were a United Airlines pilot informing passengers what European city they were flying above at the moment. "Just a few stray insurgents. Ground troops are on their way to deal with the problem as we speak."

"Easy for him to say!" Mary snapped. "He's wearing bullet proof underwear!" She referred to the Kevlar body armor most pilots wore to protect their groin from bullets penetrating the chopper from below.

"Why doesn't he shoot back at them?" Lucy asked. She pointed at the soldier positioned next to the closed door. A machine gun was mounted on a tripod bolted to the floor, ready to swing out and start shooting the moment he opened the door.

"Just waiting for the pilot to give the order, Ma'am," the gunman gave her a grin. "Not sure where the fellow taking potshots at us is located. Don't want to shoot one of our own men!"

'*Az,*' Elisabeth prayed silently, suppressing the urge to vomit as another 'ping' hit the chopper. *'If this death trap drops out of the sky, at least let me give you that kiss I've been wanting to give you before we part ways.'*

Azrael couldn't hear her, of course. He wasn't here. He'd popped in three times since he'd given her the pendant, but he'd been keeping his distance. Literally. He was back to keeping an inanimate object between them, their talks clinical and impersonal as he discussed the 'squatter' hunkered down in the midst of Najaf and what would be expected of her in her new role as gatekeeper for the carnage coming out of the city.

It was the ultimate irony that now that she'd finally warmed up to *him,* he'd backed off emotionally from *her.* She suspected their delicate dance of drawing close without touching had taken him too close to crossing a line they both knew could never be crossed. Since she'd started talking to Azrael, her fear of death was more related to how damned inconvenient it would be rather than death itself.

The way Azrael described heaven, the place his people called the Dreamtime, it was more of a great big playpen for spirits such as hers that weren't evolved enough to go out and ride their bicycles on the street alone than the heaven Earth legend made it out to be. Elizabeth had experienced enough of other people's limitations in her life! The last thing she wanted was to be locked up in some cosmic playpen until She-who-is decided to let her family come out and play again, no matter *how* well-intentioned the goddess was. Elisabeth liked being her *own* boss, thank you very much!

"We're here," the pilot called into the intercom. "Al-Najaf Airfield. Saddam Hussein's old base for keeping the Shiite south in line."

"It don't look like much," Mary complained, spying nothing but the airstrip and a couple of sheds. "I thought this was an Iraqi military base? Where's all the buildings?"

"Ain't nothing here but the air field," the gunman at the door said with a grin. "This part of the country is Shiite. Saddam didn't spend any money here. Just took it away from them."

"I see a team unrolling tents," Elisabeth pointed to troops in the process of raising a large, geodesic DRASH (deployable rapid assembly shelter). "Look at them go!" The troops raised the first shelter as they approached while a second team unrolled a second one.

"There's your new hospital, ladies," the pilot shouted into the intercom as he maneuvered the chopper in for a landing. "You'd better get your gear unpacked in a hurry. I just got a call to medevac more wounded. They've explicitly stated they're to come here. Not the unit you came from."

"You just hover above the airfield," the gunner jested, "and I'll shove them out the door."

Elisabeth went to shout something back at him and shut her mouth when she noticed the intense expression on the gunner's face. His expression grim, he started arranging additional belts of ammunition to be within easy reload reach. Wherever they were being deployed for medevac, they were expecting heavy fire. Cavalry had their own version of 'morgue humor' to keep them sane when deploying into a firefight.

"Grab your gear," Lucy ordered. As the highest-ranking nurse in their little triage unit, she was the one who juggled logistics. "Get it out onto the tarmac as quickly as possible so they can take off again. We'll commandeer someone on the ground to help us move it once they're back in the air."

"Thanks, Ma'am." The pilot executed an intricate series of maneuvers to get the Black Hawk centered over the crude 'X' somebody had spray painted on the airstrip and fought the wind. After several stomach-dropping lurches, he set the machine down so gently Elisabeth wasn't even certain they were on the ground.

"Thank you for flying Medevac Air," the gunman said with a grin as he yanked open the sliding door. "Please place all seats back in the upright position. Remove all personal luggage, barf bags, and soiled underwear. Have a nice day!"

Within seconds, their crates of medical supplies had been perfunctorily dumped onto the airstrip and the chopper was back in the air, wind from the rotating blades sandblasting dust into Elisabeth's eyes. They waited until the chopper had risen before grabbing their gear, hauling what they could towards the tent. Several soldiers rushed forward to help them.

"He said we'll have incoming in a matter of minutes," Mary said. "What equipment should we set up first?"

"Operating table," Lucy ordered, directing one of the soldiers to haul a large crate to where she wished it set up before turning to a second. "You … get that box labeled surgical supplies. Ladies … start sterilizing equipment and find the bandages … fast."

"We don't have any blood yet!" Elisabeth threw her hands up in frustration. "That won't arrive until the next shipment."

"We've got lots of nice, young blood here!" Mary had a feral grin on her face as she grabbed the bicep of a handsome young soldier and gave it a squeeze. "We just have to get it out of them. That's all."

"Good eve-v-v-ning," Lucy said in her best Transylvania accent. "Ve vont to take your blood."

"Yes, Ma'am!" The soldier was not at all appalled by their macabre humor. "I'll alert the others." At some point, every soldier made an emergency field donation. It was a fact of war.

Two soldiers unpacked and set up the surgical gurney while Lucy dumped alcohol into a metal tray. Elisabeth unloaded surgical instruments and tossed them in for emergency sterilization, alcohol splashing everywhere. They were supposed to sterilize all surgical instruments overnight in a sterilizing oven, but they had no time. Field sterilization was messy, but effective.

"Anybody got word on what the medevac unit is responding to?" Elisabeth called out, wondering which equipment to grab next.

"RPG exploded near a special forces unit moving in on foot," a soldier with a radio called out from somewhere on the other side of the tent. "Got three injured. Two seriously."

"We're not going to be ready," Lucy shouted. "Tell them to redirect the wounded to the field hospital we just came from."

"That's a negative, Ma'am," the Radio Specialist shouted. "Major Adams specifically ordered the wounded are to come here. He said Lieutenant Kaiser would understand."

Elisabeth glanced up and scrutinized the Radio Specialist relaying orders. He looked normal. No trench coat. The soldier raised one finger and pointed to his tailbone. One of the incoming wounded was not fully human.

"All right," Elisabeth shouted, stepping up to the plate. "It's us ... or nobody. We can do this."

"Mary ... better get those blood donations going," Lucy called out. "Who's got the radio? Ask them if they know what blood type the three incoming are?"

"O-positive," the Radio Specialist shouted. "A-positive. And HH-negative."

"HH-negative?" Mary said with dismay. "Where the hell will we find Bombay-phenotype blood?" HH-negative was the rarest blood type in the world. So rare that only a tiny percentage of the population possessed it.

"I have HH-negative blood, Ma'am," the young Private who had carried in Mary's crate earlier said. His expression appeared grave.

"So do I," another soldier said, a Corporal wearing the telltale long coat Azrael had explained his allies used to conceal their tails. "We'll donate whatever we can."

"But ... two?" Mary sputtered. "You're not ... East Indian!"

"My grandmother had HH-negative blood," Elisabeth deflected Mary's question. "And she was full-blooded German. From Germany. Bombay is just where they first discovered it."

"Quit yapping and start collecting blood!" Lucy ordered. "You can write your doctoral thesis on HH-negative later!"

"Yes ... Ma'am," Mary and Elisabeth said together, passing a smile between them. Mary was the outgoing one who could charm the skin off a snake. Elisabeth the talented one. While Lucy focused on the boring details that made their three-ring circus possible. Cracking the whip was one of those details.

Elisabeth beckoned the Corporal with the trench coat over to a crate and shoved a large, hollow collection needle into his vein. He looked like any American soldier of European descent, tall, dark-haired, handsome, and muscular as those who joined the military were prone to be. His ordinary-looking blood dripped down into the collection bag. If Azrael hadn't told her Sata'an descendants hid a tail, the thought would never have occurred to her in a million years.

HH-negative. Only appearing in tiny, usually geographically isolated communities. She now knew which side of the family the peculiar DNA Azrael had told her about had come from. Had Oma known she was the descendant of a mixed-race ancestor fortuitous enough to escape the terms of the Armistice due to a lucky genetic mutation?

The sound of an incoming chopper interrupted her thoughts. The medevac unit. On its way back. If one of the incoming sported a tail, how would she hide it from her fellow nurses? She realized the soldier she gathered blood from scrutinized *her* as well.

"How long have you known Azrael, Ma'am?" the soldier asked cautiously.

"Around ten years," Elisabeth glanced up from the blood collection bag. "What's your name, Corporal?"

"Emmett Tills, Ma'am," the soldier said. "After the young man whose murder sparked the civil rights movement."

"That's a nice name." Elisabeth placed a folded piece of gauze on Corporal Till's arm and slid the collection needle out. "My friends ... um. They don't ... know. If ... um ... I might need your help handling things if ... um ... your friend is..."

"That's why we were stationed here, Ma'am," Corporal Till rolled down his sleeve as soon as Elisabeth slapped a band aid over the needle hole. "Some of our best people are in there fighting alongside yours."

Although he wore the bars of an army Corporal, the young man had the demeanor of someone much older and higher in rank. Samuel Adams had explained his men embedded themselves into low-ranking positions. They were expected to roll up their sleeves and get dirty, not direct traffic from some perch above like the Archangels, who the descendants of the lizard-people viewed with contempt. Azrael had won their respect because he was not too high-and-mighty to wade through the cesspool of humanity and get his tailfeathers dirty.

"Hey ... Tills! I'm next!" a lower-ranking soldier said, fresh-faced and without a trench coat. "Quit flirting and let me talk to the pretty nurse! I've got A-positive blood, Ma'am."

Corporal Tills rolled his eyes and glanced furtively to one side in a gesture Elisabeth read to convey the soldier was not one of them. A ruckus outside the tent let them know the medevac chopper was being unloaded. Time up!

"C'mere," Elisabeth beckoned to the second soldier. "Corporal Tills? Do you have medic training?"

"Yes, Ma'am," Corporal Tills said.

"I'm going to start collection," Elisabeth informed him. "But it's going to be up to *you* to stop when the bag is full. Please be sure to mark it when you're done."

"Awww ... man!" the second soldier groused. "If I'm going to give it up, at least it should be for a pretty nurse!"

"Knock it off, Private!" Corporal Tills said not-too-seriously. "Or you'll be scrubbing out the latrines!"

"As soon as we get some latrines," the Private joked, wincing as Elisabeth shoved the large hollow needle into his arm. "Ouch! This pretty lady bites!"

"This pretty lady outranks you, Private," Elisabeth said, gently-but-firmly putting the flirting soldier back into his place. "And also thanks you for stepping forward to donate."

"Ma'am," the Private winked at her as she turned to see who was in the middle of the bustle of activity making its way into the tent. The Radio Specialist, who Elisabeth surmised was 'in' on things, directed one of the wounded into a curtained-off area, separate from the others, and beckoned for her to come.

"Report, Specialist ... uh ... Carver?" Elisabeth read the bars on his shoulder and last name velcroed to his chest. "Let me guess. George? After George Washington Carver. The father of the peanut?" She gathered by first the look of surprise, and then respect, that Specialist Carver was pleased Elisabeth guessed so readily the significance of his chosen name. Like Corporal Tills, the Radio Specialist appeared European by heritage, but he had a bit of a drawl, not English or Australian, perhaps New Zealand?

"Our man is not the first priority," Radio Specialist Carver said with a nod. "We'll keep him stable until you attend to that one over there. Then our guy. And then the third guy they're bringing in now. His physiology makes him less prone to go into shock than your guys. Our men will assist you once you finish up with the first wounded. We'd like you to assign your nurses to take care of the third wounded to keep them busy. He's got shrapnel in his arm and shoulder, but we've staunched the blood."

Azrael had explained how the Sata'an-hybrid tail conferred a survival advantage due to its ability to store extra calories, oxygen and blood in the fat-rich tissue. A Sata'an 'docked' at birth lost that advantage, rendering them no stronger or weaker than a human, while a Sata'an 'docked' later in life was usually physically weakened. This didn't stop Sata'an adolescents anxious to disappear into the human population from getting their tails cut off anyway. She stared at the radioman, wondering which he was. An ally? Or a Sata'an descendant docked at birth?

Or maybe he was like her?

Not likely. Although numerous Sata'an descendants had disappeared into humanity over the years, they lived quiet lives, sequestered into remote areas of the world where they could keep their offspring's peculiar genetic features a secret. Azrael only knew of a few cases where offspring had truly been born without a tail. It only happened when there was a genetic mutation.

"Elisabeth!" Mary called. "We need that magic scalpel of yours to do wonders over here!"

"I'm on it!" Elisabeth's thoughts were forgotten as she did what she did best. Save lives. The soldier's arm was shredded from shrapnel and burned, but he'd managed to cover his face, sparing it from horrific burns.

"This guy's arm looks like a Swiss cheese," Lucy stepped aside. "I don't think we'll be able to save it."

"We'll see." Elisabeth grabbed forceps from the tray of instruments seeping in alcohol and began to pull out chunks of metal. "Mary … where's that blood? Which one is this, anyway?"

"Mister A-positive," Mary hooked up a freshly drawn pint. "Still nice and warm. I understand there's a second pint on its way?"

"Affirmative," Elisabeth grunted, no longer paying attention to the chatter in the room. She was in save 'em mode now. "How's his blood pressure?"

"Dropping," Lucy said after pausing to check it the old-fashioned way. "Shall I dig out the bone saw?"

"Not yet," Elisabeth said. "I'm not amputating unless I have no choice." She dug through the charred flesh, picking out pieces of shrapnel and clinking them upon the metal tray.

"Any spurters?" Mary asked.

"Not that I can see," Elisabeth said. "Only this section … here … is fourth-degree. The rest are second and third. They may be able to save some function in the arm."

"These two fingers look bad," Lucy said. "They're fused together and it looks like the tendons are gone."

"It self-cauterized," Elisabeth said. "We'll leave that decision to the surgeons in Germany. Radial artery looks good. Ulnar artery was damaged by shrapnel, but appears to have self-cauterized from the burns. Can't tell if he's getting blood flow or not."

"Amputate?" Lucy asked.

Elisabeth poked at the cratered arm, unable to tell if anything could be saved. In ideal conditions, a trauma team might be able to use cutting edge microsurgery to piece together severed nerves, tendons and arteries. Unfortunately here, if the soldier wasn't getting blood flow, by the time he got to Germany, gangrene would take his entire arm and probably his life. How she wished Azrael was here! He had a way of telling when 'death' had overtaken a limb or organ. If only she had the same gift.

The soldier's wrist from three inches above his hand all the way down to his fingertips flashed black before her eyes. Everything above it looked pink. Elisabeth blinked. The image disappeared. She focused again. The blackness reappeared, slowly creeping up the wounded soldier's arm like a cancer. Oma had described how sometimes she could *see* sickness, but this was the first time Elisabeth had seen it for herself.

"Get the bone saw," Elisabeth snapped. "We're going to amputate here, three inches above the wrist. Everything below that point has been without oxygen too long. Gangrene has already begun to set in."

"How can you tell?" Mary squinted as she tried to see visually what Elisabeth just … knew.

"Don't know," Elisabeth said. "It's like everything else I do. I just do it."

Neither of her team-mates questioned her decision. One of Corporal Till's men had dug for the bone saw and started prepping it as soon as Lucy had said they might need it. Efficiency. They were treating them as though they were the doctors and Corporal Till's team was their nurses.

"Don't have any idea where the splatter mask is," Lucy handed her the portable oscillating bone saw. "Sorry. At least we had time to sterilize the blade."

"Wonderful," Elisabeth said sarcastically, pulling her regular surgical mask tighter around her face to minimize the anticipated gore. "Mary … I need you to electrocauterize the blood vessels as soon as I tie them off."

"Yes, Ma'am," Mary reached over to grab a surgical instrument that looked like a pair of tweezers attached to a wire.

As soon as Elisabeth tied the nerves off, Mary pinched them together with the tweezers. An electrical current passed between the two tines, cauterizing the vessels together so no more blood could flow through them. The aroma of cooked flesh wafted up to Elisabeth's nostrils.

"Lucy …" Elisabeth sliced through what undamaged skin remained around two inches below where she was about to cut. "As soon as she's done, I want you to pull up the skin to protect what he's got left. I'm trying to leave enough of the brachioradialas so he can use a prosthesis."

"Hand's shot anyway," Lucy said. "Even if the quacks in Germany could save the fingers, they'd never be able to unfuse them."

Elisabeth tested the power button on the oscillating bone saw. They all winced at the high-pitched sound, halfway between a dentist's drill and something a contractor might use when demolishing a house.

"My first solo amputation." Elisabeth took a deep breath and steadied herself. She'd participated in numerous amputations. Even handled the bone saw. But this would be the first time she had made the call without input from a doctor.

She wished Azrael was here, if for no reason other than she missed the steadying feel of his presence. After years of sensing him in the periphery and finally getting to know him, the fact he wasn't here bothered her.

"Blood pressure is dropping," Lucy said. "He's losing blood as fast as I can get it into him. You'd better get at it."

"Stay with me, soldier," Elisabeth touched the soldier's arm just above where she was about to cut. "Ain't nothing wrong with you we can't fix. Just stay here. Okay? If you leave, they're just going to make you come back and start everything over again from scratch. Different body. Different family. Different friends. Same bloody issues. Better to work it out in the body you already have."

Azrael had been teaching her to interpret what she'd been able to feel her entire life. She could sense the soldier hovering above his body, holding on by a sturdy thread. This one was a fighter. He had only retreated far enough to avoid the pain. If she salvaged his mortal shell, he would move back in to inhabit it.

"I'm going to try to save enough of your arm so you can wear a prosthesis," Elisabeth said into the air, not even earning a curious glance from her team-mates who were by now used to her eccentric ramblings. "You'll be able to fire a gun again within six months."

The others winced at the high-pitched whine of the bone saw as she sliced through muscle, tendon and bone. Mary moved in to cauterize the smaller blood vessels as soon as she lifted the saw out of the way, while Lucy went right in behind her to pull the skin over the stump and stitch it up with thick, ugly black stitches. They wouldn't be winning any awards, but it was done.

"Blood pressure is rising," Mary checked his vitals again using the crude sphygmomanometer which was all they had unpacked at the moment. "Pulse is still erratic, but stronger. I think he'll make it."

"Lieutenant Kaiser?" Corporal Till called from the curtained off area. "We need you."

"You two finish up here," Elisabeth said. "And then attend to our third guy. I'll take care of the man behind curtain number one."

"Need help?" Mary asked.

"It's black ops sneak-and-peak stuff," Elisabeth rolled her eyes. "Probably Prince William or some other VIP playing soldier. They don't want anyone to knowing he's here until it's time to roll the cameras and ask for campaign contributions."

"Great…" Lucy said sarcastically. "We get to play nursemaid to some pampered poodle with a paper cut while the real soldiers have to stand in line to get treated."

"This is a straight triage situation," Elisabeth said crossly. "I don't play favorites. Don't care who the poodle is."

"Yeah, yeah," Mary applied a bandage to the soldier's stump as she finished up. "We know. YOU don't play favorites. But Major Jackass Devens would have been falling all over himself to treat the guy behind the curtain first and let this poor soldier die."

"Which is why we are here," Lucy interjected. "Someone appreciates real results. Not just spin."

"Carry on, Ma'am," Elisabeth gave her two co-nurses a perfunctory goodbye salute as they both outranked her. Although she was the so-called 'talent,' she had no illusions that she could pull off the kinds of stunts she did on a daily basis without the rank and extensive knowledge of her support team. And also a hefty dose of pressure from Azrael's friends.

"Lieutenant Kaiser," Corporal Till opened the curtain for her to step inside.

A tail… Now that Elisabeth knew it was there, she could see the bulge where he kept it carefully tucked up into a special sling to keep himself from inadvertently using it to maintain his balance. As soon as a Sata'an descendant could walk he was taught to walk with his tail holstered so he learned to compensate for the imbalance. In battle, Sata'an descendants strapped spikes to their tail so it could be used as an extra fighting limb. The spike had already been unstrapped, as had the soldier's shredded flak vest.

The scent of blood filled her nostrils. Blood poured out of profuse shrapnel wounds and down the body bag they'd jury rigged to keep his body heat in while he'd been transported here. Both bags of HH-negative blood they'd gathered earlier had already been used up and a third soldier had come in and hooked himself directly to the wounded soldier in a direct transfusion. Anger boiled up in her gut as she realized what they'd done.

"Why wasn't this soldier treated first?!!" Elisabeth hissed, her voice low so her peers wouldn't hear her. "Blood loss trumps burns in a triage situation!!!"

"The other soldier is a full-blooded human," Corporal Tills said without emotion. "You're a protected species. The armistice says humans with life-threatening injuries go first."

"-I- say who goes first!!!" Elisabeth snapped. "And –I'm- color blind! I can see now why Azrael insisted my team come to this triage unit!"

"But..." Corporal Tills said.

"God and Satan can both go to hell!" Elisabeth hissed. She hurriedly checked where shrapnel from the exploding RPG had blown straight through the soldiers flack vest into his belly. "Dammit! I thought you guys were supposed to have more technologically advanced armor than us?"

"We're supposed to remain unobtrusive, Ma'am," Radio Specialist Carver said. "Your technology has advanced to the point that your body armor isn't much different than our body armor. An Alliance energy shield would be too conspicuous."

Elisabeth paused, her mouth open to speak. She had absolutely no idea what an Alliance energy shield was, but pictured something out of a Star Trek movie deflecting photon torpedoes. It was irrelevant. She pushed the image out of her mind and focused on the ruptured bowel.

"What's his name?" Elisabeth glanced up at the trench-coat clad soldier giving a direct blood-to-blood transfusion and realized he was chalk-white against his black sunglasses. "And ... you! How long have you been hooked up to him like that?"

"Your patient's name is Kennard ... Clyde Kennard," Corporal Tills said. "Private Young has been hooked up to the transfusion since before you grabbed the bone saw."

"Young ... you're out of here," Elisabeth said to the soldier who'd already given more blood than was safe. "That's an order. Tills! Either find me another HH-phenotype or you're donating another pint! And find the first guy who gave HH-negative. One pint is best, but you can donate two before it becomes dangerous!"

"Yes, Ma'am," Corporal Tills immediately rolled up his sleeve. He snapped some orders at the other soldiers in the curtained off area in a language Elisabeth couldn't understand, a language comprised of hisses and low growls.

One rushed off while a second helped the soldier who'd given too much blood to a chair. Elisabeth managed to avoid recoiling when he hissed and tasted the air with a long forked tongue, showing he had sharp teeth like a wolf. She wondered what his eyes looked like beneath the black Maui Jim sunglasses.

"Ma'am?" Radio Specialist Carver tugged at her arm. "Are you okay?"

Elisabeth looked up from the very human-looking intestines she had her hands buried in to repair into absolutely human-looking brown eyes. The

Radio Specialist wasn't wearing a trench coat. Her mouth opened and closed, unable to force herself to ask the question.

"Docked at birth," Radio Specialist Carver said as though reading her mind. "I'm wearing contact lenses."

"I'm … Az says I'm…" Elisabeth sputtered.

"You are the holy grail we all seek," Radio Specialist Carver said. "Fully human."

"It shouldn't matter," Elisabeth muttered, looking down at the patient who was probably already too far gone to save. "Dammit! No more of this … segregation! If you're going to fight alongside Coalition troops, you're going to get triaged like Coalition troops!"

"We … can't …" Corporal Tills said. "The armistice says…"

"Fuck the armistice! Lucy!!! Mary!!!" Elisabeth shouted at the top of her lungs. "Get your asses in here! I need you!"

"But…"

"You called?" Mary stuck her head in the curtain. The Sata'an-human soldier snapped to attention."

"Put a medic on your other patient," Elisabeth snapped. "His injuries are non-life-threatening. You two have just been cleared … by me … to work on this top secret patient."

"What … secret … patient?" Lucy also stepped behind the curtain.

"Lucy … Mary … meet Corporal Tills," Elisabeth said. "He's an … uh … he's a genetically engineered super-soldier. He has a tail. For balance. In battle. So does the guy on the table. His name is Corporal Kennard. You two got a problem with that?"

"Uh … no?" Mary said, not at all sure she meant it.

"Does this have anything to do with that black-winged angel some say follow you around?" Lucy asked.

"Yes!" Elisabeth stuck her hands back into the intestines of the soldier on the table. "Mary … Corporal Tills wishes to donate a second pint of blood to Corporal Kennard. Hook him up. Make sure he doesn't give a drop more than that. He's already donated a pint today."

"Two pints," Corporal Tills said. "We've got more blood than you. We can donate up to 3.5 pints."

"Whatever," Elisabeth stitched up three separate places where she had just pulled shrapnel out of her patient's large intestine. "Lucy … Corporal Kennard has a perforated bowel. We're going to have to flush the abdominal cavity with saline and then start him on a hefty cycle of antibiotics if we're going to give him a chance to live."

"Why the hell wasn't he wearing body armor?" Lucy asked.

"He was," Elisabeth tilted her head towards the shredded flak vest. "Doesn't do much good at point-blank range."

"Pulse is erratic and weak," Lucy said. "Blood pressure is barely readable."

Elisabeth tried using the sixth sense Azrael had been teaching her to use to answer that question. Not only could she sense the soldier's spirit clinging to his body, but also received images.

"Hey … soldier! Listen up!" Elisabeth gave her habitual pre-surgery pep-talk. "You want to avoid that fiery hell y'all been put in charge of guarding? Well you just keep clinging to your body while I patch it up. You hear me? You just hang on as hard as you can no matter what and we'll do the rest. Okay?"

"Suction is ready," Lucy held out a tube. "Do you want me to mop the floor or vacuum the house?"

"Vacuum the house," Elisabeth said. "I see more shrapnel."

As Lucy suctioned the patient's abdominal cavity so infection wouldn't kill him, the spirit which clung to the body on her operating table sent Elisabeth a query. It was strange, being able to communicate with a patient whose body was unconscious, but whose spirit was awake and alert. It wasn't quite what Azrael described. Much cruder. But Elisabeth intuited what carrot would entice the fallen soldier to fight to stay with every ounce of his being. She bent down to whisper the sweet compulsion into his ear.

"If you stay," Elisabeth whispered. "I will introduce you to her. I will help her understand who you are. The rest will be up to you."

For the next several hours, they pieced the soldier back together while Mary rustled up more blood. Radio Specialist Carver put in a call for more HH-phenotype donors and more donors came. The last two were blatantly not human. Mary took their lizard-like features in stride, jabbing the blood collection needles into their warm, faintly striped skin and made small talk.

"Shit," Lucy jabbed a third syringe of Rocefin into the IV as soon as she finished flushing the soldier's abdominal cavity. "How the fuck is this guy even still alive?"

"Genetically engineered super-soldier," Elisabeth said, using the white lie which was not too far off from the truth as she stitched up the soldier's abdomen. "Super-duper double-oh-seven super-spook crap. Welcome! We've all been judged worthy to come into the inner circle … although they weren't expecting us to get tossed into the lion's den the first twenty minutes on the job. Least the Iraqi's could have done was let us get through the orientation video!"

"Figured it was only a matter of time before the government started gene-splicing animal DNA into human soldiers," Mary said, her eyes wide as the soldier before her gave her a wide, sharp-toothed smile. She glanced at the name tag and rank on the soldier's uniform. "Corporal … DuBois? Shit

... did you guys start out like this? Or did you ... volunteer ... to undergo some sort of experimental treatment?"

"I was born like this, Ma'am," Corporal DuBois tasted the air with his forked tongue. "I'm sorry my appearance offends you. They don't let us out much."

"Offends?" Mary glanced at the sling the soldier wore around his arm from an earlier injury and scrapes on the side of a face that would be human-looking but not for his serpentine eyes and the faint striping visible on his skin. "We're all on the same side here. I can't ... I can't fathom ... shit! You're like Spider Man or something!"

The Corporal gave Mary a toothy grin, practically beaming as he proceeded to flirt in a most human-like manner.

"Lucy," Elisabeth said, the wheels spinning in her brain as she tried to think of a way to introduce their patient to the nurse who'd intrigued him. "I'm ... drained. Would you mind taking Corporal Kennard through post-op procedures? He gets treated here until they can airlift him to whatever super-spook hospital they usually treat these guys at. I have a feeling he'd like to meet the woman who saved his life."

"You're the one who called the shots," Lucy said. "I just vacuumed the shit out of his gut while you stitched his colon back together."

Literally.

"Talk about a shitty start," Mary jibed, referring to the bacteria-laden contents of the large intestine which had ruptured.

"If you hadn't been here," Elisabeth said, feeling over-tired and punchy, "he'd have been shit out of luck!"

All three of them snorted. Morgue-humor. Although at least it appeared Corporal Kennard wasn't going to die. Not today. His heart rate and blood pressure had stabilized the moment Elisabeth had stitched him back together and his vital signs were growing stronger by the moment. Azrael was right. The Sata'an-human hybrids were tough as hell.

"Ten-four, oh talented one," Lucy gave her the Muslim greeting of hand touching the forehead, the lips and the heart they'd all picked up from Kadima. "I shall hold our super-soldier's hand and swear at him like a longshoreman like you do until he is too terrified of me to dare die."

Elisabeth gave her a wan smile, her exhaustion suddenly real. She hadn't realized how apprehensive she'd been about working with Azrael's allies until she'd actually done it. She handed the patient over to Lucy's capable hands and began to scrub out.

"Do you really have a tail?" Mary asked the mottled-skinned Corporal she'd finished getting blood from. She squealed in surprise as he released his tail from its sling and slipped it out from the trench coat to caress one of her calves. "Oh ... I can ... see ... how that might give you an edge in battle."

"Not just on the battlefield," Corporal DuBois flirted shamelessly as his tail slipped serpent-like to touch Mary's arm. "We're very … astute … with our tails."

Elisabeth smiled as she trudged out the tent and discovered a tent-city had sprung up around them while they'd been in surgery. The aroma of overly-salted MRE heater meals and instant coffee wafted in her direction from one of the tents. The soon-to-be mess hall was already up. Everywhere she looked, men were hustling equipment to transform Saddam Hussein's desert air-strip into an American military base. It always amazed her how quickly the military could set up and break down a base such as this. With no quarters assigned yet for privacy, she made her way to a dirt wall between the airstrip and what appeared to be a field to sit down, hoping Azrael would appear.

"Oh … Az," Elisabeth sighed, leaning back against the rock and pulling her coat closer to guard against the cold. "No wonder you pity them."

Azrael was not here. Elisabeth dozed off in the middle of the field until the sound of the next chopper coming in with wounded roused her from her sleep and sent her back into the medical tent to deal with the next batch of wounded. These ones were all fully human. As were the next six batches of wounded. But Azrael did not make his appearance. Whatever he was doing, it was important enough that he didn't have time to pop in to see her.

She hoped he was okay.

Chapter 44

And angels shall enter unto them from every gate
Saying Salāmun 'Alaykum (peace be upon you)
For that you persevered in patience!
Excellent indeed is the final home!'

Ar-Ra'ad 13:23-24

Earth – March 31, 2003
Imam Ali Mosque, Najaf, Iraq

"Thee alone do we worship," the Grand Ayatollah prayed, "and thee alone we seek for help." Holy beads slipped through his fingers, the deeply ingrained ritual helping his mind expand beyond the four walls of the tiny room where demons posing as Saddam Fedayeen had locked him in the back of the mosque. Although he was not as capable of waging jihad against the Evil One as the Prophet Muhammad had been, peace be upon him, he could detect the smaller demons still lurking in his mosque.

A pleasant tingle of electricity permeated the sanctuary. He finished the last few lines of the Al-Fatiha, the opening Sura of the Quran, before getting to his feet and turning to where he sensed the familiar presence.

"Do not keep yourself hidden, Malak al-Maut," the Ayatollah said. "These are difficult times and my people are dying. If it is my time to die, I welcome thee to carry my spirit into the arms of our Beloved."

Azrael finished materializing into the room so he was completely visible. Malak al-Maut was tall, thin, and as dark as the night he shepherded the souls of the martyrs through to be reunited with Allah in Paradise. The legends described him as perfect, as all angels were purported to be, but the Ayatollah was surprised to see that this one hid a boyish countenance beneath his serious expression.

"As-salamu alaykum," Azrael greeted. "I'm not here to take you. Yet. At least I hope I don't have to take you. That's the plan."

The dark angel's expression showed concern, and also amusement. Like most devout Muslims, the Grand Ayatollah believed the path of righteousness would grant him entrance into Paradise, whether the Angel of

Death chose to escort him there personally or not. The Angel of Mercy had assured him that Paradise was real.

"I didn't think it could get any worse than that Ba'athist butcher being put in charge of this city," the Ayatollah complained. "But then a demon seized control of his body and now he is even more evil. He's killing women and children!"

"That's why I'm here," Azrael said. "We have a favor to ask."

"Ask," the Ayatollah said. "And if it is within my power, I shall grant your wish."

"You, of all the religious leaders in Iraq," Azrael said, "are sensible and even-handed. We want you to invite the American commanding officer for a parley as soon as they finish clearing the city to discuss allying against Saddam Hussein."

The Ayatollah contemplated the Angel of Death's request. Azrael waited for the cities highest-ranking holy man to process his thoughts without interruption.

"We are Shi'ite," the Ayatollah said. "Not Sunni. Our people were treated brutally under the regime of Saddam Hussein and our city stripped of its resources. The enemy of my enemy is our friend."

"Good," Azrael said. "We can count on you?"

"Me?" the Ayatollah shrugged. "I'm too pragmatic to create enemies where none should exist. I am not fooled by these demons into mistaking who our true enemy is. The problem will be the families of the patriarchs. The Al-Quds surviving families won't let the Americans anywhere near this mosque."

"Your men make suicide runs against tanks," Azrael said. "And the Al-Quds Militia has ties to Iran. Iran is flooding your ranks with young Iranians eager to wage jihad against the Americans. Coalition forces have no way of knowing who is really an enemy versus a tired old war veteran doing so under threat of having their family murdered."

The Ayatollah drummed his fingers together in a contemplative gesture as the gears turned in his head, the mind of a scholar paired with the pragmatism of somebody who'd spent a great deal of his life being marginalized by the ruling party.

"I'm not a great fan of the United States," the Ayatollah said at last. "Her leaders are every bit as guilty as Saddam Hussein for wreaking havoc in this area of the world. But her people are not the Great Satan some of my contemporaries make her out to be. Especially now that I have truly seen evil. It would not be wise to cast out Hussein, only to turn our country over to the Evil One's demons."

"The Americans are just people." The formal posture of Azrael's wings relaxed as he recognized the Ayatollah was open to reason. "The majority of soldiers amassed outside this city are good men, although every army has its roughnecks and rejects, the same as your own militias. The American commanding officer will deal with you fairly."

"I will announce I desire negotiations and enter them with open eyes," the Ayatollah said. "But I cannot promise the people of this city will simply allow the invaders to stroll in without a fight. Or that we will reach an agreement. Not when so many lives have been lost."

"That's all we can ask," Azrael said. "Hear them out. Drive a hard bargain to get what your people need. And then reach an agreement so you avoid unnecessary bloodshed."

The Ayatollah studied the ebony angel standing before him. The Angel of Death had never made himself visible before, but it was neither the first time he'd sensed his presence, nor the first time he'd been asked a favor by one of the angels. Although darker and more slender, the Ayatollah could see the bloodline of the Angel of Mercy in Malak al-Maut's chiseled features. He made the Muslim gesture of respect, touching his fingers to his forehead, his lips and his heart. It was not his place to indulge his curiosity.

"Is there anything you can do, Malak al-Maut," the Ayatollah asked, "to rid our city of that demon pulling the puppet strings of the Saddam Fedayeen?"

"You know interference by our species is forbidden," Azrael shifted uncomfortably from one foot to the other. "But … Allah has issued a fatwa decreeing I am to rid your city of the demon."

Nervous. The Angel of Death appeared to be nervous. The Ayatollah had learned from his dealings with the Angel of Mercy that even angels felt fear when it came to creatures as evil as the demons exorcised from Mecca by the Prophet Muhammad, peace be upon him. The Ayatollah had exorcised a few of his own in his lifetime, but the two who'd taken up residence in his city made his scalp crawl under his turban. Had the Angel of Mercy not taught him prayers to keep them from seizing control of his body, it would be him ordering the murder of women and children instead of the Ba'athist leader.

"The demon thought I was too stupid not to recognize when somebody tempted me to see what I *wanted* to see," the Ayatollah said, "instead of reality."

"You are descended from one of us," Azrael said. "One who possessed the ability to resist this kind of trickery. It is why we come to you whenever we need help."

The Ayatollah nodded. The only reason the demon called Chemosh kept him alive was because he needed something. Something he would not give willingly. He gestured towards the locked door where two guards were stationed outside.

"And what of my gilded cage?"

Malak al-Maut gave him a mischievous grin, a most unexpected expression from the most feared angel in Islam. He stepped up to the door and knocked twice.

"Knock, knock," Azrael said in Arabic.

"Who's there?" one of the guards asked.

"Grim," Azrael listened to ascertain the exact position of the two guards.

"Grim who?" the other guard asked.

"Grim Reaper!" Azrael dissipated the door and tapped both guards on the shoulder before they could shout and alert the other Saddam Fedayeen they had an intruder in their midst.

In a single practiced motion, he grabbed the two wraiths as both host bodies fell to the floor. Although the Ayatollah could not see the souls Malak al-Maut had just reaped, he could sense them. They were not the enormous malefactors he'd dealt with earlier, but they still made his skin crawl.

"If you'll excuse me, your holiness," Azrael said. "These two have a date with Gehenna ... um ... Sheol."

"Wa alaki s-salam," the Ayatollah made a sign of blessing upon the dark angel as he did for any other pilgrim who came to him for assistance.

Azrael acknowledged the blessing with a respectful bow of his head. With a flash of darkness, the Angel of Death disappeared, dragging the two demons along with him. The heaviness which had weighed upon his mosque disappeared along with him, the source of putrefaction dragged kicking and screaming to Sheol where it belonged.

The Ayatollah sighed and glanced towards the neat, orderly wall tiles with their repeating pattern of blues and gold. Order. He craved order. But Allah had decided he wasn't going to get any order until he created some of his own in this city.

This was his mosque. Demon, or no demon, he was the caretaker of this holy place and would not be run out like some jackal. Kneeling back down upon his prayer rug and ignoring the two bodies outside the melted door, the Grand Ayatollah resumed reciting the Quran, praying for guidance on exactly how he would pull off the favor the Angel of Death had asked of him

Chapter 45

For … God spared not the angels that sinned,
but cast them down to hell,
and delivered them into chains of darkness,
to be reserved unto judgment

2 Peter 2:4

April 1, 2003
Al-Najaf Airstrip, Najaf, Iraq

"This one looks pretty good," Mary drawled in her languid Texas twang. "Any more waiting in the queue?"

Elisabeth glanced up from the bullet she fished out of an elderly man's shoulder just in time to see Corporal DuBois sidle up behind the 'humor' of their little three-man operation with an enormous bouquet of alliums, trench coat, boonie-hat, dark sunglasses and what appeared to be a thin veneer of makeup hiding his striped skin.

"Behind you," Elisabeth said. With a furtive glance and nod, she alerted Lucy to the soap opera about to unfold in their emergency room.

Lucy gave Mary a knowing smile. Lucy dug a piece of shrapnel out of another Al-Quds militiaman who'd opted to throw his fate to the mercy of the 70th Armored Regiment rather than help the Ba'athist leader who'd seized control of their city. Only Elisabeth knew the Ba'athist leader was a demon. Literally. Or more accurately, a malignant god.

"M-m-miss…" Corporal DuBois stammered to Mary, "I … uh … found these at the side of the airstrip and thought … uh … well … thank you."

"Oh!" Mary glanced up at the Sata'an-human hybrid soldier who she'd drawn far more blood out of yesterday than should have been possible to save the life of his brother-in-arms. "Corporal DuBois! How very … um … thoughtful?"

Elisabeth sighed and focused back on the bullet which had, luckily, not hit anything vital. Azrael had warned his allies were attracted to full-blooded human females. He just hadn't warned her *how* attracted. Less than 24 hours after they'd patched up Corporal Kennard, the gut-shredded victim, and already both nurses had received numerous requests for dinner, movie-night, rides in top-secret military vehicles, including vehicles which human technology still believed to be theoretically impossible, and just about any other activity which might impress a human female enough to give a lizard-man the time of day.

She, on the other hand, was given a wide berth. Corporal Tills hadn't spelled it out, but it was obvious these men considered her to be 'Az's girl.' Elisabeth smiled, accidentally causing her patient to grunt in pain.

"I'm sorry…" she ground out in halting Arabic. "Not better." What she wanted to say was that she was sorry she didn't have a better local anesthetic to numb the pain while she fished out the bullet. How she missed Kadima!

The old man let loose an unintelligible string of Arabic words that might, or might not, be understanding. He lifted one liver-spotted hand to touch hers, nodding approval. Whether he understood or not, he was grateful she made the effort to help her enemy and treat him kindly.

"A pox upon Chemosh's genitals for sending old men to do a young man's job," Elisabeth hissed as she finally got the slender surgical tweezers around the lead and gently tugged it out.

"Who?" Lucy asked.

"Um … the Ba'athist leader," Elisabeth phrased her answer to be truthful without revealing more than her colleagues needed to know. "He's a real … um … demon."

"I thought that was *my* job description?" Corporal DuBois grinned, exposing fang-like incisors inherited from a long-dead Sata'anic ancestor.

Mary recoiled. Elisabeth winced along with her, but not for the same reason. Corporal DuBois had been knocking himself out, hoping to get Mary to give him the time of day. Although Mary accepted her new top-secret assignment, which Elisabeth had painted as nursing super-soldiers with animal DNA spliced into their genome by some DARPA mad scientist, it was a far cry from being 'color-blind' to the Sata'an descendants differences. For the first time in her life, Elisabeth was glad she'd spent a decade living in neighborhoods where she was the minority. It made her more sensitive to the discrimination the Sata'anic descendants faced for something which was not their fault.

Her Al-Quds patient also noted the fangs and glanced fearfully at the Sata'an Corporal, who had to be breaking twenty different protocols when there were human patients in their midst. Corporal DuBois was assigned to protect them in case one of the prisoners turned on them, but unlike the other Sata'an-human hybrids, he hadn't faded into the walls of the tent.

"It's okay." Elisabeth used a soothing voice to distract the old man. "Here. Look. Here's your bullet. A little souvenir to show your grandkids once the 70th Armored Regiment finishes chasing out the rest of the bad guys."

She placed the bullet in the palm of her patient's hand and closed his fingers around it. The close physical contact from a female, an American female, did the trick. It distracted the old man from scrutinizing the nearly seven foot tall lizard-man bearing flowers.

"Shukran," the old man thanked her. His face lit up with interest as he held the bullet close to his rheumy eyes, grimacing once as Elisabeth finished stitching up the bullet hole in his bicep.

Elisabeth sensed Az make his entrance someplace off to her side. Corporal DuBois sensed it, as well. He nodded in Azrael's direction. With the 70th Armored Regiment mopping up the aftermath of what had to be the biggest tank-battle since World War II, she knew he couldn't stay, but she appreciated the fact he'd taken the time to pop in.

'How goes the battle?' Elisabeth pictured putting the words into a little balloon as Az had taught her. A pleasant tingle went down her spine as Azrael lingered on the tendril she offered. It was as close to touch as she could get with an angel whose touch was death.

Vague images came into her mind. The demon-god had escaped. Frustration. Moloch's Agents still in the city, whispering suggestions to those predisposed to fight on the side of the Saddam Fedayeen. It wasn't speech, but it was communication. She was learning.

Her Al-Quds patient touched her hand, an inquiry in his eyes as he rattled off words she couldn't understand in Arabic. He wondered why she stopped, mid-stitch, to stare off into an empty corner of the tent.

"Sorry." Elisabeth gave her patient a smile to convey what words could not. "Been working too many hours. Everything's fine."

She sensed one last non-corporeal touch, urgency and regret, and then he was gone back to do whatever Angels of Death did whenever they walked amongst human battlefields. He'd explained how he was able to tell whether the soul he reaped was an evil Agent, but it was all gibberish to her. Good, bad, or indifferent, Elisabeth patched back together whomever the medics hauled in.

"This guy's all set," Lucy interrupted her thoughts. "We got any more?"

"We're all set for now." Corporal DuBois signaled Lucy's patient that it was time to go. "Until the next transport arrives. I'll take this one away to the detention area. Any restrictions?"

"I've started him on a cycle of Cephalozin," Lucy said. "He should be assigned a cot to recover."

"We're out of cots," Corporal DuBois said. "We've started bumping less-injured wounded for the more seriously injured. How high should I prioritize him?"

"Elisabeth?" Lucy asked. "Could you do that … thing?"

Elisabeth considered the wounds Lucy had just patched up using not only her training as a nurse, but also that 'color thing' Az had been teaching her to judge whether somebody's life-energy was strong, weak, or infected. Lucy's patient was shaken, but not in life-threatening danger.

"Can you get him a prayer-mat to lay down on?" Elisabeth asked.

"Consider it done," Corporal DuBois said. "The prisoners helped us string a camouflage net to give them shelter from the sun. I'll assign one of his comrades to watch over him."

Elisabeth nodded assent.

"Thanks," Lucy said.

Elisabeth finished bandaging the bullet-wound in her own patient and handed him over to Corporal DuBois for similar handling. The old man had barely flinched as she'd fished out the bullet with minimal anesthetic. If he'd been a patient back in the United States, the old man would have yowled bloody murder.

"I'm going to get a bite to eat," Lucy said. "You need anything?"

Elisabeth glanced up from the medical instruments she sterilized in preparation for the next shipment of wounded, whenever they came. It was inevitable they would come. In addition to Coalition casualties, there were reports of hundreds of Saddam Fedayeen and Al-Quds militia dead and god-knows-how-many wounded. Any break they had would be short-lived.

"Um … not food." Elisabeth gestured to the bloody mess littering the hospital tent. "But would you mind checking on how Corporal Kennard is doing after you eat? I'll clean up here."

"Sure." Lucy gave her a grin. Lucy was nearing middle-age and, as she herself put it, was as tall and plain as the South Dakota prairie from whence she'd come. Tail or no tail, the fact the handsome Corporal Kennard had awoken and been immediately smitten had the 'brains' of their little triage unit floating on air.

"Thanks!" Elisabeth checked one promise off her list. She would do what she could to encourage Lucy to cross paths with the recovering gut-shredded patient. The rest was up to him.

Now if only she could do something for poor, equally smitten Corporal DuBois, who'd taken the liberty of stopping by the mess tent on his way back from depositing their last patient in the detention area and brought back Mary a picnic lunch fit to feed a queen. Mary had the desperate expression of a gal cornered at a nightclub by a persistent guy who kept asking for a dance. It didn't matter that, once you looked past the faint stripes which marred the Corporal's otherwise human-looking skin, he was drop-dead gorgeous. Mary couldn't get past the differences.

Chapter 46

Gehenna

"Please ... No!!!" Cresil shrieked. "No ... I'll do anything ... Please! Tell Lucifer ... I'll make a deal!!!"

"Tell it to the families of the poor bastards you killed," one of Lucifer's guards hissed. "Payback is a bitch."

The Sata'an-human hybrids opened the doors to Cresil's containment canister and gave him a shove off the precipice. He screeched as he fell alongside his fellow Agent. With no host-body to inhabit, the gravitational pull of countless quantum singularities intersecting at a single multi-dimensional point in time and space sucked their corrupted spirits down to the layer of Gehenna cordoned off for the worst of the very worst.

The level inhabited by Moloch....

Cresil landed with a thud on the fiery floor of the hell-dimension shaped by Moloch into a semblance of a great hall. As a creation/fire deity, it wasn't the fires of Gehenna which kept Moloch imprisoned here, but his inability to shape a new mortal shell to counteract the gravitational pull of the birthplace of countless universes ruled by Ki. None of them was evolved enough to make it through the innermost fires of Ki's womb and emerge from the other side as Azrael had done. Not even Moloch. It was the ultimate indignity ... to be forced to watch his former wife use her own primordial essence to shape the matter Moloch had once used to create whatever caught his fancy.

Balance. The former void-creature-turned-Ki liked nothing better than to rub Moloch's face in the fact she'd been able to manifest within herself the inner peace to both create and destroy...

The Devourer of Children stalked towards the two Agents who had failed him. He was a burly, muscular god, massive in scale, with golden, feathered wings streaked with red. From his neck rose a head which was somewhat bovine in appearance, and from the top of his head sprouted a pair of horns. Unlike any grass-eating ruminant, however, the red-eyed deity possessed perfect, sharp teeth and a set of fangs that were almost vampiric in nature.

"You failed me?" Moloch hissed. "You fools gave me assurances you would not lose this war!"

Before either wraith could protest, Moloch grabbed Cresil's compatriot and shoved him into his maw, his bovine tail twitching in frustration. Cresil dodged Moloch's meaty grasp, running shrieking towards the wall of fire which presented the choice Ki gave all imprisoned here as the energy released by his compatriot's destruction reverberated through Gehenna. Eaten? Or uncreation in the unearthly fire Ki used to recycle matter as Malak al-Maut had done and somehow survived? Cresil hesitated, unable to will himself to take the final leap. None before or since had ever been able to do what the Angel of Death had done. To leap into that fire would guarantee uncreation every bit as certainly as if he was devoured by his god.

Something grabbed Cresil's leg and lifted him upside-down like a rabbit caught in a snare.

"I have caught him, Master," the lesser god laughed. "Perhaps you might be willing to share your meal?"

"Help!" Cresil shrieked.

He was snatched out of the first god's hands by one of the other major gods interred in this circle of hell; Tanit, a goddess of war. While beautiful, there was a viscous quality about her features and her voice was sultry as she stroked Cresil as though he was a cat.

"Speak," Tanit bid him. "Speak truthfully and perhaps your god will spare you."

"Chemosh s-s-said we were to do everything we could to keep the Americans focused on Iraq," the Cresil stuttered. "He-he-he said the idea was to occupy them there so your Agent in Afghanistan had time to bring your plans to fruition."

Moloch glanced down at the darkened tendrils of spirit which dangled out of his mouth like strands of spaghetti. With an unapologetic belch, the bull-god gave Tanit a sheepish grin and finished slurping up the energy released from the destroyed spirit of Cresil's former conspirator.

"Go," Tanit put Cresil down and shooed him towards a series of caverns Moloch had carved out of the fires of hell to shelter his allies. "And be mindful to pay the others the proper respect so they don't eat you. I'm surprised Lucifer interred one so meager in the seventh dimension of Gehenna. What crime were you charged with?"

"Chemosh ordered us to guard the Grand Ayatollah," the Agent said. "That void-creature you keep complaining about snuck up on us. I think he wants you to know he's still around."

Fists clenched in rage, Moloch looked up towards the gateway guarded by Lucifer and screamed his ex-wife's name so loudly that all of Gehenna trembled.

"Ki!!!"

******

Two elderly Jewish men sat, fishing lines tossed casually into the tiny stream somewhere close to the Valley of Hinnom, sharing a meaningful silence.

The ground trembled. A bubble rose to the surface of the stream and broke. The slight odor of brimstone wafted lightly into the air before being harmlessly carried away by the wind.

"Did you fart?" one of the men asked.

Chapter 47

The vast universal suffering feel as thine:
Thou must bear the sorrow that thou claimst to heal;
The day-bringer must walk in darkest night.
He who would save the world must share its pain.
If he knows not grief, how shall he find grief's cure?

Savitri by Sri Aurobindo

April 2, 2003
Valley of Jehoshaphat

Azrael was smart enough to admit when he was outclassed. Not only was Moloch's second-in-command a hell of a lot bigger and stronger than he was, but the bastard ran circles around him, outwitting him at every turn. Azrael knew of only one person in the universe capable of outthinking Moloch and his evil super-villain sidekick.

"Where is he?"

"He's ... uh ... indisposed." The Sata'an-hybrid shifted uneasily from one foot to the other.

"I need to speak to him right away," Azrael twitched his wings with annoyance. "It's important."

"Um ... you'll ... uh ... have to come back ... uh ... later," the guard stammered. Behind him, the other half-human hybrids closed ranks behind their comrades. They were acting the way they usually did whenever the General appeared, as though someone meant their leader harm. Azrael looked over his shoulder, expecting to see he had company and was surprised to discover he had none.

They were closing ranks against ... him?

"I don't give a damn about whatever strumpet he's bedding at the moment," Azrael snapped. "He needs to do his job!"

"He's ... um ... you can't ... he ... um," Lucifer's men mumbled, tails twitching uneasily.

"I need to speak to him," Azrael allowed his face to assume its stern, grim reaper aspect. "Now."

The Sata'an-hybrid soldiers stepped out of his way. Chemosh had escaped Najaf, leaving behind lower-level Agents to stir up trouble by whispering Coalition forces intended to destroy the Grand Ayatollah's mosque and kill him, not parley. But not for the wise American troop commander who'd ordered his troops to kneel before the mosque and retreat when an angry mob appeared to defend it, things would have gone the other way. Throughout Iraq, other cities fell with similar ease.

It was too easy...

There was an Earth saying, *'it takes a criminal.'* Azrael strolled towards Lucifer's personal quarters, palatial rooms he'd only ever glimpsed from the main processing room, and banged upon the door.

Nothing.

He could feel Lucifer's oversized consciousness. The bastard was here. He pounded harder. It wasn't like him to be insistent, but then it wasn't like him to go to Lucifer for help, either. Although it'd been the General who'd battled Chemosh and Moloch the last time around and thrown their sorry tailfeathers into Gehenna, it had been Lucifer who'd lured them close enough to Gehenna to *be* battled. Azrael was no good at subterfuge. Only Lucifer was devious enough to stay ahead of the game.

Except Lucifer had been strangely absent given the conflict raging around them the past few days...

"Lucifer!" Azrael shouted. "Put your pants back on and come talk to me! You can finish servicing whatever female you're bedding later!"

Silence. Not even a feminine giggle or one of Lucifer's typical hung-over groans. Azrael sniffed. The scent of bleach and disinfectant filtered through the closed doors, not the usual stench of alcohol and semen he'd forever associate with the debauch son of the Eternal Emperor.

"Lucifer!!!" Azrael shouted.

What was that human movie he'd watched about a woman who visited a cannibal in prison to help her crawl inside the mind of a serial killer? Yeah. That was what he needed to do. Touch base with Lucifer, though it'd give Hashem conniption fits, to figure out what the devious bastards were up to.

A rustle behind the door. At last! The door slid open and an elderly, plump Sata'an-human hybrid woman wearing a maid's uniform peeked out.

"He's indisposed," the maid said. "Go away and come back later."

"I need to speak to him," Azrael said. "It's urgent."

"Not now," the maid said. "Come back in a few days. After he's recovered."

He'd admit it! He had bitten off more than he could chew. It was one thing to taunt Moloch from the relative safety of Gehenna, where he could dart into the fires-of-uncreation where even Moloch couldn't survive. It was another thing entirely to have an Agent the size of Chemosh loose in the universe. All this time he'd been thinking he was the biggest, baddest thing out there and Chemosh had firmly put him back into his place.

Such a cute little void-creature...

"It might be too late by then," Azrael allowed his worry to show. It wasn't the maid's fault Lucifer was an ass. "Please?"

The maid opened the door all the way. A copper-iron scent Azrael knew well wafted his way as she did. Blood. Azrael glanced down at her cleaning cart and realized it was full of bloody towels.

"What the hell is going on here?"

"If you're not going to help him," the maid said, "then I'd appreciate it if you'd just leave. Haven't your kind made him suffer enough?" Her serpentine eyes narrowed to slits, a mother-cobra threatening to strike.

Huh?

The maid blocked the doorway and refused to budge. Nor did Azrael wish to push past her. To do so in his agitated state, even with his cloak pulled tight around his non-corporeal form, might lead to her death. Azrael had glimpsed this particular cleaning lady many times, but he'd never realized she had a place of authority above that of the guards. Cleaning lady his tailfeathers!

Was she a mistress? No. He distinctly remembered seeing the maid embrace a blind elderly human male on several occasions. She wore a mate-ring on her left hand. Although Lucifer was infamous for seducing human females, married or not, he scrupulously avoided shitting in his own back yard. Sata'an-hybrid females had been off-limits for as long as Azrael had known the Fallen Angelic.

The scent of fresh blood filled the room. Lucifer's blood.

Assassin?

"What the hell is going on here?" Azrael threw back his cape and prepared to do battle. He sized up the maid, expecting to find a squatting Agent, and found none.

"If you're going to jolt anyone out of their mortal shell," the maid stood her ground. "Jolt Lucifer. Please. You guys can't keep breaking your promise to him."

Azrael stepped back, confused. This was the strangest conversation he'd had since the day Hezekiel had come running out of Elissar's house and revealed there were Sata'an descendants numbering amongst the Fallen.

"I ... I don't understand," Azrael mumbled. "I just ... I smell ... blood."

"Of course you do," the maid sighed. "How many of our generations have you been coming here and you're just noticing this now?"

Azrael tucked his wings against his back, trying to appear as non-threatening as possible.

"Please," Azrael said. "I don't know what's been going on here and for that I'm sorry. But I really need his help. We have a situation."

"Of course you do," the maid stepped back, gesturing to the room beyond. "You always do. That's why they won't let the poor bastard die."

The maid grabbed a pile of fresh towels from the cart and gestured for Azrael to follow. The enormous sleeping quarters with its swimming-pool sized hot tub and gold-canopied bed with garish red silk sheets was neatly made up and empty. The wet-bar was wiped clean, black granite shining against carved mahogany cabinets. The maid's soft-soled shoes made a reassuring squish-squish-squish noise on the marble floor as she led him through a small door into a long, narrow hall. They followed it quite some distance, past a modest kitchenette with a table set for three people and a small, open door where the elderly man Azrael had noticed earlier sat reading a book, his fingers skimming the Braille text.

"That you, Nyx?" the old man called. He reached for the long, white cane at his side. "Who's that with you? I smell … salt air."

"It's just Azrael, dear," the maid, who Azrael assumed was Nyx, answered her husband. "He needs to see him."

"He's in no condition to be seen," the old man snapped. "Tell him to come back later!"

"It's an emergency, dear," Nyx called. "Perhaps it's time he saw for himself?"

The old man grunted something that might have been approval, or an expletive. He settled back into his chair to 'read' whatever book captured his interest with his fingertips.

Azrael was puzzled. He'd always assumed the sleeping quarters he'd glimpsed from the door were 'it,' but he now saw the garish front room was merely the parlor for a set of much smaller, simply furnished rooms. Lucifer's *real* living quarters. Nyx led him to an ordinary-looking door and paused, clutching the clean towels to her chest.

"He's had another one of his spells," Nyx's gold-green eyes filled with concern. "He usually gets them around the … um … anniversary. But sometimes other things set him off. He's been this way for the past five days."

Five days? What had happened five days ago? Azrael wracked his brains. Five days ago Sam had made a joke about Elisabeth finally giving him the time of day. Lucifer had gotten a poignant expression upon his face and congratulated him. Since then, Azrael had reaped many souls in the battles for Najaf, Karbala and Baghdad, but it had been Sata'an soldiers with canisters who'd taken each Agent off his hands, not Lucifer. That, in itself, hadn't seemed odd. Lucifer was frequently out doing whatever nefarious deeds debauch fallen sons of gods do to pass the time. But this?

Nyx pushed open the door. The scent of blood and disinfectant overwhelmed his senses as she walked past an ordinary-looking bed to a small shrine set up with pictures and candles against one wall.

A pile of blood-stained feathers, splotches of brilliant scarlet highlighted against the palette of snowy white, lay curled up on the floor entombed in the sarcophagus of his own bloody wings. Blood was everywhere. On the bed. On the floor. Only the tremble of Lucifer's feathers let Azrael know the Fallen Angelic was still alive.

"Lucifer," the maid patted his enormous white wings as though he were a child. "Sweetheart. You've got to pull yourself together. You've got company."

"Go away," Lucifer groaned. "Can't you see I'm busy?"

"I know," the maid spoke in the gentle voice a mother might give a grieving child. "But maybe it's time he saw what his kind have done to you?"

Lucifer sobbed something unintelligible while the maid used the towels she'd brought to mop blood off the floor as though it was the most normal thing in the world. The blood was … Lucifer's?

Nyx grabbed something Lucifer had clutched in one fist the way a mother might pry a lollipop out of a toddler's hands. "Let it go, Sweetheart. C'mon. Release it or I'll have to call in the others."

A knife. No. Not a knife. It looked like a piece of sheet metal pried out of an air duct? A shank. The kind of weapon one might create after someone had hidden all the knives. Nyx tossed the sharp implement out of Lucifer's reach and began dabbing at the blood covering his forearms as though this sort of thing was the most normal thing in the world.

"Why won't they let me leave?" Lucifer wept. "My life sentence was up 4,500 years ago."

Nyx crooned reassuring words as she cleaned up the worst of the blood. As she did, Azrael witnessed the gashes Lucifer must have sliced into his arm while Nyx answered the door simply scab over and heal. Azrael had always assumed Lucifer came out of whatever drunken scrape he forever got himself into by healing himself. He'd never realized the healing was involuntary.

"He's tried every way a living creature could possibly try to do himself in," Nyx explained as she cleaned him up. "Cutting his wrists. Jumping off a cliff. Suicide bomb. But She-who-is won't let him die. Doesn't stop him from trying, though."

It had taken Azrael a couple of thousand years to realize the reason Lucifer egged him on was because he was suicidal, but he'd never realized how bad it really was.

"There, there, Sweetheart," Nyx, who was obviously more of a mother-substitute than a maid crooned. "I know it hurts. But we're here for you."

More unintelligible sobbing.

Azrael looked around the tiny bedroom which was Lucifer's real sleeping quarters. Twin bed for sleeping alone. Simple bureau. Few ornamentations. The other room was a front for doing the task Lucifer seemed to feel was his goddess-mandated job. Beget offspring upon human females. This room was ... personal.

Photographs. Lucifer and a smaller man, arms thrown around each other's shoulders as though they were brothers. Smiling. So many pictures. Hunting an auroch together. Surrounded by Angelics Azrael knew had been the other Fallen. Lucifer's mate. The one he still grieved.

"Let us call her," the maid pleaded. "Please. You know she'll come for you."

"No," Lucifer whispered, his voice raspy and low from crying. "When she comes, they argue. And when they fight... He's the only one who can help her control her power."

Her? Who?

A photograph caught Azrael's eye. Lucifer. His lover. And a petite, black-haired woman with an utterly miserable expression upon her face propped up between them. Despite her lack of wings, Azrael would know that woman anywhere.

The Regent.

"I'll be right back," Azrael said.

With a flash, he teleported himself halfway across the galaxy to Haven.

Chapter 48

By night on my bed I sought him whom my soul loveth:
I sought him but I found him not.
I will rise now, and go about the city in the streets,
And in the broad ways I will seek him whom my soul loveth:
I sought him, but I found him not.

Song of Solomon, 3:1-2

Galactic Standard Date: 157,843.04 AE
Haven-2: Cherubim Monastery

"How long has he been doing this to himself and you didn't tell me?" the Regent asked.

The General retreated behind an unreadable expression, shooting Azrael his iciest 'I'll deal with you later' look.

"He deserves whatever misery he gets," the General stated flatly. "My son won't *speak* to me because of that bastard."

Son? Which son? The couple had so many Archangel offspring, Azrael wasn't sure he'd even met them all, but he'd never heard of the General being estranged from any of them.

"*Nobody* deserves to spend eternity separated from their mate!" the Regent shrieked. "You told me he was doing better!"

The room thrummed with the dark power contained within her voice. The Regent closed her eyes and forced herself to get her emotions back under control before she accidentally vaporized the walls of the Cherubim monastery.

Azrael backed into the wall, considering whether or not he should just fade right through it without first being dismissed by his commanding officer. Never, in all the time he'd known the couple, had he ever seen the Regent and the General argue. Ever. He'd just stepped into it. Big time.

"Now he knows how *you* felt," the General said in a voice so cold if felt as though the temperature dropped in the room.

"The affront was against *me*," the Regent hissed. "*I'm* the one who suffered. Not you! You didn't even have a clue until you nearly got yourself killed trying to go out in a blaze of glory! If I hadn't come for you, you still wouldn't have figured it out!"

Guilt spread across the General's face. Whatever this argument was, it was a very old one. One that had existed long before Azrael had been born.

"Which is precisely why I can't forgive him," the General's look of remorse had nothing to do with the reason Azrael had come here. "If I'd succeeded … you'd have died, too." His wings drooped so low they scraped upon the ground.

"Come," the Regent grabbed Azrael by the hand. "Take me to him. If you want something done right, you need to do it yourself!"

Ohthankthegods! Azrael focused on the processing chamber at the entrance to Gehenna and transported both of them there even though she was quite capable of transporting herself.

"Where is he?" the Regent asked.

Her bottomless black eyes flashed with anger against her pale, porcelain-white skin. Wing-spikes rustled like swords against a whetstone as they scraped lightly against the floor. Sata'an-human hybrids shrieked at the sight of the Dark Mother materializing into their midst and ran helter-skelter away from her deadly, razor-sharp wings.

"Th-th-this way," Azrael stammered. Oh. Boy. The General was going to kill him! He led her through the garish party-room to Lucifer's personal quarters. The Regent appeared to already know the way. The maid had finished cleaning up the blood and removed the shank he'd been trying to use to cut his wrists faster than She-who-is could heal them, covering Lucifer with a blanket to keep him warm.

The Regent glanced at the altar filled with photographs of Lucifer and his lover and hissed, baring her fangs. Her black, scorpion-like tail rose up as though readying to strike. The air shuddered with dark power. Azrael had heard stories about what happened when the Regent became angry, but he'd never caught a glimpse of it himself. Was she angry at *him*?

No. Whoever she was angry at, it was neither him, nor the Fallen Angelic lying upon the floor…

"Lucifer," the Regent kneeled at Lucifer's side. She placed her hand upon his wing. "What can I do to ease your pain?"

Lucifer crawled on hands and knees like a dog, his wings trailing limply behind himself, until his head rested on her lap. Azrael could feel the energy in the room shift as the Regent began to sing. Underlying her mortal song, the faint song Azrael could always hear playing in the background, the Song which had grown louder ever since Elisabeth had started speaking to him, filled the room in a symphony of music so beautiful and sad it brought tears to Azrael's eyes.

He hadn't heard the Song that strongly since Ki had asked him to descend from the upper realms to finish evolving...

"He was my friend, too," the Regent said, slipping her fingers through Lucifer's bloody blonde hair. "I forgave the both of you a long time ago."

Lucifer mumbled between sobs: "He can convince him to change his mind. I know he can. He can convince her to let me go."

Who? The Emperor? Or the General? Or was he talking about She-who-is? Azrael's mind raced to put together new pieces of a puzzle which had always eluded him.

"What really happened?" Azrael asked. "How can I act as intermediary between these two if I don't have all the information?"

"It's not what Lucifer *did* while he was possessed by Moloch the General can't forgive," the Regent said. "It's what he later found out he *didn't* do once Moloch had been cast out and he was himself again."

She looked down at Lucifer and murmured something into his ear. Lucifer moaned, a sound so low and pitiful he sounded like a cow whose jugular had just been pierced and left to bleed out for slaughter.

"What in hell's creation did Lucifer do that was worse than trying to usurp the Emperor or sending an assassin to stab the General in the heart?" Azrael asked.

"Enough questions," the Regent snapped. "Come. I've got to get him up off the floor. Pull back the covers."

Azrael felt like a fifth wheel as the Regent did the heavy lifting. She was with child again. She shouldn't be doing this kind of thing alone, but the maid had disappeared. All he could do was try to not zap Lucifer dead as she heaved him up and rolled him into bed. Perhaps he should summons the guards to help? No. It would serve no purpose to let his minions see how very far their leader could fall even though these 'episodes' appeared to be something the Sata'an-hybrids were aware of. Lucifer curled right back up into a fetal position, his wings trembling like a dying bird. The Regent covered him up.

"Go tell my husband I won't be back for a few days," she ordered. "I appreciate your having the guts to tell me Lucifer was having another episode. Usually we can see it coming and can head it off before it gets this bad."

Azrael backed out of the room, his mouth opening and closing with unasked questions. She grabbed a second blanket and curled up on top of the covers against Lucifer's back, covering him with her deadly black wings as though they were a blanket, and sang that beautiful, sad song that made him think of beauty and heartbreak and joy and sorrow all at once. Whatever Lucifer was feeling, it appeared the Regent could relate to it only too well.

It was time to go get his tailfeathers handed to him on a silver platter for interfering in whatever was the *real* reason the General hated Lucifer so much. Although, given the fact he'd just left the General's wife curled up in bed behind the biggest womanizer in the universe, that alone was justification for any normal male to hate Lucifer.

How the hell was it that, in 2,300 years of study, he'd failed to notice there was a much bigger picture overshadowing the ancient hostility between Lucifer, the General, and Hashem? Talk about an unobservant watcher!

Chapter 49

"The one who withdraws himself from the remembrance of the Merciful,
We appoint for him a Satan to be a companion to him."

Qur'an Az-Zukhruf 43:36

Earth: April 11, 2003
Najaf, Iraq

"My whole life I've looked down on him," Azrael said. "And now I find out there's more to the story than I was told."

Elisabeth threw the next batch of surgical implements into the sterilizer and slammed the door, turning the oven timer to the appropriate time to decontaminate things. The way things had been going lately, the chances of actually finishing the sterilization cycle before the next batch of wounded arrived was slim to none. She grabbed one of the gallons of bleach Corporal Till's men had purchased from a local street-vendor and placed it next to a bucket. Just in case. The rush to Baghdad had left their supply lines dangerously thin. Even an alcohol-wash was becoming a luxury.

"Did the Regent tell you what this supposed sin of omission was your commanding officer can't forgive?" She grabbed a stool and lowered herself to rest with an exhausted sigh, using her hand to prop her gimpy leg upon the bottom run.

"Your leg?" Azrael's brow furrowed in concern. He shifted his awkward perch, balanced upon his own tall stool, wings streaming loosely behind him.

It always amazed Elisabeth how, for a supposedly made-up façade, Azrael was so expressive. Not that she'd met any other angels to compare him to. Just his part-lizard friends she'd been piecing back together the past week and a half. But compared to the soldiers she was perpetually surrounded with here in the military, human or otherwise, Azrael was an open book.

"I'm just tired," Elisabeth groused. "I think I can forgive this General of yours for leaving me looking like Al Pachino now that I understand why he left the scar, but the next time he pops by, do you think you might impose upon him to get rid of the gimpy leg?"

Azrael retreated behind an unreadable expression. Not that 'grim reaper' look he often donned whenever he was perturbed. Elisabeth had grown accustomed to the fact Azrael's appearance changed with his mood, but a closed look was one she wasn't used to seeing.

"You once told me the General also has a scar," Elisabeth prompted. "To remind him what Lucifer did to him?"

"That's what I'd always assumed," Azrael said, his brow furrowed in concentration. "Although now that I think about it, that's not exactly what he said the day he and Lucifer came together to heal you. He said…"

Azrael trailed off. Elisabeth could practically see the wheels turning in his head.

"What exactly did he say?" Elisabeth asked.

"He said," Azrael said, his eyes closed as though examining the past moment on a television screen. "He said he keeps it to remind him every time he looks in the mirror how blessed he is to have found his true mate."

"True mate?" Elisabeth asked. "Is the Regent his second wife?"

"No," Azrael said. "Impossible. The Seraphim only take one mate for life. Especially him. He's full-blooded Seraphim. A broken bond will kill a Seraphim Angelic."

Even as the words left his mouth, Elisabeth could see the ugly truth dawning on him. Growing up in inner-city Chicago, she'd seen the games people played to keep others in the dark. Several classmates came from families where each sibling had a different father, others from divorced families where the parents used the kids as pawns. And then there'd been the classmate who was adopted and hadn't known until a vindictive relative had blabbed.

"This whole situation smacks of skeletons in the closet, if you ask me," Elisabeth said. "Whatever it is, it must be pretty ugly if they're still bickering about it after 5,500 years. I doubt they're going to tell you."

"Lucifer might," Azrael said. "Although … I tried speaking to him when I dropped off that last batch of squatters. He's back to being his old self."

"Arrogant, manipulative, and flamboyant?" Elisabeth asked, reciting some of the many complaints Azrael had voiced about the Fallen leader.

"More like … yeah," Azrael sighed. "Arrogant, manipulative, and flamboyant. Although, ever since it began to dawn on me there's this whole other side of him, I suspect it's all an act to keep people from getting too close."

"Sympathy for the devil," Elisabeth sighed. "I can see why the church likes to tidy things up. Things were a lot easier when all I had to do was say three Our Fathers and then Saint Michael would come crush the devil beneath his boot."

"That much is true," Azrael said. "At least the part about the General. He really did defeat Moloch. Although the only reason he was able to do so was because Lucifer lured Moloch into a trap."

"So God lets the devil exist because he needs him to watch his back from an even greater evil," Elisabeth said. "And God resents the crap out of it. Both devils. How many devils did you say there really are?"

"It's complicated." Azrael's face filled with uncertainty. "I grew up believing Shay'tan was the devil and all Sata'anic citizens were demons. And then I find out Shay'tan is just the Emperor's opposing chess partner and the Sata'anic soldiers are just people. Kinda like how you guys view Russia now that the cold war has ended."

"It was the Russian generals who told us how to go after the Taliban holed up in those caves in Afghanistan," Elisabeth said. "Though now they're all pissed off at us again for invading Iraq. Yes. Complicated. I think I understand."

Elisabeth grabbed a box of bandages that had been dumped in a jumble and began to sort them onto the empty gurney. There was always work needing to be done in the Army. Minutes spent multi-tasking now might mean saving a wounded GI later. Her mind raced through the open wound her feathered friend had stumbled into, one which had kept her own world divided in a war of bitter propaganda for more than five thousand years. Azrael watched her sort, not taking offense. He'd observed her long enough to know this was just the way her mind worked through problems.

"Nancy had a rough start, you know?" Elisabeth finally said. "Parents were never married. Her father was in and out of prison and her mother kicked her out when she was nine after Welfare Reform cut them off. And then her grandmother got deported back to Guatemala and died before she had a chance to send for her. Gangs took her in, used her as a mule to move heroin. Got her hooked. Made her turn tricks to bring in extra cash."

Azrael focused as though she preached the gospel. It was a heavy responsibility, the way an immortal creature such as Azrael and his part-lizard allies hung on her every word.

"You want to dig out that notebook of yours and take notes?" Elisabeth scowled. She didn't want that kind of responsibility.

"Do you think I should?" Azrael fumbled through the pocket of the cloak he'd taken off and tossed across his lap. He was clueless. Sweet. Gentle. Kind. Or at least as sweet, gentle and kind as the Angel of Death could possibly be when not in his fearsome Grim Reaper aspect. And absolutely clueless.

"Oh … Az!" Elisabeth smiled despite herself. How could the angel who'd single-handedly come up with the theory of rallying points God had used to send Jesus to inspire them to stop worshipping Moloch be so without guile? If the other angels were even half as clueless as Azrael, she could see why they'd need someone like Lucifer to run interference.

"I'm ready," Azrael said, pen perched above a blank page of his latest scientific journal.

All those years she'd thought her black man wrote in his great book the deeds of good and evil, and now she'd learned he wrote it all down because, without the opportunity to look through his notes for patterns, the Angel of Death was too guileless to just *know* things the way humans did after getting burned a few dozen times. All intellect … no street smarts.

"I really wish you'd been in my chemistry class." Elisabeth stepped closer to where Azrael perched upon his stool like an enormous black pigeon balanced upon a power line, his scientific journal balanced precariously on his lap as though at any moment they might all come tumbling down. He froze as she carefully slid his pencil out of his fingers.

"C-c-careful!" Azrael's glossy black wings trembled with a combination of uncertainty and longing. Elisabeth knew how much he wished he could touch her. He was terrified she'd accidentally brush against him, but he longed for her presence so badly that he no longer drew back whenever she came near.

"Has anyone ever told you that beneath your terrifying death-angel exterior you're a real marshmallow?" Elisabeth teased.

"N-n-n-n … yes?" Azrael held himself so stiffly on the awkward stool she feared the entire thing would topple over.

"I think it's kind of sweet," Elisabeth said. She took the strange, thick pencil and drew an enormous heart on the open page. She then drew a stick-figure angel holding a stick in the middle of it with a marshmallow on the end. "That's you. Marshmallow angel. Black and crispy on the outside, but take a bite and it's all sweet, gooey goodness inside."

She stared into black-velvet eyes that had no bottom and no end. Sam had told her they had no idea how Azrael existed in this realm. It shouldn't be possible, he'd explained, without something to anchor him here. A willing vessel of some sort. Or an unwilling host. And yet, here he was. Her beautiful, dark angel. The most terrifying … and gentle soul she'd ever met.

She sensed his spirit touch hers, the only part of her he could touch, and the question he didn't dare ask because he feared knowing the answer. Their two subconscious minds, it seemed, had been performing an intricate mating dance long before they'd stopped playing games and just started talking to one another.

'Yes … I –do- love you,' Elisabeth thought to herself.

His sharp uptake of breath confirmed her suspicions that he could read her mind if she left it open enough for him to see. His eyes swirled darker, if that was even possible. Losing herself in them was like being caught in an ocean current, not caring which way the tide would turn, but trusting that the destination would be a pleasant one.

'If only I could touch you,' the thought touched the edge of her mind. *'I would ask you to be my mate.'*

His thought? Or her own wishful thinking? Azrael broke eye contact, glancing down at the crude stick-figure angel she'd drawn.

"You deserve better," he mumbled. His wings drooped to the ground. The withdrawal of his spirit felt like abandonment.

"Oh!"

CRASH

The clatter of a dropped tray at the entrance of the tent jarred them out of whatever each had been about to say.

"Lucy," Elisabeth said to her wide-eyed team-mate with annoyance.

With a poof, Azrael was gone, teleported god-only-knows where to avoid being seen.

"W-w-was that an angel?" Lucy stammered.

Elisabeth gave her a tight, wan smile. Talk about your bad timing!

"Is it any weirder than having a boyfriend with a tail?"

Lucy turned pink all the way down to her collarbone. Corporal Tills had gotten a portable shelter assigned to Corporal Kennard to help him recover *here* instead of airlifting him to wherever lizard-people were normally airlifted to. She didn't have the heart to tell Lucy her romantic interest's friends were not only rooting for him by pulling strings with the *real* military to keep her recovering boyfriend close enough to woo her, but had also set up a sizeable betting pool as to whether or not the recovering gut-shot Corporal would be able to land his 'big fish.'

"Clyde said there really *was* a death angel following you around," Lucy said. "It's just … seeing him makes it real."

Elisabeth mouthed platitudes and finished sorting the bandages as her mind chewed over the information which had her feathered friend so worried. It was *her* world caught in the middle, after all. Somebody had to figure out a solution so Earth didn't end up road kill because of a bunch of idiotic immortals couldn't play nicely together.

Chapter 50

I am the terrible time, the destroyer of all beings in all worlds,
Engaged to destroy all beings in this world;
Of those heroic soldiers presently situated in the opposing army,
Even without you none will be spared.

Bhagavad Gita 11:32

Earth - April 12, 2003
Tikrit, Iraq

The General surveyed Saddam Hussein's royal palace built on the banks of the Tigris River. With Lucifer limping along on only three cylinders since his last 'episode,' the Regent had taken the rare step of circumventing all parties involved, including her husband, and reasoned directly with She-who-is to sanction a rare, joint mission. For the first time since Lucifer had summoned help to eradicate Adolf Hitler, an entire flock of Archangels had accompanied the General to Earth to team up with a platoon of Lucifer's Sata'an-human hybrids.

"Sir?" Azrael asked. "Is something wrong?"

"This is where it all started," the General said to the half-dozen Archangels assembled under his command. "The Armistice that protects this planet was signed by the two emperors right where that palace sits today."

"Why do you think Moloch's Agent chose this spot to build his palace?" Azrael asked. "It's rather brazen. Don't you think?"

"To thumb his nose at the two emperors," the General's eyes hardened as he gazed at the ostentatious symbol of excess rising above the banks of the Tigris River. "The Agents thrive whenever they incite bickering between the two emperors."

Azrael didn't add that Agents *also* thrived when the General and Lucifer were going at one another. Or the Emperor and Shay'tan, for that matter.

"I see activity," Vohamanah, one of the Archangels, pointed to a box truck that drove up to the palace gates and idled, waiting for the guards to authorize passage.

"Get ready to move into position." The General touched the pulse rifle strapped to his thigh. "Our intelligence indicates they're destroying all evidence of their activities. We need to preserve what we can so we have a better idea of what they've been up to."

Although Archangels carried swords, primitive weapons were inadequate to fight the modern weapons humans now had at their disposal. They were immortal, but they weren't gods. Time spent reconstituting their bodies meant days, weeks, even years spent in the ascended realms piecing back together their mortal shells. In a battle such as this, they wouldn't take any chances. The General nodded to where Azrael lingered on one side so he wouldn't accidentally zap his fellow Archangels.

"Check for squatters," he ordered.

"Yes, Sir."

Azrael moved slowly so he didn't create static electricity, a dead giveaway the 'shadow' moving towards the palace in the pre-dawn light was anything but, he stretched hundreds of thread-thin tendrils into Hussein's summer palace to ascertain the position of the Agents located inside.

The other Archangels did the same thing using modern Alliance surveillance equipment, while the Sata'an-hybrids circled around the exterior of the compound, ready to cut off any who attempted escape. Their equipment could see what was happening inside the building, but only Azrael could tell from this position which were ascended wraiths squatting in a body versus plain old bad guys drawn to Moloch for money, prestige and power. Azrael drifted back and solidified into his preferred form.

"Saddam Hussein has already fled," Azrael said. "So have his sons. I'm only sensing one squatter, Abid Hahmed Mahmud, his Presidential Secretary."

"What about the truck?" Vohamanah asked.

"They're loading crates of paperwork," Azrael said. "I wasn't able to look inside, but they're leaving the art behind. It must be important."

"That sounds like what we want," the General said. "All right, focus."

The Archangels clasped hands and bowed their heads, clearing their minds as they reached out to touch one another's spirit. Although not quite mind-reading, it enabled them to send and receive mental images during battle. While only a few had inherited the ability to wield the cloak of Shinobi-on-mono mastered by the Regent, the invisible warrior, every single one of them could harness the Cherubim killing incantations handed down from the original Cherubim monks.

"*Namu Tobatsu Bishamonten!*" the Archangels murmured together, saying the ancient prayer to the Cherubim god. "*Akuma o seifuku suru tame ni, watashi ni nanji no tsoyo-sa o fuyo!* [to subjugate the demons, grant me thy strength!]"

Azrael could not touch the group that huddled before him, but he whispered the prayer anyway, wishing he could harness the blue ray of the Cherubim and not have to *feel* things quite so deeply whenever he went into battle. He sensed the energy around him shift. The Cherubim energies created a state of balance halfway between the light-energy of She-who-is and the dark-energy of the void. Controlled destruction.

"Go!" the General gestured for the Archangels to move into position. He waited until they were ready to storm the palace before turning to Azrael, his eyes ice cold and devoid of emotion. "Go reap that Agent, Malak al-Maut."

Azrael teleported directly into the palace. The squatter wearing the mortal shell of the Iraqi Presidential Secretary Mahmud shouted orders to hurry up and remove all evidence of Moloch's activities from the stronghold.

"You're forbidden to interfere!!!" Mahmud screamed. He began to disentangle his consciousness from his host-body so he could escape before Azrael could kill his host.

Gunshots sounded as Archangels flew through windows and Sata'an-human hybrids kicked down doors, taking out the mortals who followed Moloch.

"You're not supposed to interfere, either," Azrael gave him a dark grin.

"Go to hell!"

Mahmud dropped the host body upon the floor like a pair of dirty underwear. With no mass slaughter to open a portal to Gehenna, Mahmud avoided being sucked back in. If She-who-is caught the disembodied wraith traversing the astral realm she would evict him, but eternity was a large place to monitor. The body continued breathing while Mahmud threw himself between the dimensions to escape.

Azrael followed. He realized the moment he emerged on the other side it had been a mistake.

"Malak al-Maut," Mahmud laughed. "Our god has prepared a welcome feast in your honor! He shall dine upon what's left of your life energy as soon as he uses it to escape!" Mahmud threw himself through a small portal and slammed shut the hatch.

Azrael tried to follow and realized, for the first time since he'd become a creature of the void, that he couldn't simply pass through the wall of the chamber. The walls were shielded like his ... cloak? The chamber vibrated as power built to its apex. He was trapped inside a nuclear power plant. A nuclear power plant retrofitted with a tachyon particle accelerator. Saddam Hussein's palace had been a ruse to lure him into a trap.

"Oh ... crap!"

Billions of tachyons slammed him into the wall. Particles tore through his spirit. He had physical mass? When had he begun to develop physical mass? Azrael realized he now possessed fragments of DNA.

It hurt! It hurt! He reached for the reservoir of primordial chaos he sometimes fed upon and realized he was cut off by the shielding chamber. The energy released by his own pain caused a putrid green circle to open up behind him. Particles tore at his hand, the place where the mass he'd begun to accrue was densest, and began to tear him apart. The portal grew larger. Azrael desperately clung to the sides of the particle accelerator, trying to keep his spirit from getting sucked in. In his injured state, he'd be easy prey!

"Elisabeth!" Azrael screamed as he realized *why* he had physical mass, who she was, and what she had carried across time.

Laughter rang though the particle accelerator as the Agent gloated at Azrael's foolishness in thinking he'd remain invulnerable forever.

"Elissar…" Azrael's spirit began to fray, destroyed by the very anti-matter he wielded as a creature of the void. He wrapped his tentacles around the tiny, broken fragment of his DNA, the memory of which was all she'd been able to carry with her when she'd come back to find him.

"Ki…"

Azrael sent out the mental plea as his consciousness began to dissipate. All that mattered was he hang onto that tiny fragment of DNA and the slender tendril of spirit which connected him to the twin-spark who'd been searching for him for 2,300 years, but because of the cruel rules of this universe, had been forbidden to *remember* him.

The reactor shuddered. A deeper, more powerful vibration rattled the chamber. A horrible, terrifying sound.

An explosion.

The sensation of being torn apart was suddenly gone. Its power source eliminated, the portal disappeared. The chamber dissolved into primordial goo. Azrael shot out like a cannonball and splattered against the wall. He peeled off like a pancake and plopped on the floor, tentacles in a jumbled mass. He writhed in pain as he realized who Ki had sent to free him.

"You dare prey upon my prodigy?"

The bat-winged Regent hovered over Azrael's limp form, more beast than human as her flesh turned black with power. Molecules vibrated with each flap of her bat-like wings as a singularity of destruction began to throb within her. Clawed fists clenched in lethal anticipation as she bared her fangs.

And people thought HE was scary …

She stalked towards the Agent like a panther moving in for the kill. Her razor-sharp scorpion tail rose above her back like an arm wielding a sword, ready to strike. With each step her visage grew larger, more terrible than even Moloch himself. The ground trembled, as if the Earth understood the Regent could uncreate it with a single thought.

Azrael twitched, unable to regain control of his tentacles. He'd heard the sister of the Guardian was terrifying, but he'd never seen it. The others went to great lengths to keep her calm ... and humanoid. Now he understood why.

"You are forbidden to interfere," Mahmud squeaked in terror. "The Armistice says all you can do is lock me in Gehenna."

The Regent stared at the petty god with her pitiless black eyes. "Your laws do not apply to the Lords of Chaos. I enforce the ancient decree. All who upset the balance shall be uncreated!"

Her scorpion-like tail twitched like a cat stalking a mouse. She fed upon the Agent's fear the same way Moloch fed upon the spirit of his victims, rustling her wing-spikes to increase his terror. Unlike Moloch, her food-source was not the life-energy of the young and innocent, but those wraiths too old, too tough, too powerful and depraved to be digested by the other gods who sought to keep the balance. She was a carrion bird, come to feast upon all that was cancerous.

"No!" Mahmud shrieked, trying to leap out of her path.

The Regent struck out with one leathery wing and skewered him upon a deadly wing spike. He begged for mercy as she bit into his neck, tearing out chunks of spirit-light with her enormous fangs. Mahmud received the *same* mercy he'd just given to Azrael ... none. Corrupted spirit-light spurted onto the walls like blood until Mahmud finally stopped screaming. Although she could have simply uncreated him with a flick of her wrist, the Regent, it appeared, preferred her destruction up close and personal.

'What have I done? Please. Stop. You're scaring me.' Azrael twitched helplessly, unable to give voice to the terror screaming through his damaged mind.

The Regent lifted her head and howled, a deep, horrible sound, a lioness heralding her kill. She dissipated the chewed, bloody mass of what had once been Mahmud into primordial nothingness and absorbed its essence, causing her to grow larger and even more terrifying than she had been before. Azrael tried to reach towards her and realized it was a mistake. His sorry condition only fueled her rage.

"Not enough!!!" she screamed. Her voice caused the ceiling above them to shudder and disappear, exposing the dawn. "I am hungry and I need to feed."

Azrael felt the Song of Destruction in her voice grow louder, causing the damaged reactor to whine in harmonic resonance with her anger. Concrete buckled as the rebar became malleable in answer to her song. The molecules which made up the walls released their sub-atomic bonds and melted into puddles like a Salvatore Dali clock, bending towards her as she summoned their essence to feed her growing rage.

The Regent pulled twin-swords from her back, her mortal weapons of choice, and two more arms sprouted from her torso as though *she* was one of the four-armed Cherubim. Her horns grew longer and sharper, every aspect of her being a deadly weapon. She grabbed a chunk of steel rebar from the destroyed reactor and, with a wave of her hand, reshaped it into a scythe. Kalika. The Dark Mother, preparing to walk the Earth.

If Azrael had attempted to wield that amount of power, the entire galaxy would have already been destroyed. He tried to form words. To soothe her. To rein her in before she wiped out the planet.

'Ki! Help! Please? What did I unleash?'

The Regent lifted her head to the rising sun and howled, every shred of her humanity fleeing as she opened the reservoir to her brother's power. The Earth shuddered as it ceased spinning clockwise and, with a jerk most mortals would mistake for an earthquake, caused the rising sun to slip backwards beneath the horizon.

"Mo ghra [my love]," a voice called. "Azrael is still with us. You're frightening him. Le do thoil, gra [please, love]. Let me comfort you and dry your tears."

Azrael recognized the voice of the General, come to soothe his mate. The Regent crouched, tail twitching, ready to spring away and resume her killing spree, more animal than humanoid.

"I grow weary of these pathetic games the other gods play with Moloch," the Regent snarled, twitching her spiked tail to dissolve some rubble into primordial nothingness. "I shall awaken my brother and we shall destroy him together."

"You brother has not yet found his true mate," the General stepped before the enormous beast which towered over him like a behemoth. "Without the bond, he can no more control his power than *you* can. Would you deny your brother the chance to find the love that we have found?"

"Moloch devours Earth's children!" the Regent cried out, not anger in her voice this time, but sorrow. "If we don't find a way to destroy him, eventually he will succeed!"

"Yes, my Queen," the General agreed. "We shall find a way to destroy him. But not today. Today ... our daughter who grows in your womb has been forced to know your power before she is ready. Our children wait just beyond the wall, upset their mother is so angry. And Azrael lies badly injured on the floor. He needs you to help him heal."

Black tears spilled forth from her eyes like rivers, dissolving the floor. They fell on the General like gentle rain, dissolving the armored vest he always wore over his heart at her insistence and exposing the scar everyone knew about, but none had ever seen. Her tears destroyed all they touched, but *he* was unharmed. It was as though, with each teardrop, she cast off the power she was loathe to control. Rivers of blackness formed upon the floor as she shimmered and shrank back down to her normal size, still a four-armed creature, but small enough to seek comfort from the Archangel who stood before her. With a sob of anguish, she dropped her swords and flung herself into her husband's arms.

"It's okay, mo ghra," the General soothed his mate. "You got here in time. Azrael is saved."

"He won't take my healing!" the Regent wept, great black tears streaming down her ebony cheeks. "He never would. I don't understand why?"

Azrael knew why. He tried to speak and failed, but the involuntary flailing of his tentacles brought his efforts to the General's attention.

"Azrael ... tell us what you need," the General asked.

Azrael could no longer form sounds, but he knew what he needed. The question was, would she help him? Or would she run screaming in terror? Reaching a tendril of consciousness towards the Regent, the only person he could touch without killing, he projected the single thought into her mind.

"Elisabeth."

Chapter 51

'Tis a fearful thing
To love
What death can touch,
To love, to hope, to dream,
And oh, to lose.
A thing for fools, this,
Love,
But a holy thing,
To love what death can touch.

For your life has lived in me;
Your laugh once lifted me;
Your word was a gift to me.

To remember this brings painful joy.

'Tis a human thing, love,
A holy thing,
To love
What death can touch.

Judah Halevi or Emanuel of Rome – 12th Century

Earth - AD April, 2003
Kirkuk, Iraq

"Elisabeth!" Kadima urgently tugged at the back of her uniform.

"Kinda busy!" Elisabeth fished shrapnel out of the leg of a carpentry/masonry specialist unfortunate enough to drive over an improvised explosive device. "This gal was lucky. The armor plating they welded to the floor took most of the shrapnel. She'll be on her feet shooting bad guys in a matter of weeks."

"Oh ... my ..." Mary stammered.

Elisabeth had a bad feeling about this patient. Or something. It felt as though she wanted to crawl out of her skin, but she was so damned busy she hadn't had a chance to focus on what the hell was giving her pins and needles. It didn't help that, around twenty minutes ago, birds had fallen from the sky and every dog for twenty miles had started yowling after the explosion … or earthquake … or whatever the hell it was had hit.

"Holy shhh … uh … I mean … um…" Lucy sputtered.

"Elisabeth!" Kadima hissed again, tugging at her shirt. "Somebody is here to see you!"

Elisabeth looked up into the most unearthly blue eyes she'd ever seen. More than seven and a half feet tall, the massively muscled Archangel stared down at her with an emotionless expression. Rather than the medieval armor churches depicted angels wearing, he wore the remnants of a military uniform that looked as though someone had dripped battery acid onto it, exposing bare skin which looked every bit as mortal as any other soldier running around the base outside Kirkuk. It was the ornate insignia on his otherwise tattered shirt which clued her she was speaking to a very high ranking Archangel, indeed.

"Come with me, please," he reached out one hand to take hers.

Elisabeth stared up at the mountain of a man who dominated the tent. Fair-skinned, dark-haired, dark-winged, with beautiful, chiseled features that looked like an older version of Azrael, the archangel stared down at her from a massive height. There was no emotion in that face, not even that *'you'd better obey me or else'* look sported by higher-ranking military officers. Elisabeth glanced down at the soldier in whose leg her hands were buried.

"I'm in surgery, Sir!" Elisabeth snapped. "What is it with you guys? You think you can just barge in and I'll drop everything?"

"Azrael has been badly injured," the Archangel said, a shadow of concern crossing his face. "He needs you."

"Injured?" Recognition of that terrible feeling forced Elisabeth to pause fishing shrapnel out of the patient's leg. "I thought…"

"Azrael has been badly injured," the Archangel repeated. "The Regent thinks you may be able to help him. Will you come with me?"

"Go!" Kadima hissed. "Don't you know who this is?" She made the Islamic gesture of respect and greeting, touching her hand to her forehead, lips and heart and murmured something in Bosnian.

"I thought … we couldn't touch you?" Elisabeth warily looked at the enormous hand which reached to take hers.

"Only those harnessing the power of the void must be cautious about who they touch," the Archangel said. "We must hurry. It's not good to leave the Regent alone when she is this upset."

"Let me finish," Elisabeth said. "Please. And then I'll go. I can't just leave this soldier to bleed out on the operating table."

The Archangel placed both hands upon the leg Elisabeth had been picking chunks of shrapnel, floor board and rock out of for the past half hour. The room felt as though they were standing near high-tension power lines, but the sensation was pleasant. His stern features softened as he transformed from soldier to healer, giving him a bit of a tender, vulnerable expression. Slivers of shrapnel worked their way to the surface as the leg-wound began to close up, scab over, and scar as though she were watching a high-speed video of the natural healing process.

"S-s-saint Michael?" Elisabeth blurted as the insignia of rank finally clicked. "Um … Kadima? Could you please make some excuse why I'm not here and make sure this soldier is taken care of?"

"Of course," Kadima said. "Now go! Harold isn't going to believe this!" By the tone of her voice, it wasn't a question as to whether her husband would believe her, but rather that the General *himself* had made an appearance in their ranks.

Elisabeth reached up to take his hand, marveling at how enormous he was compared even to Azrael. Larger than life. That was how Azrael described his famous commanding officer. He wasn't kidding!

"It won't hurt," the General reassured her. "I'll bring you to him now."

Except for the hum of energy, the General's hand was every bit as warm and human-feeling as hers, not cool like she remembered Azrael's had been. Elisabeth didn't have time to gulp with fear before there was a moment of nothingness, as though she free-floated in space and *she* was space as well, and then she was someplace else.

The General held her hand firmly until she caught her balance. She was in a concrete bunker?

No … mangled equipment sat in the center of the room. The roof had been torn off and, just at the horizon, the sun was beginning to rise, not the middle of the night as it had been in Iraq. To one side a second angel kneeled on the floor, caressing an enormous black squid and speaking to it in a soothing language she couldn't understand.

Elisabeth startled as she realized that was no angel. The woman was as dark as Azrael, with enormous spiked wings, horns, a spiked tail, and four arms. Strapped to her back so they crisscrossed between the juncture of the wings sat twin swords. A scythe lay on the floor beside her.

"Kalika," Elisabeth whispered, recognizing the image from a small statuette Nancy had kept on the mantle of her house. Destroyer. The Black Madonna. The woman Azrael called 'Regent.'

The Dark Mother looked up, her bottomless black eyes swirling with vast power. Tears streamed down her cheeks as she clutched a tentacle to her chest and wept.

"He won't let me heal him," the Regent sobbed. "I'm not sure how it happened. He can't ... touch ... you. You usually ... you have to ... he didn't ... you couldn't. But ... somehow ... it happened. He bonded with you and only *you* can heal him!"

"I don't understand," Elisabeth said. Horror dawned on her as she realized what, or more accurately, *who*, was crumpled in a tangled mass of tentacles on the floor. "Azrael? Is that you?"

"He can't answer you, child," the General said. "I warned him it was not wise to taunt Moloch by leaving a calling card. The Evil One decided to make an example of him."

Elisabeth stared at the pool of black sludge shuddering in pain. She'd seen his natural form once before. It wasn't pretty. But watching how tenderly the Regent clutched his tentacles to her chest convinced her it really *was* him.

"It's instinctive for their species to bond with the one they love," the Regent said. Black tears dissolved the floor beneath her. "He won't let me heal him because he's chosen *you* to be his mate."

"M-m-me?" Elisabeth stammered. "Really?"

Her heart did a little flip-flop as the Regent voiced the words that had been very much on her mind lately. She was unable to hide the hopeful lilt to her voice.

"If you can't find it in your heart to return even a small part of what he feels for you," the Regent said, "his spirit will dissipate."

The only thing that can kill an Archangel is a broken heart... Azrael's words came back to haunt her. He twitched like some poor creature that had been electrocuted. The General kneeled behind his weeping wife and pulled her into his arms.

"If you have any feeling for him at all," the General pleaded, "you must help him heal. He's been through enough already."

Elisabeth stared at the Archangel and the Dark Mother clinging to one another, blowing to smithereens her last few notions of heaven or hell. She had no concept of bonds or the other things the two heavenly creatures spoke of, but even if it hadn't been running through her mind lately that she was in love with him, she knew she'd do whatever she could to help him because he was her *friend*. It would have to be enough...

"Tell me what to do," Elisabeth said.

"There is great risk," the Regent said, "if he's wrong. But I don't think so. Now that I know what I'm looking for, I can see the threads which stretch between you."

"At some point in the past you two chose to bond," the General said. "Enough for you to begin to heal him."

"What are you two talking about?" Elisabeth asked. "Please ... speak in ... some ... Earth language? Neither one of you is making any sense."

"Ever since the day you touched him," the Regent said. "He can feel his hand as though it were real. If you touch him a second time, we think it will give him greater access to the Song so he can finish healing."

"The Song?" Elisabeth asked.

"The Song of Creation," the General said. "The source of power I used to heal the leg of the young woman you were operating on. Only a mated pair can hear the Song of Ki."

The quivering blob distracted her. She didn't need to be a psychic to see Azrael was in enormous pain.

"Az," Elisabeth dropped to her knees beside the Regent. "I'm here. Tell me what to do. They didn't teach me this stuff in nursing school."

Tendrils slithered on the ground, shuddering from the effort of moving. It took nearly a minute for Elisabeth to realize what he struggled to do. He'd landed on top of one particular tentacle that he was trying to free. Elisabeth pointed.

"That one," Elisabeth said to the Regent. "I think he needs help freeing that ... uh ... limb?"

The Regent crooned to Azrael in a language that sounded as though it were the root of all Earth languages. After a moment, she helped Azrael free the errant limb.

"Now what?" Elisabeth asked as the tentacle shakily rose and paused a foot or so from her forehead.

The Regent caressed a separate tentacle and nodded, as though she could hear him speaking.

"He's having trouble communicating," the Regent said. "But I think that's the tendril of spirit that was connected to the hand you touched the day of your accident. He thinks it will be safest for you to touch him there."

Elisabeth gulped. As much as she'd tempted him to touch her, telling him she wasn't afraid, the truth was she -was- afraid. As a child, she hadn't known what the stakes were. Now...

"You don't have to do this," the General said. "If you hadn't survived once before, we wouldn't even ask. But... "

Elisabeth noted the way the General rubbed between the leathery wings of his ebony-skinned, terrifying visage, void-mattered wife to calm her. Talk about subduing darkness!

Azrael's tentacle began to weaken. What was it Az had said happened to souls who got lost? They just ... dissipated? Disappeared and became nothing. Undone. The worst thing that would happen to *her* was she'd get an all-expenses paid trip through the lint-filter they called heaven and a second, or third chance at life. Preferably not in a body with a gimpy leg and a big ugly scar across her face. Azrael was …

Azrael was the angel she'd spoken to each week in the lobby of First Saint Paul's church. The yellowed, broken-winged angel at the top of the Christmas tree she'd fed cookies. The silent, invisible angel who'd watched over her, protecting her, after her parents had died. His distraught eyes had haunted her dreams and stood between her and any other man who'd ever tried to woo her even *before* he'd jumped in front of a bullet to save her. If the roles were reversed, Azrael wouldn't hesitate to put himself in danger for *her.*

"If I pass into the dreamtime, Az," Elisabeth grimaced as she prepared to be jolted out of her body. "Promise me you'll come looking for me again?"

The black tentacle touched her forehead. Coolness sank into her flesh, but the sensation was not unpleasant. She could feel the power which vibrated through his spirit, the compulsion for matter to release the bonds that held it together and return to the simpler form of primordial chaos, but the compulsion did not appear to extend to *her.*

'Elisabeth…' Azrael whispered into her mind. *'Mo ghra … ta tu an gra i mo shaol.'*

Pure light radiated through her brain as, for a moment, she could see him as he had been before his tangle with Moloch had turned him into a creature of the void. Emotion sobbed from her lips as she saw a beautiful, guileless boy: friendship, agape, terror, pain, loss. She felt as though she were wringing her hands, helpless as some other physician had worked to save him, and then sent him off for a lengthy rehabilitation that to her had been merely minutes, but for him had been more than 2,300 years.

The memory faded.

Elisabeth touched the appendage which pressed against her 'third eye' like a priest sprinkling water upon an infant's forehead during baptism. As her fingers brushed his tentacle, it felt as though a star went supernova inside of her heart. A *new* emotion took up residence with the old ones, love, hope, joy that at last he had healed enough for them to be together. Tears sprang to her eyes as, not only did images of what he wanted to tell her poured into her mind, but also the emotion behind those images.

'Mo ghra.' My love. He called her 'my love' in the language of the angels. Beautiful angel, or dark wraith, she did not wish to ever again be parted from this sensitive creature who loved her.

"Me too," Elisabeth whispered, feeling awkward about professing something so … personal … in front of an audience.

She wrapped her fingers around the tentacle, noticing the way his entire form trembled at her touch. His flesh felt as though a cool fog wafted off the ocean and touched her skin. The first three inches felt more solid than the rest. The spot where she'd touched him once before? Even as she touched him, she felt the appendage grow firmer, more corporeal in her hand. She pulled the trembling limb to her lips and kissed it.

"Awake, Lazarus," Elisabeth whispered. "For you are reborn."

The Regent burst into tears, but they were *happy* tears this time. Clear. Not the black tears of destruction.

"It appears my wife is right," the General said, the tremor of dark feathers betraying the emotion he kept from his stoic face. "You are what he needs to heal."

Elisabeth looked down, expecting to see her body had dropped to the floor. She shifted her weight to make sure she was still alive.

"We need to get him out of here," the Regent said. "I destroyed the Agent responsible for leading him into a trap, but Chemosh is still loose. They were nearly successful in using his life-energy as a power source to punch a hole into Gehenna."

"How will we move him?" the General asked. "None of us can touch him and *you* are with child. You've exposed our daughter to enough void-matter for today."

"Goat dung!" the Regent said. She glanced around the room as if sizing it up, and then waved her four arms as though she were a conductor leading an orchestra. The room shimmered and Elisabeth felt a sudden dislocation.

"Azrael is at risk until he recovers. Let Moloch dare touch him *here!*"

The General flapped his wings as though catching his balance, but nothing in the room changed except the fact it was no longer dawn shining through the melted ceiling of the nuclear power plant, but brightest noon. Instead of the sweltering heat of the Iraqi desert or the strange, tropical humidity of wherever it was the General had transported her to, the air was cool and crisp like autumn air. Strange scents assailed Elisabeth's nostrils, the scent of a land the likes of which she'd never visited before.

"How will we cover *that* up," the General crossed his arms and gave his wife a stern look. "That reactor wasn't even in Iraq. Now it's just a big hole in the ground in North Korea."

"Not my problem," the Regent gave her husband a haughty look. The two continued to quietly 'disagree' in the language of the angels, but from the way the General's expression softened, Elisabeth could tell who had won.

Azrael's tentacle curled tenderly around her wrist, sending a pleasant thrill down her arm straight into her heart. An image leaped into her mind. Or more precisely. A song. The song which had stayed with her the last time she'd touched him, but had faded the longer he'd remained hidden from her. It sounded distant and far away. But it was beautiful. So beautiful it filled her heart with joy.

"I hear it too," Elisabeth stroked his tentacle and noted the way her touch resonated within her own heart. Touch. What Azrael craved more than anything in the world. The more she touched him, the more she could feel the song strengthen the connection which had always existed between them and the more solid he felt beneath her fingers.

"He's like you once were," the Regent laced her fingers through her husband's hand. "He just needs to feel connected to the one he loves."

Elisabeth realized the stern, emotionless General was crying. He pulled his petite wife into his arms and cupped his hand protectively over her abdomen. Not only was the Regent barely five feet tall and slender as a reed, but she was also around five months pregnant.

"You put our unborn daughter at risk moving the entire facility here," the General scolded his wife, nuzzling her neck. "You had other options."

The Regent physically shifted shape. Four arms melded into a single pair of human arms, flesh turned porcelain white against ebony wings and hair, wing-spikes, tail and horns…

Well … even on a *good* day the Regent was still deadly as hell…

Petite and beautiful … but deadly as hell.

"Talk to him," the General said. "About … little things. Things you've seen together or discussed, or things you would *like* to see with him in the future. It was how my wife kept me in this realm when –I– was that badly injured."

Through the tatters of the General's uniform, Elisabeth noted the scar over his heart, the one Azrael had told her about. She touched the scar that ran from her own temple to her lip. The General nodded. For the first time since the day she'd woken up a cripple and looked in the mirror, she understood the General really *did* mean it to be a badge of honor.

"Archangels will be stationed just outside the door," the Regent said. "But I think he'll do better if you spend this time with him alone. He needs to *feel* you."

The Regent focused and then flicked her wrist. Elisabeth could feel energy swirl around her as though solid matter had become as malleable as water and caught up in a powerful current. The molecules in the room shifted, still molecules, but as she watched they reassembled themselves into whichever shape the Regent had formed within her mind. No longer were they in the spent core of a melted nuclear reactor, but a tiny, primitive mud-brick house with a cozy fire lit in a beehive hearth. Azrael's form lay propped upon a crude sleeping platform that appeared immune to his tendency to dissolve matter. The Regent pointed to her scythe. It turned into a puddle of black goo, and then reassembled itself into a primitive wooden stool next to the cot. For her. To sit at Azrael's side.

For the first time the General smiled, an image Elisabeth had never seen captured in *any* of the numerous Earth-depictions of the angel who had crushed Evil beneath his boot. He pulled his wife into the circle of his wings, leaving only her tail and a stray wing-spike peeking out of her husband's much larger wingspan. The pair disappeared in a flash of white light.

"Let's see how much I can safely touch?" Elisabeth said gently to Azrael. "I'll be careful. I promise."

She slid her hand down his tentacle, registering the subtle changes in the coolness and solidity of his form and how energized the compulsion she could feel radiating out of him was. She could get all the way down to where the limb joined his torso before the sensation became uncomfortable. He struggled to pull the other tentacles away from her, fearful he might hurt her. Better to wait. Give him time to adjust to her.

The 'safe' tentacle shakily moved up in front of her forehead once more. Elisabeth paused, allowing him to touch her mind. A flood of emotions poured in, bringing tears to her eyes. Loneliness. Fear of rejection. Love. Joy. And of course the song. As banged-up as he was, Azrael drank the feel of her touch like a man too long deprived of water in the desert.

She pulled up the chair the Regent had formed for her and sat down next to him, understanding this would be a lengthy recovery.

"Sleep, my sweet marshmallow angel," Elisabeth soothed him. "I will stay at your side however long it takes for you to recover."

She supposed she should be repulsed by the tangled black jumble of tentacles which draped off the platform like a rag-mop, but as a nurse, she'd long ago learned to ignore a man's injuries and focus on keeping him alive. She stroked until she fell asleep in the chair, clutching the lone tentacle to her chest. When she awoke, three tentacles possessively circled around her as though she were a favorite teddy bear. Whatever she had that he needed, it had spread. She could tell by the soft rise and fall of his body that Azrael had drifted off to sleep.

The song reminded her of an old hymn Oma used to sing. Stroking the parts of him that were safe to touch, Elisabeth sang the words, imagining, as she often did with her other patients, that she loaned him her will to live.

"We shall walk through the valley and the shadow of death," Elisabeth sang in her earthy alto. "We shall walk through the valley in peace."

Somehow, it didn't seem to matter, in this place amongst the angels, that she had not been blessed with the heavenly voice of one. All that mattered was the gentle spirit drinking in her touch loved her. And she ... if she let down the walls she'd built around her heart because every time she let somebody in, they died, she knew she loved him in return.

The underlying Song grew louder.

Chapter 52

How poor are they that have not patience!
What wound did ever heal but by degrees?
Thou know'st we work by wit, and not by witchcraft;
And wit depends on dilatory time.

Othello - William Shakespeare

Galactic Standard Date – 157,324.07
Haven-2 – Cherubim Monastery

Hideous. He was hideous. And yet she had tended him, first when he couldn't hold any shape other than a tentacled blob, then later as he'd relearned every single step of how to reshape his hideous black nothingness, which now had some mass, back into the tall, thin form he'd kept hidden beneath a cloak for the past 2,300 years. A spark of hope settled into his chest that perhaps she might not reject him after all? But with that spark came fear, for who would love Death?

"The General can take you home now that I can get around by myself," Azrael said. He hid his mangled features deep within the hood of his cloak so she would not see his fear.

Elisabeth stiffened. "Is that what *you* want?"

'No,' he thought to himself.

"It's been two months," Azrael spoke aloud. "The Regent thinks I'm out of danger. It would be unfair of me to ask you to stay any longer."

"You still haven't relearned your original shape," Elisabeth said. Her lips turned briefly downwards before she retreated behind that no-nonsense expression she usually assumed for her patients. "The Regent said you'll heal faster if I am here."

Yes. But every day she stays increases the chance it will break my heart when she -does- reject me and leaves…

"There are lives back on Earth you could be saving," Azrael said softly. He stepped closer, wishing he dared gather her into his arms.

"Nonsense," Elisabeth jutted out her chin. "If you think I'd bail on one of my patients before they're healed, you can just forget it."

She looked exhausted, his beautiful Elisabeth. For two months she had refused to leave his side … and it showed. She was stubborn. He feared she would allow his injuries to drain the life out of her the same way Hayyel's mate had refused to let *him* go, or as she would have done for Nancy if he hadn't intervened and put a stop to it. Usually she *hated* using her cane, but her weariness settled around her shoulders like the hated lead cloak *he* wore to dampen his destructive tendencies. He was being selfish, asking far more of her than any creature of darkness had a right to beg.

Did she have any idea how lovely she looked with the Haven sun reflecting off her pale, blonde hair as though *she* were a ray of sunlight?

"You don't have to … I mean … stay … if you don't want to …"

Azrael's hand tingled like a hungry dog, aching for the sensation of her touch. What was he doing? Inviting her to leave when what he wanted more than anything in the universe was for her to *stay?*

Elisabeth wore a vulnerable expression as she laced her fingers through his, the first part of him that had regained form. A shiver of pure pleasure radiated through his entire body. Touch! Oh! How long he'd yearned to feel the simple sensation of touch again! That spark of hope expanded, grew larger until it cast out the hunger which had gnawed at him for thousands of years and replaced it with a *new* hunger. To bond with her and make her his mate. Something about his eager wiggle must have reassured her, for her eyebrows shot up with skepticism.

"For ten years you follow me around like some stalker-dude," Elisabeth chided. "And now that I *can* touch you, you're trying to send me away?"

"Oh … no!" Azrael stammered. "Of course not! It's just … I mean … you didn't *ask* for any of this. I don't want to wear out my … um … welcome?"

"The only thing that's wearing out is my butt sitting in this darned chair," Elisabeth hid her insecurities behind her usual grouchy demeanor. "I'm glad the Regent made it because otherwise I'd be sitting on the floor. But … dang! Couldn't she have made me something a little more comfortable?"

"I think this is a replica of the house where she healed the General," Azrael said, not mentioning that his sleeping platform was *equally* uncomfortable now that all of a sudden he had a bit of physical mass to make him *feel* it. "It's … um … symbolic. I think they hope…"

Azrael trailed off mid-sentence. He knew what they hoped. They hoped Elisabeth would grow to love him as much as he loved her so they would become a mated pair. Was that even possible? Even if she did wish to deepen the emotional bond which had developed between them, there was no guarantee he could perform the final act of merger which would bind them as one soul for all eternity. Even after two months of recuperation, Elisabeth could only touch the group of tendrils he had reshaped back into some semblance of a hand.

Then there was the distressing fact that, once he'd regained enough of his faculties to assume a vaguely humanoid form, Elisabeth had withdrawn to that arms-distance she'd always kept between them. Interested ... but wary.

"When do you think it'll be safe to touch your face," Elisabeth touched his hood. "I'm not sensing that uncomfortable feeling quite so strongly there anymore."

Azrael pulled the hood tighter. There had been this Earth movie he'd watched once about a race of hunter-people who came to Earth in spaceships to hunt the hunters for sport. The hero in the movie had pulled off the alien's mask and said 'you're one ugly motherfucker.' That's what he looked like right now. One ... ugly ...

"I'd really rather you didn't," Azrael's voice was a mortified whisper. "Please. Let me get my act together a little more."

Azrael saw his own black visage reflected in her eerie silver eyes as she traced the scar which ran down her own face.

"I used to say the same thing in the mirror to *myself* every day."

"You were a beautiful child," Azrael's heart choked his throat. "Who grew up to become the most beautiful woman I've ever seen. And I've lived a long time." He swallowed, fighting down the sensation he felt every time he looked at her that he wanted to cry, though whether those tears were sadness or joy he did not know. Perhaps a little of both?

Silence stretched between them as Azrael soaked up the warmth radiating from her hand. Not awkward or uncomfortable. Simply ... silence. As though there were no words capable of expressing what either wished to say, so they let the silence say it for them.

"Do you feel up for a walk today?" Elisabeth finally asked. "I'd hoped to visit the temple of the Cherubim god?"

"Sure," Azrael said. Beneath his hood he smiled, though he did not let her see it. "The Temple of Bishamonten is one of my favorite places."

It was close enough to the little sanctuary the Regent had reshaped out of nothingness for him to walk there like a mortal man, even though the cloak weighed heavy upon him and he tired easily, not used to the weight of suddenly having mass. The scent of flowers tantalized his sensitive sense of smell, the closest thing to 'touch' he'd experienced until now, along with the buzz of countless insects as they walked down the deceptively simple gravel walkway through meticulously tended gardens. At its center sat an ancient temple where, inside, an enormous statue of the ant-like Cherubim god stood, resplendent in his armor. The Cherubim had been the original guardians of the Eternal Emperor. Now ... only Bishamonten himself occasionally visited these realms.

"It's the blue ray of Bishamonten which gives Archangels the blue glow to their eyes when they go into battle," Azrael pointed up at the enormous, four-armed, ant-like statue. "It gives the wielder the ability to see clearly and suppress their own discomfort."

"Like meditation or something?"

"You have this movie ... Star Wars," Azrael said. "It talks about a force being with you. It's something like that. Only there's no dark side to turn you into Darth Vader. Either you use it correctly, or Bishamonten strikes you dead."

"So Bishamonten is like, Yoda?" Elisabeth glanced up at the statue.

"I've never heard the guardian of the blue ray called that," Azrael laughed. "In real life he's over thirteen feet tall with sharp spikes and claws protruding out of every facet of his exoskeleton. Even before you add the armor."

"What about the power you wield?" Elisabeth asked. "Is there a guardian for that power, too?"

"Yes," Azrael said. "The Regent has a brother. He-who's-not. But you have to be very careful about using *that* power because chaos does not take sides. It simply -is-. But it *does* naturally seek balance, so perhaps *that* is the energy you would consider this 'force?'"

"Does it have a dark side?" Elisabeth asked.

"Yes," Azrael said. "But anyone who misuses void matter usually ends up destroying *themselves*. Especially if they create a ripple in the fabric of the universe large enough for HIM to notice somebody is abusing his essence. Or in this case, the Regent. She babysits his reservoir of power while he's off on sabbatical doing ... whatever. Whatever fourteen-billion-year-old void creatures do when they need to take a break from running the universe."

"I feel as though I'm in some sort of weird dream," Elisabeth sighed. She clapped her hand towards her mouth in a vain attempt to suppress a yawn. "Oh ... sorry! I haven't been getting enough sleep!"

They admired the fresh cut flowers the Regent personally set at the feet of the statue every morning. Elisabeth looked at the flowers. Azrael looked at *her*.

"This place just has such a ... I don't know ... Zen ... feel to it," Elisabeth yawned again. "Like a Buddhist retreat."

"What we do for work takes a lot out of us," Azrael eased himself down onto a bench set up for contemplative purposes. "We are intermediaries between the old gods, who sometimes forget what it was like to be mortal, and mortal creatures who don't understand that being a god has its limitations. The Archangels keep the monastery exactly as the Cherubim left it when they evolved out of here so we have someplace to replenish our spirits."

He watched, fascinated, as Elisabeth closed her eyes and drank in the atmosphere. It was peaceful here. He shivered with pleasure as she nestled against his cloak, mindful to keep his damaged wing-tentacles tucked beneath which still vibrated discordant, dangerous notes. His wings had been the first portion of him which had been incinerated in the fires of Gehenna the last to relearn their shape. His nostrils flared, inhaling her scent. His ears picked up the way her heart sped up as he adjusted his less-healed arm beneath his cloak so it would not directly touch her flesh and then nestled the limb around her shoulders. She smelled like … sunshine.

"Oh … Az …" Elisabeth asked. "What am I supposed to do with you?"

'Love me?' Azrael thought silently to himself.

"Just be my friend," he said aloud.

Elisabeth curled her legs beside her on the bench and leaned into him, trusting him not to zap her. Within moments, she dozed off, exhausted from too many nights tending him. He carefully lifted a strand of blonde hair out of her mouth, staring at the beautiful, tempting lips parted slightly in sleep that he hoped to someday kiss.

'Old friend,' Azrael prayed silently to the statue of the fierce-looking god who held a spear in one hand, a small pagoda representing the giving of knowledge upheld in the other. *'If you've got any wisdom to impart about winning Elisabeth's heart, I'm sure open to suggestion.'*

The old god, of course, did not answer. He hadn't descended all the way down into these realms for thousands of years. But Azrael thought he sensed a tendril of the old god's consciousness perk up with interest. The Cherubim god reportedly kept an eye on his pet project, the Archangels.

Chapter 53

For this affliction has a taste as sweet
As any cordial comfort. Still, methinks,
There is an air comes from her: what fine chisel
Could ever yet cut breath? Let no man mock me,
For I will kiss her.

William Shakespeare - The Winter's Tale

Galactic Standard Date: 157,324.10
Haven-2 – Cherubim Monastery

"Picture the white light of She-who-is coming through the top of your head," the Archangel Rahmiel, the Regent's oldest daughter, coached Elisabeth. "Pull it down through your heart and out your hands as you work. It should feel warm."

Other than the fact the archangel possessed black-feathered wings like her father and not the leathery, spiked wings of her mother, Rahmiel could have been a carbon copy of the Regent. Eldest of the General's offspring, Rahmiel appeared not much older than Elisabeth. She was the only archangel Elisabeth had met with black irises, reminiscent of her mother's solid black eyes which *had* no white to them, instead of the blue-tinged irises every other archangel possessed by default, though sometimes her eyes changed color depending upon which source of energy she drew upon that day, or blending them, like now, so that she possessed black iris's surrounded by a thin ring of blue.

"I feel nothing!" Elisabeth exhaled with frustration. "I don't know why you guys think I can do this!"

"How do you heal your patients, then?" Rahmiel asked. "You said your grandmother taught you?"

"Not … this," Elisabeth said. "Oma was a devout Lutheran. She prayed all the time. And sang. Hymns. Lots of hymns. I just adapted them to help my patients."

"What sort of hymns?" Rahmiel asked.

"Oma had a hymn for just about any problem," Elisabeth said. "Skinned knee? It felt better. Not enough money? It came. Scared? She'd teach you a hymn to make it go away. Mama used to call it her 'gift.'"

"Were these hymns what your people call witchcraft?" Rahmiel's black eyes sparkled with curiosity. "The invoking of an ascended being to provide relief?"

"No!" Elisabeth said. "At least … no more than any other god-fearing Christian does. Everything was Jesus-this and Jesus-that. They were just … hymns! Like you sing in church."

"Yeshua has more important things to do than fix skinned knees or bring money," Rahmiel laughed at her. "Your grandmother must have possessed pre-ascended abilities in her own right."

Elisabeth shrugged.

Rahmiel appeared perplexed. "I don't understand how your people can possess pre-ascended abilities and not develop them. Don't you wish to ascend to a higher plane of existence?"

"How many times you been to Earth?"

"I've never been to Earth," Rahmiel said. "The Armistice forbids all but the General and one observer unless the factions agree otherwise."

"Then how come you sent Azrael there to get chewed up and spit out by an evil god?"

"*We* didn't send Azrael there," Rahmiel said. "He was mortal then. He was filling in for Hashem's authorized observer at the time. They had no idea he could … uhm…" Rahmiel trialed off.

Elisabeth had the distinct impression the angels had lots of not-so-angelic dirty laundry flapping on the clothesline, the same as any mortal family. God and Satan were chess buddies. Not only did angels marry, but the Archangel Michael was married to the Dark Mother and had a gazillion children. A sex goddess ruled the universe. And to top it all off, Lucifer was the de facto Emperor of Earth.

Oh … and Earth was the Hellmouth…

Any moment now, vampires and werewolves would leap out of the bushes and start tap dancing and singing campy stage-tunes. Hellmouth. The Musical.

"Before you knew what?" Elisabeth gave her a sharp look.

She adjusted her gimpy leg, which had begun to cramp after two hours of sitting cross-legged on the floor. Around them, other mortal creatures whose genetic profiles showed promise of developing ascended abilities were trying to learn the same lesson … with much greater success.

"Before we knew Azrael was capable of wielding void-matter," Rahmiel said. "Like Mama does."

"He was only seventeen years old!" Elisabeth hissed. "You didn't even warn him there was a malignant god on our world looking for ascended DNA to feed upon! As primitive as we are, at least our Earth religions teach us not to mess around with the Devil!"

She shoved her cane into a gap in the floorboards and heaved her aching body up off the ground. A groan escaped her lips as she tried to put weight on her gimpy leg and realized it had fallen asleep.

"Why don't you let me heal your leg?" Rahmiel asked. "You don't need to be hindered by it any longer."

"It is a badge of honor left by your father!" Elisabeth snapped. "Remember?"

"Papa wasn't the one who left that injury there," Rahmiel said. "It should have healed already. He thinks it's the echo of a spirit-injury carried forward from a past lifetime."

Elisabeth scowled, but did not grace Rahmiel with an answer. All her life she'd dreamed of talking to angels and discovered she had one following her around. Now ... for months now dozens of them had been crawling up her ass with a microscope to see what made her tick.

"Are all humans so prickly?"

"Listen," Elisabeth said. "I came because your father said Az was hurt and he's my friend. It's what I do. Fix people who are broken. But ever since I got here, I feel like that guy in Alice's Restaurant."

"I don't understand," Rahmiel raised one eyebrow in confusion.

"Ever since I got here," Elisabeth said. "I've been hung down, wrung down, wrung up, and all kinds of mean nasty ugly things. I'm sick of it! I'm just a nurse!"

"You're more than a nurse," Rahmiel retreated behind that darned unreadable expression all the angels seemed to have mastered. "If you and Azrael plan..."

"There is no plan!" Elisabeth snapped. "You got that? He's my friend! Nothing more!"

Rahmiel winced. "That's what we're afraid of."

Elisabeth didn't know what was going on. The more Azrael healed, the more tight-lipped and distant he became. She could have sworn when she'd first touched him, he'd called her 'my love.' But now? She wasn't so sure. Was he pulling away because his people didn't approve of her? She was, after all, only human. And weren't angels forbidden to get involved with humans? They were, after, all, pretty pathetic compared to not just any old angels, but Archangels.

"Why do you all feel compelled to study me?" Elisabeth's hand jutted out with frustration. "Are you hoping you'll find some errant gene that will make me … what? Worthy to hang out with you guys? Or are you just trying to figure out what the hell Az sees in me?"

Rahmiel was silent, as though weighing what she wished to say. "We just wish to understand you. That's all."

"Why?" Elisabeth shot back.

"Because if you are to become one of us," Rahmiel said. "You need to understand our ways."

"Do you see any wings sticking out of my back?" Elisabeth pointed to her back. "I thought I was only here until Az gets better?"

Rahmiel hesitated.

"I *am* only here until Az finishes healing," Elisabeth asked. "Right? And then you'll take me home?"

Rahmiel fidgeted, her cold-bitch Angel demeanor slipping as pink crept into her cheeks.

"I'm a prisoner?"

"Not … a prisoner," Rahmiel said. "More like … protective custody."

"I'm in custody?!!" Elisabeth shouted. The other creatures stopped their stupid white-light meditations and all looked at her. Cripes! Some weren't even humanoid. There were bugs and slugs and frogs. All hanging out in a bizarre cumbaya ceremony learning to do what she had done her whole life instinctively.

"I'm sorry," Rahmiel stammered. "I didn't mean to offend you."

"I want to go home," Elisabeth said in clipped, authoritative words the way a drill sergeant spoke to new recruits. "Now."

"I can't," Rahmiel said.

"I want to go home," Elisabeth said again, her knuckles gripped white on her cane.

"Rahmiel!" a voice called from nowhere. A flash of darkness appeared at their side, coalescing into the Regent. "I'll take it from here."

Oh … shit! Now I've done it. The boss-woman cometh.

"Yes, Mother," Rahmiel bowed. She backed up several steps to bow a second time before moving to another part of the room.

"Walk with me, mate of Azrael," the Regent said.

Deadly wing-spikes rustled as the Regent tucked them against her back to make them appear as small and non-threatening as possible. Not counting her enormous wings, she barely came to Elisabeth's tall, German chin. Elisabeth wasn't fooled. She'd seen what the Dark Mother could turn into when she was really, really pissed.

"Yes, Ma'am."

Elisabeth fell back on her Army training. As so-called 'Queen-Regent of Chaos' the Regent was the highest ranking person around here. Even the General deferred to her, unless they were in private, in which case she'd noticed the relationship dynamics shifted and the Regent deferred to *him* the same way any other wife sought to crawl into the shelter of her husband's arms. Although the General also deferred to someone called the Eternal Emperor; who deferred to the creation goddess who was also a sex goddess; who deferred to someone named Ki; who had delegated authority to this absentee Dark Lord; who'd appointed the Regent to act in his stead.

Sheesh! The chain of command around here was more convoluted than a meeting at the White House where multiple branches of the military mixed with the President, Congress, and a half-dozen countries' foreign dignitaries. No wonder the immortals couldn't get out of their own damned way!

Elisabeth followed the Regent out into the garden. Gravel crunched beneath their feet as they wandered through meticulously maintained gardens containing flora and fauna Elisabeth had never dreamed of.

"Azrael is very attached to you," the Regent said at last.

Elisabeth was silent, the tap-tap-tap of her cane on the gravel her only answer.

"The question is," the Regent continued. "Are you as attached to him?"

"If I didn't care for him, Ma'am," Elisabeth said. "I wouldn't be here."

The Regent nodded. They continued in silence until the path approached the temple of the Cherubim god. The enormous carved doors looked ridiculously oversized for a woman that petite as she shoved them open so they could stride inside. Several angels and a bug-man bowed reverently and scurried out.

"Be seated," the Regent ordered.

Elisabeth sat on the simple wooden bench which, although sized for larger creatures, was still reasonably comfortable.

"Bishamonten," the Regent said softly, fondly stroking the armor of the statue. *"Akuma o kyōda suru tame ni, watashi ni no chikara o kasu."*

The language was neither English nor the angel-language everyone else around here spoke of which she'd picked up just a few words, but the soles of Elisabeth's feet tingled as she sensed the shift of energy in the room.

"You can feel that," the Regent asked. "Can't you?"

"Yes, Ma'am," Elisabeth said.

The Regent nodded with approval. Whatever she was looking for, Elisabeth realized she'd just passed some sort of test.

"You have questions," the Regent made a great show of arranging white calla lilies in a vase and not meeting her eyes. "You've picked up on the undercurrents of dark, hurtful things which make you hesitate to give us your trust. That distrust prevents you from bonding properly to Azrael."

"I don't like sitting in the dark, Ma'am," Elisabeth said. "I've been caught on the short end of the stick too many times to not notice when things don't add up."

The Regent grunted in satisfaction.

"He said you had a good head on your shoulders," the Regent said. "Good. He needs that. Azrael is brilliant, but he's too trusting."

"I noticed that, Ma'am," Elisabeth said. Despite her uneasiness at being summoned, she couldn't help but smile at the thought of Azrael awkwardly perched on a stool, taking notes.

Satisfied with the flowers, the Regent turned and scrutinized her as though she could see straight into her heart and soul. It felt like being cast naked into a crowd. Elisabeth stared into those all-seeing black eyes which swirled with unimaginable power, understanding that to flinch would be a mistake. She resisted the urge to chew her lip.

"You wish to know why your world is ground zero for our war against Moloch," the Regent asked.

"I was led to believe that wasn't anybody's doing, Ma'am," Elisabeth said. "He just ended up there and it's something we all need to deal with."

The Regent nodded. She plucked a stick of incense from a holder and lit it using one of the candles at the feet of the enormous statue. The scent of sandalwood and flowers filled the air. A slender tendril of smoke curled back upon itself before dissipating into the air like a symbol of eternity.

"I sense you know what it's like to long for something that doesn't make sense," the Regent said. "People say you're crazy. So you silence that small, quiet voice that clamors for you to look at what's right in front of your eyes."

"My earliest childhood memory is of seeing the fire-damaged statue in the lounge of First Saint Paul's church and thinking it was a friend," Elisabeth said. "My parents used to tease me about my obsession with angels. I always thought my invisible angel friend would pop in at any moment to play with me. Even before I met Azrael."

The Regent nodded.

"Echoes of past lives," the Regent said. "One of She-who-is's favorite tricks is to wipe out your memories. *She* justifies it as a chance to start over without being hindered by your past-life mistakes. *I* say it's just an easy way to get people to act the way you want them to act without justifying your actions. It is something upon which we fundamentally disagree. But…"

The Regent waved her arm like Vanna White turning letters on Wheel of Fortune.

"*SHE* shaped all of this, so unless we want to go shape our *own* universe to live in, we must all abide by *her* rules."

The Regent moved to arrange some beautiful white flowers that reminded Elisabeth of the Easter lilies First Saint Paul's had always kept on the altar after someone had a funeral the day before. The scent was so intoxicating it made her want to sneeze.

"What does that have to do with Azrael?" Elisabeth asked, and then added on a gut impulse, "or you and your husband?"

The Regent snorted, but it did not sound as though she took offense.

"The Seraphim take one mate," the Regent said. "Not just for life, but for *all* lifetimes so long as they remain mortal. A mated pair will find each other no matter *how* many lifetimes they live until they've evolved enough to be freed from the wheel of rebirth *together*. The urge is instinctive, without conscious thought. Seraphim descendants truly cannot grasp that humans can *choose* to mate for life. Or not. I think you know what I'm talking about?"

"Yes, Ma'am." Tommy Rodriguez jumped into her mind. That had been a mistake!

"Yes," the Regent read her thoughts. "It was. You're not the only mortal who ever made a bad choice out of loneliness. But you need to understand that a mistake like that can get an Angelic killed."

She turned to Elisabeth and tapped her own chest. "We have a saying. The only thing that can kill an archangel is a broken heart."

Elisabeth let those words sink in. So *that* was what had Rahmiel and the other archangels so flighty about the fact she was sniffing around Azrael. But how do you kill someone who was already dead? Sorta dead. Actually, now that he'd regained some of his physical form, did that technically make him alive? She suspected even *they* didn't know.

"Azrael told me that a long time ago," Elisabeth could not help but feel a little bit offended at her concern. "Is there anything else I should know, Ma'am?"

"There are *many* things you should know," the Regent said softly. "We'd like to teach you. If you're willing to learn."

Elisabeth wasn't sure whether to be flattered or angry the Regent served up the same shit-on-a-shingle for dinner that her daughter had served, only with ketchup. Protective custody her ass!

The Regent laughed, her concern disappearing behind an expression that made her look more like Titania, the fairy queen, than a harbinger of destruction.

"You must show me what this distasteful meal they serve in your military tastes like," the Regent said, her laughter a soft tinkling sound echoing off the rafters of the temple. "It sounds like the food Hashem feeds his mortal armies. Remolecularized food cubes."

Not only had the Regent picked up on her visual image of the slop they plopped onto trays in the mess tent, but also the cause of her angst.

"Am I a prisoner here, Ma'am?"

"What do you remember of your past lifetimes?" The Regent's bottomless black eyes swirled with power. Elisabeth squirmed under her intense gaze.

"Nothing, Ma'am," Elisabeth said. "Azrael tells me we're not supposed to remember our past lifetimes. He discourages me from even trying."

"A kindness, I suppose, given how horribly you died," the Regent shrugged. "In that I think he and She-who-is agree. But I believe in full disclosure. What else has She-who-is has wiped from your memory?"

"Sometimes I wonder if maybe I am Az's friend who died" Elisabeth said. "Your husband said he thought I might be her."

"Of that I am certain," the Regent said. "I can see through She-who-is's ruse. But there's another name attached to your soul, an even older one which predates this universe. Your subconscious whispers it to you from time to time."

"Yes," Elisabeth said. "When I dream of fire, it feels as though I'm Elissar. But I'm also somebody else. I'm angry because I've been searching for someone like Azrael for a very long time and I don't want to leave him behind."

The Regent's black eyes became even more intent. She turned to gaze up at the enormous statue, her expression reverent. "What about you, old friend. What do you see?"

The Regent cocked her head, as though listening to an internal voice. Whatever the old god said, an expression of sympathy appeared on the Regent's face before turning into laughter once more.

"Ahh ... *Eosphorus*. That explains much," the Regent said to the statue of the Cherubim god. "Hashem will not be pleased to discover he now has *three* of you to babysit, but Shay'tan will be tickled."

"Ma'am?" Elisabeth asked, perplexed.

"You have much in common with my husband," the Regent said. "You need Azrael to help you heal as much as *he* needs *you* to help *him* heal."

The Regent waved her hand in front of Elisabeth's chest. It felt as though she tugged a brick out of the wall she'd built around her heart since her family's death to protect it. The ever-present hymn grew so loud if felt as though she were standing in the middle of the Chicago Symphony Orchestra. Tears gathered in her eyes as she sensed her connection to Azrael and sobbed. The emotion she feared filled her heart with joy.

"Don't lose him a second time," the Regent slipped her arm through Elisabeth's as though they were sisters and led her out of the temple towards the cottage. "He waited 2,300 years for you to come back, and then he found you again. It's time to let go of your pain and trust him. He's not the one who damaged you."

The Regent led Elisabeth out to the meticulously tended garden. All pathways led to this sanctuary, like the hub connecting the spokes of a gigantic wheel. Their conversation turned to less weighty matters as the Regent pointed out the various flora and fauna which were native here and educated her about the history of the Cherubim who had taken her in and trained her while she'd been in that vulnerable, intermediate state halfway between a mortal and an ascended being. They stopped to smell the flowers, the scent of the air near a bubbling brook, a handful of moist earth near the stream. Each time the Regent urged her to close her eyes and *feel* the subtle energy which lay beneath all matter, coaching her how to look into each delicate life-form and see the tiny spark of life that inhabited everything from the tiniest insect to the most powerful god.

As they approached the tiny mud-brick cottage, the Regent waved her hand in front of Elisabeth's chest a second time. A sensation akin to having electricity turned on and off again in her heart made her aware of the connection Rahmiel had been unsuccessfully trying to teach her to feel.

"If you have any doubt he will search for you and find you again no matter *how* many lifetimes it takes for you to regain your immortality," the Regent said, "here is your proof."

"Elisabeth? Is that you?"

Azrael burst out the door, hastily rearranging his physical form so he appeared as Elisabeth had first seen him, her beautiful dark angel. He couldn't hold the shape long before his wings devolved back into tentacles, but the rest of his body was holding up pretty well. It wouldn't be long before he'd heal enough to bring her home.

Home … where was home? Did such a place even exist?

She stared up into that beautiful black visage that reminded her of some gangly science nerd she might sit next to in chemistry class. The *real* Azrael. The one she could happily pore through a nursing text with for hours on end and discuss such abstract topics as biochemistry or ways to piece back together a broken collarbone until the wee hours of the morning. Home was where *he* was…

"Azrael," the Regent said. "Bishamonten has agreed to take Elisabeth under our protection. As soon as Vohamanah can teach her to use the blue ray to contact us if Moloch attacks, you may both return to Earth."

"Thank you, my Queen," Azrael bowed.

The Regent reached up to tousle his hair as though he were a small boy. Azrael wiggled like a puppy being given a treat. She leaned towards Elisabeth and whispered:

"He's very shy. You'll have to give him some encouragement or you'll be waiting for him to build up the guts to make a move for a very long time."

Her informality disappeared.

"Your wings are coming apart at the seams, ceann beag. Tuck them behind your back before you accidentally zap your mate. They're the only part of you that's still a danger to her."

Azrael's form was too dark to show any color other than black, but if it was possible for midnight black to blush, he did so now. The Regent disappeared in a puff of darkness, leaving them alone.

"Why do they keep calling me … mate?" Elisabeth feigned innocence. "Is it some sort of military rank like the Australians use?"

Azrael almost choked.

"Um … uh … they think … ah … because … um … because we … ah … you can touch me … um … it must be because … um…" Azrael stuttered. His wings devolved into tentacles as distraction caused him to lose focus.

"The Regent said everything except your wings are safe to touch," Elisabeth searched his dark eyes.

"Y-mm-maybe?" Azrael stammered.

Elisabeth touched the beautiful, high cheekbone she'd been longing to caress for a very long time. Azrael's breath caught in his chest as though not sure what to do next. He tentatively reached out and did the same. She traced his beautiful, dark features, cheek to ear, and ran her fingers down his strong jawline. Although he felt more solid now than he had several months ago, there was still an otherworldliness about the way he took shape beneath her fingertips, as though he were made of stardust and *she* was his sculptor.

She stood on tiptoes and brushed her lips against his, the sensation feather-light as though she were kissing fog. He gasped with surprise, not sure what to do until some older, more primal instinct kicked in and instructed action where intellect failed. He pulled her against his chest, drinking the chalice of her lips as though it were sweet wine. A sensation akin to electricity tingled wherever his form came into contact with hers, but it was pleasant. Extremely pleasant. Fire ignited in her chest and slid like water down to her feminine core. She wished to do a hell of a lot more to her beautiful angel than just kiss him!

"*Mo ghra* [my love]," Azrael trembled with emotion. "You have no idea how long I've dreamed of this moment."

The ground they stood upon trembled, but the sensation was not threatening. Azrael's power was tied to his emotions. To overwhelm him with physical sensation after thousands of years of sensory deprivation would probably not be wise. She needed to acclimate him to the sensation of being touched again, just as the Regent had just acclimated *her* to the notion of sensing the energy that underlay all matter so she'd be more aware of being touched by her immortal lover. She forced herself to break away, caressing his cheek as she stared into his velvet black eyes.

"Soon," she smiled. "First we have to do something about your poor wings."

Tugging him along behind her, they slipped back into the tiny cabin and shut the door. Elisabeth led him over to the sleeping platform and gave him her most sultry, come hither look.

"W-w-we should…" Azrael stammered. "I want … but … it's a big deal … um … we should … um … ask and … um … we only … and … um … there's an … um … ceremony and … um … my wings are too dangerous!"

"I know," Elisabeth silenced his apprehensions with a kiss and heaved his heavy cloak off her chair. It weighed so much she could barely lift it. She wrapped the unwieldy garment around *herself* so it covered her from head to toe, smiling at the puzzled look on Azrael's face.

"I'm not sleeping in that cold sleeping loft another night," Elisabeth said. "Move over!"

He stood there like a tall, gangly beanpole, wing-tentacles twitching with uncertainty until he realized she wished to spoon. He clamored in behind her, awkward as a puppy, and aimed his wing-tentacles harmlessly into the wall. With a sigh of pure contentment, he snuggled into her back and gingerly placed his arms around her as though she were made of glass.

Azrael wouldn't be getting any sleep tonight. He would soak up the sensation of her warmth, muffled as it was by the heavy cloak, and teach his body to solidify against it until his physical form learned to become solid.

"I've loved you for a very long time," Azrael whispered into her ear. His hands cautiously explored the feel of her cloaked body nestled against his. "If you'll have me, I'd like to take you to be my mate."

"For life?" Elisabeth relished the echo of his happiness in her own heart. Whatever the Regent had done to make her *feel,* it had removed the heavy brick which had weighed down her heart for longer that she could remember.

"For *eternity,*" Azrael said. "Our species doesn't do it any other way."

"Then if you zap me in my sleep," Elisabeth whispered. "I shall die a very happy woman."

Within moments, she was asleep in her beloved's arms.

Chapter 54

To be idle is a short road to death
And to be diligent is a way of life;
Foolish people are idle,
Wise people are diligent.

The Buddha

Earth: December 13, 2003
Al-Dawr, Iraq

"Go!" Sam Adams hissed. At the moment he wore his Sergeant's stripes. The stripes he'd been wearing the first time Elisabeth had met him at the Army recruitment office in Chicago, although unbeknownst to her, he'd been keeping tabs on her long before he'd made himself known.

Six hundred Coalition Special Forces fanned out to surround Objectives Wolverine One and Wolverine Two. Several members of the First Brigade were embedded Sata'an-human hybrid agents, but they weren't taking a leadership position. In fact, most of them were just along for the ride. A little insurance policy to make sure the Agent squatting on Saddam Hussein's mortal shell didn't escape if their intelligence was good.

"You can come out now," Sam whispered as soon as the last soldier disappeared around a corner. "About time you got your tailfeathers back to work."

Azrael faded into view.

"How'd you know I was here?" Azrael asked. A genuine smile graced his ebony features at the sight of his old friend.

"Standing near *you* is like scuffing your feet on the rug and then touching your sister's bathrobe," Sam grinned, exposing his slightly-pointed teeth. "You make my 'fro all aglow, bro!"

Azrael laughed. Although the Angel of Death had never been a stick-up-your-arse like the other Angelics, he'd never been a creature of mirth, either. Az's eight-month 'vacation' to Haven with his pretty lady friend had agreed with him.

Sam surveyed the progress of his troops using infra-red glasses. He was expected to put his tail on the line along with the men under his command at the first sign of trouble. At the moment everything was quiet. He didn't have demonic spider-senses like the Angelics, but he'd been doing this kind of work long enough to tell their quarry was most likely not on the premises of Wolverine Two.

"How's things been going in my absence," Azrael asked.

"Oh … the usual," Sam said. "Chemosh jumped hosts again into some radical Shiite cleric named Al-Sadr and disappeared somewhere into Iran. Remphan is still squatting on Osama Bin Laden and hiding in the caves of Afghanistan. Kewan's squatting on Kim Jong Il in North Korea. And now Tanit is on the loose occupying bodies unknown."

"Tanit escaped?" Azrael said with a frown. "That's bad. I had a hell of a time rounding her up the last time she got out. She's another big one, though not as bad as Chemosh."

"Yup," Sam said. The signal came from the compound ahead. "Hey … gotta run. You gonna hang around for a while?"

"Sure," Azrael said. "I've got a favor to ask. But go ahead. I'll wait. Been a while since I reaped a squatter."

Sam crept forward, careful to scrutinize the ground for disturbed soil which could indicate freshly-dug IED's. Unlike his buddy the Angel of Death, dead for him was dead. He was rather partial to his body and not overly keen on having it suffer a horrible, painful death. He'd much rather die in his sleep, like his grandfather had, or a nice, painless hand-holding from Azrael when his number was up. Until then, he'd be careful.

"We got nothing, Sir," the Army specialist said. "The building is clear."

"Search it and see what you can find," Sam ordered. "These guys don't look like your normal run-of-the-mill homeowners. Something's up."

Sam gestured at the so-called 'family' that had too many men and not enough women to be normal. Collaborators. He didn't need to be part-demon to sense there were people here who didn't belong.

"Where is Saddam Hussein," the Iraqi-American Special Forces translator asked. "We know he was here."

"We're just a family of poor farmers," one of the men said in Arabic. "We have no connection to Hussein."

Sam caught the subtle way the mother had her children huddled together, close to an elderly man. A twenty-something man who bore too strong of a resemblance to be anything other than her son glowered at them with hatred in his eyes. A believer in Saddam Hussein, but not a squatter.

The woman kept glancing fearfully at two men who'd positioned themselves on either side of the children. The man speaking must be her husband. The two on either side didn't belong, but Sam got no sense they were squatters. Mortal hangers-on, along for the power ride. They existed everywhere sentient creatures existed, evil gods or no evil gods. Someone in the family, either the husband or the son, had given Saddam Hussein refuge and the woman knew it. He'd bet his life on it.

"You, take her out of here," Sam ordered. "Leave the children with those two so-called uncles. Yes, the ones her husband claims are his brothers. Let's see how much she trusts them with her children."

The woman began to wail with terror. The husband snapped at her to shut up and glared at the Special Forces translator in defiance. Yes. Those two didn't belong.

"Get them out of here," Sam pointed to the two collaborators. "Turn them over to Red Dawn command. They know something."

Word came over the radio that Objective Wolverine One had also come up dry. The First Brigade milled about in frustration, searching every nook and cranny of the two farms. He was here. Somewhere. Sam was no Angel of Death, but he'd learned to sense when a squatter was close by. It was time to go see what that favor was Az wanted and maybe ask for a little favor in return. If he was up for it. Word was Az had gotten chewed up and spit out pretty bad that last mission.

"Az," Sam called into the darkness. "Hey! Az!"

Az faded back into view, inches from his face.

"Oh! Shit! Man! Don't do that to me!" Sam blurted out, his heart racing in his chest. "Fuck! Thought you were going to zap me for a minute there!"

"Sorry," Azrael said. "Elisabeth's been spoiling me. After eight months of being touched, it's going to take time to adjust to the fact nobody *else* can touch me. Yet. The Regent thinks eventually that will change."

"You ask her to marry you yet?" Sam asked.

"She said yes," Azrael grinned. "The Regent thinks I've healed up enough to not zap her out of her body on our wedding night. That's the favor, by the way."

"I ain't taking care of *that* deed!" Sam joked. "You're just going to have to get your tailfeathers corporeal enough to bed the little lady yourself!"

By the way Azrael choked, Sam could tell it was the *last* thing he'd expected to pop out of his mouth.

"Although I'm sure Lucifer would be happy to oblige," Sam added. "He doesn't have any qualms about bedding somebody else's wife. He'd probably even let you watch."

"Enough!" Azrael roared in laughter. "I need a best man. Not a surrogate ... whatever!"

"Thought as much," Sam said. Not that Azrael had ever let any of the Sata'anic-hybrids he worked with get close, but the Angel of Death had become downright sociable the past ten years. Elisabeth's doing, he suspected. She'd been the missing piece he'd needed to stop genuflecting to the holier-than-thou immortals who forever interfered just enough to screw things up, but never enough to actually help.

"You getting married here? On Earth?"

"Ceres Station," Azrael said. "The factions all wish to be present. There's no way Lucifer will let that many busybodies down on his planet."

"Wise move," Sam's heart did a happy little skip-jump of joy at the news. Ceres station! And as best man he was certain he'd be allowed to accompany the bride!

As a descendant of a Sata'anic soldier, he was bound by the same rules which bound everyone else. He wasn't supposed to leave Earth unless he built himself his own spaceship and got there under his own steam. Since using advanced technology was also forbidden, he had to use the materials and technology of whatever period he lived in. Humanity was finally moving in the right direction, but it was unlikely any Sata'an-hybrid would still be alive by the time humans got around to inventing their own hyperdrive. But if Az could manufacture some exception, even if it was only to the asteroid belt of this solar system, he'd sure like to go along!

Ever since mankind had become technologically advanced enough to start exploring space on their own, not even the emperor's observers had been able to shuttle back and forth with impunity as they had in the early days of the Armistice. Too many Earth satellites with eyes aimed at near-Earth orbit. The Russians thought the occasional strange radar blip was the Americans. The Americans thought it was the Chinese. And the Chinese thought it was the Russians. They were being forced to keep a lower and lower profile.

It was only a matter of time before humans figured out there was a big fat cat in the bag squirming to get out. Then maybe, at last, his people would be free of this accursed armistice which prevented them from simply turning to the neighbors they'd been living amongst for 5,500 years, unfurling their tails, and saying 'hi.'

"He's over there," Azrael interrupted Sam's happy musings.

"Huh?" Sam asked, visions of space-shuttles travelling through the stars as his full-blooded Sata'anic ancestors had done dancing in his head.

"The squatter," Azrael pointed to a small outbuilding that was positioned halfway between Objective Wolverine One and Wolverine Two. "He's over there. Around seven feet underground."

"Oh!" Sam grabbed his radio. "Red Dawn command. Red Dawn command. This is Wolverine Two. The fox is in the henhouse located about a half klick between the two objectives. Over."

The radio erupted with chatter as Red Dawn Command mobilized the troops to converge upon the quarry. The Coalition forces Sam was embedded in here today had absolutely no idea some of the so-called 'spooks' in their midst were really what their legends believed to be demons.

"You going to reap this one for us, Az?" Sam offered. "It would be an honor."

"Nope," Azrael said. "Saddam Hussein is one of those squatters with unusual requirements. He can't jump anyplace without another genetically compatible host. Elisabeth thinks it's better if we let the Iraqi people try him themselves for war crimes."

"Wise woman," Sam said.

"Agreed," Azrael said with a grin that made him look like a teenager. Some Angel of Death! All he needed was a pocket-protector and a pair of thick, coke-bottle glasses and he'd be mistaken for some mathematics dweeb straight out of Cal Polytech.

Sam returned his focus to the job at hand. Dragging Saddam Hussein's sorry ass out of the grave he'd dug himself. Filthy. Matted hair and beard. He'd buried himself with $750,000 US dollars and a couple of AK-47's, but didn't use them, surrendering and begging for mercy. The only reason he surrendered so peacefully was because Azrael hung over their shoulders, just corporeal enough to be visible to the quasi-ascended Agent and let him know resistance meant an instant all-expenses-paid trip straight into Moloch's grinning maw.

A wedding! On Ceres station! Sam couldn't wait!

Chapter 55

There is no man who lives and,
Seeing the Angel of Death,
Can deliver his soul from his hand.

Targum Psalm 134:45 (A.V. 48)

Sol System: December 25, 2003
Ceres Station

Although archangels could ram their spirit through the time-space continuum to get from one place to another, mortals required *technology* to traverse the stars, something both emperors possessed in infinite quantity. Azrael grinned as Elisabeth stepped off the shuttlecraft wearing a simple white dress. She leaned on Opa's cane, a reminder, no doubt, of the family who couldn't be here.

"She looks breathtaking," Shay'tan rumbled in his ear. The old dragon adjusted his significant girth with a sigh. "I always did love weddings."

Kadima scurried out behind her and adjusted her white khimar, wide-eyed as she stared out into the space-hanger turned garden and the two alien militaries which had lined up to witness today's event in a formal honor guard. In a spat of generosity, She-who-is had terra-formed the underground facility into a habitable biosphere, complete with flora and fauna. You needed a survival suit to wander outside, but inside Ceres Station had become a paradise.

Sam stepped off behind them, pausing to admire a very different view than the one admired by the ladies. Spaceships! Lots of spaceships! And aliens! Including his full-blooded Sata'anic ancestors! For all Sam's teasing about Azrael being a science nerd, Sam was a bit of a sci-fi geek of his own. Sam kept a Star Fleet uniform and pair of Vulcan ears to go LARP-ing at Star Trek conventions as his favorite character, Lieutenant Tuvok.

"Hey ... wow!" Sam hurried ahead of the bridal procession to join Azrael at his place before the two emperors. He eyed the enormous red dragon who'd been his ancestor's god with suspicion, resplendent in his jeweled robes of state, and the rather ordinary looking bushy-haired man who stood opposite him, wearing a simple white robe. "Spaceships … and gods. If you were to zap me dead right this moment, I don't think it could get any better than this!"

"Our guest-of-honor has yet to arrive," Azrael said. "The Regent warned me she'd make a stage entrance perfectly timed to steal the show."

As if on cue, the overbearing presence he associated with the Architect of the Universe pressed down upon the base. Milliseconds before She-who-is finished ramming her enormous spirit down into a teeny-tiny humanoid shell, the Regent loudly commented about how beautiful Elisabeth looked to detract from She-who-is's attempt to upstage the bride. Oblivious, the goddess who ruled All-That-Is glided up to Azrael with more allure than any Hollywood starlet.

"Azrael," She-who-is purred in a breathy voice. Her sparkly golden dress was much more elaborate than the simple white gown Elisabeth had chosen for today's ceremony. "I hope your bride appreciates my efforts to make your day a special one."

"Typical," Shay'tan rumbled deep in his belly. He rolled his golden eyes and gave Azrael a conspiratorial wink. "It's always got to be about HER."

She-who-is shot Shay'tan a dirty look. The old dragon donned an expression of pure innocence and moved his paw to his head, his snout and heart in a gesture of respect. The Architect of the Universe appeared mollified. She turned to gather genuflections from the other VIPs who'd assembled for the wedding. As she did, Shay'tan shot out his tail and caressed her gossamer wing. She-who-is slapped the offending limb, but Azrael couldn't help but notice HER pleased smirk.

Lucifer led Elisabeth up to the living gazebo. Her long blonde hair was braided with flowers, with a simple hand-crocheted white veil covering her hair. Azrael glanced between She-who-is and his bride-to-be and noticed the goddess had waxed melancholy, her mascara smudged as she hastily wiped away a tear. With a wave of HER hand, the flowers in the living gazebo changed color from gold to white to match the baby's breath in Elisabeth's hair. Their scent wafted through the flight hanger, a tantalizing aroma.

Lucifer stood before his adoptive father whom he had not seen for 5,500 years with an unreadable expression before bending to kiss Elisabeth upon both cheeks. Now that Lucifer and Elisabeth stood side-by-side, the physical resemblance was eerie. Azrael caught the strange expression that crossed the Emperor's face as *he* realized it, too.

"He is the mate I chose for you the last time you were in this realm," Lucifer whispered with tears in his eyes. "I'm glad you found each other again." His snowy feathers rustled with emotion as he gave Azrael her hand.

Azrael trembled at the pleasure of Elisabeth's small hand curling around his. She peeked through blonde eyelashes and blushed as Azrael lifted it to his lips.

"I see you," Elisabeth said with a hushed voice, the first words she'd spoken to him in *both* lifetimes he had known her. Her cheeks turned pink as she realized everyone had heard.

Lucifer blinked to cram the emotion back behind the mask of arrogance he usually wore to hide his feelings and stepped out of the way to bear witness with the other guests. The General stiffened, giving him an icy look. The Regent elbowed her mate in the ribs, forcing him to acknowledge his adversary with a nod. Lucifer turned towards his adopted father and appeared crushed when the Emperor turned away. Both She-who-is and the Regent sighed with rare agreement. The Emperor's inability to forgive his son had long ago grown stale.

The Eternal Emperor stepped forward and took charge.

"Dearly beloved," the Emperor said, "it's not often the powers that be reach unanimous agreement on any topic, but today we celebrate the marriage of our loyal servant, Azrael, to the human female, Elisabeth."

"I can't believe God *himself* is presiding over their wedding," Sam whispered to Kadima.

"Allah," Kadima corrected. "Allah himself is presiding over the ceremony."

Kadima almost leaped out of her skin as the enormous red dragon which stood behind her rumbled with his too-deep voice.

"The concept of god or the devil as preached by your Earth religions are amalgamations of many different religions," Shay'tan said. "As you can see, there are many gods, including higher gods who even *we* worship." The old dragon cast his eyes skyward towards some deity who was not in the room.

Elisabeth gave Azrael a knowing look. She'd never been subjected to the whole motley crew of oversized egos jammed into a single room before, but no sooner had they announced their engagement than the power-brokers had started popping by the Cherubim monastery at inconvenient times to pay their respects. There'd been this one time out in the gardens…

"I understand you have your own vows?" the Emperor asked.

"Yes," Azrael said. He patted his pocket and the scrap of void-resistant paper he'd tucked in there just in case he forgot his vows even though he'd spent the last three weeks memorizing them. He held Elisabeth's hands level with his heart as he stared into her beautiful silver eyes.

"So many people dream of that one great love," Azrael's heart filled with warmth as he recited the vows which had flowed effortlessly onto the page. "That fateful look across a smoky room where you say, this person is for me. Eros. The heady, almost frantic need to be with the object of your affection. But such love rarely lasts. The supernova which burns so brightly in the night sky soon burns itself out."

Tears welled in Elisabeth's eyes as she squeezed his hand and nodded. The words he used now were how she'd once described her attraction to the young man who'd proven unworthy of her.

"There is another kind of love," Azrael continued. "Agape. The love you feel for a best friend. It's the ease with which two people can sit together in total silence and be content because words are not necessary to communicate how you feel. It's the urge to run home and tell the other how your day went because you want your joy to be *their* joy as well. It's the ability when life forces you to spend time apart, whether a few hours or many years, to pick right up where you left off as though no time has passed at all."

Now it was the Regent who began to sob. The General pulled his mate back against his chest and wrapped his arms around her shoulders, bending to whisper reassurances in her ear.

"And then one day you realize you've been in love with that person all along," Azrael said. "And you never saw it coming because it crept up on you so naturally, so quietly, that you can't imagine any outcome other than spending eternity with your twin spark because no one in the universe will ever meld so perfectly with your soul. I ask you, Elisabeth Kaiser, to become my mate for life."

Tears welled in Elisabeth's eyes as she nodded, chewing on her lower lip. He squeezed her hands.

"Elisabeth?" the Emperor asked.

"Azrael," Elisabeth said, her voice trembling with emotion. "All my life, I dreamed an angel watched over me, shadowing each painful step as I made my way through the world. No matter what hardship came, I always knew you were there, loaning me your quiet strength. Then one day I discovered you were real, the best friend my heart had been crying out to find."

She reached up to touch his face. As she spoke, her golden-white hair picked up the light, making it appear as though she wore a halo.

"It took time for me to trust what my heart had always known," Elisabeth said. "That no matter what happened, you would never abandon me to suffer alone. That no matter what forces tried to rent us apart, that somehow, you would always find me again. I love you. And I wish to never be parted from you."

This time, it was the General who wiped his eyes and covered the errant emotion with a cough. The Regent smiled and nestled further into her husband's wings. Darkness, gloriously subdued by the General's light.

"I understand you wish to exchange mate-rings?" the Emperor asked. It was a rhetorical question. With Azrael prone to dissolve any matter he wore whenever his emotions were sufficiently aroused, the Emperor had gone all-out synthesizing a pair of mate-rings that were resistant to the vagaries of void-matter.

"Sam?" Azrael asked.

"Ring … oh … um," Sam got a sheepish expression. He made a great show of pretending to rummage through his pockets.

"Ho-ho-ho!" Shay'tan slapped his sides as he picked up on the fact it was all an act. The old dragon appeared to appreciate a little humor.

Sam pulled the ring from his breast-pocket where it had been all along. He held out his fist and waited for Azrael to open the palm of his hand to drop them in since handing them to him was out of the question.

"Very funny," Azrael said. He took the rings and turned back to his bride, her silver eyes gleaming with happiness as he took her left hand and placed the ring at the end of her finger.

"My beautiful Elisabeth," Azrael said as he slid the ring down into place, black tears streaming down his cheeks. "Take this ring as a symbol of my everlasting love. That no matter what forces may try to separate us, we will always find our way back to one another again."

Elisabeth's eyes glittered silver with tears. She took the second ring and placed it at the end of Azrael's finger.

"My beloved Azrael," Elisabeth said. "No matter what form you may take, whether it be the kiss of fog against my cheek or the caress of flesh upon flesh, know that somehow I will always know it is you." She slid the ring down his finger into place.

"And now you must recite the vow of our ancestors," the General said.

"We breathe," Elisabeth said. "As one breath."

"Our hearts beat," Azrael said, "as one heart."

"Our souls merge together," they spoke in unison, "as one soul. So that come what may, not even death shall keep us apart."

"Then by the powers vested in me by … me," the Eternal Emperor said. "I now pronounce you mated for life."

The deities in the launch bay began to clap. Behind them, two galactic empires' militaries gave a rousing cheer and threw their caps into the air.

"You may kiss your bride," Shay'tan rumbled, giving Hashem a poke. The old dragon was an earthy fellow. He wasn't about to let his uptight chess partner forget the best part of a wedding ceremony.

Azrael pulled his bride in for a kiss, mindful not to accidentally zap any of their esteemed wedding guests as he encircled her in his arms and wings. He'd waited more than 2,300 years to find her again and another decade to be able to touch her. He wasn't about to let either emperor's silly prohibitions against public displays of affection prevent him from letting the whole world know Elisabeth was his!

"Does this mean I finally get to pin your wings to the bed and have my way with you?" Elisabeth whispered when he finally let her come up for air.

"Mmmm.hmmmm." Words flew out of his brain as that part of his anatomy he'd unconsciously reshaped centuries ago woke up and started clamoring for attention, a reaction it had never occurred to him to manifest until the day she'd given him his first-ever kiss.

He glanced towards their wedding guests and realized Lucifer had absented himself from the post-wedding festivities. His back and snowy white wings were stiff as he stood at the bar, alone. The outcast. No matter how many hangers-on he gathered around him seeking political power or prestige, at the end of the day Lucifer always stood alone. They watched him pour himself a brandy, lips twitching in suppressed misery, and down the entire glass.

"Go," Elisabeth's eyes filled with compassion. "Keep your promise."

He reluctantly let go of her hand, ignoring the puzzled glances the others gave him as he left his bride's side and plowed his way through well-wishers who dove out of his path. He stood, waiting, until Lucifer realized he was there.

"Azrael?" Lucifer glanced behind him at the other deities staring with confusion in their direction.

Azrael held out his hand.

"I promised that when I found her again," Azrael said, his voice hoarse with emotion. "I would take your hand in friendship."

Emotion danced across Lucifer's ethereally handsome face. Confusion. Surprise. Relief. He closed his eyes and sighed, his lips moving in silent prayer as he focused on the connection he could still feel to the mate he had loved, and lost.

"Take good care of Elisabeth."

"No!!!" the Emperor shrieked. The old god who co-ruled the galaxy and now, more and more, the entire universe, leaped towards them.

Lucifer's hand closed around Azrael's outstretched one, his lips curved up in a smile.

"Thank you," he exhaled with his dying breath.

His mortal shell slid peacefully to the ground, snowy white wings forming a graceful arc as they settled around his body in a whisper of feathers.

"Azrael!!!" She-who-is shrieked as she realized he'd just circumvented the protections she'd put in place to prevent Lucifer from killing himself.

As an Agent of Ki, Azrael's power came from a higher source than that of her daughter. In a flash, Azrael pulled Lucifer's spirit out of that place and flashed him to the entrance of the Dreamtime.

Chapter 56

Is death the last sleep?
No--it is the last and final awakening.

-Sir Walter Scott

Ascended Realms
The Dreamtime

The entrance loomed before them as it had always appeared to Azrael, a great, blank wall with no apparent entrance except for those who were welcome to enter. Only lifesparks that were between mortal shells could pass into the playpen known as the Dreamtime.

"It's blocked," Lucifer said with an unhappy sigh. "It's *always* blocked. I got you in trouble for nothing." His snowy white wings drooped despondently as he waited for She-who-is to yank him back into his body.

"Wait," Azrael said. "There *must* be a way to enter."

Lucifer ran his hand across the veil.

"Won't you destroy it if you touch it?" Lucifer asked.

"That's what I always assumed," Azrael said. "Actually … nobody knows. The one time I ever asked *HER*, she hit on me and then got angry when I turned down her advances."

Lucifer rolled his eerie silver eyes. "Typical. Every time I plead with her to let me go, *SHE* waxes cryptic and tells me it's not up to her. *You're* here every day. What *do* you know about this place?"

"Supposedly passage is a one-way ticket whose only exit is rebirth into a new body," Azrael said. "But Elisabeth's brother passed through the veil when he died, and then he pulled himself back out again, frantic to find her. He wasn't evolved enough to reconstitute his body, but if you *are* evolved enough, I think you may be able to pass back and forth."

"Like a child safety gate," Lucifer said. "The big people can just step over the gate, while the little people press their noses through the wire and whimper for snacks." He pressed his forehead against the veil and whispered: "Please, sister. Let me go?"

Sister?

Azrael was surprised She-who-is hadn't appeared *herself* by now to stop them. *Had* this place been created by She-who-is? Or had she had help from her now-abandoned husband, the Dark Lord? Or her mother-goddess, Ki? Or maybe it was one of those constructs like humans built? Like a bridge? Once it had been built, anybody could cross it, not just the architect who had designed it.

"Perhaps now that I can control my power a little better," Azrael said, "I can touch the wall and see if I can't make just a tiny hole?"

"Won't that disrupt it?" Lucifer's brow furrowed with concern. "I'm selfish, but not *that* selfish. She built this place to keep the soul-sparks safe from Moloch."

"I touched *HER* once," Azrael said. "It interrupted her hold on her mortal shell, but it didn't hurt her. If this place is an extension of her spirit, then touching this barrier shouldn't cause any lasting harm. I hope…"

Lucifer's chiseled features glistened with a hope that was almost giddy. That side of Lucifer he'd only ever caught glimpses of, the side he suspected would have been the dominant one had Moloch not gotten his hands on him and warped his personality, made the Fallen Angelic appear almost brilliantly innocent.

'Morning Star…' Ki whispered into Azrael's brain.

"This should not inconvenience you for long, your Majesty," Azrael apologized to the thick, white veil which blocked entry. Using one finger, he touched a spot above his head and drew a line all the way down to the floor. The veil parted.

"Thank you," Lucifer's white wings trembled with emotion. He slipped through the entrance Azrael held open like a curtain.

Azrael hesitated, not sure whether he should step inside. Now that he knew he could get in, he was confident he could get out again the same way. He sensed other spirits waiting for Lucifer's long-overdue reunification. A dismayed cry filtered through the veil.

"He's not here!"

Azrael decided now was as good a time as any to peek into the paradise he'd been barred from entering. Careful to touch the veil as little as possible, he parted the curtain and slipped inside the place he'd visited several times each day for millennia, yet never seen. As described, it was a simple white room, but beyond it swirled whorls of light. A beautiful, dark-winged Angelic who was otherwise the spitting image of Lucifer kissed his head as though he were a little boy. Her eyes were filled with tears.

"He's not here, son," Asherah said. "Ki took him."

"SHE lied to me?" Lucifer clenched his fist.

"SHE never told you he was here," Asherah said. "What she said was…"

363

"I could never reunite with my mate in the Dreamtime," Lucifer sighed. "I thought it was meant to be a punishment."

Asherah turned to a square-jawed, white-winged Angelic at her side who possessed the same white hair and silver eyes as Lucifer.

"Lucifer, this is Shemijaza. Your *real* father. Or at least your biological one. He was determined to be here when you finally crossed over."

The tall, fair-haired Angelic held out his hand. Lucifer hesitated. His wings trembled with emotion as he faced the Angelic who had sired him. Shemijaza. Moloch's prior unwilling host until the bastard had realized he had a more malleable option available in Shemijaza's fifteen-year-old boy. Father and son embraced.

"How am I supposed to reunite with him?" Lucifer cried out. "I'm not evolved enough to access Ki's realm!"

Azrael's lip twitched with regret. *He'd* gone there once, after Ki had saved him, but he was no more knowledgeable about how to get there on his own than Lucifer was ... or any of the other old gods stuck hanging around She-who-is's universe. He had killed Lucifer for nothing.

"Ki released your mate from the upper realms around the same time he released Elisabeth," Shemijaza said. "He's back on Earth in a new mortal shell."

Lucifer's resolve stiffened. "Where?"

"I don't have that information," Shemijaza said. "All I know is that you finally improved Earth's bloodlines enough for Ki's other Morning Stars to incarnate back into mortal form through the children of the fallen."

"There's a war coming," Asherah said. "And once again, chol beag, *you* are at the center of it."

"A war?" Azrael asked.

"The same bloodline that allows the soul-fragments of Moloch's devoured children a second chance at existence," Shemijaza said, "also provides opportunity for Moloch to find a new host."

"If you don't find your soul-siblings before *he* does," Asherah said, "Moloch may just get his hands on one of them."

"It is prophesized that someday the Morning Stars will all awaken at once," Shemijaza said, "and their combined brilliance shall either shine bright enough to destroy Moloch once and for all, or he shall seize that power for himself and destroy Ki. It's imperative you find them before Moloch does."

"You must return to Earth, *ceann beag*," Asherah tussled Lucifer's hair as though he were a small boy, "and use the lessons you have learned this lifetime to make the *right* choices this time. Your mate incarnated back into human form to do battle at your side, but he is without his memories. You will need to find him."

Lucifer gave Azrael a hopeless look. "How will I find him if I don't know what he looks like and *he* doesn't know to look for me? I mean, really? He's going to go searching for a Fallen angel?"

Azrael remembered what Elisabeth had told him about how she'd talked to imaginary angels even *before* she'd had her accident.

"Around the time Elisabeth's new mortal shell would have been conceived," Azrael said, "I began to feel drawn to Chicago. I couldn't understand *why* I suddenly found that city so fascinating, but it became my favorite place. I found myself returning there again and again. Has something like that happened to you?"

A smile lit up Lucifer's face. A genuine one; not that fake one he flashed to sway politicians and woo women into his bed. It struck Azrael how much Lucifer looked like She-who-is.

"Will you guide me home, old friend?" Lucifer held out his hand. His expression was wary, not the practiced handshake of a politician, nor a plea to undo his own death, but a query of a different sort. *Are* you my friend? It was the personality Azrael caught glimpses of whenever Lucifer wasn't busy acting like an asshole, pretending to be somebody else.

"I just killed you," Azrael reminded him. "Remember? I've never been able to put a spirit back into a body I've touched."

"He's an ascended being," Asherah said. "All he has to do is will his spirit back into his body. No harm's been done except a bit of oxygen deprivation. He'll be disoriented due to cell-damage, but he's evolved enough to heal it himself."

"What is it humans say?" Azrael clasped his forearm to Lucifer's. "The horse knows its own way back to the barn?"

"That's car, nimrod," Lucifer said. "The car knows its own way home. Horses went out of fashion with the last century."

"I can't ride in a car," Azrael said. "The electrical system shorts out any time I get near one."

"You can't ride a horse either," Lucifer said. "Not without killing it."

In a flash, Azrael transported them back to Ceres Station.

Chapter 57

Our friend Lazarus sleepeth; but I go,
That I may awake him out of sleep.

John 11:11

Sol System: December 25, 2003
Ceres Station

Elisabeth watched the Eternal Emperor cradle Lucifer's body, tears streaming out of his golden eyes as he tried to will his Fallen son back to life. If seeing the Regent nestle into the General's arms was weird, *nothing* had prepared her for meeting the deity she'd assumed was god with a capital 'G' … and then learning his touch did *not* contain the spark of life as was depicted on the ceiling of the Sistine Chapel.

"Son, please!" the Emperor touched Lucifer's chest. "Wake up!"

"He's gone, old friend," Shay'tan rumbled. One clawed hand reached out to touch the Emperor's shoulder. "This is what he wanted."

"Why?" the Emperor wept. "Why did he leave without saying goodbye?"

'Because the first thing you did after not seeing him for 5,500 years was to turn your back on him,' Elisabeth thought to herself. *'That's why…'*

For the past few weeks, Lucifer had taken her under his broad, white wings and prepared her to assume her role as … whatever. Whatever plans he and the Regent had cooked up for her, not only was *she* in the dark, but so was Azrael. They didn't seem to be *bad* plans. In fact, everybody seemed quite happy Lucifer would no longer be running the show. Not that anybody had asked *her* if that was what she wanted to do.

Personally, she'd rather let somebody *else* be in charge. But after having witnessed Haven and this whole, gangly group of super-ego's, she could see why Earth-folk needed to get their act together and start exerting a little more control over their *own* fate instead of pleading to God or Allah or She-who-is or whoever to come and save them. Heaven … or Haven as they called it … was a mess!

Ironically, Hades seemed to be much better-run…

Elisabeth realized she had company. She turned to gaze into the brilliantly-lit golden eyes of She-who-is.

"Do you like the decorations I created for your wedding?" She-who-is asked.

Elisabeth bit her tongue. Why hadn't She-who-is gone barreling after Lucifer if *SHE* was the one holding him here? *SHE* seemed oddly dispassionate about the whole thing. Lucifer claimed he had no memories of any lifetimes prior to *this* one, but if what Azrael believed was true, not only had Azrael circumvented *HER* protections, but her new husband may have just killed She-who-is's actual *brother*.

"Um … yes?"

"I engineered them from scratch," She-who-is gestured towards the ivy which grew up the inside walls of the cavern carved out of the dwarf planet, thick with white, pleasant smelling flowers that looked like roses. "They feed off the exhaust cast off by the afterburners of the shuttlecraft so they can survive here with minimal artificial light."

"Um … that's nice," Elisabeth said, not sure what else to say.

"Without a void creature to feed me constant sub-atomic particles," She-who-is said. "I've had to get creative about recycling matter. But with a void-creature for a husband, you shouldn't have that problem. Perhaps I could give you pointers?"

Elisabeth stared into She-who-is's brilliant golden eyes. This was the *strangest* conversation she'd ever had!

"Um, yeah, that would be great," Elisabeth stammered.

"I thought perhaps you might try transplanting some of them into the caves of Gehenna?" She-who-is gestured to the roses. "The fumes cast off by the pit should provide ample fertilizer for them to adapt to the caves." Her gossamer wings gave a crisp snap. "Personally, I could never *stand* being underground. No wonder Lucifer's always depressed."

She-who-is took her hands and squeezed them. Her lips curved up in a genuine smile as *SHE* bent in and gave her a peck on the cheek. It struck Elisabeth how much She-who-is looked like Lucifer, except for the fact her wings were gossamer instead of feathered and she had pointy ears.

"I'm glad you're back," She-who-is said. "Maybe with a void creature to protect you this time, you won't get eaten?"

Elisabeth had *no* idea what SHE was talking about. Wailing from the direction of Lucifer's body pulled her out of the surreal chat with She-who-is, back to the drama unfolding between the Emperor and his Fallen, now-dead son.

"Please!" the Emperor implored She-who-is. "Bring him back."

She-who-is gave the Emperor a patronizing, insincere grimace.

Shay'tan lowered his considerable dragon-like girth to kneel and placed a clawed hand on the Emperor's shoulder to comfort him, a sight Elisabeth would never forget for so long as she existed.

"Let him go," Shay'tan said. "This is what he's always wanted. He's in the arms of the one he loves now."

Elisabeth didn't miss the way She-who-is blanched.

Hmmm…

The subterranean cavern filled with the scent of ozone as the Eternal Emperor attempted to reanimate his adopted son, but just as happened when Elizabeth shocked a human body with a defibrillator, Lucifer's body jerked upwards, but with no spirit to inhabit it, it was all for naught.

The hair stood up on the back of her neck. A feather-light tendril of consciousness touched her forehead.

'Lucifer's mate wasn't in the Dreamtime,' Azrael whispered into her mind. 'He's been reborn into mortal form. We've got to help Lucifer settle back into his body so he can find him.'

A second spirit touched her mind.

"So how do I do this?" Lucifer asked. "The last ten billion times I got forcibly shoved back into my body, it was She-who-is doing it. Not me."

"I have no idea," Azrael replied. "I've never been able to un-kill somebody I've killed."

The Regent's head shot up. She gave Elisabeth a black-eyed look that pierced straight to her soul. There was no hiding anything from those too-perceptive eyes. The Regent nodded approval.

'How do you keep your patients alive, mo ghra?' Azrael asked.

'Beats me,' Elisabeth spoke low enough that those currently wearing mortal shells would not overhear her. 'I just do it.'

'Think!' Azrael pleaded. 'You two are of the same bloodline. If –you- can do it, chances are –he- can do it.'

'I just talk to them,' Elisabeth said. 'Convince them to stay. They do the rest. I just loan them a little extra energy.'

It was strange, having a conversation with two invisible people while simultaneously pretending to be listening to actual real-life *gods* jockey for position now that a major player had just been removed from the picture.

'Lucifer,' Azrael said. 'Try to settle back into your body. Elisabeth believes it's the patient's will to live which keeps them here.'

'I don't get it,' Lucifer groused. 'He's a god. Why can't my adoptive Father see me?'

"Lucifer," the Emperor cradled Lucifer's limp body. "Please come back!"

'A gift?' Azrael suggested. 'From She-who-is? Or maybe Ki? To teach him a lesson for being such a hypocrite?'

Lucifer tried to make his body move. It wasn't working. Not even when the air inside Ceres Station filled with static electricity as the Emperor channeled the power of the universe to attempt to call back his adopted son.

She-who-is stood over the Emperor, her hand on Shay'tan's enormous scaled shoulder, tapping her exquisite designer high-heel on the floor to the tempo of her gossamer wings as though she was impatient. There was not a hint of sorrow in those golden eyes. In fact, *SHE* wore the same look a mother bird might when shoving its fledgling out of the nest, waiting for it to fly. Elisabeth was *certain* SHE knew Lucifer hovered above his body, trying to figure out how to get back into it.

'Elisabeth,' Azrael whispered. *'It isn't working. Please. Help him.'*

She thought of all the times she'd been forced to kiss Major 'Doc' Deven's ass to get him to step aside and let her work on a patient when the Doc was ready to let the poor bastard die. At least the Emperor was, belatedly, realizing he didn't want the son he'd spurned to be dead.

Elisabeth's hair stood on end. Sparks filled the cavern as the Emperor used his ascended powers to 'zap' Lucifer again. Elisabeth winced. What was it Doctor Abdullah had said? It's not like jump-starting a car. It would take more than a syringe full of atropine to fix this mess.

"Your Majesty … um … Sir?" Elisabeth asked. "If you don't mind … there's something I'd like to try?"

'I'm sick of watching them treat Lucifer like crap,' Azrael whispered into her mind. *'All this talk of welcoming home the prodigal son, but after 5,500 years the Emperor still makes his -own- son crawl. Make him earn it.'*

Shay'tan jerked his long, serpentine neck in Azrael's direction, and then looked at Lucifer's body. The old dragon gave it a sniff. A toothy smirk appeared on his face. He looked towards the invisible Azrael and winked with his large, luminescent golden eyes.

"Perhaps if you tell the boy how you really feel about him?" Shay'tan rumbled. "I mean … you *did* just spend the last 5,500 years telling everyone your son was the devil. Another devil. Actually, you do that a lot. Call everybody who disagrees with you the devil."

Elisabeth placed her hands over Lucifer's heart and tried using the white light Rahmiel had unsuccessfully tried to teach her to use. It didn't work any better now than it had then, though the fact the goddess whose energy she purportedly tried to channel stood over her, tapping her foot with bored impatience didn't help her concentration. The Emperor met her gaze, tears in his eyes.

"He chose that boy over me," the Emperor whispered. "He chose your *world* over me. He could have ruled my empire, and he threw it all away."

'Knock knock!' Lucifer whispered into her mind. *'Who's there? Homer. Homer who? Homophobia…'*

"Well that explains everything," Elisabeth said. "He's dead, and you still can't forgive him. No wonder he doesn't want to come back."

'But I –do– want to come back,' Lucifer protested.

She-who-is gave Elisabeth the *same* enigmatic smile Oma used to give whenever she made excuses that she couldn't do some task because it was too hard. Ooh, boy. Was this some sort of test?

"Then get your ass back into your body and stop making excuses!" Elisabeth snapped at Lucifer. She felt the disembodied wraith flailing helplessly beneath her fingers strengthen at the compulsion in her voice.

"That's it!" the Regent said. "The power of persuasion. You're the same bloodline. Lucifer's primary mode of transmission is sound."

'You need to swear at him like a longshoreman, mo ghra,' Azrael whispered into her mind. 'The same as you do for your patients.'

A light bulb went off in her head. She'd just spent the last eight months talking to Azrael to coax him back into physical form.

"Stop picturing your spirit as a complete body," Elisabeth said. "It's energy. Your nervous system makes your body move by sending electrical signals to your muscles. You've got to think on a much smaller scale. Start with your heart. Your body needs oxygen. Attach a single tendril of spirit to tell it how to beat."

His pulse came to life beneath the fingertips she had pressed to his neck.

The Emperor gave a cry of relief.

She-who-is gave her a bemused look that communicated, 'and you two are just figuring this out now?'

"Now send each command into your lungs to order them to contract and exhale," Elisabeth said.

With a gasp, Lucifer began to breathe. His entire body shimmered and, just for a moment, felt every bit as incorporeal as Azrael's before solidifying beneath her fingertips. Lucifer's silver eyes shot open.

"Arise, *Luciferi*," Elisabeth touched his forehead as though dispensing absolution, "and *choose* this time to herald the dawn."

The Emperor buried his face in Lucifer's neck, sobbing, oblivious he knelt on snowy white wings or tore out some of his long lost son's feathers. Shay'tan gave Azrael the 'all clear' to finish materializing back into the room. Lucifer trembled and, with an expression as though he could not believe what was happening, cautiously slid his arms around his father's neck and embraced him, the prodigal son returned.

"Why I *do* believe this means Lucifer's life sentence is up?" Shay'tan slapped his opposing emperor/god on the shoulder as though he'd just won a wager. "Doesn't it, old friend? He did, after all, just resurrect from the dead."

She-who-is edged towards the bar and poured herself a stiff drink. It struck Elisabeth how much She-who-is's manner of moving reminded her of Lucifer's. Her perfectly painted lips grimaced as the alcohol braced her, and then moved into a thin smile.

Lucifer disentangled himself from his sobbing adoptive father. The Regent elbowed her husband. The General hesitated, and then reached down to help Lucifer up.

"Thank you," Lucifer said, his expression wary.

"C'mon, c'mon, c'mon … don't blow it…" Azrael murmured from her side, corporeal once more.

The General did not speak; just stared at Lucifer with those deep, blue eyes. His expression was, as always, unreadable. The Regent elbowed her husband in the ribs a second time, hard enough to make him grunt in pain.

"You're welcome," the General said.

Azrael breathed a sigh of relief.

Elisabeth turned to her brand-new husband.

"I do believe you owe me one wing-whacking good time." Elisabeth lowered her voice to a sultry tone. "Can we please get out of here now?"

Azrael took her hands. She gasped as he teleported her between the dimensions to the cozy little honeymoon bower he'd dropped hints about, but refused to discuss.

"Oh … Az!" Elisabeth stared up at the three-moon moonrise over a pristine purple ocean. "It's beautiful!"

The houseboat rocked gently on an endless sea. Nearby, other houseboats were tethered to moorings. Beneath them, nearly transparent pods floated like enormous pearls as far down as she could see, their twinkling lights making the ocean appear to be a snow globe Christmas scene. Off in the distance, a magnificent city floated across the horizon, spacecraft flitting from the spaceport to satellites clearly visible in the sky.

A high-pitched squeal not unlike that of a dolphin came from the water. Azrael answered. A dolphin-like creature with a human-looking face and fingers at the end of each flipper peeked out of the water and asked another question in a high-pitched language. The dolphin wore clothing.

"The Mer-Levi are a sister-race of humans," Azrael explained. "Their ancestors came from the same homeworld your ancestors originally came from. The Merfolk Navy intermarried with the Leviathans the same as the Fallen intermarried with your people. They're now part of the Alliance."

The dolphin-creature made another inquiry and then disappeared. Moments later, he reappeared with a tray of fresh fruit and sushi on a bed of kelp. A maître'd? Azrael replied to the dolphin-man. The maître'd reared up on his tail and disappeared back into the water.

"I thought you'd like to see where Earth might be in a few hundred years if given the right example," Azrael said. He led her towards the tiny hut in the center of the floating platform. All of a sudden, his wings fluttered as though he was bashful.

"This is the part where you're supposed to pick me up and carry me over the threshold," Elisabeth teased.

Azrael reached out to tuck an errant strand of hair which had escaped her French braid.

"I see you," he said, his eyes black with desire. He bent down to give her a perfect kiss before scooping her up and carrying her into the cabana.

Chapter 58

Life is eternal and love is immortal;
And death is only a horizon,
And a horizon is nothing save the limit of our sight.

Rossiter W. Raymond

December 25, 2003
Leviathan Homeworld

Azrael released his bride, the brush of her flesh against his nearly-corporeal nothingness the most precious gift imaginable. He was still ... insubstantial. Little more than a wraith comprised of silt-fine void matter that could pass through her flesh as though it wasn't even there the moment he began to experience great emotion ... or arousal. Elisabeth insisted she didn't care, but Azrael was worried. Would he disappoint her?

"You're doing that thing again," Elisabeth's hand slipped reassuringly into his. "Stop analyzing everything and *feel* it for a change."

Azrael gave her a shy smile. "What if I lose control of my power? I only just relearned to shape my wings."

"Ours is a spiritual bond that has transcended two lifetimes," Elisabeth splayed her fingers across the heart. Warmth spread beneath her touch, taking the edge off that ever-present hunger.

"I've never done this before," Azrael pressed her hand against his chest. "I'm not even sure what to do."

Elisabeth raised one eyebrow in amusement, merry skepticism dancing in her silver eyes.

"You've been tracking human behavior for how long?" Elisabeth laughed. "And you mean to tell me you've never walked in on two mortals doing the down and dirty?"

Azrael gulped. What was it pretty girls like Elisabeth called boys like him? Nerds? Yes. He was a nerd. Tracking data on something and *experiencing* it were two different things. Would he be adequate to satisfy her needs?

"Az." Elisabeth caressed his cheek, passing a finger beneath his eyes to capture a black, void-filled tear that would have destroyed anyone else. "Are you okay?"

Azrael's lip twitched with a wistful longing. "My mother would have loved you. I wish she was still here to meet you."

"She *is* here," Elisabeth reminded him. "Somewhere. Remember? She-who-is told the Emperor she released Janiel to Earth thirty-seven years ago."

"You know what I mean," Azrael said. He gave her a wan smile. Somehow, his moodiness didn't seem very … romantic. 2,300 years old and he didn't have a clue how to romance his beautiful bride. Any moment now, he'd blurt out the fact he was as terrified of *her* as most mortals were of *him*.

"Undress me?" Elisabeth led him towards the bed. The waterbed rocked beneath her weight as she crawled onto the center, her breasts bobbing enticingly beneath her simple white gown. He'd seen them once before, that night when she had given herself to a boy who was not worthy of her love. He'd dreamed of them many times since then, her small, pert breasts shining white against the darkness. He wished to see them again.

"I … um," Azrael stuttered.

She'd been gentle until now, teasing him as they'd curled up together each night, teaching him how to solidify his body against hers. The broken fragments of DNA she'd carried across time were proliferating throughout his spirit, repairing their strands and replicating new ones of matter amongst the fertile soil of void matter of which he was comprised. The Regent felt, given enough time, he would one day become as solid as *she* was, capable of shifting between forms at will.

Would Elisabeth be satisfied with him until then?

"You're ruminating again," Elisabeth chided him. "Stop thinking and get out of your own head. You're worse than the Emperor!"

Her touch jolted Azrael out of his melancholy. Or would it more aptly be named terror? He let go of the illusion of cloth sliding over his upper body to show the illusion of muscles rippling beneath his skin, as though he really *did* have a physical form. These days, he had *some* form, but most of what people thought of as his body was still an illusion, silt-fine void matter held together by an act of will to form a sand castle which would dissolve back into the beach with the incoming tide.

"What if I accidentally zap you while we're … um?" Azrael had been okay until this moment. The Regent had reassured him it would be fine. But Azrael didn't feel reassured.

"Then I'll cling to my body like I did the last time you tried to jolt me," Elisabeth ran her hands down his chest. "In case you forget, I don't die easily."

"No, you don't." Elisabeth's ability to resist void-matter was on par with the General's.

"You won't be repulsed if I … um … devolve?" Egad! That would be awful! Although his current form was pleasing to behold, he didn't think she'd find it quite so wonderful if she found herself in the embrace of a gigantic black-tentacled … squid.

"I cared for you when you were injured, remember? I've seen all of your forms. It's what's inside that matters."

He kneeled above where she lay supine, her body curved into a pleasing 'C' shape as she propped herself up with her elbows behind her. Wings flared, he noted the gentle rock of the houseboat beneath them. The malleable form of this entire water world … water bed … water house … felt as though this realm existed as a halfway point between his formless existence and her solid one.

Her hand slid down from his cheek, down his neck to his bare shoulder, his flesh naked beneath her fingertips. He shuddered with pleasure as her hand slid further down his bicep. She raised his hand to her lips, kissed his knuckles, and then placed it upon a soft, firm breast hidden beneath her dress. The room vibrated with a pleasant shudder. Just for a moment, the Song of Creation and Song of Destruction came together in rare harmony.

Oh! That had never happened before! He could see by the surprised gleam in her silver eyes that she had sensed the shift as well. Her lips curved up in a smile, softening the scar which marred her otherwise perfect face, that beautiful scar which had brought them together again. He kissed it, his lips trailing from her temple to her lips, relishing the sensation of the pink imperfection sliding beneath his mouth.

"Make love to me, Azrael," Elisabeth's eyes were platinum with desire.

For thousands of years, Azrael had kept an iron grip on his emotions, afraid to feel any great depth lest he let things get out of control and destroy. But now the emotion which warmed his chest and spread throughout his physical form was different from the emotion he'd previously suppressed. Anxiety. Excitement. Terror. Love. His hunger still demanded to be fed, but it felt more like the hunger one would feel gazing upon a hot fudge sundae than the emptiness of a starving beast. Ice cream? He dissipated her dress, exposing two perfect mounds of vanilla deliciousness with erect cherries taunting him to take a taste of the forbidden fruit.

Her groan of pleasure as his lips closed around one pert nipple and suckled it incited a pleasant reaction within his own body. Never had it occurred to him to manifest an erection until the day she'd led him into their tiny cottage and taught him how to spoon against her back. Not for the first time, he wondered how he'd known to recreate the body part now straining against the illusion of pants long before he'd crossed paths with her again this lifetime. A growl of pleasure escaped his lips, causing a low vibration not unlike a cello warming up before a performance. Two songs, anxious to harmonize as a single orchestral piece.

"This whole planet is going to know what we're up to," Elisabeth giggled. She nipped his lower lip, the flesh there finally substantial enough to feel pain. He closed his eyes and relished the sensation. Pain … and pleasure. Actual *physical* pain and pleasure. Not just all in his head. It was the most heady sensation he'd felt in a very long time.

"Emperor Shay'tan rented out the entire hotel for us as a wedding present," Azrael said. "Including the rooms submerged beneath us. He uh … thought … um … he said the whole galaxy knew he'd won his bet the last time an Agent of Ki merged with a mortal."

Elisabeth slipped her hand to touch his insubstantial black wings. Her hand passed through the nothingness of his feathers, each caress depositing memories of DNA and encouraging it to grow.

"I wish I could remember our time before," Elisabeth frowned. Her puckered scar made her look sad.

"We were both still children," Azrael kissed the lonely pucker and trailed his kisses to whisper in her ear. "I can most definitely tell you we were *not* doing this!"

To derail her melancholy, he blew bubbles upon her neck. Her shriek of laughter bubbled within his own heart, causing joy.

"Then I suppose we didn't do … this … either." Elisabeth caressed his manhood. "Did we?" She giggled as his wings flapped of their own volition, hitting the lofty ceiling of the room and causing the chandelier to jingle like wedding bells.

"Definitely not," Azrael gave an earthy growl.

"Then let nothing come between us again?" Tears welled in her beautiful, silver eyes which were becoming more and more luminous each day they spent together, nestled in the safety of each other's arms. The eyes of a pre-ascended creature. She needed him to help her heal as much as he needed her. Without the other, they were both incomplete.

The Regent had pulled them aside and tutored them about what must happen next. Cross-species bondings were risky for Seraphim descendants, but Azrael didn't think Elisabeth would have carried his DNA forward in time if she hadn't wanted to be with him. It was with great solemnity that he touched her slender lace G-string.

Elisabeth nodded, his own vulnerability mirrored in her silver eyes. She chewed her lower lip as he dissipated the remainder of his own shaped clothing and then slid her slender panties down her hips, leaving them both naked before one another. His eyes were drawn not to her feminine mysteries, but to the scars which ran down her damaged leg. He had never seen her completely naked before, so he had never noticed the scars looked as though a shark had taken bites out of her leg and hip

"We breathe," Elisabeth's voice trembled as she began to recite the Seraphim lifemate vow. "As one breath."

"Our hearts beat," Azrael's bottomless black eyes held her silver-eyed gaze, "as one heart."

"Our souls merge together," they spoke together, "as a single soul. So that come what may, not even death shall keep us apart."

The air grew thick with expectation; as though the gods themselves were listening to them make their commitment. Although words were not necessary to bond, the intent focused their energy.

"Just breathe," Azrael whispered as his mouth descended upon hers, no longer anxious or unsure as every ounce of his being focused upon making his beautiful Elisabeth *his* for all eternity. "All we have to do is breathe."

Elisabeth slid her hands around his back as she guided him into position to complete the mating act. It wasn't sex which caused the bond, but the deliberate intertwining of their life energy into a single soul. The act of procreation had been beautifully engineered to facilitate this bonding by necessitating the physical joining of two bodies.

Azrael's heartbeat pounded in his ears, his breathing rapid even though he no longer needed to breathe. The head of his manhood brushed against her silky curls and grew more substantial. The instinct to bond tutored his body what it needed to do. Errant strands of DNA rushed to his manhood to not only make it more erect, but also more *real.*

Elisabeth's pupils dilated until her eyes were nearly as black as his. She wriggled her hips to relish the feel of his very solid manhood brushing against the entrance to her feminine mysteries.

"Does this make me the Blue Fairy?" she grinned.

With a groan, Azrael sank into the place some ancient god had engineered so they would fit together. He froze, nearly overwhelmed with the sensation of her body closing around a part of his anatomy that was so … intimate. She nestled against his torso and waited for him to adjust to the sensory overload before allowing herself to succumb to the urge to rise up to meet him; to ride towards the ecstasy both could taste just on the other side of the next delicious push into each other's flesh.

A sense of urgency came upon him, urgency to complete the act which would bind her to him forever. He exhaled and slowly slid his manhood from the warm sheath of her flesh, trembling with the loss of no longer being fully inside of her.

"Are you okay?"

Azrael nodded, afraid to speak lest the power in his voice dissolve the walls of the room and leave their activities exposed to the outside world. Her eyes. He focused on the flecks of light dancing deep within her beautiful silver eyes which had been the first thing which had captivated his interest both lifetimes that he had known her.

"Breathe," Elisabeth repeated. "All you have to do is breathe."

His wings stretched the full width of the room. Electricity surged through them. They flapped of their own volition, trying to shake off the painfully pleasant tingling one might feel when one's foot fell asleep and then woke up again. Alive. Elisabeth made him feel alive.

With a laugh of pure joy, he slid into his beautiful Elisabeth a second time, relishing the tingling which spread throughout his body as he felt not just her body, but her spirit rise up to stroke his, testing for the places they could join together and merge as a single soul, just as their physical bodies stroked and tested for places they could join together in the act of becoming man and wife. He knew it was *her* mortality he felt tingling through his flesh right now, not his own, but it felt good. It felt like…

"*Grá mo shaol* [love of my life]," Azrael laughed aloud, wanting to shout his joy to the world, "you make me feel alive!"

Elisabeth wrapped her legs around his thighs, limiting his ability to withdraw, and pulled his head down for a kiss. In all the movies Azrael had ever seen, one's first mating was supposed to be apprehensive, or heady, or filled with panting and groaning, but all he wanted to do was shout for joy how much he loved this woman who had travelled across two lifetimes to be with him.

"Alive!" he pushed into her again, trembling like a stallion at the starting gate of a racetrack. "I feel so alive!"

"You're funny," Elisabeth laughed. This was not the way romantic encounters were supposed to go, and she seemed as giddy as he was. In fact, he could feel each passion-filled giggle as he pushed into her a fourth and fifth time, her laughter reverberating throughout his wings and out into the larger room, amplifying the sound, the vibration, the … joy!

Tendrils of spirit, darkness and light, stroked, tasted, touched, and found its counterpart on each other's body, testing for which tendril wished to be joined with which, a sensation not unlike being licked by the rough tongue of a cat. Breathe. All he had to do was breathe.

He captured her mouth and relished the feel of each exhaled breath she made into his lungs, passing the same breath back and forth many times until they both came up for oxygen, laughing at the pleasant burning. Air! He needed *air* when they made love and it felt very, very good!

The tension which had been building began to spread, causing the texture of their lovemaking to change. Friends. Twin-sparks. Lovers. Mates. His wings gave up holding their shape and transformed into thousands of microvilli like the long, slender tailfeathers of an emu. For as long as he had known her, Elisabeth's life-energy had been invisible, hunkered down within her body as though she wished to hide her essence. Safe in the shelter of his arms, she unveiled what she had kept so carefully hidden. Each dark tendril wrapped around the slender white tendril it had chosen of her spirit and coaxed her non-corporeal form to open like the petals of a flower. Memory of a similar, much larger form he had once seen comprised of the exact same light leaped into his mind.

Primordial light in its nascent, still vulnerable form. The exact opposite of what *he* was, only she was the same size as him because she'd been fed upon and nearly destroyed by Moloch. He knew now what she was, his Elisabeth, and why Ki had chosen him to guard her.

"*Mo bandia, mo ghrá* [my love]," he whispered with awe as he realized what she, herself did not yet remember, a mercy bestowed upon her by her bigger sister. "I will protect you with my very existence."

Nails dug into his back, causing a sweet blend of pain and pleasure as she rose up to meet him with more urgency, greedy, hungry, her breathing a frantic pant. The hunger which had been building in his own loins grew more insistent, clamoring for him to stop thinking so darned much and just finish what he had started. Tendrils of spirit bound themselves together, every ounce of their being yearning to be joined as one. Breathe! Their breathing synchronized as they pulled each other closer, the urge to become one so overpowering the flesh which kept their bodies apart began to merge as their heartbeats synchronized into a single beat.

"Azrael," she arched her back and drove her hips upwards as she shuddered in anticipation of the precipice both could feel themselves perched upon, ready to fall.

"Say it," Azrael cried out, wishing to hear her say the words. He touched her cheeks as they prepared to fall over the edge together, to look into her beautiful, silver eyes which glowed with the light of what she really was as she spoke their commitment aloud.

Elisabeth opened her mouth to speak, but instead of words, the rays of light that were her true form radiated out into the room, causing it to shift dimensions as she cried out in ecstasy. Elisabeth had her *own* song to sing, not merely the echo of her mother's song. Rays of light intertwined with his primordial darkness, illuminating it, giving shape to the fertile silt that was his void matter, dragging him over the precipice along with her.

Azrael's back arched, his formless wings flapping of their own volition as the bass-string of a cello joined her flute. His heart exploded with joy as his physical seed spilled into her mortal shell. His. She was his. Forever. He could feel rays of light wrap around his heart even as his own, dark tentacles stroked and kissed hers. The bonds wrapped around one another and solidified into a single tree reaching between their hearts into the upper realms towards eternity. She was his. For all eternity.

"I love you more than life itself," Elisabeth whispered, her mortal vow blending with her immortal light and song. "And I shall never be parted from you. Ever. Again."

He realized he was crying.

"I love you more than my own existence, mo ghrá," Azrael wept. "And not even Moloch himself will keep me from you."

They floated there in that place that felt as though they were cradled in the branches of a great tree beneath the stars, carried along in the joyous song that was a blending of their own, unique song, and the much stronger Song of Creation. Every touch, every caress, every kiss, every warm thought increased that beautiful duet where his song and hers came together into a single melody. The Song of Creation and Destruction reunited as one. Her hand brushed across his cheek, her expression tender.

"Your tears," Elisabeth said. "They're clear."

She held the glistening drops in front of his eyes. Clear. Like dew clinging to a blade of grass on a summer morning. Not black, creating destruction wherever they fell. Simple water.

"I guess that makes me a real boy now?"

They floated in the Song of Creation as they nestled into each other's arms. He saw the places her spirit had been fed upon, where physical scars mirrored spiritual scars, the places her light was dim, where Ki had pieced together what little she could find and nurtured her back to sentience just as she had nurtured *him*, many pieces missing where Moloch had dined upon her light and failed to completely destroy her. She rested her head upon his chest, listening to his heartbeat, and sighed. Content. It made him happy to see her so content.

After a time basking in the Song, he could sense Ki nudge them back towards the material realms. Elisabeth instinctively pulled her spirit back into the mortal shell she had grown to hide it, to avoid broadcasting what she was for Moloch's agents to find. Remaining hidden would make it easier for him to protect her.

"Are we being cast down?" Elisabeth asked. The energy grew heavy as they were guided back to their own dimension. Lungs demanded air, muscles resisted gravity. It felt as though just for a time they'd dropped a heavy weight then picked it back up again.

"No, gcroílár m'anam [heart of my soul]," Azrael said. "We have work to do. That's all."

He didn't add that he knew, what, exactly, that mission entailed. Until his beautiful mate had healed enough to deal with whatever traumatic memories had caused her such horrific damage, he would not enlighten her that she was the first of *many* siblings now roaming the Earth, all clueless they'd been sent back to Earth to destroy their accursed father.

Nestled together in their wedding bower, Azrael covered her with one ebony wing instead of a blanket. They whispered their hopes and dreams to one another until the wee hours of the morning, when at last sleep overtook them. They had a long road ahead of them, but together, Azrael knew they could conquer anything.

Even her father...

Epilogue

O Lord of lords, so fierce of form,
Please tell me who You are.
I offer my obeisances unto You;
Please be gracious to me.
I do not know what Your mission is,
And I desire to hear of it.

Bhagavad Gita 11:31

April, 2004
Fallujah, Iraq

Azrael stared across the scarred village, debris littering the cobblestones of what had once been a lively, vibrant marketplace. No merchants hawked their wares now. All had fled in the wake of the vicious Al Qaida insurgents targeting any who did not buy into their rabid agenda, their hatred fueled by whichever Agent had moved up in rank to take Saddam Hussein's place. It saddened him to see the once-proud Babylonian Empire reduced to rubble. Would Muhammad be horrified to see that suicide bombers now worshipped Moloch in his name?

A curious sensation caught his attention moments before a group of Coalition soldiers moved out of the shadows, M-16's pointed in a coordinated sweep of the marketplace. A platoon sent to rout out insurgents. Al Qaida lay stationed on rooftops and in buildings. The rustle of insurgents moving into position to ambush the soldiers rippled through the marketplace like the all-too-infrequent Iraqi breeze.

Azrael resisted the urge to protect one side against the other. Maintaining his impartiality had grown difficult as Elisabeth had definite opinions about whose side he should favor. Death should never take sides. The best he could do was alleviate any fallen soldier's suffering, no matter how misguided their ideology, and see to it the battle remained one between mortal armies, not disembodied evil gods.

The rat-a-tat-tat of a Kalashnikov pierced the silence. The soldiers dove for cover and fired back. An IED exploded, hidden beneath the rubble. Drat! His rules against impartiality didn't apply to the loathsome devices, battle tactics of a coward. Soldiers screamed in agony as their fragile mortal shells were blown to smithereens, unaware they no longer had bodies to mouth those screams.

Still no sign of the squatter, but that peculiar sensation grew stronger, drawing his attention to an African-American soldier writhing on the ground. Azrael flitted to the man's side and flared his wings to provide a protective umbrella, an 'interference' he justified as 'I need to put my wings *someplace* while I make up my mind whether to take them or let them live?'

The man's flesh was nearly as dark as *his* was. Should he alleviate this soldier's suffering? Or were his injuries survivable? Elisabeth's ability to defeat him ... and teach others how to defeat him as well ... had blurred the line. Intestines writhed like grey snakes swimming through a bloody red stream where the soldier's entrails had been blasted out of his abdominal cavity. This man was already dead; his spirit just hadn't made up its mind yet to let go of his mortal shell. Even Elisabeth would approve of ending this man's suffering. Azrael made himself visible and reached down to take the soldier's hand.

"Come with me, brother," Azrael looked into the dark-skinned soldiers eyes. "It is time to take you home."

The man's eyes were wild with pain, so black and dark it felt for a moment as though he were staring into the eyes of the Regent. That peculiar throb grew stronger, more powerful, and more ... ominous. The entrails writhing along the ground grew black and began to curl in upon themselves. Black ... tentacles? The soldier screamed in pain, but instead of words, he screamed a sound Azrael knew well.

The Song of Destruction...

The ground shuddered and began to collapse inward upon itself, a vortex of power so vast it made even Azrael cringe in fear. Tentacles moved towards the rubble littering the marketplace, absorbing the bonds which kept their molecules together and absorbing their energy. An Agent? No. No Agent knew the Song of Destruction or Moloch would have been freed eons ago. The man's face contorted in agony, so black and beautiful he appeared almost a statute of a martyr.

"Corporal," Azrael read the bars off the man's beige desert camouflage. "Who are you?"

The Song of Destruction grew louder as the black tentacles clutched at any matter within reach and shoved it into the gaping black hole left in the man's abdomen by the improvised explosive device. Rubble, a piece of his rifle, and the engine block of a parked car which had been detonated along with the bomb were shoved into the increasing vortex and disappeared. It occurred to Azrael that perhaps *he* might be in danger? He backed away, not sure how to prevent such an event when it was *somebody else's* anger fueling a void-matter incident and not his own.

A flash of blinding white light appeared in front of the dying man. Alliance uniform. Dark hair. Black-brown wings. The General kneeled at the dying man's side, unharmed by the deadly black tentacles even though they wound around his arm the way an injured soldier might squeeze the hand of a medic.

"You must temper your power, brother, or you will destroy this world," the General said gently to the dying man. "Come. Your sister will heal these wounds."

"I cannot," the soldier cried out. "I cannot subdue the hunger any longer."

The General touched the man's cheek, his expression one of pity.

"You have come so far, brother," the General said. "Would you give up hope before you have found the gift your sister has given me?"

The General's touch brought whatever the void creature needed to control its power. Black tentacles grew smaller and faded, leaving nothing but the shattered intestines of a dying man, but already the man had begun to heal. The General picked up the soldier and cradled him against his chest.

"Forget what you have seen here today," the General ordered. "And speak of it to nobody. Not even to this soldier if you should ever happen upon him again. The fate of not only this world, but the entire universe depends upon him not remembering who he is until he has completed his mission."

With a flash of blinding white light, the General and the dying soldier disappeared, leaving Azrael with the memory of the man's bottomless black eyes, vast with power. He had seen that face once before, those stern eyes staring out of a sculpture shaped by the Regent's own hand. The man she called her brother.

What was He-Who's-Not doing on Earth, disguised as a mortal?

Also available…

Sword of the Gods: The Chosen One

At the dawn of time, two ancient adversaries battled for control of Earth. One man rose to fight at humanity's side. A soldier whose name we still remember today…

Earth: 3,390 BC

Pain.

The first sensation he recognized was metal piercing flesh. He gurgled in agony as lungs scraped against the steel rod which had pierced his breast, pinning him to the deck of his ship like a butterfly. He could not even scream. The best he could do was pant small, shallow breaths.

Blood welled in his throat, burning and gagging as he exhaled. The stench of blood filled the air. The scent of his impending death. One wing lay shattered beneath him, bone piercing skin and feathers. The other had no sensation at all. He tried to move his arm, but it was broken. The other arm and wing were pinned beneath the collapsed bridge. He could not feel his legs. He had no idea whether they were pinned, broken, or severed completely from his body.

ANNA ERISHKIGAL

Sword of the Gods
The Chosen One

His head hurt as though someone had hit him with a club. He tried to remember his name, who he was and how he had gotten here, but his mind drew a blank. It did not matter. No living creature could sustain these kinds of injuries and survive.

'So this is it,' he thought. 'The end…'

Alone. A single tear escaped, the sting of salt as it passed over a cut oddly sharp through the pain of his other injuries. Alone. He had always known he would die alone.

He closed his eyes and prayed to pass quietly into the void, to feel his life slip from his body so that his pain would end, but he did not. Even close to death, some part of him, the part that remembered who he was, whispered. Fight. Survive. Live another day. Smite those who had done this to him, even though he had no recollection of who he fought or what he was fighting for.

Long after he should have passed from this world, Mikhail continued to fight for each and every breath.

Also available...

A Gothic Christmas Angel

The Ghosts of Old Miseries are never far behind...

Dumped by her boyfriend on Christmas Eve, Cassie Baruch thought her pain would end when she aimed her car at an ancient beech tree. But when a gorgeous black-winged angel appears and tells her 'this ain't no stinking paranormal romance, kid,' she realizes death hasn't solved her problems. Can Jeremiel help her exorcise the ghosts of problems past and find a little closure?

A Gothic Christmas Angel features the purple-winged Archangel Jeremiel who guarded the entrance to the Eternal Emperor's genetics laboratory in *Angel of Death*. Not just a holiday novel, this modern paranormal spin on *A Christmas Carol* and *It's A Wonderful Life* was written to give people hope they can come to grips with the ghosts of miseries past.

Excerpt:

The angel flexed his muscles and stared at his hand as though he was bored. Truth be told, the angel was way hotter than Mauricio. A naughty thought flitted into her mind. Maybe...

"Forget it, kid," the angel looked at her with disgust. "Even if I wasn't, oh, a few thousand years older than you, the last thing I'd do is fall for a kid who doesn't even have her head screwed on straight."

Oh, great, and he could read her mind...

"I thought angels were supposed to comfort the living?"

The angel laughed; an obnoxious, raucous sound. "You're dead, kid. Remember?"

Cassie glowered at him. "Are you a fallen angel?"

The angel laughed even harder. It reminded her a bit of the way the football jocks laughed when they played a prank on somebody and laughed at them as a team.

"Listen, kid," the angel said. "I ain't here to save you. I ain't no fallen angel. And even if you weren't dead, this ain't no stinking paranormal romance where a hot angel falls from the sky to rescue you from your oh-so-boring, tedious mortal life. You ... are dead. You got dead because you drove your car into a tree." He shrugged. "It happens. So just go into the light like a good little girl so I can move on with my already shitty day."

"What light?"

"The light you're supposed to see when you're dead," the angel said.

A Moment of your Time, Please...

Did you enjoy reading this book? If so, I would be most grateful if you would do me the honor of revisiting whatever distribution platform you purchased it from and leaving a written review. This book took more than a year of my life to write working diligently for 5-6 hours each day. Unfortunately, without the multi-billion dollar advertising budget of a big commercial publishing house, most independently published and small-press books do not make back the cost to produce them (much less eat while writing them) ... *unless* ... readers such as yourself pass along word to others that you enjoyed it. In this day of online shopping, websites rank which books you see and readers decide what books to buy based on reviews left by other readers. I would be oh-so-grateful if you would do me the honor of leaving a written review.

If this book came your way via a gift or a loan from a friend, you can still share the love by leaving a review on one of the reader-centric review websites:

www.Goodreads.com
www.Shelfari.com
www.LibraryThing.com

Feel free to contact me or leave feedback at my Facebook page. I love hearing from you and I *do* write back!

Be epic!

https://www.facebook.com/pages/Sword-of-the-Gods/266590273421583

About the Cover Photograph

The Angel of Death monument in Wroclaw, Poland memorializes the 1940 murder of 22,000 Polish military officers, policemen, intellectuals and prisoners-of-war by the NKVD in the forest of Katyń by order of Josef Stalin during World War II.   Designed by Warsaw sculptor Tadeusz Tchórzewski, the striking monument depicts the sword-wielding Angel of Death on a high pedestal over the figure of Katyń Pieta - the Matron of the Homeland despairing over the body of a murdered prisoner of war. Symbolic granite walls/graves flank the scene, with the names of the POW camps and places of mass murder inscribed on them. Anguished, terrifying and gruesome in turn, with detail down to the bullet hole in the back of the fallen officer's head, this evocative monument was unveiled in 1999 and can be found in the park next to the Racławice Panorama.

The cover photograph used for this book was digitally remastered from the one above taken by *~xartez*, a local Polish photographer, and used with his kind permission. Please visit his website to enjoy his other magnificent photographs and purchases prints.

http://xartez.deviantart.com/art/Angel-of-Death-35266069

ABOUT THE AUTHOR

Anna Erishkigal is an attorney who writes fantasy fiction as a pleasurable alternative to coming home from court and cross-examining her children. She writes under a pen-name so her colleagues do not question whether her legal pleadings are fantasy fiction as well. Much of law, it turns out, -is- fantasy fiction. Lawyers just prefer to call it 'zealously representing your client.'

Seeing the dark underbelly of life makes for some interesting fictional characters, the kind you either want to incarcerate, or run home and write about. In fiction, you can fudge facts without worrying too much about the truth. In legal pleadings, if your client lies to you, you look stupid in front of the judge.

At least in fiction, if a character becomes troublesome, you can always kill them off…

Contact Anna at:

Facebook: https://www.facebook.com/anna.erishkigal
Goodreads:
https://www.goodreads.com/author/show/5823115.Anna_Erishkigal
Google+: https://plus.google.com/u/0/102296607002432216166
Pinterest: http://www.pinterest.com/annaerishkigal
Twitter: https://twitter.com/AnnaErishkigal
Blogger: http://www.anna-erishkigal.blogspot.com

Other Books by Anna Erishkigal

Sword of the Gods Saga: (epic fantasy/space opera)
-The Chosen One
-Prince of Tyre
-Agents of Ki
-*The Dark Lord's Vessel (coming soon)*
-*The Fairy General (coming soon)*

Children of the Fallen: (paranormal fantasy)
-Angel of Death: A Love Story
-A Gothic Christmas Angel (A Novella)

Leviathan's Deep: (science fiction/contemporary fantasy)
-*La Sirène (coming summer 2014)*

SERAPHIM PRESS

CAPE COD, MA

www.seraphim-press.com

25724430R00222

Made in the USA
San Bernardino, CA
10 November 2015